SEVERED

By Peter Laws

SEVERED

PETER LAWS

Allison & Busby Limited
11 Wardour Mews
London W1F 8AN
allisonandbusby.com

First published in Great Britain by Allison & Busby in 2019.

A CIP catalogue record for this book is available from
the British Library.

First Edition

ISBN 978-0-7490-2321-8

Typeset in 11.25/16.25 pt Sabon by
Allison & Busby Ltd.

The paper used for this Allison & Busby publication
has been produced from trees that have been legally sourced
from well-managed and credibly certified forests.

Printed and bound by
CPI Group (UK) Ltd, Croydon, CR0 4YY

For the strong, brilliant, and thoroughly inspirational Julie. You're like a sister to me. Oh, wait. You are my sister. Lol.

'And at three in the afternoon Jesus cried out in a loud voice, "*Eloi, Eloi, lama sabachthani?*", which means "My God, my God, why have you forsaken me?".'

Mark 15:34

PROLOGUE

Excerpt from The Rough and Ready Travel Guide to Rural Britain, 2018 edition

'Everybody calls it the Crooked Church. Each map and tourist leaflet, every walking route and history guide. Local villagers and passing cyclists never use its proper name, St Bart's. They say, "Ah . . . you'll be wanting the Crooked Church of Chervil village." It's been described that way for a hundred years. As soon as I arrived I saw why, because it really is one of the most physically wonky places of worship in Britain. Even more pronounced than the twisted spire of Sheffield Cathedral.

'Records say it happened in December 1886, when a coal-mining company misread their underground maps. Some fella told another fella the wrong way to dig and – boom! – the ground began to sink up top. Nobody noticed at first, though a farmer did say his land felt a bit more hilly than usual. A week later, the choir at St Bart's was suddenly showered with what looked like snow. True, it was Christmas Eve, but what actually poured on its members was powdered stone from the ceiling of the chancel – the section of the church where the Communion services are served.

Then the head of an angel statue fell clean off and plummeted with a loud, downwards whistle. They say it smashed off the altar, exploding into bits. Parishioners ran for their lives, screaming of world's end.

'It wasn't the apocalypse, just a bit of subsidence, but the congregation didn't know that. They gathered behind the long, drystone wall (which, to this day, still runs along the dirt road by the church). Horrified, they watched the west-end chancel, and two sycamore trees, slowly sink into what everybody assumed was going to be the groaning pits of hell. Yet the only part of the church that really dropped was the chancel. It sank a full six inches – with a groan "that sounded like the Devil himself" – then all was still.

'Nobody was hurt, thankfully, and a posse of brave (and superstitious) locals spent their late Christmas Eve frantically putting girders up inside. By early January the chancel was fully reinforced and the crevice below filled in. Somebody from the Missenden Mining company got fired, services began again – though it's said those early congregations prayed with one eye shut and another on the stone saints and apostles above them, whose heads looked heavier than ever.

'The church has stood with this quirky slope to it ever since. In 1901, Rev. Gerald Cartwright even immortalised the name in metal. With an eye to tourism, he had a huge wrought iron sign bolted over the entrance porch saying WELCOME TO THE CROOKED CHURCH. The sign, which still remains, has brought the church to the attention of the world.

'In late 2018, St Bart's found an unlikely surge of infamy when photographs of it became an Internet meme (a repeated and adapted image shared worldwide). The odd shape and entrance sign has become a social media shorthand for critics of the so-called "crooked" church in general. Made from stone, in typical seventeenth-century style, today's visitors will find a modest but reasonably beguiling place of worship. Yet its bizarre shape and backstory, along with the current social media fame, make the Crooked Church a unique diversion on any cycle or drive through the Chiltern Hills.'

SUNDAY

THE FIRST DAY

CHAPTER ONE

Reverend David East stood on the frosty gravel path to his church, watching his house across the dirt road. The tall trees of the vicarage swayed and rattled and a few beads of melting ice dripped from the gutters, but there was no movement from Micah's room. His black curtains were closed . . . again. No sign of him at breakfast. Again.

He plunged each chilly hand into the pockets of his tatty brown coat and started to pray, 'Father, would you . . .'

He paused because someone was whistling, filling the air with a chipper, happy tune.

He looked up and felt the first genuine smile of the day.

It was Miriam Aimes coming along the farm road, with her backpack tightly strapped to both shoulders. A decade younger than him – mid to late forties, he reckoned – she always seemed to bounce to church. Like a stage-school kid on the first day of rehearsals. God, he loved her enthusiasm. Even Micah said she was 'cool' once. Hearing his mouth form a positive word about another Christian felt like a genuine, unequivocal miracle.

When she saw him waving at her a massive smile lifted her rosy cheeks, but the sunlight was fierce, so she slipped her huge, curved sunglasses on. He watched her springing up the gravel path and was happy to log a guilt-free, godly thought. Miriam wasn't just the youngest and most recent parishioner to join his congregation – she really was, by a country-mile, the prettiest.

'How about this weather, Dave?' She sidled up to him, blonde curls bouncing under her bobble hat. 'Is it crazy, or is it *crazy*? Snow one day, storms the next.'

'And blazing hot sun in between. It's all over the place,' he nodded. 'Forecasters on the radio are baffled.'

'Maybe God's planning something. Something wonderful.'

'Maybe . . . you always see the good side.' He saw his own face beaming back from her sunglasses. What little hair he had spun wild and high in the breeze. When he palmed it down, it shot straight back up in a new gust. They both laughed, but his eyes soon drifted back to Micah's bedroom. He sighed. 'So tell me this, Miriam. How do you get teenagers to see the good side of church? How do you show them it's not crooked?'

'Easy,' she said. 'You love them. Don't be his vicar . . . and don't be his dad. Be his friend . . .'

'Simple as that, ey?'

She saw his eyes flicker. 'Micah will come back, you know.'

'And how can you be so sure?'

'Because Jesus always seeks the forgotten. And he always finds them too . . . never forget that, Dave.'

His smile was back. 'Miriam, my dear' – he opened his palm to the path – 'your faith is contagious. Shall we?'

They turned towards the bent silhouette of St Bart's, where a fat, fierce sun sat skewered on the steeple. He saw that blasted iron sign too, bolted over the entrance. WELCOME TO THE CROOKED CHURCH. He shook his head at it and started walking down the path, lined with gravestones facing in. The long-dead gang, welcoming him to work. Once inside, the warmth from the church radiators hit and they both sighed, but when he closed the door, Miriam froze.

'David,' she said. 'Look.'

He turned and saw something he hadn't seen for twelve months. Something astonishing. It was Micah, in his usual black combats and top, in the sunken chancel, crossed-legged on the floor. He was on the other side of the Communion rail, sitting in front of the altar. He was staring up at a stained-glass Jesus, dying colourfully on the cross.

David put a hand on his chest, and whispered, 'Oh, my.'

'See? Now, go to him.'

His shoes clicked a bright rhythm on the stone floor as he headed up the aisle, and he felt that familiar – yet always strange – pressure in his knees as he moved down the six-inch slope to the sunken chancel. Micah sat in a perfect rectangle of multicoloured light.

Don't be too jolly, he hates that, but don't be all deadpan either. He'll think you're grumpy about som—

'Heeeey, son!' It came out like Barney the Dinosaur. All finger pistols. He dialled it down. 'I thought you were still in bed.'

Micah mumbled like always.

'Sorry, son. Didn't catch that.'

'I said, I've been over here a while.'

'You have? Well that's a-okay with me.' He pushed through the little gate in the Communion rail and plonked himself down. They both sat cross-legged, looking up at Jesus. He was painfully conscious ('painfully' really was the right word) that they used to do this together each Sunday morning. He first started the pastorate here ten years back. Micah was six back then, and they'd sit here and pray for the service each week, while Zara hovered back at the vicarage, clearing up the breakfast bowls and gathering flowers for the altar. The idea of them sitting here like this, after

17

such a long time, made him want to burst into laughter and tears simultaneously, but then David's nostrils started to twitch. There was a dank smell coming from nearby. From Micah, perhaps? Possibly. Actually, make that probably. The kid wasn't much of a fan of the shower these days.

David tried to catch his eye, but only saw a profile of hair. He often wore it across his cheeks, to hide the acne. Poor boy. He was ravaged with it. 'So . . . um . . . what prompted you to come today?'

Micah shrugged.

'Did you come to pray, maybe?'

'To think.'

'Well it's the perfect place for that. Remember how we used to sit here and talk to God?'

Micah nodded, and David's heart tingled.

He leant in and whispered, 'Would you like to stay for the service, son? Absolutely no pressure.'

There was a long, ticking pause, and David watched for the usual shake of the head. He prepped his well-rehearsed broken-hearted response of 'fair enough. Maybe some other time'. After a year of saying that phrase, he'd become an expert at faking understanding, while being broken-hearted. But something else happened that made him gulp. A bona fide answer to prayer. The mass of hair nodded.

'Well, Micah, that just about makes my day. Heck . . . my week.' He really wanted to say 'year', but instead he put his hand on Micah's shoulder. The curve of black jerked away from his fingertips. Like a spasm.

'Son? Is everything okay?'

The hair shook out a nod, but the face didn't turn. No surprise there, either. Micah didn't like looking people in the eye these days, especially his dad's. Just something acne-ridden teenagers do, he supposed.

'Well, if you ever need to talk . . . I'm here. But do you mind stepping back from the altar and grabbing a pew? People are arriving and we need to set up for the Eucharist.'

Micah sighed and pushed himself up. 'Fine.'

David stood to light a few candles and called out a happy hello to the organist, who was now settling onto his stool. Mighty power chords filled the church with wondrous sound.

'Goodness.' David checked his watch. 'Ten minutes, folks.'

Micah sat in a pew with his head down, reading a leaflet over and over while David grabbed his bag and headed for the vestry, trying not to whistle. He was going so fast that he collided with Gwen Skeggs. She was waiting for him at the door. Her face was white.

'Gwen? What's wrong?'

She twisted a handkerchief around one bony finger. 'Can we talk, David?'

'Erm . . . we're about to start. Could it wait till after?'

Shiny dentures pressed into a grey bottom lip.

He slid his hands over hers. 'Course we can talk. How about you come into the vestry? The rest of them can wait a few minutes.' He touched the door handle. 'And guess what? Micah's in church, praise God.'

She sucked in a breath and seemed to stagger back. One hand grabbed the door frame.

'Gwen, love. Whatever's the matter?'

She tugged her jumper into place, 'We'll talk later, then. After the service.'

'Why look, you're trembling.'

'Later.'

'But . . .' David called out after her. 'You'll be first on my list, Gwen, okay? Top of the pile!'

He said a quick prayer, knowing what it was. Her wayward son Kyle was probably in debt again. He'd seek her out at the end and pour her a good strong tea, just how she liked it. But for now, he wasn't going to let his jolly mood dissolve. In the vestry, he pulled on his white surplice-robe and black tippet (the long piece of material that Micah used to call his holy scarf). Then he did his usual quick stare at the photograph on his desk. The one where all three of them were on Skegness beach. Him and Zara with a ten-year-old Micah, flashing teeth and smiles between them. This was from before Zara cut her black hair short. Before she hacked it off in a rage. He'd always liked how it flowed around her shoulders. He kissed his fingertip and tapped it gently against her windswept cheek. 'And Jesus . . .' he prayed, 'find her too, and bring her home. Soften her heart.'

The vestry door rattled open.

'Vicar?' the church secretary nodded.

'Victor?' he nodded back.

'Showtime.'

David flattened his robe down and went to the door. 'God's going to move today, Vic. I can feel it.'

He pretty much glided up the pulpit steps and he threw out his usual opening line like a birthday ribbon. 'Welcome, one and all, to this morning's service of praise and . . .' he paused, 'celebration.'

Micah was gone.

David saw the empty space in the pew, just as he said the word 'praise'. So the jolly tone of his sentence drooped at the end, in a sound wave shaped exactly like this crooked building. His autopilot minister voice kicked in, saying generic things about God being great as they all shared the peace, but his eyes sprang like a lizard from pew to pew, from corner to doorway. He couldn't see Micah anywhere.

Back in position he thought he heard a movement in the chancel behind him. But when he turned he saw nothing but the headless stone angel high up in the rafters. The slice of her neck looked ragged and sharp. He thought of Christmas Eve just gone. How he'd willed that angel to fall again, as he sat in here alone. Two weeks after the new, short-haired Zara had finally walked out. He'd laid back on the altar and willed that stone body to drop and smack his head right open. Demanded God do it, until he shook off his selfishness and knew it wasn't to be.

He drifted through the prayers and the homily on auto-pilot. Then, eventually, he heard his own voice announce the Eucharist and he clumped down the creaky pulpit steps. Miriam looked up from her service book and mouthed the words 'are you okay?' He dearly wanted to say no, but he'd rather not cry in front of everybody. Nobody would want that. So, he just threw her a happy, dead-eyed smile. He headed down the slope to the chancel and noticed the sun had changed. The stained glass threw no more light on the floor.

He stood behind the altar: a wooden table now covered in a brilliant-white tablecloth. This was the exact spot the angel's head had smashed into pieces two centuries ago – you could still see the marks in the wood. The exact spot of his suicide prayer a few weeks ago. When he'd lain on his back and begged for God to kill him for Christmas, not long after the last happy parishioners had left midnight Mass.

Focus, he told himself. *Even if your family don't need you any more, this congregation do.*

He opened his arms and that rank smell flooded his nostrils again. Like somebody turning on a switch. How odd. It smelt like a public toilet. Which suddenly made him feel spiritually oppressed. Like something ungodly was prowling. A cold shadow blew him a kiss.

Welcome to the Crooked Church, with its selfish, broken, piss-poor priest.

He blinked and announced a hymn – 'Eternal Father Strong to Save' – and the hefty organ kicked in. Only now it sounded louder and far less pleasant than before. These were chords straight from a horror movie. The Phantom of the Opera sat in the organ loft now, springing his hands wildly off the keys, while David's mind played old, silent-movie memories of Zara, weeping in the bathroom and hacking off her hair. 'You don't care about us,' the flickering title card said, as she stood wide-eyed at the blackening sink, 'we get the dregs . . .'

He blinked her image away and turned around to the stained-glass Jesus, up on his cross. He raised the silver goblet of wine. 'The Blood of Christ,' he said, projecting it to the universe and to any dark force that was pressing in on him now. Because something was pressing in on him. Not so much the presence of something, but more like the absence of something. He could feel the absence of God. Which was the exact moment he noticed the back corner. The strange bulge in the long curtain he'd asked the church to add, years back, because he liked the orthodox style. There was a lump in it.

Nobody else seemed to notice. They were too busy pushing their old groaning bodies up from the pews and hobbling down the sloping aisle. They were lining up and singing and kneeling at the rail, with the audible creak and crunch and crack of old bones. But their heads were bowed and their hands were out and most importantly their eyes were closed. Tongues were set to loll out and flick a gluten-free Jesus back in.

David was the only one with his eyes wide open. He saw that bulge shift a little, just a few feet from where he stood.

A Micah-sized lump.

He thought, *Wow, there he is and this is good . . . he's listening after all.* Then he felt confused and embarrassed because Micah really shouldn't be on this side of the rail. He should be with the others, kneeling. Not lurking behind a curtain, which was just plain weird, acne or not. The hymn ended and somewhere behind him, someone made a very deliberate, get-on-with-it cough. He turned back to the congregation and in the silence, he opened his hands across the altar. A magician, setting up his most famous trick. He read the usual passage from Corinthians 1, then said, 'For whenever you eat this bread and drink this cup you proclaim . . .'

He saw the shadow just then.

A puddle of very cold greyness spilled onto the white tablecloth in front of him. Since all eyes remained closed, nobody really saw what that shadow was, but David did.

'. . . the Lord's death until he comes again . . .' He turned his head to see Micah, who was standing in the strangest of stances. He had both hands behind his back. All solemn, like a funeral pose. His eyes were lost behind that mass of straggled hair that the old ladies always told him to cut. It was worse than ever right now, because he'd deliberately dragged and raked it not just over his spotty cheeks, but right across his entire face. It looked so damn ridiculous and immature. So savage. The hair was wet, maybe from tears, but who was he kidding? It was probably sweat. And that stink, dear Lord, that public toilet stench. The church seemed to be growing darker.

People were noticing now. Eyes were opening. He heard confused mumbling behind him.

'Micah,' David whispered, quite firmly. 'I'm sorry, but you shouldn't be on this side.'

Micah said, '*Eloi, Eloi, lama kataltani.*'

It was such a bizarre thing to say that David's brain was too busy processing it to see Micah's arms move. But then he noticed that Micah was holding something very long. It looked like a thick table leg, with a wedge on the end. Something big, and heavy and rusty-looking.

David was so disorientated by this. The table leg. The wedge. The swinging of it up, so that it was really only when he felt the impact against the side of his head that things became—

Thud.

He spun around like a dancer towards the others then fell into the altar. He hit it so heavily that it almost tipped over. Both hands slapped the white cloth, fingers splayed, crunching the white sheet into a ripple of thick folds. He thought, *my son just bloody well punched me in front of the entire—*

Then someone screamed.

The Communion wine had tipped over. It was gushing across the cloth, and he was furious that it might stain. Until he saw how the silver goblet stood untouched, full of red wine. He felt a fast, warm trickle fill his ear and he started to blink rapidly. Wails of horror shot from the crowd at the second impact. Something sharp cracked into the back of his skull. That was when the world truly exploded into pain. His scalp went warm and wet. His head felt way heavier, because it now carried extra weight. He let out a hideous grunt and it made people gasp. Then his head yanked and felt lighter again.

'Son . . .' He turned his head and was terrified to hear his own voice was no longer clear and well projected. His Bible college tutor had always taught him – *you must always speak to the back row!* Now his voice was gurgling and bubbling saying, 'Son . . . Son . . . no . . .'

'Please, Dad . . .' Micah said. 'Don't look in my eyes.'

David held up his hands in defence, so Micah swung for those too. He missed, and David heard the *thwoop* of wood and metal slicing the air. Miriam, and a few of the others, had finally unfrozen themselves from shock. They were climbing over the Communion rail, booming loud voices at Micah to put the axe down, while David's panicked mind kept obsessing: *but we don't own an axe. How odd. We've never needed one.* Like that was the most important element to ponder right now, and not the fact that his son was clearly aiming for his neck.

David heard old ladies talking to God like never before. They screamed their prayers out. Full marks for enthusiasm. The church was exploding with genuine lament at Biblical levels. He thought he heard God eagerly say: *This is exactly how it sounded when all those Egyptians found their dead first-borns.* Then he realised that wasn't God saying it at all. It was Satan, filling his ear with excited whispers. Like those screams were music to him. Others were running for the door.

Micah, blood-spattered and panting, was sobbing and he now turned to the stained-glass Christ. He said, '*Avi, Avi . . . Lama kataltani,*' then he raced off across the chancel, heavy axe still in hand. He slammed his shoulder against the side door just a few feet away, and it sprang open. A huge, snarling beast of a wind rushed into the church and blew all the candles out. When the wind roared David knew it was the devil, sighing with contented achievement. David watched his son dwindle on the path outside while Victor and a few others tried to run after him. Yet those young legs made Micah a bullet, and as David's vision blurred, he saw the old men stop on the path, gasping and gripping their knees. A strange thunder rolled above them. The sky was dimming.

Miriam dropped and both knees splashed into the blood.

'Jesus, please . . .' She cradled David's head, staring up to the stained glass. 'Jesus . . . Jesus . . . please . . . *please* come . . .'

Her prayers melted into a squelchy sort of murk, and instead he imagined her voice was Zara's voice, saying she'd changed her mind and accepted his apology. That she'd come back to love him again, but the satanic wind had another cruel message. It said:

It's too late, David. Cos you prayed you'd die in this chancel. That Christmas Eve prayer's been all signed off and contracted now. No turning back. You belong in the ground. Which was the only time a tear came. He felt it roll from his eye and drop.

'The thunder . . .' David whispered. 'Micah hates the thunder . . . best get him home . . .'

'Jesus . . .' Miriam closed her eyes. Tears welled through the lashes. 'Jesus, *please* . . .'

'And tell him it's not crooked, okay?' His own voice was fading. 'Tell him we love . . . and we're not crooked . . . we love . . .'

He watched the bent ceiling of the Crooked Church turn blue, then grey above him. Then this bizarre demonic weather sent storm clouds around the church, sweeping and squeezing so tight that the chancel turned jet-black. He wondered if the old mineshaft below might have finally opened its mouth as wide as it had wanted to. That two hundred years ago was only ever a dry run for this.

Then he felt himself sink into the ground, deeper and deeper, and could feel the dirt of the churchyard filling his eyes and mouth and nose. Then all senses were gone. All senses but one. Sound remained. He could hear the Devil's chuckle in the muffled drumming of distant rain above him, and the clicking of well-dressed bodies that had slid from their coffins, patiently crawling through the deep soil to find him.

CHAPTER TWO

Professor Matt Hunter pounded his feet down the grass hill, trying hard not to slip on the frost. Around him other parents, school staff and schoolkids were running too, sliding, stumbling and frantically trying to grab the giant inflatable duck that was heading for the water.

Geoff Butler, a frankly ill-looking conservationist, was rattling his bones down the hill too. He'd introduced himself to the crowd earlier, tapping the mic and welcoming them in a measured, thoughtful tone. Now he cried out his words in a breathless, scrawny wail, 'Do not let it hit the pond. It'll smother the real ducks!'

Matt's laugh spluttered out, but he swallowed it for politeness, and kept running.

They'd lived in their new hometown of Chesham, Buckinghamshire for four months now. So this morning when he and his family rocked up at this local park event, the plan was to mingle with the locals. The fact that it was a fundraiser for local duck conservation was neither here nor there. Matt liked ducks a lot, especially with pancakes. Yet this morning was primarily about local integration.

The social install of the Hunter family into a new community was an important project. So ducks it was, and they all turned up eager and fresh-faced, ready to make new friends.

Lowndes Park stood on a long downward slope. So, when the giant inflatable duck broke free of its moorings a few moments ago, it naturally headed down. Then a crazy-fast wind came out of nowhere, making 'Daphne' (as she was apparently called) tumble and roll much quicker than any of them could run.

He heard the rhythmic *tap-tap-tap* of plastic behind him as his wife Wren ran up in line with him, a box of Tic Tacs rattling in her jeans pocket. Her arms swung in a demented power run.

'If we catch this . . . they'll love us . . .' she gasped, '. . . we'll be like . . . local heroes or something.'

'We'll get the key to Chesham . . . the secret codes and handshakes . . . and how about this . . .' He caught his breath. 'The first one of us to grab Daphne . . . chooses the takeaway tonigh—'

'Stop that duck!' She surged ahead, Tic Tacs at full pelt.

Laughing, he cranked his own speed to T-1000 levels while further down the slope he saw little kids and pensioners scurrying to the sides and diving behind bushes. They knew what was coming. A large pond waited below, with real and oblivious ducks chugging along the now-choppy water. Beyond the pond was a busy road where cars trundled back and forth, slowing to see the spectacle. Daphne hit a bump in the hill and a gust of wind sent her reeling eight feet in the air. This made everybody slow down, just at the sheer awe of it, and way back up the hill he heard all the schoolkids who'd sponsored this duck squeal with delight. Then she bounced back into the wet ground again and rolled, faster than ever, rattling a long beard of frosted mud-chips up her chin.

Matt took a deep breath, gaining on Wren with each step. 'Chinese!' he chanted. 'Chinese! Chinese!' He quickly stopped his mantra when he remembered others might hear him. Particularly the Chinese guy a few clips ahead.

Down by the pond a family with two small children were sheltering under a tree. The dad was one of those walking-chunk types. All muscle with a washboard chest, bursting through a grey tracksuit, and baseball cap. He was striding directly into the flight path, while everybody else down there ran to the sides. His kids were clapping out his name, *Daaah-dee! Daaah-dee!* The mum (also chanting) had her phone out to catch the magic.

The panic in Geoff's thin voice hit previously unreached octaves. Now he shouted in tones that only dogs could hear. 'He's an idiot! He can't tell how big she is! He'll die!'

Ignorant of these warnings, *Daah-dee* marched into the dead centre of the duck's trajectory. He rubbed his neat little beard then fixed his eyes on Daphne's giant, rolling, goofy stare. He locked his hefty legs into place and stuck both of his massive hands out – Iron-Man-style. He could have shouted something epic like 'Ye shall not pass!' but he hollered his own line instead. 'End of the liiiiine, braaaaaaah.'

Matt winced, and everybody winced with him, when Daphne eventually fused with tracksuit. She slammed hard. People gulped, genuinely shocked at how loud the crack was. He heard Geoff say, 'Dear God. His spine.'

Matt and Wren stopped laughing just then. When Geoff said the word 'spine'. In fact, nobody was laughing now. The chants of '*Dah-dee*' clipped off midway and the mum wasn't filming any more. Now she was scrambling down the hill towards her buried knight, while the entire crowd of runners slid to a stumbling, silent stop around the now-stationary duck.

'Hold her!' Geoff shouted. 'Case she blows off again.'

Twenty hands grabbed her fleshy skin and Matt dropped to his knees. He lifted the giant curve of yellow and there he was: Daddy Chunk, flat on his back, with both of those mighty hands locked like twin vices on the duck's chest. One of his nostrils was filled with blood.

'Holy crap,' Matt said. 'Are you hurt?'

He winked and shouted to his wife, 'Did you get it? Did you get it?'

Her eyes flashed with panic, and she quickly started filming again.

Matt laughed and reached his hand out to help him up. 'We've got her now.'

The guy rose to his feet and brushed himself down while the entire park cheered. Naturally he lifted his arms Rocky-style and did a bobbing victory circle on his feet. His entire back and legs were drenched with mud, but the two kids and the woman still flung their arms around him.

Wren, who had fallen behind, came running over. Her Tic Tac signal rattled to a stop. She grabbed Matt's waist. They stood together and watched for a moment, listening to the cheers.

'We've failed,' he whispered into her wet hair. 'The locals are never going to accept us until we catch one of these. You know that, don't you?'

She put a hand over his, closed her eyes, and with a solemn nod she whispered, 'We'll keep trying. We'll train.'

Everybody watched the now-punctured Daphne slowly deflate. The rain picked up, spattering her dissolving curves. People started heading off, while Geoff and a few of his colleagues started sitting on her and rolling around, pressing out the latent air. Matt offered to help, but Geoff said, 'No. No. She's a tricky fold.'

Finally, their two daughters Lucy and Amelia caught up, panting. They'd been up top, in the queue for drinks. That task was abandoned now. Their eldest, Lucy, raked a hand through her wet hair and looked at her fingers, horrified. At sixteen, bedraggled, newborn calf was not the look she was going for. 'Er, let's get inside before we drown.'

'Wait.' Their seven-year-old, Amelia, came up next to Matt and slipped her hand into his. 'She was a very good duck, Daddy.' He could hear the smirk on her face.

'That she was.' Matt stood up straight, pressed his heels together and saluted the sinking material. Amelia did the same. Wren snorted.

'Oh, God . . .' Lucy groaned and marched towards town. 'I'm getting an espresso.'

'Espresso you say?' Matt flicked his head around. 'A fitting tribute, yes . . .'

They ran off after her, lifting their jackets over their heads, laughing for the entire minute's wet sprint to the shops.

CHAPTER THREE

There was a large, two-floor coffee shop on the high street, so everybody from the duck fiasco rammed into it, much to the wide-eyed gawp of the baristas. It was heaving inside, with bodies everywhere, wet with rain and sweat. The hot, panting breath quickly fogged the huge windows. Matt saw a lone kid quietly draw a set of breasts in the corner of the glass, laugh, then smear it away with the cuff of his jumper just before his mum brought drinks to the table. Sodden jackets were hung from hooks, chairs and anything else that jutted and almost everybody was chuckling and comparing video angles of when the duck went airborne.

Even the man himself turned up. *Dah-dee* turned out to be a top-flight financial advisor called Marshall Webster. The entire place erupted with a rugby-roar cheer when he walked in, and he was inundated with offers of latte. Everybody else was inundated with his business card. Nobody refused. Matt saw an old lady try to high-five him and totally miss. She gave him a jiggling hug instead.

Matt and Amelia stood in the epic queue. She had her nose on the glass display case pointing at each cake in turn. '. . . and I'd eat that . . . and that . . . and I'd eat that . . . that . . . and that . . . and I'd—'

'One,' he said. 'You'll eat one.'

Her 'pffft' threw a mist on the glass.

It took them a good minute to battle to their seats. Amazingly, Wren had found them a table in the far corner downstairs. They all sighed as they sat down, and he swiped a fistful of napkins across his wet fringe. The first sip of caffeine brought deep moans of delight. 'Where's the other one, Wren? Where's Lucy?'

'Talking to her new teacher. He's over there . . .' Wren jabbed her doughnut at the steamed-up windows, where Lucy sat on the arm of a sofa. A skinny young man with trendy white-framed glasses was talking to her. His quiff was improbably tall. A man and a woman were with him and were much older; both wore cardigans, and both were red-faced. The man's sideburns were so thick and curly, even a Vegas-era Elvis would have said they were too much.

'So, which one's the teacher?' Matt asked.

'The quiff,' Amelia said. 'Lucy says he's the new RE guy.'

'No way,' Wren sunk a sugar into her coffee. 'He looks what . . . twelve?'

Sideburns set his teapot down and looked over. Their eyes met. Matt smiled at him but Sideburns didn't reciprocate. He held the gaze, turned something over in his mouth and looked away.

'See, Wren. Total smash with the locals.'

The young teacher suddenly stood with Lucy. He threw a satchel over his shoulder, grabbed his coffee and said something to Sideburns, who shook his head firmly and folded his arms. Then he and Lucy began their epic push through all the bodies.

Matt nudged Amelia, 'Budge up, Midget. We need your chair.' She climbed onto his knee.

They did that thing people do in coffee shops when preparing for a table visitor. They sat more upright, brushed a few crumbs off their jumpers. Amelia attempted her version of table cleaning by flicking lumps of muffin across the room, but Wren raised a finger. It was time to switch to pleasant, presentable, family mode.

When Lucy finally reached the table, she grabbed the espresso. 'Mine, I take it?'

The young teacher stood awkwardly behind her, one hand holding his cup, the other tugging his quiff into place. He could play keys in an 80s German synth band any day. The strap of his canvas satchel pressed hard across his skinny, rib-lined chest.

Matt sprang to his feet. 'Hey, I'm Lucy's stepdad, Matt.' He just came right out with it these days, the stepdad part. She seemed to prefer that at the moment. 'And this is Wren, Lucy's mum. And Amelia.'

'Hi.' He put out his hand and Matt noticed a very slight tremble to it. 'I'm Sean Ashton. I just started teaching RE at Lucy's school.'

'Great. Well, pull up a pew, Mr Ashton,' Matt said.

The young man bit his lip for a moment, then he looked over his shoulder at Sideburns and co. They were staring, with nothing even approaching a smile.

'Your friends too, if they'd like,' Matt said. 'We'll squeeze them in.'

'They prefer the window, thanks . . . and they're not my friends, they're my parents.' He coughed. 'Though I suppose there's no reason why your parents can't be your friends . . .'

'I can think of a few reasons,' Lucy said, then laughed at her own joke.

Sean finally sat, with his satchel resting neatly on his lap. He lay both hands on it, one over the other.

Wren was good at sensing tension. She was good at breaking it too. She smiled at him and said, 'I absolutely love your glasses.'

'Thanks. They're recent. Got them for the new term.'

'Well, they're great. And you know, I always loved RE at school. Back in my day, we used to make unleavened bread and stuff like that. Do you still do that?'

'Not really. Well, I don't, anyway. It's my first teaching post out of college, actually.'

'Yikes.' Matt remembered (with a shiver) those early days as a newly qualified lecturer at university. The mistakes he made, the times he lost his notes. The afternoon he made a nervy and ill-advised joke that George Lucas should be tried for war crimes, after making *The Phantom Menace*. And him receiving a formal, written complaint, one hour later. 'How's it going?'

'Well, I'm enjoying the challenge and opportunity.' That sounded like a sound bite. Something you'd read in a leaflet. 'It's good to work in my hometown. Nice to see my parents more often.' That last bit sounded like a sound bite too.

'So, how do you know Lucy?' Wren said. 'As far as I know she doesn't take RE.'

'That's true, but I've just seen her around school and most people know she's related to . . . well . . . to *you* . . .' Sean shimmied on his chair, shifting his position. Now he was looking directly at Matt. 'So, I was wondering . . .' He patted the satchel and went to undo the clasp, but then he paused sharply for a moment. He glanced over his shoulder at the window again. His mum was waving him back over, frantically.

'Sean?' Matt said. 'Do you have a machine gun in there?'

He sucked a deep breath in, then turned back round. 'No gun. But . . . I was wondering if you had a pen?' The clasp popped open and he slid something out. A hardback book. He turned it around to face them all.

'Oh . . .' Lucy sank back into her seat. 'That.'

In Our Image: The Gods We Tend to Invent by Professor Matt Hunter

Matt whistled. 'See kids, I told you we weren't the only ones to buy it.'

'It's actually quite profound, Professor,' Sean patted the cover,

'. . . in terms of religion it's extremely thought-provoking. So, do you have a pen?'

Matt reached into his jacket and pulled out a biro. 'Should I make it out to Sean?'

'Yes please. S-E-A-N.'

'Gotcha.'

'And can you write . . . *To Sean* . . .' he ran his hand across the air, '*embrace the mystery. Matt Hunter.*'

'Um . . . okay,' Matt flipped to the title page and started scrawling.

'That sounds like an aftershave advert,' Amelia said, '. . . *embrace the mystery, Matt Hun—*'

Lucy cupped her hand across Amelia's mouth, so the words became a mumble.

When he finished, Wren leant over and grabbed the pen. 'Now I guess you'll want my autograph. Because I live in the same house as him and I've seen him on the toilet and everything.' She clicked the pen on. 'Oh, the bathroom tales I could tell . . . for example—'

Matt swiped the pen from her hand and dropped it back into his pocket. Sean laughed. It was the first time his mouth had really moved from a nervous slit. 'Thank you, Professor,' he looked back at his parents. 'I appreciate . . .' They were gone. Both of them, vanished. His smile evaporated too. '. . . I appreciate it. But if you'll excuse me.'

'Sean?' Matt leant in. 'Is everything okay?'

'. . . Perhaps we could talk again sometime. Somewhere more private? I've a million questions about your book.'

'I'd love to. Let's do it over a pint.' Matt slipped him his card.

Sean stared at it, then dropped it into his pocket. 'I'd like that. Well look, it was nice to meet you all. See you in the hallways Lucy, and thanks for introducing me to your dad.'

'Step . . .' she said.

'Sorry . . . *step*dad.' He tipped his quiff to her. 'Amelia . . . Wren . . .' He waited for a second. 'Matt.'

They watched him go back through the crowd and Matt went to speak, but suddenly Yoda started calling out from his trouser pocket. *A call you have! A CALL you have!* He fished for his phone as the voice grew louder. It was stuck in his damp jeans.

'You have got to change that ringtone,' Lucy said.

Wren winced as it grew more frantic, 'Matt. People are looking.' *A CALL you HAVE!*

'Sorry.' Matt finally yanked it from his pocket. '*A CALL YOU HAVE! A CALL YOU—*' He answered, and with a finger in one ear and the phone to the other he rose from the noisy table. He wondered (hoped) if the unknown number might be that guy from eBay he'd called last week. The one who was selling the old, retro Donkey Kong cabinet that Matt desperately wanted for his small but growing arcade collection.

It wasn't.

'Err . . . hello?'

A woman's voice crackled on the line. A vague hint of Africa in her accent. 'Professor Hunter?'

'May I ask whose speaking?'

'This is Detective Sergeant Jill Bowland. I'm with the CID. Got a minute?'

CHAPTER FOUR

'You're the religious professor, right? The ex-vicar who helps the police now and then?'

'Correct.'

'Great . . . I read that you live in Chesham now.'

'May I ask what this is about?'

He heard her clear her throat. 'I'm calling about the incident up in Chervil village, which is just up the road from you.'

'Incident?'

'You haven't seen the news?'

'Sorry, I've been busy this morning.' He didn't mention ducks.

'Ah, right. Well, there's been an attempted murder at the Anglican church in Chervil, right in the middle of the morning service. The victim is Reverend David East. He's in a coma.'

'It happened in the service? Sheesh. Was it . . . terrorism or something?'

'I don't think it is, no. East knew his attacker.'

'Knew how?'

'It was his son.'

Matt groaned.

'Anyway, he's called Micah. He's sixteen and still on the run, and we're having trouble tracking him down. Maybe you can help.'

'I'll try. Fire away with your questions.'

'Actually, Chesham's only a sixteen-minute drive from Chervil. Could you come?'

'When?'

'Now.'

He paused, looked back at the girls, giggling around the table. 'That should be fine.'

'Excellent. Meet us at the Crooked Church. Heard of it?'

Who hadn't? He'd seen its photograph a hundred times in YouTube videos and atheist Internet forums. It was the gif that kept on giving. 'It's called St Bart's, isn't it?'

'That's right. It's too remote for a satnav but it's signposted from the centre of the village. It's right at the end of an old track so you'd be blind to miss it. Thanks for this . . .' A pause. 'Oh, and I presume you'll know a little about' – she cleared her throat again – 'devil worship?'

A burst of cackles from some teenagers behind him.

'A fair bit, yes.'

'Great. I figured you would. Then you're my expert for the day.' She gave a muffled holler to someone at her end. 'Just don't dawdle, Professor. He's still out there. And he still has the weapon.'

'Which is?'

'An axe.'

'Jeez. I'm on my—'

Click.

'. . . way . . .'

She was gone.

He headed back to the table to find that Lucy and Amelia were playing Pass the Pigs, an old game he'd picked up in a charity shop the other day. Wren wasn't playing. She was scrolling through her phone, staring.

'Daddy? Ready to be beaten?' Amelia blew into her hand, tossed two rubber pigs onto the table, then punched the air. 'Yes! Makin' bacon!'

'Sorry folks, but I have to go.' He grabbed his still-damp jacket. 'I'm heading up to Chervil.'

'You're what?' Wren gawped up from her phone. He saw the local news app shining from her screen. He leant over and caught the headline, VICAR IN CHURCH AXE ATTACK. 'You're going for this, aren't you?'

'Um . . .' he shrugged. 'Yes.'

'Says here he's still on the run.'

'Wait . . .' Lucy sat up. 'Who's on the run?'

'Wren, they just want a bit of advice . . .'

She stared at him, then pushed up from the table. 'Two seconds, girls,' she said, as Wren found a spot out of earshot. 'Look, I don't want to be a nag or anything . . .'

'But . . .'

'It's like you've got a bat-phone these days. Got a psychopath? Call Matt Hunter.'

'Hey. It's nice to be wanted . . .' He smiled.

She didn't smile back. Not at all. He just saw the colour in her cheeks go. 'Wasn't Hobbs Hill enough? And Menham?'

He waited a moment. 'Look, it happened in a church. Maybe there's something I can offer. I know faith stuff, Wren. It's kinda my thing.'

'So, it's a thing now?' She put her palm on his chest. 'Can't you just stick to books and lectures and pub quiz Bible rounds? And . . . can't they find someone else?'

'It's a sixteen-minute drive away.'

Lucy slapped her hand hard on the table behind them. A pig skittered off the edge. 'I said . . . who the *hell* is on the run?'

Wren quickly span around. 'Oh, Luce . . . I'm sorry . . . It's not your dad. It's nothing like that.' She assembled her face into an unconvincing smile. 'It's just some kid from Chervil. Nobody major.'

'What kid?'

Matt pulled out his car keys. 'I really have to go.' He high-fived Amelia and nodded to Lucy, then he turned to Wren who was still standing. He planted a kiss on Wren's cheek. 'I'll be in touch.'

She whispered into his ear, 'You better. Cos if you get hit by an axe, I'll kill you.' Then a very genuine, 'Just be wise, okay?'

He pushed through all the bodies, making his way to the exit, as those familiar, horrendous snapshots of Menham and Hobbs Hill flickered in his mind again. These were images that had lodged so deeply in his subconscious that he knew he'd never shake them. They were there for life now. Emotional tattoos, he'd heard them called. And usually, they only simmered up in the quiet nightmares that woke him now and then. Usually around 3 a.m. The nightmares he never mentioned to Wren, or to anybody, in fact. The nightmares that occasionally even slipped into waking life. Black figures in the corner of his eye. Strange groans in the cusp of his ear. Black rabbit shadows, springing across his bedroom ceiling.

All just echoes of past trauma, Google had told him.

He slid through the crowd, where thick hairy arms slid against his, and was glad to be out in the street again, pulling in fresh air. How strange, he thought, that even after all that grotesquery, he still perked up now that another police call had come through. Granted, most of his growing police consultancy work was pretty mundane. Last month he helped shut down a religious relics scam on eBay. That took an afternoon. But not since Menham, a few months back, had he been called in for anything violent or extreme. How bizarre, he thought, to feel both fear and excitement right now.

The rain kept falling, so he flipped the collar of his jacket up and rushed through the puddled backstreets. He passed boutique gift shops and cafes that were stuffed with dry people, looking at him with amused sympathy. He found his Lexus and climbed inside, slamming the rain out. It was just as he pulled on his seat belt that he spotted an old green Land Rover with an impressive tsunami of mud up the side. It was parked by the ticket machine with the engine running. The wipers frantically slid from left to right.

Sean Ashton sat in the front passenger seat. He had his head down while his dad, Mr Sideburns, sat in the driver's seat, loudly berating him. Matt was too far away to hear actual words, but he could tell it was an air-quivering shout. In between the chairs, Mrs Ashton was in the back seat, one pudgy hand on Sean's shoulder, the other twisting her cardigan with anguish.

Matt considered getting out. He could rattle a knuckle off Sean's window and check if he was okay. But maybe he'd make things worse. Those two hadn't exactly seemed into Matt, earlier. Besides, the time really was a-ticking and there was an axe man loose, and all. So, he swung the car out of his space and headed for the exit. He only stopped once on the way out. That was to avoid the flapping lump that lay on the floor. He slowed down, drove around it, then wound down his window to see what it was.

His first and so far only book, *In Our Image*, lay face down in a black puddle, while the cold wind flapped it like a dying fish. He drove on and saw they'd torn pages out. Loads of them in fact, because he kept seeing white sheets flutter past him as he left the car park. They were turning into papier mâché, slapping against wet car doors and sodden walls. He wondered which of those sheets had his signature on, and if the ink had already started to melt and warp his name. As he drove past the park, he saw a group of Boy Scouts near the pond. They were stuffing a torn, ruined and now fully deflated Daphne into a litter bin.

CHAPTER FIVE

The first time Matt had ever seen (or indeed heard of) the Crooked Church was on a TV panel show. He and Wren were eating ice cream in bed one Friday night, watching comedians rip into the week's news events. They'd started discussing how the Church of England were making a huge national push to fight inner-city poverty, while at the same time being one of the biggest landowners in the UK. For the entire segment the presenter flicked up a picture of a church porch with a wrought iron sign across it, and everybody chuckled. A few hours later, screenshots and parody songs of 'Welcome to the Crooked Church' were racing down Internet delivery tubes.

Paedophile priest in the news? Copy and paste a shot of St Bart's. Philandering evangelical with a Liberace toupee and personal jet? Copy. Paste. An atheist website even did a range of T-shirts saying 'Welcome to the Crooked Church' with a huge cartoon of a clumsy God sitting on the church roof and crushing it. For a while St Bart's was the poster-child for ruined religion. He'd sent a few pics of it himself when it first went viral and he'd always fancied a little drive up to see this place for real sometime, since it was so close. Today he'd get his chance.

It was easy to find.

When he arrived the rain had dropped to a drizzle, but the dirt track had held on to it, storing it in deep puddles. The track splashed and rocked his car as he followed the signs. His indicator clicked a dull beat as he pulled up next to a long stone wall, wipers sliding, and there it was through his trickling side window: the outline of the weirdly wonky St Bart's. He killed the engine and heard rain slowly patting the roof. Then he buttoned the top collar of his coat and stepped out into the mud.

There were cars everywhere, parked haphazardly. Front tyres sat up on ridges, nudging tree trunks. A few were police cars, but civilian ones were scattered too. The ones that took up the most room were two outside broadcast vans.

The sky rumbled again, and the clouds, now gunmetal grey, made the church look crazy-dark for a Sunday afternoon. If anything, the slant of the Crooked Church was even more pronounced in real life. It looked in mid-collapse.

As he weaved through the cars, he was conscious of the hedgerow on his left, and wondered if a figure might spring out with an axe and shout a pre-chop 'Boo!'. Over the hedge he saw what looked like an old farmhouse, built from the exact same stone piles as the church and wall. The rectory, he assumed; not slanting, but close to it.

A Sky TV rig with tinted windows was parked ridiculously close to the church gate. It touched the car behind too. He had to smear his knees across the headlights just to get through and found that it was actually too tight to make it. Crappiest parking ever, he thought. Then the van doors popped open.

Like a domino effect, three other vehicles did the same further up the road. Reporters sprang out.

'What's your business here today, sir?'

Another called over, 'Where's Micah East?'

Matt saw a bearded man whisper into the ear of a woman with scary cheekbones. Her thin eyebrows sprang instantly when she heard what he said. She pushed towards Matt while a camera suddenly swung its lens at him, over her shoulder.

'Professor Hunter?' she called out. 'Can we have a moment please?'

He considered hopping the bonnet of the van and sliding across it, going all Starsky and Hutch to get through. But the thought of sliding off and landing arse-end in a puddle on national TV brought wisdom. He realised then that the parking wasn't crappy at all. In fact, it was very impressive parking, seeing as it was done precisely to trap any visitor for a few precious seconds.

'Professor? Can you answer a few questions?'

'Sorry, but you know more than I do.' Matt smiled. 'Genuinely.'

'Then why've they called *you* up today? Is there something bigger going—?'

'All right, all right,' a voice barked on the breeze. 'Let the man through.'

A police officer in a thick, high-vis jacket was crunching heavy boots down the church path. He had one gloved hand on the opposite shoulder, tugging a walkie-talkie to his lips to pass the message on. 'He's here.'

Questions exploded through the rain. 'Have you found Micah yet?' 'Any word on Rev. East? Is he out of his coma?' 'Give us a moment with the professor. Sixty seconds – tops.'

The policeman just gestured to the sky. 'It's going to chuck it down any minute, folks. So how about you get in your cosy vans and relax. And move this bloody van back, now.' He slid a wet pincer-glove around Matt's elbow. 'Sorry about that, Mr Hunter. This way.'

The van rolled back, and Matt finally made it through the

metal gate. The path was lined with headstones and as he walked between them he watched the Crooked Church loom slowly over him. He spotted the famous wrought iron sign over the church porch, which glistened and dripped in the rain. How tempting to take a selfie under it, but no. This wasn't the time. Especially when underneath it, a thick wooden door creaked slowly open, Dracula-style. Standing in the glow of a warm bulb was a tall, impressive-looking black woman in her late fifties. She had short grey hair, cropped and shaved at the back and sides, but the fringe was thick, and it swept across her forehead, fashionista style. One of her hands was stuffed into the pockets of a long, elegant black coat; the other played with her ear. To be honest, Matt thought she looked like an older Uhura from *Star Trek*, with that little Bluetooth headphone sticking out of her ear. He got the urge to say 'Permission to come aboard'. A classic sign that he was nervous. He put his hand out and said, 'Hi,' instead.

'Come into the warm, Professor. Come into the dry.' She had a smooth, Radio 4, book-at-bedtime voice. A storyteller's vibe. 'I'm Detective Sergeant Jill Bowland.' She was one of those hard shakers, so her wedding ring pressed a stinging crease into his finger. She'd also smoked a cigarette recently, that much was obvious.

He put out his hand, 'Good to meet—'

'One second.' Her eyes flicked over Matt's shoulder as she frowned and tutted. 'Marcus. Go back and tell them to move every single one of those vans. Put them right down by the corner. And tell them if we can't get our cars out quickly, the sky will fall on them. Okay?'

The officer nodded and jogged back down the path.

'Sorry about that. It's good to meet you too.' She offered her hand again, and he noticed something slightly out of keeping with her look. Despite her meticulous fashion sense, there was a thin and clearly home-made bracelet on her wrist, with little cubes and beads of clashing colours. She let him inside with a smile. 'I'm afraid I haven't read your books, Professor.'

'Call me Matt. And it's book. Singular.'

'Well, that's handy to know. I have a rather epic book queue at home. But naturally I'll shoot you to the front. This way . . .' She waited as he wiped his muddy shoes on a bristly brown mat that said 'Jesus Welcomes You'. When she closed the church door firmly behind him he heard the iron latch echo as it fell into place, and then they were alone.

'Any news on the son yet?'

'Not yet, though it feels like we have half of Thames Valley police tracking him down as we speak. I'm just tying up a few loose ends here.'

'What sort of loose ends?'

'It's probably best you see. Follow me.'

As they walked, he saw pews with knitted kneeling pads, and over by the north wall he noticed children's books and soft toys. A poster said 'Ickle Fish' – the Sunday School he presumed. And on the south wall, he saw a row of about thirty small votive candles, burning slowly in memory of the dead.

He didn't need to ask where they were heading. It was obvious.

Down at the sunken end of the church was a truly bizarre sight: a large, glowing white cube. It was a white, plastic evidence tent, with some sort of industrial spotlight inside. He'd seen police use these lamps before – when bodies were concerned. They'd fire down heat rays from tripods and pick up every detail of grit, hair and gore. It looked strangely pretty, that cube. Like the holiest of holies, filling the chancel with brightness. Their faces started glowing as he felt a strange pressure on his kneecaps.

'You can feel it?' Bowland said. 'The slope?'

'Wow,' he nodded. 'It's really pronounced.'

She stopped by the Communion rail and handed him a white

cloth. It looked like one of those muslin sheets you clean baby-sick up with. 'For the smell,' she said.

He copied what she was doing and cupped the cloth across his nose and mouth, then she bent over and unzipped the tent door. The acoustics amplified the zip dragging up. It sounded like a huge wasp was in there, waiting. A bright spike of vivid light fell across her shoes, then she went inside. He followed her in and squinted as his vision filled with light.

'Hope you're good at holding your breath, Matthew.'

It was like another planet, another bright dimension. It sure as hell wasn't the holiest of holies, put it that way. There was no Ark of the Covenant. No radioactive baby Jesus, glowing in sprouting hay, just a harshly lit tableaux of a Communion altar. The hefty wooden table had a white cloth messily hanging half on it, half off. Only it wasn't very white any more. Over half of it was caked with a wheelie bin's worth of blood, and on the floor, a vast reservoir of dark, sticky red was filling the stone cracks. Reverend East may be comatose in a hospital bed right now, but it felt like he'd left plenty of himself behind.

'Aw, it reeks . . .' Matt squeezed the cloth on his nose.

'Yes. Micah hit some major arteries. Seems like he was repeatedly going for the neck.'

'Which means . . .'

'He was trying to take the head off. At least it looks that way.'

'Lovely.'

'Thankfully the boy had appalling aim, plus axes are pretty heavy, so . . . he missed a lot.'

Some of the blood had browned and dried at the edges, but many of the larger stains had thick, sticky-looking patches in the centre that still looked wet to the touch.

'It's astonishing that he survived this,' Matt said.

'The congregation are calling it a miracle, though of course we'll have to see about that . . . the doctors reckon he won't make it through the night.' She took a step forward. 'So . . . about Micah. He's sixteen, doesn't drive. His mountain bike is still propped up in the vicarage porch, so we doubt he's gotten far beyond Chervil village. But there's hundreds of acres of woods and countryside out there, so he could be anywhere. Might be holing out in an old farmhouse maybe. We've been searching for two hours but the rain's holding us back. We can't get the cars up some of the roads.'

'Is there a mum?'

'Yes. Zara East, forty-eight years old, but she's away travelling at present. We're not sure where exactly but we're trying to track her down. No siblings.'

'What about motive?'

'Well, this is where you potentially come in . . . I'm looking into some rumours' – she bit her lip – 'that Micah might have been involved in devil worship or Satanism . . . but we'll get to that in a second. Just look over the scene. Tell me your first impression.'

Intrigued, Matt ran his eyes across the stained cloth again, and the silver goblet of wine, filled to the brim with a mixture of wine and blood. He spotted a loaf of bread sitting in a pool of coagulated blood. That particular sight made both his stomach and his heart lurch. He saw a flash of his mother, dead at her kitchen table, seeping into her Sunday dinner. 'Well it looks fairly chaotic to me, but most of the blood is on the altar specifically. The place of sacrifice . . .' He turned to her. 'When exactly did it happen?'

'Micah hid behind a curtain. He stepped out during the Eucharist or Communion . . . those are essentially the same thing, aren't they?'

'Yeah, but when in the Eucharist, exactly?'

'Just before he blessed the wine.'

'Jesus's blood, you mean . . .' He rubbed his chin. 'Where are you getting this Satanism thing from?'

She shifted on her feet. 'Bear with me, there's a few things. Firstly, Micah's lived here since he was seven, that's almost ten years. The congregation say that for almost all of that he's been a lovely boy who loved the church, until about a year ago when he seems to have fallen out with his dad. Since then he's avoided the church, been rude and threatening to some of the older ones.' She looked down at her notes. 'That's when he started dressing differently. Long black hair, black clothes . . .'

It sounded strange to laugh in here, but he couldn't help it. 'Black jumpers doth not a Satanist make.'

'He was also heard to chant something just before the attack. People were too far back to hear it, but they said it was a repetitive, strange language' – she glanced at her phone again – '"something scary, ancient and satanic".'

'He could have just mumbled. Teenagers mumble.'

'There's more. One of the elderly parishioners, Gwen Skeggs. She told me something odd.' Her voice dropped a notch and she leant in. 'She's on a rota to do church flowers once a month. She came in last night to arrange them, ready for this morning, and she looked down the aisle. She saw Micah standing on the altar. Right on top of it.'

'Doing what?'

'Pulling his jeans down.'

Matt winced. 'Dare I ask what he was doing?'

'He was urinating all over the wood. Had a circle of candles burning, too. Gwen got the shock of her life and rushed out. She climbed into her car and drove straight home. Poor lady was pretty shaken by it, though she's sure she wasn't spotted. She said he was too busy praying in this strange language . . . and before you ask, she didn't know what it was. Just that it was the same as what he used this morning.'

'I see . . . so, did she tell Reverend East what she saw?'

'She tried at this morning's service, but she never had the chance.

She insists . . .' Bowland waited for a moment. 'The boy has the Devil in him.'

Matt took the cloth away for a second and took in the blood smell. Now he could finally understand the other foul stink that lingered here too. It smelt like a toilet here. A gruesome toilet. 'Teenagers do get angry. They lash out, sometimes symbolically. Especially at the stuff their parents value. It doesn't mean he was a full-on Satanist.'

'Agreed, but there's something else over at the vicarage. Have you seen enough here?'

'I've seen plenty. Smelt plenty too. Plus, I'm kinda freezing my nuts off in here.'

She frowned at him. 'You're cold?'

'Aren't you?'

For the first time, he realised she'd unbuttoned her jacket. 'I'm rather warm, actually. The lights.'

He shrugged and felt colder still. Resisting a shiver, he said, 'I must have rain down my shirt. Lead the way.'

He was glad to be out of the tent, and though the air was still a little tainted, he breathed it in eagerly as they headed back up the aisle. He turned back to look at the tent for one last time, just as a breeze seemed to make the flaps of the tent twitch a little, like they'd left somebody in there. The wind made a noise too: not a high-pitched whistle, but the sad exhalation of a low moaning breath. Perhaps there were candles burning down there too. Perhaps that's why the shadows on the wall seemed to move.

'Professor?' she said, in a tone that made him blink. 'Let's not dawdle, eh?'

CHAPTER SIX

The world outside felt shockingly gloomy after the glaring light of the cube, but at least his nostrils were free of middle-aged blood and teenage piss. Not a cocktail he'd be ordering again in a hurry. Around him, the wet wind rattled the frantic trees, but it hadn't managed to shift the sun-blocking clouds, nor did it manage to threaten Bowland's titanium haircut. At least the reporters had moved. They'd parked their vans down the road, as instructed. Every door still clicked open though, the second he and Bowland walked down the gravel path.

To their snapping, loud questions she called out a loud and clipped, 'We'll update you at 4 p.m.'

'But have you found him ye—'

'4 p.m.' She turned to Matt and smiled. 'Got to be firm with them. Like toddlers. Now, follow me.' They crossed to the other side of the dirt road and pushed through the creaking rectory gate. Someone shouted for permission to film inside the vicarage. She chuckled at Matt. 'As if.'

The patchy grass of the front garden was ravaged by the cold weather, and over by a wooden fence Matt saw what must have been the East's Christmas tree, lying flat on its side on a bed of mud. Globules of rainwater dripped from its browned branches. She rummaged in her pocket and pulled out a set of keys with a plastic tag on it. They made a tinkling, fairy-godmother sound as she opened up. Matt was immediately hit with the coldness inside. He ran his hand up and down his arms. 'Now, come on. It's like a fridge in here.'

She nodded. 'This time I agree with you. The boiler's broken. Seems like it's been that way for weeks.'

He ran his eyes across the rectory. It was much older and much bigger than the 1970s suburban semi Matt was given as a church minister. Yet the age and size of it had clearly brought problems as well as potential. The walls had many lightning cracks across the plaster and the entire place reeked of mould and damp carpets. Wooden beams ran through the ceiling, exposed and splitting. He saw doors open into an old-fashioned kitchen and the lounge was strewn with newspapers and old-looking books, splayed on their spines. He thumped an armchair and the air turned instantly foggy with floating, whirling dust.

'Would you look at that.' He passed his arm through it like a star field. 'Guess Reverend East hadn't mastered the whole cleaning thing.'

'I mastered cleaning years ago. She's called Fenella. Twelve pounds an hour.' Bowland put a hand on the bannister, 'Come on. It's upstairs.'

The old wooden staircase groaned with a ghost-ship creak, and they emerged into a wide landing filled with bookshelves. Each shelf sagged in the middle under the weight of biblical commentaries and Bible dictionaries. He recognised some of the titles. Most had been published in the early 1980s. You could always tell when a vicar had been at Bible college – they buy a shitload of holy books around then and never seem to update them.

All five doors up here were closed, and Bowland nodded at the porthole window in the landing. 'Bit creepy, living next door to so many dead bodies.'

'Funnily enough, my bedroom in Chesham has a very similar view.' Matt bent over and peeked through the trickling pane. He saw tombstones out there, swamped in the rainy gloom. The only thing that didn't look grey were the windows of the chancel, glowing with the blood-filled cube inside. 'You know there's a lot to be said for having quiet neighbours.'

'Not that quiet.' She went to push the bedroom door open, but hesitated, fingertips on the door handle.

'Are you okay?'

She waited for a moment. 'You don't believe in this spiritual stuff any more, do you? You're not a believer.'

He shook his head. 'Why do you ask?'

'Just curious.' She pushed the door open and clicked on the overhead light.

He squinted at the dull, pathetic glow. 'I never knew you could buy one-watt bulbs.'

Bowland clicked on a torch instead.

The stale smell of sweat, farts and general musk lingered. The place was a teenage cliché. An unmade double bed sat in the centre of the room. Jeans, tops and trousers, mostly dark grey, brown or black, were scattered everywhere in chaotic-looking piles. In the corner he saw an old, first-generation Xbox, covered in dust so thick it could cover coins. Sticky-looking wires trailed to a deep, old-style portable TV, perched on a pile of old encyclopaedias. The only thing in the room that looked reasonably clean was a large halogen heater by the bed.

Matt blew inside his fists. 'Any chance we can put that on?'

'Might as well . . .' Bowland leant over and clicked it. The room suddenly bloomed with an orange glow. They opened their palms at it, like a couple of hobos in the street.

'First time I've seen a teenager's room without any posters,' Matt said. 'No rock stars, no girls in bikinis, no skaters or footballers . . .'

She nodded. 'Least he had the bugs for company.'

'What? Where?' Matt sprang his gaze to where she was pointing. Up in the far corner of the ceiling, just above a strange little half-sized door, was a fat, hefty-looking spider. It crawled slowly across an intricate web, clearly made from weeks of unbroken effort. It scuttled even faster when the perfect circle of torchlight fell on it.

Bowland lowered the beam to the door directly beneath it, then walked towards it and got down on her knees. 'Come on. You need to see inside this little cupboard.'

Distant thunder rolled outside.

He lowered himself alongside her, smelling her perfume and crunching his kneecaps into the carpet, conscious that above him, the thick-looking spider sprang and bounced along its flimsy frame. 'This bolt looks brand new.'

'Yep, and pretty expensive too. Took me a while to smash it off, but I did. I'm a sucker for a kettlebell class.'

'I'll bear that in mind.'

She curled her fingers around the handle and pulled. The carpet was too thick underneath, so the little door dragged in spasmodic jerks as it opened. It looked like a pure black hole inside, until she fired the torch at it.

'You mentioned the lack of posters . . .' she said.

'Wow.' He crawled forward a little. Inside were piles of magazines strewn across the slatted wooden floor. They were stacked in haphazard clumps, but what made him frown was what had been done to the covers. Somebody – Micah, he assumed – had punctured all the eyes out with a pencil.

'They're pretty much all like that. Even the porn, though he didn't have much of that, to be fair.'

Most of the magazines were for films and computer games, and looked like last year's editions, but any shot of an actor, singer or celebrity had ragged holes for eyes. Underneath he saw the garish colours of a porn mag. A pig-tailed woman was sucking her middle finger like a lollipop. The entire top half of her face was torn out.

'Yeah,' Matt said, '. . . I'd certainly file this under weird.'

'Get closer. I need you to look up *inside* the cupboard. At the ceiling.' Her eyes flashed. 'Get on your back.'

He paused, saw her nod, then twisted himself around.

'That's it. Right back.'

He put his back on the carpet and Bowland slapped the torch into his open palm, 'You'll need to actually crawl in there.'

'It's filthy in here.'

'Just hang on to your dry-cleaning receipt.'

Before moving in he flicked the torch up a little and felt his stomach quiver as it fired onto the bedroom ceiling. The epic spider web stretched directly above him, and it looked way bigger from this angle. Now two black shapes were scuttling across it, bouncing and swaying, looking horribly too heavy for the structure they'd created. If one of them opted for a SWAT-team drop, it'd scramble right into Matt's gawping mouth. He clamped his jaw shut and quickly shimmied through the narrow door until his head, shoulders and chest were inside the cupboard. Under his shoulders, the eyeless army from all those cold magazines pressed against him.

'If one of those spiders drops on my gut, you'll whack it, right?' he called back. 'Shoot it in the head if you have to.'

He heard her now-muffled voice. 'I'll handcuff it. Now look straight up.'

He flung the beam to the top of the cupboard and moaned at

57

another spider web, with disturbingly thick cords, until the swaying shadows calmed down and he got perspective. Despite the little door, the cupboard was much taller than he expected inside. And these thick shadow lines weren't cast by spiders. A bunch of crucifixes dangled on rough string, stapled to the ceiling.

He blinked. Tilted his head a little. 'Woah,' he said. 'They're all upside down.'

'Yeah. There's thirty-three of them. We counted.'

'Thirty-three? That's how old Jesus was when he died.'

'You think that might be significant?'

'Maybe,' he shrugged. 'Maybe not.' He watched them dangling. Little crosses of various sizes. Some made of wood, some of metal, others that were little more than twigs and branches tied together. And all of them inverted.

'What's all this black stuff on them?'

'Were getting it checked out. Seems like soot.'

'He burnt them?'

'We don't think so. Seems like he burnt something else and rubbed these crosses with the ash. We'll find out what. See what we mean about devil worship now?'

'Well . . .'

'I was thinking if this was from some sort of organised Satanist group or something, it might give us some leads in tracking him down. A coven of witches, maybe?'

He slowly moved his gaze from cross to cross. 'I think you can rule out a coven. Witches don't really use symbols like this. Heck, they don't even believe in the Devil. Satanists do use the upturned cross as a symbol for liberation, but most are law-abiding citizens, especially the Church of Satan members. Attacking people with axes is going to put them in prison, and believe me, losing personal freedom is the last thing a Satanist wants.'

'I see,' she said, sounding distracted.

'I'm just doubtful this is part of some organised group . . .' He realised he was talking to the crucifixes and not to her. Plus, his arms were going numb. 'Hang on, I'm coming out.' He shimmied back out, dreading one of the spiders dive-bombing into his face. 'It's more likely that he's just done all this on his own . . .' He trailed off when he noticed something. She was gone. The halogen fire was off too. The room was now only lit by the dull glow from the pointless bulb, and the circle of his torch.

'Er . . . hello?' he shouted to the room and what came back was a scuffle of noise from the cupboard behind him. He craned his head back and saw a fat rat scamper across the magazines. He yelped, sprang to his feet and quickly brushed the dust from his shoulders. He went to call her again and heard footsteps on the landing. 'Bowland? Are you there?'

She appeared in the doorway, a phone clamped to her head.

'Where'd you go? There's a killer rat in—'

'Let's move.' She spun away. 'Now.'

'Wait . . .' He raced after her and watched her hammer down the rickety stairs, one hand pinning the phone to her head, the other yanking car keys from her belt. He quickly realised what was happening and took the stairs two at a time to keep up.

'Where exactly?' she said into her phone as she threw the front door open; her black coat swung out in the gust of wind. 'On our way.'

As they hurried through the front garden, Matt heard the throb of a helicopter overhead. 'Where is he?'

'A barman just found him hiding in their beer cellar. Couple of miles away. Maybe you can talk with him.'

'So, they have him?'

'Not yet, but we've got a visual on him.' She zapped her key fob in the air and her car, positioned and ready to roll, blinked awake. Behind her, the Crooked Church looked even darker and more forbidding than before. Down the road the other police cars –

and some of the news crews – were already surging off. She shouted at the remaining news cars to get out of the way and her volume sounded like pure thunder. Then she called to him, over the roof of the car. Her tone back to friendly. But still urgent. Very urgent. 'You better ride with me, Professor.'

CHAPTER SEVEN

The squirrel stood completely still, staring right at him through a mist of falling snow. Even when the flakes landed on its hilarious, bushy eyebrows the animal never twitched, never blinked. There were no little sneezes to break the mood.

Do the same, Ever thought. *Be super still, so the little fella doesn't run off.*

He held his breath. Made himself as stiff as he could. He mentally toured his own body, freezing each muscle in turn. Eyes locked, heart paused.

Funny. If the others wandered past they'd think they'd stumbled into a photograph. Like the ones Milton had in his room. He kept old books with pictures of beaches and mountains and other things Ever hadn't seen. Standing here, he became his own picture. The little boy in a bright-red Puffa jacket, with a springy squirrel ready to leap on his shoulder.

But of course, nobody would see this moment because the others hardly ever came to this part of the stream. There were higher, more interesting patches to play in, where the stream was wider, the trees more climbable and the view of Comfort Hill more pleasing and big. But Ever avoided those higher spots because they were a little too distant from the farmhouse for his liking. He felt much safer having his home in sight. If a Hollow ever came creeping up here, at least he'd be in running (and screaming) distance.

Not that he'd ever actually seen an unexpected Hollow up here, but he knew they were out there, watching. Especially at night, when the shadows came and it got so dark that even the poor little moon had to hide behind a cloud. Whenever the moon hid, it meant the Hollows weren't far away. He'd hear the distant drone of their machines. He'd watch the glow of their lights poisoning the horizon.

Of course, he'd seen a few up here, through the years. But at least they were expected. Every now and then they had to let one or two Hollows come to the house. Prosper said it was a strange game the demons liked to play, and that it was best to just go along with it. They'd never come as themselves. They wore their human suits instead, looking kind and well dressed. They'd wander through the farmhouse asking him questions like, did he have plenty of bedding, did he like eating food, and they'd check if he could add and spell. Prosper told him to just answer their questions and keep his head down. Those visits were, without a doubt, the most terrifying experiences of his life, but then they'd leave and he'd not see another for a whole year. But he wasn't stupid. He knew they still came back unannounced, creeping up here, after dark. When the game was over and the skin was peeled away. When they came as their true selves, just to watch.

Milton said he saw one of these watchers one night. It was after he got up in the middle of the night for a wee. Milton was old, so he weed a lot, and he got up one hot spring night and opened the bathroom window as he let himself go. He saw a Hollow near their shed, sitting on their fence. He said he was so shocked that he dribbled all over his slippers. It was three in the morning, and after switching off the bathroom light, he sat at the window and watched it for two hours. Two whole hours! He said it just sat there, perched near the gate, watching them sleep as it nibbled its claws. Then it was gone. Next morning, a slipperless Milton told them all about it over the most intense breakfast ever. Since then, Ever decided he'd only ever play near the house.

So what if Merit laughed at him for not playing higher upstream? What did she know? She wasn't brave because five-year-olds aren't capable of bravery. Any courage they had was more to do with ignorance than strength. But he was ten, and at that age the heart starts learning sense. He wasn't a coward, he was wise, which was why he was so excited that it would end soon. Yep. After today, all the Hollows were going to fall up into the sky. Every single one of them. Right up into the clouds, then *pop!* they'd be gone.

Trying not to blink he stared at the squirrel, at this mass of grey fuzz, and the fuzz stared back. Two statues, collecting time. The only thing moving was the snow.

This weather was so weird.

Raining one day, sweaty-hot the next, and this afternoon, a random, but totally wonderful blast of snow that sadly didn't settle. It just seemed to dissolve against whatever it touched. All this nutty weather was a sign, of course. Prosper said it was 'the last pang of a confused, dying world'. He said it showed a universe in panic. Like any dying thing panics. Yeah, the weather was a sign, without a doubt. And Ever certainly knew how important signs and symbols were. They didn't just point to things; symbols could change the world.

Uh-oh.

A big flake of snow dumped itself right on his hooter. It started to melt almost instantly, trickling into his nostril. Imagine that, he thought. Fluff, literally from clouds, falling for miles, just to make him sneeze and scare the squirrel away. He rolled his eyes up and fired an angry thought, right at heaven. *You want to ruin everything, don't you?*

The clouds responded, and heaven sent a batch of new, wet splats, to threaten the moment even more. How spiteful. How immature. How—

A gunshot rang out.

He flicked his eyes to Comfort Hill and then there was silence.

He saw familiar shapes come up over the curve. Prosper and Milton stood up near the chapel, laughing and firing into the sky. He actually preferred the sound of gunshots to what he normally heard up on the hill. The grown-ups made funny old sounds in that chapel. Especially on big days like today. Sobs and groans. Wails and screams.

When Ever looked back, the squirrel had already sprung off the stones. Their frozen moment now thawed and over. The tuft of tail bounded upstream, off into the cold.

He sighed and soon the sigh became a prayer. Sighs often did that, he noticed. 'Make everything work today. Make all the Hollows fall up and die. Amen.'

He clambered back up the little ridge towards home and saw Prosper and Milton were heading there too, leaving the high chapel and coming down the long dirt path. They shot one more bullet into the sky while Milton cupped his hands around his mouth to shout his name.

'Hey, Big Man!' The old man's voice bounced through their valley. 'End's comin'!'

Ever hollered a jolly message back, 'And it's comin' soon. Wohooo!' They cheered while Ever ran across the field, arms wide open, making curves and circles in the falling snow, all the way to the farmhouse.

CHAPTER EIGHT

Wren had this physics rule of thumb that she was trying to enshrine into Hunter family law. If they were out in the car, and it was raining, the driver had to minus at least ten miles per hour from whatever the speed limit was. That way, should a kid, dog or herd of Bigfoot run out into the road, there'd be a decent amount of stoppage space. Clearly, this rule hadn't reached the Bowland household, because when it was raining, she liked to take the speed limit and add thirty on top.

Now, on the soaked country roads of 40 mph, they were whipping past hedges at a thoroughly ungodly 70, and on the longer stretches with a 60 limit she was well over 90, sometimes at 100. Matt felt his body slide and press hard into the passenger door and he gripped the handle that hung from the ceiling. She'd instructed him to grab that, back at the vicarage. As soon as she'd turned the ignition, in fact. As she swung around the bends, he could hear the beads of her homemade bracelet tapping against each other, and he saw a couple of loose CDs sliding around in the footwell. Dolly Parton's *Here You Come Again* was one of them. Dolly's happy clown face beamed up at them both, kicking her jeans out in a winky, homespun grin. A leopard-skin coffee cup rattled in the holder. On the side it said, 'Best Grandma Ever'.

Another police car surged in front while another one bit and chomped from behind. They must have been brilliantly trained in driving, because they all kept top speed. For seventy per cent of the ride it didn't feel like they were going to slam into one another. Every now and then he'd check on the helicopter by leaning forward and looking up through the windscreen. Through the rain it looked like a giant mechanical dragonfly, swooping and diving. From time to time, the huge insect even spoke from above. Buzzing through the dash radio it said, 'We've seen him', 'He's heading west.' Then a very certain, 'He's heading for the wind turbines.'

The entire body of the car tipped to the left as Bowland swung a hard curve, and then Matt finally saw what the helicopter could. About half a mile down, across the field, three white towers were spinning their blades against a cement-coloured sky, and just beyond them, a train was whizzing past, cutting a track between two fields.

'We've lost him,' the radio buzzed.

Bowland slammed her palm off the steering wheel and groaned.

The radio again. 'We'll check the trees by the line. Stand by at the turbines.'

It didn't take long to reach the turbines, though it was bumpy as all hell getting there. A long stretch of frozen mud ridges made his bones shake, and his voice became a rapid, mad vibrato: 'Thanks for the massage.'

'Okay, we're stopping.' She didn't say this as much as yodel it. Her earrings were having a fit. 'Hold tight.'

She locked her brakes hard, and they both sprang forward in their seat, seat belts locking, shoulders stinging. Tyres dragged deep canyons in the ground and as he grabbed the dash with open hands his little finger slid and knocked the CD player on. Dolly Parton filled the car, the opening pulse of '9 to 5'. She reached over and knocked it off, immediately. Which was kind of a shame. Then she killed the engine, and they watched the helicopter fly off ahead of them at a tipped angle. It swung by the train line, then seemed to hurry back as if it had seen something. It hovered in one spot, right above the turbines. The air was filled with spinning blades. The trees and hedges nearby swayed and bowed wildly.

'They've stopped,' Matt said. 'They must have him.'

The radio buzzed in response. 'We think we see him again, hiding inside the furthest tower. Proceed with caution.'

She flicked her belt loose, and so did he.

'No way,' she glared at him. 'You stay here.'

'You said I should talk to him.'

'Yeah, but after he's secure.' She opened her door and the helicopter throbbed louder than ever. 'Can't have him chopping your head off, can I?'

'I'll—'

'Stay.' She slammed the door shut and ran off, the tail of her long jacket flapping. Amazing really, he thought, watching this glam granny bound around the countryside like a superhero, barking out instructions. When Matt's granny was this age, her special skills were making farm scenes out of dried pasta and smelling of onions. Funny how genetics work out. He watched her fling her arm back towards the car, then he heard a click. All the doors locked. *Hey!* he thought. *Professors die in hot cars!* Then he relaxed. She only did that to lock Micah East out, not to lock him in. They'd pop open if he pulled the handle, probably. Possibly. He didn't try the handle to test it.

He cupped his hands against the window and watched what he could of the action, but the rain-soaked glass threw the entire world underwater. He saw them checking the hedges and trees as they moved towards the turbines. With no way of lowering the windows or starting the wipers, he might as well have been in a submarine. He shrugged and sat back into his heated seat. Maybe he should have brought a book.

Another train thundered past, and as he watched the blur of it, he thought he heard the police shouting over by the turbines. Which is when he saw the black smudge run from one hedge to another, barely twenty feet away.

He sprang up in his seat.

The black figure moved again.

Oh, shit.

From the hedge to a crop of trees.

He looked back towards the turbines, and saw the police spreading out, pointing signals to each other, only none were in his direction. The helicopter still hovered there.

Dammit. He had to tell them.

He stared at the dashboard at what he assumed was the police radio. 'On switch?' he asked, as if a voice would answer back saying, 'Right here, Matt.' He jabbed at the buttons instead and a display cropped up saying, 'Enter code'.

'Crap.' He looked up and stared at those hedges again, but all that rain meant he couldn't see a thing. He'd have better vision swimming in a pool of milk, without goggles. But still . . . he had to tell them. He took a breath, brewed up a shout, and tried a quick test. He pulled the handle from inside. Like he'd thought, the locked door popped open easily. He quickly closed it and pushed the lock down again, and they all clunked shut.

Okay. He had this. He'd open up, shout for them, and drop right back into the car and lock the doors again. He'd only have to put one foot out of the car the entire time. This was genius.

Sometimes people don't think things through.

It's like pressurised circumstances force them into particular actions. Army guys and police folk get trained in the quick-thinking mindset, but Matt was a university professor. He usually had ample time to make responses. So when he opened the door, planted his one foot down and stood up into the rain, he cupped both hands around his mouth so he could shout to the police. He did it as loudly as he could. 'Over here.' But as he formed the 'o' with his lips, the figure in black rushed up from the back end of the car. Matt span and saw a wet caveman lunge through the rain. He slapped a very wet hand across Matt's mouth and pulled him from the car, spinning him and dragging him to the floor.

Matt called out in a muffled roar but he cut it short the instant something sharp pressed against the base of his spine. The corner of that infamous axe, ready to sever his spine, perhaps? A thought bubbled up that made him want to punch himself – *Should have beeped the horn, ya dick. Should have beeped the horn.*

Micah held Matt there, both sitting on the wet soil, hidden between the cars.

'You've got to drive me out of here,' Micah said. He stunk of that cruddy odd cocktail from the church . . . blood and urine.

'I don't have the keys.'

Micah hissed into his ear, 'Don't lie to me.'

'I swear to you, I'm not. It's not my car. I'm just a passenger.'

The kid groaned desperately, and his breath was pure panic.

'Micah, listen,' Matt spoke into a hand that was slowly loosening to let him speak. 'We can talk. Let's ta—'

'My dad,' he whispered. 'Have they moved the body from the church yet?'

'The body? But he's alive . . .' Matt felt a flash of hope. 'So, this isn't murder, all right? You're not in as much trouble as you think.' He wasn't sure why he assumed this information would be helpful. Perhaps he just imagined how relieved his own teenage self would be, if his lashing out wasn't permanent. So, Matt said it again, 'You didn't kill him.'

This hopeful titbit did nothing to lift Micah's spirit. It was the absolute polar opposite.

'No . . . no . . . no . . .' He gave out a horrified, lurching moan. '*That's* why you're still here.' Then he made another sound. Was he crying?

'Micah,' Matt said. 'Why did you do this?'

'I had to,' he sniffed and whimpered. 'Had to.'

'But why?'

'You know why,' he sobbed. 'To stop you all. To stop the Father.'

'I told you, your father's still alive. Now, I'm just going to turn around.'

'Don't you dare.' Micah pressed the sharp point harder into Matt's coat. Then the boy gasped.

The helicopter was swooping back now, and all the police and Bowland too were coming with it, charging from the turbines back to the cars.

'Keep talking,' Matt said. 'What is it you want to stop, exactly?'

'They know,' he said in panic. 'They know I'm here.'

The helicopter got to them first. It swung overhead, blasting deafening power into the ground, pressing out every blade of grass, every strand of hair.

'I'm not a policeman, okay?' Matt shouted over the blades. 'And I know what it's like to want to hurt your dad.' Matt started to turn his head.

'Don't you dare look at me, demon.'

Matt frowned. 'Demon?'

'If you do I'll . . . I'll cut your eyes out. So, it won't work, Hollow, it won't work.'

'What won't work?'

A spotlight erupted from the helicopter. It threw a brilliant, perfect circle over Matt and Micah, alien-abduction style. Then the giant dragonfly cried out words in a deafening, mechanical buzz. 'Put the weapon down. You're surrounded. Put it down.'

The sound of shouts and pounding feet was getting closer. Maybe fifty feet away.

'Tell me about the crosses,' Matt said. 'And the church altar.'

Micah's hand fell loose and the pressure from the blade vanished from the base of his back. Matt felt himself pushed forward. He stumbled forwards, hands outstretched into the damp, but still hard mud. When he spun back around, he saw Micah had already flung himself to his feet. In his hand was a ballpoint pen. There was no knife.

'Micah, wait!' he called out, but he was already shrinking. He was running back towards the trees where he'd been earlier, as the white, spectral circle from above followed him in perfect time.

Matt raced after him, just as the others were closing in. He heard a bevy of policemen thirty feet away, roaring out demands for Micah to stop running. In amongst it, he heard Bowland's panting voice shouting, 'Stand down, Professor. Stand down!'

But Matt kept running, because he knew what would happen next. Heck, they all knew. It was obvious. Micah span dirt under him so he might reach the train track. So he might reach the train that was hurtling down the line at what, in the distance, looked like a slow-ish speed. True, if Micah could get across this track before the rest of them, he'd at least have a chance of losing them again. Though Matt doubted the kid could ever escape the helicopter above.

But there was a horrible inevitability about it, because the train was obviously too close. The nearer they got to the track, the less slow the train seemed to be. It wasn't a passenger train. There were no commuters sipping warm tea at the windows, or bored yawners catching up on their Netflix queue. It was just a giant, wrought iron, black centipede dragging fifteen skips of what looked like heavy coal.

'Micah, no!' Matt shouted out. 'You won't make it.'

Micah surged ahead, anyway. Towards the end, Matt saw the already exhausted kid veer to the left a little, as if going at the track on an arc of just a few extra centimetres might just get him across.

It didn't.

The last thing they all saw was Micah raising his hands in the air, so he could shout at the sky. Calling out something indecipherable. Then they heard the monstrous roar of the train that didn't slow at all, but seemed to speed up in those few final seconds.

Matt squinted his eyes shut, but like his shout from the car before, his brain hadn't prepped him for the timing. It went in slow motion. The heavy lids of his eyes closed, the eyelashes spiked into one another, like a portcullis dropping. None of this was fast enough.

It was interesting, he supposed. From a purely biological point of view. That the brain can register images in a thousandth of a second, because just as the forest of lashes closed, he saw the train pick up the figure of Micah and carry on moving, and then his eyes were shut tight. For a silly, but genuinely hopeful second, he thought the kid might have somehow grabbed onto a railing and was holding on. Using some super-cool parkour skills, to make an epic getaway.

But he opened his eyes again and the train was screeching its brakes in a nightmarish scream, and out of the corner of his vision he saw the strangest sight he'd ever seen. A leg, as if it was still running, was tumbling down from the sky.

CHAPTER NINE

Ever pushed through the wooden gate and looked up the path at his home. Everybody's home, really. Wisps of smoke were just about visible from the chimney, which made his tongue instantly tingle. A big day like this meant they'd cook toast on the open fire in the lounge. He loved it when they did that. Huddled together, all bundled up in prayer and honey and laughter and crumbs.

He squealed as the snow turned into heavy rain, and he raced up the path. He looked back at the men who were both running too, but they were heading for the shed for some reason. At least they'd stopped shooting. Ever didn't wait for them. *If I get inside now, I'll get a seat on the couch before they do. Prime toasting space. Ha!*

He pushed through the door and smiled at the warmth inside and noticed the glow. With it being a special day, all the lights were off. Mum had lit soft rows of candles, instead. They threw strange, swaying shadows across Donald – the big deer head that hung on a plaque, near the ceiling. Donald's mouth smiled at him, then stopped smiling, smiled again, then stopped. At least the eye sockets were empty. They'd been scooped out ages ago. Though in the dancing light, it almost looked like there were movement in those sockets too. New, deeper eyeballs growing and trying to push through.

He shoved his boots into his section of the huge metal rack and skidded on his socks across the hallway to the lounge. He ploughed right into Pax's legs. She was stepping out of the kitchen and she stumbled backwards when they clashed.

'Pax.' He felt terrible. 'I'm so sorry.'

He needn't have worried. As usual, she was oblivious. Pax meant peace, after all, which was true enough, because she never used many words. Right now she just stood there, chewing the overlong sleeve of her raggedy old cardigan. 'I . . . dreamt . . .'

Ever waited. 'You dreamt . . .'

''Bout Hollows.'

'Oh.'

'They came. Burnt us . . .'

'Hey . . .' he took her hand, 'it's just a dream.'

'Too slow to stop them.' Her eyes glistened. 'Sorry . . . Ever died . . .'

'Oh, Pax. Come here.' She was pretty tall, so when he threw his arms around her hips he had to speak into her tummy. 'Just forget about those stupid Hollows, okay? And forget that brain of yours, too. You'll get a new one soon. You'll be the cleverest person in this whoooooole family.' He pulled back, staring up at a child of twenty-four. Prosper called her slow. Uncle Dust said it was brain damage. Milton just called her a retard. But Ever? He called her 'sleepy', because that's precisely what she was. But she'd wake up soon. They all would. He squeezed her hand. 'End's coming, Pax.'

'Is Mummy coming too?'

'Soon, I think.'

His own mum appeared in the kitchen doorway. That rope of

long, plaited hair hung off her shoulder and, as usual, she had that thin scarf of hers, tied around her neck. 'You kids ready for a feast?'

His eyes popped. 'Totally.'

'Then take Pax and grab a seat in the lounge, Merit's eating in there already. But be quiet, Ever. Uncle Dust's still praying.'

He threw her a thumbs up and headed in.

They found the sofas and armchairs had all been pushed back, and right in the centre of the large space was a figure, crouched over. Dust had his forehead pressed on the floor, whispering into the wood.

Pax's five-year-old, Merit, was sitting on the sofa, legs dangling as she quietly ate toast. Pax sat down next to her like a robot but did nothing except stare at the fire. So Merit slipped her mum's fingers between her own, and manually locked them together. Then she kept on munching her food.

Uncle Dust finally looked up from the floor. He raked his long hair from his eyes and scooped it into a ponytail, then he sat in the armchair by the window, slipping his little ringed glasses back on. He caught Ever's eye as he tapped his glasses into place. 'Hiya,' he mouthed, then winked at him.

Ever did the same wink back, but Dust had already turned to look out the window, gazing at the rain.

Ever went over. 'Uncle Dust?'

'Yup?'

'It's still going to happen, isn't it?' Ever waited. 'It's still going to end?'

The front door crashed open, and any sacred silence in the house vanished. The hallway filled with men's laughing voices as Prosper and Milton strode in. Prosper, long-armed and gangly, with his perfectly bald and perfectly reflective head, and Milton, older than any of them, all tattooed arms with thick, bone-crushing fists on the ends and cheeks puckered with little scars.

Milton nodded to Ever and warmed his backside by the fire. 'Hiya, Big Man.'

'Hi,' Ever said.

'Hey, Dust,' Prosper was frowning. 'Why so glum?'

'Glum? Who's glum?' Dust laughed.

Prosper flashed his little teeth. 'You are. Feels like a funeral parlour in here. Feels like somebody died.'

'Relax, I was praying. Just easing the way.'

'Pah,' Prosper shook his head. 'The time for prayer's over. Me and Milton have just been melting this snow with praise . . . with dancing!' He slapped a thick hand on Milton's shoulders. 'Maestro, please.'

Milton vanished into the hallway, then came back with his accordion in place.

Merit stopped the slow chew of her toast, 'Yay!'

Even Pax let her cardigan drop from her mouth.

Milton curtsied in the centre of the room and started wheezing out busy, happy chords while Prosper clapped a constant rhythm. His claps were always that little bit too loud. Each slap of his skin sounded like a whiplash.

Prosper looked over at Ever's mum, who was leaning by the door. 'Don't just stand there, Verity. Come and rattle these floorboards.'

She chuckled, then flung the tea towel away. 'Ahhh, why not.' She started clapping and came over to Ever, tugging him up too. Then, as music filled the room, Merit and Pax slid off the couch to join in. And finally, Dust. He started tapping his hands on his knees as he sat in his chair.

'End's coming, hallelujah,' Prosper whirled in a circle. They all did. 'Hope is blasting Hollows to the moon!'

Milton spun too, his fingers flying wild and busy on the buttons and keys. It was only when Ever stopped to catch his breath that he noticed Uncle Dust. He was back on his knees again, over by the rain-spattered window. His scarred hands, that were always so great at flinging him high into the air, were now locked together in prayer. Prosper saw this, and just rolled his eyes. 'Louder, Milton,' he shouted. 'Faster.'

Milton spun more quickly.

'End's coming! End's coming.'

Chanting. Laughing. Clapping hard.

'Hallelujah it's coming soooooooon—'

Prosper trailed off when Milton lost his balance and staggered headlong towards the fire. The whole room gave a panicked 'Whoa'.

Dust leapt up and grabbed him, stumbling him into a safe landing on the sofa.

The kids cheered but Prosper stood there, quietly. His gargoyle face flickered in the firelight.

'Verity?' Dust said. 'I reckon it's time we had this toast of yours.'

'Coming up.' She vanished for a moment, then came back with a tray of bread and jars, each with knives sticking out. They all scooped up slices and stuck them on forks, dangling them over the flames. Ever was trying to jab a fork into his when he heard his name.

'Ever . . .' Prosper said.

He swallowed. 'Yeah?'

'Made a new friend today?'

Silence.

'I saw you talking to the squirrel.'

He nodded. 'It's the cutest little—'

'Hollow?' Prosper licked his bottom lip. 'Could be one of them, you know.'

Ever shook his head, 'No way.'

'Don't you know? It's not just humans who turn. I've heard animals can too. And when they turn Hollow the Father makes them walk tall like people, and they even talk like people. And worse than that they love to kill, just like people love to ki—'

'Prosper . . .' Dust said. 'That's enough.'

He ignored him and leant forward. 'You didn't look in its eyes, did you?'

Ever shivered.

'Did you?'

Ever jumped when a hand touched his side. He relaxed. It was Uncle Dust, hitching him up onto his hip. 'It was a squirrel, okay? And what's it matter? It'll be over soon.'

'That it will.' Prosper sunk back into the sofa. 'Just want you to be safe, that's all. Don't want to lose anyone today, of all days. Closer to the end we get, the more they'll come to find us. They have tricks, remember. Tricks.'

Mum was sat on the floor, catching her breath. 'Prosper?'

'Mmmmmm?'

'It is still happening today, isn't it?'

'Course.'

'But Hope . . . Have you heard anything yet?'

'Relax.' He checked his watch. 'It's not quite lunch yet, Verity.'

'Erm . . .' She nodded at the clock on the wall. 'Lunch was an hour ago.'

Prosper blinked, looked at his watch, then tapped it. His smiled faded. He pushed himself up from the sofa and walked to the window. He stood there for a long time watching the farm track, winding his watch and looking up at the clock on the wall. He had big cheekbones, which in certain lights, and certain unsmiling moods, made his face look like a skull. Like now. A minute became ten. Then ten became twenty. They all just sat there, looking at him, breathing awkwardly. When he finally turned back, he had jam smeared on his cheek. 'Weather isn't changing,' he said.

'Is it supposed to?' Dust asked.

'I expected it to right at the end, yes. A huge storm. And hail. Lots of hail.'

Milton, sensing the sudden tension, grabbed the accordion. He started squeezing chords again but Prosper shot out a hand. 'No.'

'What is it?'

'Dust, you're right. We need to pray.'

Dust stepped forward. 'Do you think something's gone wrong?'

'Is it time for the other path?' Mum put a hand on Ever's shoulder.

'Shhh . . . slow down. We need to pray, right now.' He put a hand on Dust's shoulder and pushed him hard to the floor. 'Everybody. Come on.'

They did as they were told.

They all knelt together, as hands grabbed hands. The circle filled with the sounds Ever didn't much care for. The moans, the grunts, the whispers, the ancient language that he couldn't understand. But at least they prayed for something he longed for more than ever.

The end of God and heaven.

CHAPTER TEN

He's in there, Matt thought; *he's in there, somewhere.*

He and Bowland were sat in the high-backed chairs of the intensive care unit at Stoke Mandeville, staring silently at Rev. David East. Here was a minister who only hours ago had offered the blood of Jesus to his congregation. He wound up giving them buckets of his own instead. He was surrounded by what looked like four different IV drips, along with a chaotic mix of monitors and gizmos bolted to stands. Some of the machines looked modern and slick-looking, with sharp screens of numbers and lights that beat in slow, rhythmic sequence. But some of the tech looked decidedly vintage. Like something you'd use to pump old car tyres up with in the 1960s. Or measure radiation.

There was a face amongst it all . . . though it was almost impossible to find it under all the stuff they'd stuck to him. A huge white plastic breathing piece was strapped to his face, winding off him like a kooky elephant's trunk. Most of his head was wrapped in thick bandages and dressings. It was almost, *almost* funny. The obligatory comedy sketch of a 'man in traction'. But actually, it wasn't funny. Not one bit.

Matt broke the silence. 'They tied those dressings really tight, didn't they?'

'Once they stapled his scalp and skull together, they had to.' Bowland crossed her legs and reached for her phone. 'Let's just hope it'll hold.'

An image flicked across Matt's brain. Of the good reverend's head exploding like a watermelon and both he and Bowland having to duck. He sighed and looked to the floor. Then, he did more than sigh. He shuddered. Some cruel little voice pointed out that this particular explosion image wasn't something he'd made up. It was actually a very real memory from a few hours earlier, when the same thing happened to this man's son. Just before Matt's maddeningly slow eyelashes shut it out.

He shook his head. Best to pretend that he hadn't just seen a teenager explode. Nah. That was just a silly memory from an old zombie movie he'd seen once. An old Monty Python sketch. His stomach lurched. His heart too.

'You okay?' Bowland said.

He reached into his reserves and pulled out a smile. He was always good at that. Acting okay when he wasn't sure if he actually was okay. When you're a church minister you perfect those skills. 'I'm fine. I just had a crazy morning before I met you.'

'It was crazy before?'

He told her about the duck. She gradually started to laugh. He liked the sound of it, and the warmth in her face as she did it. He decided that if he'd met Jill Bowland in the street he'd figure she was a photographer or a clothes designer. Not a policewoman. Welcoming the distraction, she skipped going back to the case for a while. They talked about her only daughter who'd moved to Taiwan, and how Skype calls to her grandchild were never quite the same as the real thing. And how she'd been a policewoman for forty years and that her late husband was one too. The mention of him made her glance at the clock and she snapped out of the break. She started checking over the case notes on her phone instead.

Now that her jacket was off, he noticed how large and stiff her white shirt collar was. It fired from her like spikes. With her free hand, she rolled a bead of her home-made bracelet between her fingertips. 'So just to clarify . . .'

'Again?'

She smiled. 'Yes, again. To clarify . . . when Micah grabbed you, you're absolutely sure he said nothing else than what's here?'

'That's all he said. I told him his dad was still alive. I figured that'd be good news, but it wasn't. He panicked. Then he thought I was some sort of demon and wouldn't look at me properly. Explains why he carved all those magazine faces up . . . he wasn't into eye contact. The only thing I didn't hear properly was what he shouted out before the train hit.'

'You, and everybody else. That train was loud.'

The room vanished.

Thud.

Squelch.

Trainer laces, whistling through the air.

'Matt?'

He smiled again. 'Yup?'

'Are you sure there's nothing else you remember?'

He shook his head. 'Just that I didn't see the axe.'

'That's because you wouldn't have. We found it in a field, rammed into a tree.' She tapped her phone off. 'Right, well I better get on then . . .'

'What's next?'

'Next, we drill down into Micah's computer and talk to his friends and teachers. Try to figure out his motive.'

'And the upturned crosses, the urinating on the altar . . . ?'

'We'll look into all of that, but that might all be academic now.'

'But all that talk about devil worship and covens?'

'That was when I didn't have a clue where he was. I thought if he was part of some group, it might help us track him down . . . but hey, we tracked him down anyway . . .' She trailed off and looked back at the robo-vicar, wheezing and beeping across the room. 'But all this talk of demons and eyes and paranoia . . . I reckon it's just a messed-up kid. Like you said, it's probably not part of some wider group. In which case we'll peg this as domestic violence and we won't need to pass this on to SOCU.'

'Wow, you guys love your acronyms. What's SOCU?'

'Serious and Organised Crime Unit. I reckon this might not be for them.'

'I'd class this as a pretty serious crime . . .' He noticed she wasn't listening. 'Um . . . hello?'

'One sec . . .' Bowland pushed herself from the chair and walked towards the door where a straggle of blonde hair vanished from the small square of glass. Bowland pushed it open and Matt got up. He saw a woman standing in the corridor with two hands wrapped around a white pot, pressed to her belly. A single white orchid swayed from the pot. She'd tucked her blonde hair behind both ears.

Bowland smiled. 'Can I help you?'

'I don't mean to intrude, but the clock says it's visiting hours.'

'And you are?'

'I'm Miriam Aimes, from the church.' She held the plant awkwardly in one hand and held out the other to shake. 'David was in my arms when the ambulance arrived.'

Bowland's shoulders relaxed. 'That's fine. We're just trying to keep the press out of here. They're going in pretty hard on this case.'

'I know. There's a few of them in the car park outside. Vultures, every one.'

Bowland waited. 'Have you been with the church long?'

'Not really. Just a few months.'

'Does that mean three, four, five?'

She bit her lip, 'Three, I'd say.'

'And you know Reverend East well?'

'A fair bit, yes.'

'And Micah? Would you say you knew him very well?'

She shook her head, 'He didn't come to the services . . . Wait . . . you are the police, right?'

Bowland pulled out her ID. 'Miriam, can I ask a few questions, please?'

She looked down at the flowers. 'Can I put these in the room first? I think the smell might brighten him up.'

'Be my guest.' Bowland stepped aside and let her through.

Miriam nodded politely at Matt as he stepped aside, then he watched her walk towards the bed. The sight of East made her hover mid-step, then she seemed to sway unsteadily.

She slid a hand across her mouth. 'Oh, dear Jesus.'

'Whoa, let me take that,' Matt slipped his hand around the white pot, just before it toppled. 'Take a seat.'

'Thank you.'

She sank into the chair, eyes brimming. 'Can we touch him? Can we hold his hand?'

'Best not,' Bowland said.

Miriam just stared at his hand, wrapped in bandages like a little kid's mitten. She put her hands together to pray but pushed them against her face instead.

Matt mouthed to Bowland, *Shall we give her a minute?*

Bowland just sniffed and said, 'Can you describe what happened in the service this morning?'

'I gave a statement already.'

'It'd be helpful to hear it again.'

She wiped her eyes. 'It was absolutely horrendous. Like something from hell. David led Communion and Micah just jumped out from behind the curtain. I had no idea he was there. None of us did.'

'And we're told Micah spoke before he attacked.'

'Yes. It sounded like gobbledy-gook to me. Nobody could make it out.' She moved her gaze back to David, tilted her head, then a tear came again. 'Do you want to know the most heartbreaking part? It's that Dave was so pleased to see him there. He thought it was . . . was a miracle. That Micah was finally back in church. To be honest, I thought so too.'

Matt spoke up. 'Do you know why Micah stopped attending in the first place?'

'The same reason millions have stopped . . . he didn't believe it any more. That's all. He's not some devil worshipper, anyway.'

'Why do you say that?'

'Because that's what Gwen's telling everybody. She reckons he was in league with Satan cos he wore dark jeans, but I think it's a lot less dramatic than that. Micah just fell for the lie.'

'And what lie is that?

'That every church is a crooked church.' She looked up at him for a long moment. 'Even the wisest of men fall for it.'

Matt waited. 'So did Micah turn from Christianity altogether or did he find an alternative?'

For the first time, her sweet face turned to a scowl. 'Alternative?'

'I mean did he find another faith, or did he turn his back on all religion?'

'Another faith? An alternative? That's nonsense. There is no alternative to Christianity. Jesus is the only route to heaven. That's not me talking, it's there in black and white. If Micah did choose another faith, then he might as well have chosen no faith at all.'

Bowland's voice was like a soothing balm on the tension. 'Tell us about the mother.'

She shrugged. 'There's not much to say.'

'But you've met her?'

'Once, I think, though she didn't say much. She didn't come to church, so there wasn't any chance to know her. Kept herself to herself, as they say, so I wanted to respect that. She went off travelling anyway . . . Have you found out where she is yet?'

'We're working on it.'

'Good, because she should be here, by his side.' She paused, and her face grew tight with worry. 'And Dave? Is he going to pull through?'

'The doctors aren't hopeful.'

'There's always hope,' she said. 'Because there's always prayer.'

'Miriam,' Matt said. 'Why do you think Micah did this? I mean, lots of people lose faith, but they don't take an axe . . .' He trailed off.

She shrugged. 'How could I even begin to guess?'

'Not even a theory?'

She stared at the floor for a long moment. 'Maybe he just didn't like his dad.'

The door suddenly opened and a gaggle of three pensioners (if that was the collective noun) came bustling into the room. They were laden with fruit, drinks and snacks, the likes of which David East would probably never be able to eat for a month. Maybe never. And a banana too. *Try stuffing that down his food tube*, Matt thought. Their chatter turned into groans and gasps when they saw their vicar splayed out on the bed. A nurse heard the commotion and swung her head in. She saw the crowd and boggled her eyes. 'Do not overcrowd this room. A few of you need to step out for a bit. Take it in turns. You can go two at a time.'

One of the old ladies muttered, 'Like the ark.'

The nurse put a hand on her hip, waiting for someone to comply. Bowland did. 'Well, thank you for your input.' She handed Miriam a card. 'Perhaps when you're done, I'll chat to you and the other ladies some more. But I'll give you time to pray first.'

Miriam nodded. 'We appreciate that.'

Bowland led Matt outside and tugged him down the corridor a little. They stopped by a window overlooking the car park.

'So, what do you think?' she said.

'Well, there's clearly more going on here than Micah just losing his Christian faith. He wasn't ambivalent towards it, he was rabid against it,' Matt said. 'Plus, there's all the stuff he said when he had me at knifepoint.'

Her eyebrow shot up. 'Erm, ballpoint.'

'Okay, ballpoint.' Matt ran a hand through his hair and looked down the corridor. 'I just wish we could hear this language that Micah said, before the attack. Someone must have heard a snippet. Big echoey room like that, someone must have picked it up somehow . . .'

'Don't worry, I'll dig into that . . .' She glanced at her watch. 'But look, I think for now you might as well . . . hey, where are you going? Hey!'

Matt heard her call after him, but he didn't turn. He was already heading back up the corridor, pushing through the door to East's room.

CHAPTER ELEVEN

They prayed on the lounge floor for an hour. Until Ever's trembling kneecaps burnt. The only time they stopped was when something utterly bizarre, and more than a little terrifying, happened. Prosper went to the corner of the room, and with his penknife he prised one of the boards up.

'What's he—'

'Shhhh.' Dust put a finger against Ever's lip.

Prosper pulled out a metal box, and inside was a small bundle, wrapped in a hand towel. When he started unwrapping it, the others started praying even harder, but Ever kept watching as the towel fell open. The little black thing appeared, with buttons and numbers on it.

The phone.

Ever groaned. This was a bad sign. They shouldn't have had to use it.

'There's a plug for it,' Dust said. 'It's in the study—'

'I know where it is.' Prosper let the metal box crash to the floor.

Then he took the phone to the study and they waited some more. Through the window, the sky had turned almost black with rain.

Mum saw Ever gawping at Prosper's door and put a hand on the back of his head. She pushed it downwards. 'Pray. Don't look, pray.'

Strange noises came from the study. A sort of buzz and weird beep. Then a long stretch of horrible silence. But nothing was as bad as the sound that came next. A screech of despair and the boom of crashing furniture. Ever, on instinct, leapt to his feet.

He gasped. 'There must be Hollows in the house.'

Dust shook his head. 'That wasn't them screaming.'

When Ever looked again Prosper was at the door. His face was white and the dome of his bald head was white too, and his knuckles were dripping blood.

'So?' Dust stood up. 'Was there a message?'

'Hope says . . .' he whispered into the air.

Pax looked up at the sound of her mother's name.

'Says what?' Dust asked.

'He failed . . .'

Mum put a hand to her mouth. 'What do you mean, he failed?'

'You mean Micah?' Ever said. 'Is he okay?'

Prosper didn't answer. He just stomped towards the fireplace as if he might throw himself into the flames. He slammed both fists against the mantelpiece, which made a glass vase spin into a perfect circle. His mum's dried flowers were in it, and Ever watched them tip off the edge and crash to the floor.

As well as those cheekbones of his, Prosper had rather large eyes, and whenever he closed them, the lids bulged in a terribly circular way. Like two ping-pong balls, ready to burst out. Not a pleasant look from a man with no hair. They did that now. As Prosper prayed, his eyes heaved against his closed lids. When he finally spoke again, it was through a terrifying wall of clenched teeth. 'Damn this world,' he whispered. Then he opened his ball-eyes and looked with disgust at the watch on his wrist. He tore it off and flung it to the floor. 'Damn this filthy fucking pit. Damn every stinking pig and piglet in this entire fucking cruel, sadistic . . .'

He went on and on and on like this. Spitting out his furious petitions to the fire. By now, Ever was shivering, so it was good to feel his uncle's arm slip around his shoulder again. Even better when his lips pressed close to his ear, risking a whisper, even though everybody in the family knew that when Prosper prayed like this, they all had to be totally silent. But Dust was shivering too, and he said the words anyway. It looked like the fire was going out.

'Don't be scared, Ever,' Dust said. 'I'm here.'

CHAPTER TWELVE

Matt held the door open so the women in both the room and the corridor could listen. 'Ladies, I'm very sorry to interrupt you. But do you record the sermons at your church?'

One of them screwed up her face. 'Record? Like a tally?'

'No.' He tried not to groan. 'I mean how churches often record the audio of the sermon or homily so they can put it online or they—'

'We don't have a website,' Miriam laughed. 'We're not that modern.'

'. . . Or they record it for members of the congregation who are housebound. Don't you ever do that?'

'We don't. Sorry.'

Miriam smiled, 'So, if you'll let us get back to praying . . .'

One of the old ladies put her hand in the air, and it stopped everybody talking. She pushed her tongue into her cheek. Probably more than her tongue, actually. Her dentures might have dislodged as she pondered it. Either way a large bulge appeared, and then quickly vanished and Matt heard a click. Face symmetrical again, she lowered her hand. 'Malcolm tapes it, sometimes.'

'No, you're wrong,' one of them said, 'he just switches all the speakers and doo-dahs on. Though the old coot barely knows what he's doing with those, to be honest.'

Denture woman shook her head. 'No, I'm sure he used to put stuff on a little tape machine for Phyllis Packman. She's stuck up in The Meadows. I'm sure he used to do that. He was there this morning.'

Bowland dug into her jacket and pulled out a notepad and pen. 'We'll need his details.'

'I know them,' the old lady said, then she scrawled them out and handed it back. 'Now can we keep praying, please? We don't want to waste our visiting time talking about Malcolm, of all people.'

Bowland nodded, and a minute later, she and Matt were back down the corridor again.

'So,' Matt started fastening his jacket up, 'how about we head to this Malcolm's house, and check for the tapes?'

She smiled. 'I'll send someone over, and I'll let you know when we get them.'

'Ah, it's no bother. It's only late afternoon, and I haven't got much—'

'I think you need to go home and rest, don't you?' She blinked slowly. 'It's been a hectic few hours, the doctors have checked you over . . . You've seen a lot today, Matt. And I don't just mean the runaway duck.' She rummaged in her purse and handed him not one card, but two. 'The top one's me. Give me a call if you have any more thoughts on this, but either way, I'll be back in touch about the tapes. Good call on that, by the way. I've never been in church since I was a little kid, so I forget some of them keep up with the times.'

'Even if it is audio cassette,' he smiled, and took the cards, turned them over.

'The other one's our staff counsellor. You can talk to him about what happened today. Or anything else, if you need it . . .'

'Ah, I'll be okay really, but I appreciate—'

'Listen to me . . .' She leant in closer. 'Not many people see a kid hit by a train. Including me, okay? So I may well be calling this number one of these nights, do you get me? So don't be an idiot and throw this card away.'

He looked at her, pictured her soothing her grandchildren to sleep. 'Okay . . . and thank you.' He pocketed them both and shook her hand. 'Just call me when you hear those tapes. And if the ladies say anything interesting.'

'I will.' She headed back up the corridor where Miriam was already out of the room. She was sending the other two old ladies in for their tag team prayer session. Miriam caught his eye briefly, waved a quick goodbye, and turned away. He turned too and headed for the lifts, shoes squeaking along the floor.

Of course, everywhere he looked he saw teenage boys. They were flicking through their phones, winding the curl of their fringe, or staring out of windows. And only one out of every five reminded him of Micah. So, they were the only ones that made him look away. Just in case they shattered into glass in front of him.

A policeman had kindly driven his car over, from Chervil. He was told it was in Car Park B. Before he headed out to find it, he decided to replenish his sugar stocks. He grabbed a cookie-dough milkshake from a vending machine. The metal shelves slowly, and laboriously, shimmied out his drink, so he gazed at the TV while he waited. A news reporter was standing in a blue cagoule, trying hard to stay upright on the wind-battered coast of Clacton-on-Sea. Behind her, huge waves were launching up across the promenade. The rolling headline underneath said: MORE WILD WEATHER TO COME.

Finally, the milkshake thudded into the tray. He grabbed it and glugged half of it down in the lift. Pure liquid cake: bliss. He pushed through the front doors of the hospital and tried to guzzle the rest of it, but he almost gagged on it instead when a small crowd of people rushed up to him at the door. Two reporters got so close he almost lost his balance. With a pop, he pulled the bottle from his mouth, and used his sleeve to wipe the trickle from his chin. 'Do you mind—'

'Professor Hunter.' A microphone almost smacked his front tooth out. 'Why did Micah East try to decapitate his father?'

Another voice: 'Was it devil worship? Are the rumours true?'

A TV camera surged at him like a bullet.

He put up a palm. 'No comment.'

'Is this part of a wider network, Mr Hunter? Might there be more attacks in churches? Is that why they called you?'

'No comment.'

'Would you class this as satanic terrorism? Do you have anything to tell us?'

'Yes, I do . . .' He pushed through the crowd. 'I'd like to finish my milkshake, please.'

'What did you see when the train hit, Professor?'

It was the only time he stopped. 'I said "no comment", and I said it very clearly. Now please . . .'

They must have realised it was useless because the news people slinked away from him, like zombies going after better brains. They gathered themselves back at the entrance, waiting for Bowland or East's visitors, no doubt.

He started firing out the invisible beam from his key fob and found his car eventually. It was waiting like a sweet little shuttle, eager to chug him away from this craziness. *Howzabout we get you back to normality, ey, Matt?*

He nodded and slid behind the wheel. He quickly texted Wren.

Heading home for that takeaway! Then he hovered his thumb for a moment and added. *Love you SO much.*

He spotted a notification from Facebook.

Sean Ashton sent you a friend request

'Who the heck is Sean Ash . . .' he trailed off. 'Oh . . .'

He clicked on the RE teacher's face, and saw a killer profile pic. Sean looked like a model, with his white glasses and mega-quiff stuffing the screen with style and quirk. With an exaggerated wink, he was grinning open-mouthed into what must have been a very decent camera lens. This was like a magazine shoot, posed with bright teeth shining. On his head sat a pair of retro headphone cans, a curled black cord around his fingertip. To be fair it looked super staged, but still, it was really rather cool. Way more hip than the profile shot Matt Hunter had, of him sitting in a wheelbarrow with both of his thumbs up. Laughing like a mad goon.

He hovered his thumb across the phone again, wondering if it was really good practice to make friends with someone who might end up teaching his kids. Then he remembered the last time he saw Sean, sat in a Land Rover, being hollered at by his dad. It made him think of Micah, and David East, and how that all ended up.

'Accept.' He tapped him into the inner circle and flung the phone into the passenger seat. He turned the ignition, and his phone pinged again.

A message from Sean Ashton

'Eager,' he said. He'd read it later.

The journey back to Chesham was longer than he expected. The car was cold, and it took a long time to warm up, but at least the rain had eased off. So unlike Bowland's car earlier, the view from these windows was clear and crisp. Which wasn't great, actually. He almost wished the rain was back. The clear view gave him plenty of opportunity to see the ghoul of Micah East waving at him, and slowly bursting apart, on multiple street corners.

CHAPTER THIRTEEN

So strange how quickly the mood of a day can change. As quick as the weather.

When Ever woke up this morning, they'd all skipped to the top of Comfort Hill. Literally skipped. They filled the chapel with songs and prayers and shuffling shoes. They danced and they cheered. Today was the key day, after all. The day their special symbol would restore the world. But now the songs were gone, and he sat banished in his tiny bedroom, instructed to kneel and pray for the kingdom 'like never before'.

It was hard to concentrate with all those muffled groans and shouts from the grown-ups downstairs. He couldn't make the words out, but there was a level of desperation in the house that he'd never heard before. It scared him so much that he kept switching from an ear to the door to an eye at his bedroom window. Just to make sure the Hollows weren't walking across the fields in an all-out assault. They weren't, but from the occasional word he could make out, the people downstairs were talking about the Hollows a lot.

It was only when he heard a rattling outside his door that Ever flung himself back to the floor. His prayer-hands slapped together but his door didn't open. Instead he heard a sound he hadn't heard in a long time. The unlocking of the padlock which hung from the attic door. Ever flicked a panicky eye open. Why would they go up there? Then he started answering his own question.

Is that where we'll hide? Was 'the other path' up there? Whatever that was.

Footsteps thudded above him, then he followed a low scraping sound that creaked across the ceiling. Frowning, he pressed an eye to the keyhole and heard boots slowly clanking down the attic ladder, then the keyhole flashed with the jeans of Prosper and Uncle Dust. Ever was terrified that the door would swing open and reveal his rebellion. But curiosity won. He held his breath and his jaw dropped open.

It was the TV.

Dust and Milton were lugging the TV to the top of the stairs.

Prosper whispered across the landing, 'And don't forget the box thing. The remote.'

'Got it,' Dust said.

Astonished, Ever watched a flash of dark grey plastic pass by his keyhole. It was the television set that he'd been told he must never, ever watch. Prosper had often preached that the world of television was 'a land filled with eyes'. He knew that Prosper used it on extremely rare occasions. Just to keep up with what the Hollows were up to. Milton even ventured into town once and bought a special little box to make it work. But Ever had never, ever seen it switched on.

He sat on his bedroom floor for ten minutes, chewing his fingernails, half expecting to hit bone. Then another sound entered the house. It was a strange beat of music, the type of which he'd never heard before, and with it a loud, jolly voice talking. A loud, jolly, Hollow voice.

He threw himself back from the door and scurried to his prayer space, panting. He said it over and over again, 'Lord, Lord good and true. Never let me stray from you.'

He'd said this prayer – one of his favourites – precisely nine times, until he heard the whispering at his window. His eyes peeled slowly, very slowly, open.

Ever . . . it said.

He looked at the window and the closed curtains.

Evvvvvver . . . it said.

The wind.

Evvvvvver . . . it said.

His mind?

Ever . . . it said. *Go . . . go . . .*

He stared at the door while something invisible prickled across his skin.

This is for you, Ever . . . go and look . . .

He sensed a hand slip into his. A cold hand.

'Lord?' he whispered. 'Is that you?'

Yessssssss. Now go, Ever. Go and loooooook.

He walked to the door, pushing it open a fraction. Holding his breath, he shocked himself by stepping out onto the landing, dreading that Prosper might climb the staircase and see him. Not shouting but speaking in that low disappointed tone he sometimes used. Saying 'Did you look in that squirrel's eyes? Little slug? Did you?' But under it all he heard the wind from his window, and it seemed to speak with an authority even more compelling than Prosper's.

It said, *You're meant to see this.*

He reached the top bannister and peeked down the stairs. He could clearly see the lounge, through the archway, but it was filled with the backs of their heads in flickering silhouette. Nobody was looking his way. They were all cross-legged on the floor, gazing at a screen he couldn't see.

Looooook. Try three steps down.

The voice, it turned out, was wise, because three steps was perfectly adequate. From there he saw the most amazingly bright window of light in the lounge, filled with colours and shapes. And across the screen he saw words, only they didn't look like anything he'd seen in a book. These ones moved. They flew and danced like pure magic, while drums and other instruments he couldn't place pounded out a scary, exciting melody.

Then it wasn't exciting any more, because a Hollow appeared, staring out of the screen. Ever flicked his eyes away. He heard the others draw in a sharp breath too.

He dropped his eyes to the back of his mum's head. She, along with all the others he could see, had put her hand across her eyes for protection, but every now and again she'd look up in very short bursts. Apparently, if you had a lot of faith you could hold their gaze for a few moments. The really pious, a whole ten minutes maybe. Though it was risky, Milton always said. *The clever ones only need a few seconds to climb in.* This last thought was petrifying because what if his family, in a moment of weakness, got caught up in the stare from that Hollow woman on screen? What if they sat there hypnotised and warped, until they all turned around on all fours, and crawled up the stairs, or up the walls, calling his name?

The screen shifted from the Hollow to another image entirely. A building with a point on it, which looked a little like their chapel. Only it was much, much bigger, and it looked all slanted and strange. This one wasn't made out of tin sheets either. It looked like rock and stone. He'd been told about these places since he was young, but he'd never really seen one: a Hollow church.

Prosper and the others moaned with horror at something on the screen. A giant building, which he knew was a hospital. Someone had managed not to die, and some Hollows were calling it a miracle. All this talk of survival threw the others into a grim bout of scraping. Feet and fingernails dragged on wood. Lips were whispering desperate prayers, then he heard Milton say, 'We'll never find another in time. We have to take the other path.'

Until Mum shouted.

That was the strangest part of all. When she threw a word into the intense crazy jabbering. And it really wasn't a word he expected to hear. Yet it made everybody stop what they were doing so they could stare at her.

She said, 'Hallelujah.'

He saw the lower half of Prosper's body and legs stomp towards her. 'Verity? What the hell?'

Mum kept staring through her fingers at the TV screen, shaking her head and laughing.

'What's wrong with you?' Prosper said.

She said it again. 'Hallelujah.'

'Oh God.' Milton was on his feet. 'She looked in its eyes for too long. She's turning—'

Mum clapped her hands together with such a snap that Ever flinched.

'What is it?' Uncle Dust put a hand on each of her shoulders. 'What's so funny?'

'It's a miracle,' she pointed at the screen. 'It's a miracle.'

Dust looked at the others, and shrugged. 'We don't understand.'

When she spoke again she said it through tears, but there was a strength in her voice. A wonder. 'That's him . . .' She pointed at the man on the screen. 'Praise be, that's the one.'

By now the others were on their feet, so he couldn't see any of the screen now. It didn't matter, because the wind in his room was back.

This, Ever . . . it said . . . *this is for you . . . go . . . look . . .*

With a trembling hand he started to walk down to them all.

CHAPTER FOURTEEN

A huge, three-voiced, female roar exploded into the Hunters' kitchen.

'Pick it up!' Lucy slapped a hand on her forehead. 'Mum, quick! The four-second rule!'

Wren stared at the naan, face down on the floor. Then she shrugged. 'I read that the four-second rule's a myth. That the bacteria covers the food instantly.'

Amelia dropped to her knees and flung it onto her own plate. 'Well, I read dirt is good for your immune system.' Before anybody could stop her, she stuffed a hefty corner into her mouth. 'Mmmmm,' she said. 'Healthy dirty.'

'Table's ready.' Matt stood at their large circular dining room table, all set with mats, glasses and cutlery. He glugged red wine into two wine glasses that didn't match. He and Wren were experts at smashing one out of every set they bought. 'Ladies, let's go all out . . .' He waved his hands across the table. 'I'm thinking mood music. I'm thinking candles, I'm thinking' – drum roll on the table, and a pathetic attempt at a French accent – '. . . *rest-a-raunnnn*.'

He dimmed the lights with a single flick, lit a candle and tapped on some music he figured sounded civilised – the jazzy soundtrack to an old Charlie Brown cartoon. Eager hands shot over the food, cracking poppadums, tearing naan and flicking lids of cartons with thumbs. Until Amelia stood up and put a finger in the air. 'Wait,' she said. 'Waiiiiiiit.'

They all hovered, bread flopping from their hands.

'Hands together . . .' she said, '. . . eyes closed.'

Lucy shook her head. 'My korma's getting cold, you toilet.'

Matt almost choked.

'I'm serious,' Amelia said. 'Hands together, heads bowed. I'd like to pray. It's my right.'

Wren and Matt frowned at each other because the Hunters didn't do grace. They were a dive-in and chomp type of family. But Wren closed her eyes and bowed her head, and after a glare from Amelia, he did the same. The stance unlocked some old muscle memory. Reverend Matt Hunter at many a village fete, providing that absolutely vital local role – the sayer of grace at community buffets. Then another memory came, sweeter and much more painful. Him as a kid at his mum's table, doing this at every single mealtime growing up. 'Isn't Jesus great' on her lips.

Amelia cleared her throat. 'We dedicate this wonderful meal of food, to those we have loved and lost.'

Matt opened one eye and looked at her. Snoopy-jazz slinked quietly out of the speakers. He thought of Micah East flying through the air.

'For those who lost their lives today . . .'

He looked at Wren. She was biting her lip, awkwardly.

'So, in short, God, we want to say thank you to Daphne the Duck, for all she did for us and for all the other fuzzy wuzzy ducky wucks in—'

Her attempt at a toast, a prayer, or whatever it was, turned into a high-pitched squeal when a piece of contaminated naan bounced off her forehead. She opened her eyes and laughed. '*Now* we can eat.'

They laughed and talked about the usual range of scattered subjects. Wren, an architect, had a series of big meetings this week. She was designing a brand-new preschool in a very posh part of Buckinghamshire. She said her joke about adding a 'discreet cage system' for the really naughty kids didn't go down well. She'd be working on her presentation tonight. Lucy had a biology test on Thursday, which she said was mostly about airborne diseases. She punched the air in mock excitement at what she called 'her glorious, thrilling life'. Amelia couldn't stop talking about the news, and the country's apocalyptic weather. A huge storm was coming, apparently, and as usual, people feared that Brits would not be ready for it. Matt mostly just listened and nodded at all this – soaking up the sounds of normality. He certainly didn't talk about his adventures in Chervil today. Seeing a boy of Lucy's age shatter into a flying wet mess was not dinner table fare. But the thought of it still flashed as he separated his rogan josh. He pushed it away.

Wren looked at him, 'Finished already?'

'I'm just as full as a pot-bellied pig.' He leant back on his chair and slapped a hand off his gut. 'But I better make a bit of room for liquid, cos guess what I'm doing later tonight?'

'Aren't you finishing that article . . . the one about cow gods or something?'

'Hinduism, Wren,' he smiled into his wine. 'Nah, I've bumped that till tomorrow. Tonight, Professor Hunter is' – he ran his hands across the air – 'out on the town.'

'Oh, is he now? Who with?'

'Wait for it . . .' He grinned madly at Lucy. 'Mr Ashton! Yes, Lucy, it's true. I plan on being best mates with all of your teachers – but only the trendy ones. And someday we'll all go surfing together and they'll teach me how to skateboard so I can show off to your friends' – he licked a palm and pushed his hair up – 'and I'm a gonna be the funkiest fella in all of Chesham, and make no mistake, Daddy-O.' He shot a finger pistol at her.

'Kill me,' she said.

'Of course, I jest.' He set the wine down. 'Actually, he just wants to chat about my amazing book, and I know you were working tonight, Wren, so . . . I figured I'd let him buy me a brew. Though, Lucy, I'll almost certainly try his glasses on and take a selfie—'

A call you have! A CALL you have!

Yoda's voice buzzed from the hallway, buried inside a trendy little apple crate. All their phones lived there at dinner times. A new family rule.

'Darn. I better get this.' He stood and headed for the hall, calling back, 'And leave those. I'll do the dishwasher.'

A CALL YOU HAVE!

'Jeez, Yoda. Calm down.' He fished the phone out and answered it at the mirror, laughing at his makeshift quiff. 'Yello?'

'Matt,' she said. 'It's Bowland.'

He stopped posing. 'Oh, hi.'

'Listen, you were right. There was a tape and I've got it here in my office right now. Got a minute to hear it?'

'Absolutely.'

CHAPTER FIFTEEN

Ever took another step down. Then another.

Maybe Prosper would see him walk into the lounge and get furious. He might even drag him up to the chapel again, all bald head and bulging eyes. Force him to spend a terrifying night up there, all alone. Like the last time Ever tried to spy on their secret meetings. But it was the voice. The sweet, cold whisper that made his feet move.

Go . . . brave Ever . . . go.

They were so caught up in their whispering that they never even heard him creak on the second-to-last step. They were so animated with confusion, shock and what looked like a growing sense of astonishment, they didn't even see him step right into the room. Soon *his* face and *his* body was flickering by the light from the box of eyes.

'*Ever?*' It was Pax, of all people.

She turned, which made everybody else turn. He braced himself for the shouts, or worse, for Prosper's low voice of frightening calm.

But none came. He just saw the black shapes of his family, set against the white glow of the TV. And they were speechless.

He said what he thought would be the right thing to say. He said, 'I want to help.'

That's when Mum dissolved into tears, proud ones, while Milton burst into claps and laughter. Prosper just stood by the fire staring at him, a smile sliding across thin lips. 'Wow,' he said. '*Wow*.'

The only one who wasn't smiling was Uncle Dust. He looked at Ever with pale cheeks and a twitchy mouth. The other face in the room, the Hollow, was staring out from the world of eyes. He took another chance and tripped a quick gaze at it, just to see what they'd all been so taken with. It was a man, with a bottle in his hand, trying to push through a crowd of other Hollows. Underneath words were sliding across the screen, like a book made real. The Hollow's name was Matthew Hunter.

Ever quickly looked away, just in case. And by the time he looked back the TV was off. Now arms were sliding around him, under his armpits and under his knees, lifting him to the ceiling and bouncing him on a wave of baffled laughter. He saw Milton hurry to the corner to dig out his accordion.

'What's going on?' said Ever, a slow smile growing on his face. 'Is it still going to work? Are we going to be okay?'

'We are now, boy,' Prosper laughed so much that his shoulders shook. 'We are now.'

'But how?' Dust whispered into Prosper's ear. The only one in the room not laughing. 'How?'

Prosper grabbed Dust's ponytail and jiggled it. 'Come on. It's obvious, isn't it? It's gloriously, wonderfully obvious. Ha!'

The rain was falling, and the wind was up, so it didn't drop straight. Ever saw it turn in happy circles at the window. Much like Ever's family did for the next half an hour, dancing as the rain danced. He had no idea why this was happening, only that it was, and that he liked it, and that it was infinitely preferable to the wails and screams from before. He saw Prosper and Dust talking feverishly in the kitchen, then at one point he saw Prosper go into his room to find that phone again. 'I'll tell Hope.' He seemed excited.

Ever was amazed they let him stay up so long, and how they plied him with toast and cake and many hugs besides. He couldn't even guess why he'd suddenly been invited in, but it was too wonderful to question it. He just took Milton's hand and danced, falling into a crashing heap on the sofa as they sang and prayed and sang again. The only sad part was that Merit never saw it. She was up in bed, where all kids should be. Ever kept glancing at their secret lookout by the bannister, hoping the noise had woken her. He wished she could see this. How much they were fawning over him.

When it was finally time for his room, that was okay, because now he was tired and baffled, but filled with the type of peace that makes beds warmer and moons more full. Mum came into his room and tucked his blanket under his chin, just how he liked it. She tickled his nose between two knuckles.

He asked, 'What's going on, Mum? What's changed?'

It was the only time her smile fell. She put her fingertips inside the scarf on her neck and scratched her scars. She often did that. It got itchy under there.

'Mum,' he said. 'What's wrong?'

'It's a horrible world out there.' She lay a gentle palm against his head. She stroked the mop of his hair. 'It's evil.'

'But the end's still coming, isn't it? It's coming soon?'

She pressed her lips against his forehead and kept them there for a long time. 'Yes . . . because it's a miracle . . . you're a miracle.' She pulled back, wiping a tear from her face. 'Rice pudding and jam for breakfast. How about that?'

His jaw dropped. 'Whoa.'

Then she was gone, and his light was off.

It took him ages to drift off, his mind was racing so much. It didn't help when he heard the sound of the front door open. He twitched the curtains and saw that the moon had turned the world blue. But at least it wasn't hiding behind a cloud, which was a good sign. Comfort Hill and the entire field in front of the house were glowing. He leant towards the window and felt cold glass press against his nose. Three black figures were marching towards the shed. Dust, Prosper and Milton. Then suddenly he heard the growl of an engine and headlights threw long beams across the field. Their van rolled out and he watched it slowly head up the track, leaving a glowing red trail of exhaust fumes. He hadn't seen that van moving in a long time. He watched it disappear over the ridge, knowing full well that eventually, that road went down to the Hollow towns and the Hollow cities. He thought about Pax's mum Hope. She was out there, somewhere. Maybe they were going to get her and bring her home.

He gazed at the moon, wondering why they'd been so interested in the Hollow on the screen before. Matthew. That was a Biblical name. Who knows. Maybe he wasn't a Hollow at all. Maybe he was good. He might even help them end things. The family certainly seemed pleased to see him. These thoughts brought the whisper back, and it sounded soothing and gentle.

It was saying,

Sleep, Ever. Sleep. Don't worry about tomorrow. Let tomorrow worry about itself.

Be brave and trust, because this is for you . . . but above all, sleep.
So he did.

CHAPTER SIXTEEN

He needed privacy for this, so he hurried across the back garden to his precious office, the cabin. Home to all his books and work and his two arcade cabinets. He flicked on the downlighters and sank into a chair. 'Right, you're on speakerphone, okay?'

'Okay,' she cleared her throat. 'So this fella Malcom records the services for one of the old ladies. And he uses an old portable cassette player. It's the only thing he had but the woman at the home only had a tape player anyway. But at least he rigged it to the sound system. Quality's not great, but it's good enough. It certainly picked up the attack.'

'And the words Micah said?'

'Yes, though I can't make much sense of them. I'm hoping you can. Malcolm let me borrow his player, so I'll get it onto digital soon, but for now . . . I'll just do it old school, okay? I'll hold the phone up to it. Ready?'

He slapped a yellow A4 notepad on his lap, swung his feet onto the desk and popped a pen on with his chin. 'Commence.'

He heard her fumble with something at the other end. 'Bear with me . . . this thing's an antique.' Her voice sounded distant. He heard her tut and say 'Stupid thing.' Then he heard a dull clunk of a plastic switch and a sudden hiss. He could see the spools turning around in his mind. Cassettes were making a comeback, he'd heard.

The voice of Rev. David East suddenly crackled from the tiny speaker.

. . . So you see, even King David, who let God down so spectacularly, was given a fresh start. Which means even the most wretched sinner will always be welcomed with open arms. Even me, and yes . . . even you . . . so let's turn to receive that very same grace, through bread and wine now.

Bowland called out in the background. 'Malcolm says that clump is David East heading down the steps.'

There it was. *Thud, thud, thud.*

Matt closed his eyes and quickly constructed a virtual interior of St Bart's in his mind. The high wooden pulpit; the sloping route back to the chancel; the wooden exit door to the right. He squinted, trying to erase the giant glowing cube that was there before. This morning it would have just been the stone floor, the railing, the altar—

Just as he thought that, he heard the squeak of the gate on the tape, and what sounded like an echoed laugh.

'Was that Micah laughing?' Matt said, eyes still closed.

'Just the congregation. Keep listening.'

Nothing much was happening, so Matt tapped the volume up a little. He jumped when Rev. East started instituting the Communion.

For I received from the Lord, that which I also passed onto you . . .

He mouthed the words along with East. How many times had he himself said those words in church?

The Lord Jesus on the night he was betrayed, took bread . . . and after giving thanks he broke it saying, this is my body, which is for you. Do this, in remembrance of me.

The breeze suddenly geared up a notch outside, and he heard the big oak behind their back gate start whipping its branches against the cabin. He cranked the volume a little louder.

And in the same way after supper, he took the cup, saying this is the new covenant in my blood. Do this whenever . . . East trailed off for a moment, as if distracted by something. Matt heard him clear his throat. When the voice came back it was odd and unsteady. *Do this whenever you drink it in remembrance of me. For whenever you eat this bread and drink this cup, you proclaim* . . . the voice trailed off again.

'He's seen something,' Matt said. 'He sounds fright—'

. . . *the Lord's death, until he comes again.*

'This is it,' Bowland said, almost in a whisper. 'Brace yourself.'

Matt grabbed his pen, shut his eyes tight and pushed an ear towards the phone, considering that perhaps he'd rather not hear this after all.

Too late.

Eloi, eloi . . . Micah's voice. *Lama kataltani.*

Matt's eyebrows shot up, and he scribbled the words down.

A new sound. Some sort of impact that sounded very slight on the tape, yet it still made Matt jump and scrawl a ragged accidental line on his pad. Footsteps staggered on the stone floor. Then it was hard to make anything else out, because the background filled with noise. Screams, mostly.

He could picture it more vividly than he expected, or indeed wanted. The swinging teenage arm, the long wooden handle slicing the air, the block of sharp metal hacking and burying itself into his scalp. Then being yanked back out again. The sympathy he'd had for Micah East was, he suddenly noticed, fairly non-existent now. A groan of revulsion flowed out of him. Those screams. It was impossible not to visualise the congregation wailing and tearing their hair out, while Micah slammed the axe . . . and this was the very worst part. He could hear East pitifully pleading with his own child, for mercy.

Son . . . he kept saying . . . *son* . . . *no* . . .

Micah's response was suddenly in English. He said, *Please, Dad. Don't look in my eyes.* Matt scrawled that down. Then soon after, that odd phrase came again, only it was shuddering and desperate now, and slightly different this time. *Avi, Avi . . . Lama kataltani.*

He scraped his pencil on the paper again in sharp, capital lines.

AVI, AVI

There were new sounds in the chaos now. Feet were running and a door was flung open, followed by a roar of wind and horrified shouts. The voice of a woman came. It was more clear and crisp than before because she must have been close to East now, and to the little mic, clipped to his robes. This must have been when she held him.

Jesus, please. It was Miriam's voice. The woman from the hospital room. *Jesus . . . Jesus . . . please . . . please come . . .*

Click.

The hiss of the tape suddenly vanished and Bowland's voice came back, 'That's all folks.'

Matt noticed his forehead was buried into his palm. He let out a long sigh, 'So why did the tape stop then?'

'That's when Malcolm realised it was still running, so he yanked it off. Didn't want to record a man's last moments, is how he put it,' she sniffed. 'So, Professor . . . that sounds less like gobbledy-gook and more like a language to me. Tell me I'm right?'

'You're right. It's a language.' He checked his pad, and asked her to play that section again, just to make sure he'd written it correctly. Then he shook his head, confused. 'It's very odd, though.'

'What language is it?'

113

'It sounds like Aramaic.' He heard her silence. 'It's best known for being the everyday tongue spoken in Ancient Palestine. It's thought to be the language that Jesus spoke, though there's some debate on that.'

'Do you know someone who can translate it?'

'Yeah, me . . . give me a sec.'

'Excellent. I'll wait.'

He swung his feet off the desk and set the pad down. He hunched over it, pencil tapping against his chin, mouthing each word. 'This really is quite strange. What Micah said is very, *very* close to something from the New Testament. Something Jesus said on the cross. Only most translations put it like this . . . *Eloi, eloi lama sabachtani.*'

'Which means?'

'My God, my God, why have you forsaken me? Obviously, that's a pretty significant thing for the Son of God to be saying but you'll find it clearly in the Bible . . . hang on . . .' He pushed his chair back. It was on wheels, so he could slide to one of his many bookshelves and grab what he needed. He rolled back and slapped out a heavy dictionary of ancient Hebrew and Aramaic. He started flicking through the pages . . . 'But Micah doesn't say *sabachtani*, which is the "forsaken" part. What he says sounds more like "kill" or—' He ran a finger down the page and stopped suddenly. 'That's it. *Kataltani.* That's more like . . . like the word "murder".' He slashed a hard pencil line under the phrase again. 'So what Micah shouted, just before he tried to kill his dad was, "My God, My God, why have you . . . murdered me?"'

'Then later, when he changes it a bit?'

Matt checked his pad again, and didn't have to look this one up 'Avi means "father", so it's. . . *Father, father, why have you murdered me?*'

The wind surged outside and scattered dirt against the patio doors. He looked at it. Blinked.

'You still there, Matt?'

'So, he's quoting Jesus, but not quite.' Matt tapped the words with his fingertip. 'God . . . father . . . murder. It's a very unusual way to put it.'

'Well, how about you think on it and let me know if it's actually significant?'

'Will do.' He finally looked up from the pad. 'And did you check his laptop yet? Find anything?'

'Only that it was smashed. The screen, at least. Looks like he smacked it with a brick.'

'And the contents?'

'Nothing major. We rigged it up to a computer and found all the usual teenage stuff. He'd deleted some porn, but that was over a year ago. There was nothing since. Lots of schoolwork.'

'How about devil worship stuff? Upturned crosses?'

'Not a thing. Just a lot of searches about how bad the weather's been lately, and a lot of stuff about the Bible. New Testament, mostly.'

'Where in the New Testament?'

She paused, 'Matthew, Mark, Luke . . . John.'

'The gospels . . . was it only them?'

'Actually, yes. Just them.'

'So the Jesus bits, basically . . . okay.'

'Oh, and the TV in his room, and the Xbox. The fuses were missing from the plugs, so he couldn't switch them on. With that and the magazines I'd say he was having a bit of a media detox, wouldn't you?' She let out a breath. 'Anyway, I reckon that's enough to ponder for now. It's Sunday night and I need to finish writing this crazy day up. What are you up to?'

'I'm off out for a pint.'

'You civilians make me sick.'

'Hey, there's nothing stopping you pouring out some wine and getting that Dolly album on.'

'Ooo, tempting,' she laughed. 'Well look, thanks for your help today, and with the translation, but listen. Now that Micah's dead I do have other priorities. So, I reckon our wisest move is to wait and see if East wakes up and ask him straight out. If anything comes to you in the meantime, you let me know, okay? Because, I'd personally love to know what the hell today was about.'

'Ditto.'

'Goodnight, Matt.'

'Night.'

He hung up and stared at the words he'd scrawled out.

'My God, my father . . .' he whispered, 'why have you murdered me?'

Frowning, he tapped his fingers on his desk, tempted to fire up his computer to see how the death of Micah was being reported. But he shook his head. Time to switch off. Time to breathe. Time to—

'Load the dishwasher,' he said.

He closed up the cabin and hurried back to the kitchen to find they'd already done it. He apologised to Wren and Amelia who were in the lounge, practising her spellings for school tomorrow. He checked his watch, knowing that he had enough time for a quick shower. By 8.20 p.m. he was pulling his jacket on in a cloud of aftershave, then he grabbed a bag and leant in to Wren and Lucy. 'Just heading out with my boyyyeee.'

He stepped outside, amazed at how clear the sky was. The stars didn't just shine. Some of them seemed to flash.

He was meeting Sean in the Jolly Sportsman, which was only a ten-minute walk from his house. He shut his gate, plunged both hands in his pockets and strolled past the church, shivering at how cold it was. It was hard not to play over the events of the day, but he wiped them out with a jaunty whistle of 'Spanish Flea'. It was hard to think of falling legs when that was playing, though not impossible.

Which was when he saw the large, long shadow moving across the church next to his house. It made him stop dead and look over, the whistle dying on his lips. The exterior spotlights were all blazing but the lights inside the church were off. The poorly attended evening service must have been finished, but he was still almost certain he'd seen someone standing among the graves.

He shook his head and told himself not to be an idiot. He'd been seeing dumb shadows all day. To be honest, he'd been seeing them off and on since the mindfuck that was Menham and he knew full well that tall black rabbits lurking in the bushes were little more than lack of sleep, and maybe even a dollop of stress. Today hadn't exactly been a spa break, had it?

Besides, everybody knew the churchyard had an open public path that lead to the estate. He looked at the graves and wondered if the shadowy lump behind a leaning cross was actually a person, crouching. Or a tall black animal thing ready to pounce. He tilted his head and leant to the right. He saw a shadow on the gravestone and nothing more. He thought of that card Bowland gave him. The one for people to talk to. But then a quicker solution came to mind. One that was far more attractive right now.

He said a word into the night, and the word was 'beer'. The sound alone managed to make his tongue sparkle and launched him into an eager power walk into town.

CHAPTER SEVENTEEN

Night came to the city.

Headlights, street lights, shop lights. They all sparkled in the puddles. The snow from today hadn't managed to settle anywhere. But Sam Price assumed that thick lines of it must be covering the Chiltern Hills. It'd be like a ski resort up there, he imagined. He'd have loved to have seen it. To have a snowball fight with a bunch of mates up there and build a massive snowman with a big old set of knockers, just to make them laugh. But of course, he couldn't because there was no car to get up there and no money for a bus, and let's face it, no friends either.

Instead, Sam just did what he always did. He crawled under the metal fire escape behind the all-night laundrette and tried to sleep against the wheelie bin. It was a proper little cubbyhole under these steps, stuffed with cardboard that sometimes wasn't even needed since the laundrette had an extractor fan. It pumped out a blast of heat right now. Wonderful. He assumed this patch would be stolen from him any day now, but right now, it was his.

Sam was fifty-six, though any passing shopper with a car and a house key would no doubt disagree. They'd insist he had two decades on that, maybe even three, because matted grey hair clumped together in strands does not a young buck make. And vodka had a habit of shrivelling skin. They never mention that in the adverts. It's all party time and glamour in those. But it dries you out, that stuff. Turns your face into Billy the Kid's saddlebag.

He laughed to himself and listened to the fan throbbing its usual rhythm.

Whup-whup-whup.

He thought back to the evening he'd had, and the smile dropped. He'd stormed out of the Salvation Army soup kitchen again, after one too many lectures from the God squad. He even tossed his rancid-tasting coffee across the room. He felt terrible after that. He'd hammered on the window trying to apologise. But the hammering just scared them, which was so silly. Sam Price wouldn't even hurt the most unreasonable fly. It's just that they suggested he use their phone to contact his brother all the way up in Glasgow. They didn't appreciate that Sam and his brother couldn't exist in the same space. If they ever met in the same room, if their fingers ever touched, the universe would implode.

He'd be banned from the place now.

'You're a disaster, Sam,' he whispered to himself, an echo of his mum's favourite phrase. Whenever he dropped a mug or cut her sandwiches wrong, she'd say, 'You're a disaster, Sam.' Which, strangely enough, was the exact thing Sam's ex-wife said to him, when he lost his head teacher's job. After that really awful Ofsted, when the school board kicked him out, Carol found him sitting on the bathroom floor and she'd said those exact words. She cried when she said it, which only made it worse. 'You're a disaster, Sam.' The only way to stop those words stinging was to thicken his skin. And what better way to thicken skin than Lidl's own-brand vodka.

He dragged his sleeping bag across him, listened to the fan and whispered, 'Night, Mum. Night, Carol . . .'

Someone whispered back.

It was incredibly faint. He strained to listen and heard nothing but the fan.

Whup-whup-whup.

Then there it was again. A weird hiss was speaking. He pushed himself up on his elbows and looked down his body to the entrance of his home.

Across the alley, he saw a man on all fours, looking at him.

Whup-whup-whup.

Bumps, many of them, broke across his skin.

The man looked large and well built, an average fella by all accounts, except that he was on his hands and knees and was staring.

'Um . . . hello?' Sam said.

The stranger's lips were moving, but they made no sound.

Sam was used to shivering out here. Aw, who was he kidding? Since he lost everything, Sam Price was an absolute world authority on shivering. But the deep tremble that broke through his body right now was new to him. This was a different kind of cold. So he spoke firm and sharp with his head teacher voice. The same tone he used to use for breaking up suspicious groups of teenagers in the playground. 'Excuse me,' he said, 'but what are you up to?'

The stranger's lips stopped moving, but the hands and knuckles . . . they started pushing through the dirt.

He's crawling. Look at that, Sam. He's crawling to get you.

'Now look here, this is my place!' Sam said, then he noticed something. Something that gave him courage. 'And you're a coward, aren't you? Can't even look a bloke in the eye when you're mugging him?'

Something flashed in the stranger's hand. Something unmistakeable. A stubby little . . . *oh shit* . . . a stubby little Stanley knife.

Fear hit him like a brick and his body jerked into action.

He rammed his shoulder against the giant, heavier-than-hell wheelie bin. Forks of pain sparked from the chronic ache in his neck. A skiing injury, from the days when he was rich enough to still find snow enjoyable. The stranger stopped crawling and paused for some seconds. Perhaps he was startled by Sam's terror, or amused. Then all his limbs sprang into frantic life, scrambling forward in a horribly quick, insect-like scuttle.

'Christ,' Sam slammed himself against the bin again and amazingly, it shifted a little. A gap appeared. He spun himself round onto all fours. *Yeah, I can crawl fast too, ya big bull—*

A hand grabbed the heel of his boot.

'Get off!' He kicked out hard and the fingers slipped away. He sprang out from the fire escape and staggered to his feet, dizzy with shock. The buildings settled into their correct angles, and he bolted down the backstreet.

It was a long alley this, he'd always thought that. Full of twists and turns with nothing but bins and corrugated doors for company. Those doors lead to jolly restaurants and happy, air-conditioned shops on the other side. But this side was his world. Filthy and forgotten, with angry-looking graffiti and pools of urine and shit, and sometimes even semen. Yeah, drunk folk and shopworkers sometimes nipped around the back for kisses that never stopped. Seeing that was always far less arousing than he hoped it would be. One night, it even made him cry.

He pounded down the long, dirty alley now, while behind him his pursuer pushed bins to the side. The stranger's boots hit the puddled floor in a steady slap. He was way too scared to look round, but he knew a side street was coming, next to Muchacho's, the Mexican restaurant. The one with the cute neon cactus on the door. He took that hard right and pulled empty boxes down behind him, so that this chasing freak would slip on the cardboard.

He felt a sudden elation of ingenuity and something he rarely felt in his life: achievement. God, it felt amazing. He could cheer, because the old, smashed fence was at the end of this alley. The one with the broken board that never got fixed. This would be his shortcut to the other side, to the mother planet, where he'd call out to the beautiful people for help. So what if they backed away like they usually did? Their fear of contagion wouldn't break his heart this time because at least he'd be safe and seen.

He pushed through the fence.

It didn't budge.

Um . . .

He pushed again.

Nothing.

They'd fixed it. He almost laughed at the irony of it. That for months this fence had been broken but now, on the precise night he really needed it, it was nailed coffin-tight.

You're a disaster, Sam. A dizzz-arrrr-sterr.

Sam turned and shuddered when he saw the man again. Only, at first, he was just a set of dirty fingers grasping the corner bricks. Then he became a tall giant filling the space. The moment that really set Sam's heart on fire was when the tall man split into two men. One very tall. One shorter and more bulky. They walked through his pathetic cardboard trap like it wasn't even there.

Sam's knees cracked in pain when he dropped to the floor. He called out 'Help' and automatically gripped the plastic cross that hung from his neck. A gift. Not from the mission, but from his wife Carol. She, who had never been to church since the cruel nuns of her youth, had given him this cross one breezy autumn day, when she accidentally stumbled across him begging in the street. She bought him this cross and gave him a handful of twenty-pound notes, then ran off in a flurry of tears. He thought she might come back one day. He'd even saved up some begging pennies to buy her a coffee.

She never did. Her cross used to light up in the dark, like those glow sticks people buy at firework parties. But it hadn't shone in a very long time.

When he saw that fat little knife again, he heard his own voice cry out, and he knew it was Carol he was calling for. Not for help, though. He was apologising to her. He really had pushed her so far away. But then he stopped speaking because the two men came very close indeed. And then a third appeared. The three shadow men pulled a rag from thin air and they flung it across Sam's eyes. The alley vanished as one of them pressed their lips to the side of Sam's head.

Sam felt hot breath on his ear. And the breath said,

Hollow . . .

Funny, he thought. Carol used to call him that, too.

CHAPTER EIGHTEEN

Matt turned up at the pub a little early, so he was expecting ten or so minutes of eBay-lurking on his phone. But the second he swung the door open he immediately spotted that Sean Ashton was already there, sitting in a brown leather chair by the fire. His hands were crossed on his lap while the fireplace flickered in his glasses. And next to him, Matt saw an identical empty chair, waiting.

He glanced across the ales as he shrugged his coat off, then he headed over, setting his bag by the chair. 'Hi, Sean.' He put his hand out.

Sean snapped into life and sprang up. 'Professor, hi. Thanks so much for coming.'

'Oh, it's my pleasure. And it's Matt, remember.' He put both palms towards the fire. 'So, what are you drinking?'

'Erm . . . what will *you* be drinking?'

'Well, I just spotted an ale on draught called . . . wait for it . . . Rinkydink and there's another called Lord of Steel. So I'm going Rinky, then Steel.'

Sean bit his lip and stared at the bar, deep in existential thought. 'Or there's coke, wine, lager, tea. They're bound to have Tappoline.'

'Ooo, what's that?'

'Water . . . from the tap,' Matt smiled. 'Or Council Pop, as my dad used to call it.'

Sean laughed, and finally seemed to relax. 'I'll have the same as you, please. I'll go Rinkydink.'

'Hero.' Matt headed to the bar, tapping out a rhythm on the brass railing with the edge of his debit card. It was only when the barman got halfway through pouring that Matt spotted the strength. 'Six point four? Sheesh. I think we're going to need some roughage with that. Two packets of crisps, please. Dealer's choice.'

Hands loaded, he headed back to the glow of their seats, and set the drinks down.

'Cheers,' Sean said.

They clinked, and Matt leant back into the leather chair, which was hot against his back. He took a deep, exquisite sip. One of those long sigh-with-your-eyes-closed sort of deals. He wiped his lip and cradled the pint for now. 'So, Sean . . . how was your day?'

'Hmmm. Not great. Quite challenging, actually.'

'Oh?'

'I've been prepping an RE class this week. It's on one of the most incomprehensible concepts in Christianity . . .'

'Let me guess. Why Christians wear socks with sandals?'

'Not that tricky. That's PhD level. . .' Sean giggled into his drink. 'I just have to explain that little thing called the Trinity to a bunch of sixth-formers. Who, speaking frankly, have a habit of asking horribly intelligent questions. They keep saying how the word isn't even mentioned in the Bible.'

'They're right, it's not.' He sipped. 'But the concept's definitely there. That God is actually three distinct personalities: Father, Son and Spirit.'

'Which makes God sound . . . schizophrenic.'

Matt set his drink down and leant forward. Diving back into a little of his day job was probably just what he needed right now. 'You got a pen? I promise it's not to autograph your beer mat.'

Matt flipped a Starbucks receipt over and flattened it out on the table. He started scribbling three overlapping circles that became a three-dimensional sphere. 'For what it's worth, this is how I explain it. The Bible seems to present God as *three* divine beings: God the Father, God the Son and God the Holy Spirit. You even see hints in the book of Genesis when God creates the cosmos. He doesn't say "I will make humans in my image". He says, "Let *us* make humans in *our* image." There's more than one creator at work. And of course, I'm using "he" as a shorthand here. God transcends gender labels.'

Sean shook his head. 'That sounds awfully like polytheism.'

'Only if you start in the wrong direction. When you teach the Trinity you don't begin with the concept of one God, then try and make that three. Start with three personalities as your base plate, and then figure out what makes those three *one*.'

'You mean like water can be ice, steam and water. Three distinct things, but it's all the same thing too. Maybe I could bring some ice into class—'

'Don't. They'll miss the point.'

'Which is?'

'Water, ice and steam can only be one thing at once. The Trinity, however' – he tapped on his 3D circle – 'that's three distinct, separate personalities. What makes them one is their relationship. It's why the Bible presents the Devil as precisely not a Trinity. He's just one single entity, exclusively self-centred.'

Sean stared at the circles. 'It's still a bit abstract.'

'Then just think of the word "God" as the collective noun for the Father, Son and Holy Spirit in relationship. Without each other, they're not God any more. But that love makes them so close, they're classed as one single God.' Matt laughed. 'Course, whether all this stuff is just a steaming bunch of crud is another matter entirely. Leave that to your students to decide. I tend to think we invented God, Satan and all of it.'

Sean waited for a moment. Said nothing.

'But the idea itself is pretty radical,' Matt went on. 'It's unity without uniformity, which ironically is a very trendy message these days. How many times have you heard politicians or pop stars yearn for a society that celebrates diversity but stands as one? What they're asking for is the Trinity model in a nutshell.'

'I'm not sure the fundamentalists got the diversity memo, are you?'

'Sadly, no. They tend to see God as one singular personality, one monad. So they wind up with only the Father being truly God, Jesus is his second in command who isn't really divine, and the Holy Spirit ends up as some wispy special effect or a ghost. Which is more down to Plato than the Bible . . . but hey, I'm seriously waffling now. And Sean, I do get paid to waffle.'

Matt smiled and noticed Sean's pint glass was three-quarters empty already. Matt's was three-quarters full, from all his yakking. For a while they just listened to the pleasant crackle of the fire, and the low sound of darts thrumming against the dartboard.

Then finally Sean suddenly spoke. 'You saw me, didn't you?' He turned from the fire, slowly. 'In the car park this morning. You saw my dad shouting at me.'

CHAPTER NINETEEN

Scratch.

The sound made Ever groan in his sleep – not enough to wake him, but enough to turn him onto his front. He plunged his cheek deep into the warm cushion until—

Rattle. Thud.

This time, he did stir. Enough to flutter his eyes half-open. Slowly his vision adjusted, and he turned his gaze to the glowing blue curtains above his bed, because the scraping and scratching was coming from out there. He thought about calling for Uncle Dust, but then remembered his mum had told him off for doing that in nights past. There was, however, enough curiosity to make him swing his feet out of bed. The floorboards felt like ice against his bare feet, but they didn't creak. He stepped towards the window and pulled the curtain back just a touch.

The hill, the field, the stream . . . they all floated in the dull blue light from a moon, which was – a shiver ran through him – which was hidden by a bank of cloud. The distant hills looked like piles of dark powder, and between them, he saw the skin-tightening glow from the Hollow towns and cities.

He opened the curtains some more.

Thud.

Shaking, he leant forward and pressed his cheek against the cold glass, trying to get a decent look at the side of the house. He saw the dirt road, and the path leading up to the chapel. And the metal shed where they kept all their farming tools and sacks of . . .

His eyes bulged.

A rope.

The shed had a rope tied around it.

That wasn't right. That wasn't normal.

But there it was. A thick rope was wrapped around the entire shed, looped through the double-door handles up front, and tied in a hefty knot. What's more – and this was the part that really had his skin prickling – he could see those shed doors were pulsing with a slow, unpredictable rhythm. Something in there was quietly scratching and knocking at the door, trying to get out.

His bottom jaw jerked open in a spasm when he heard 'Psssst. Psssst'. He saw the figure on the grass outside. The lopsided shoulders, the wild hair.

'Pssst' – Milton turned his finger, telling him to open up – 'come to the window, ya daftie.'

Ever swung the window open and leant out. The air was freezing.

'What you doin' still up?' Milton whispered, looking this way and that. He was carrying a shotgun. 'You should be all tucked up.'

Ever whispered back. 'What's in the shed?'

'Tools and such.'

'Very funny. Is there a Hollow in there?'

Milton bit his lip and looked around again. 'Don't worry. You'll get your go with it.'

'Huh?'

'Just get back to bed. You'll wake Merit.'

'Just her?' Ever's voice was a low hiss. 'Aren't the adults asleep too?'

'Course they aren't. They're on their knees,' he said. 'Now sleep.'

He'd heard that phrase a million times – on their knees. It made him look up at the chapel where he saw the dim, black outline of the roof. He could just about make out one of the windows. The tiniest hint of a candle flickered inside.

'They're up there, taking back the world,' Milton said, proudly. 'And you'll take it back too, okay? But for now, go to—'

'There's a Hollow in the shed, isn't there?'

Milton winced.

The shed doors started pulsing again.

'Why is there a Hollow in the shed?'

'You'll find out in the morning. But don't you worry. We've got that monster tied up, nice and tight. And I'm going to guard your room for the whole night, okay?'

'What about Merit's room? Why aren't you guarding her?'

'Cos I'm keeping you safe. That's my job. Now sleep.'

'Milton . . .' Ever put a hand on the window frame. 'I'm scared.'

He tilted his head. 'Truth be told, so am I. But just remember Jesus . . . he's with us. Every day in every way.'

Just as he said that, the entire farm brightened as the huge moon emerged from behind a thick cloud. The light fell on the shed, and the pulsing door immediately stopped.

'See,' Milton said. 'He's with us. Now get some shut-eye, Big Man.'

Ever's spine tingled and he crawled back into bed, quilt up to his nose. It took him a long time to fall asleep, not least because whenever the moon hid, he heard the scratching in the shed come back. It made him wonder if the Hollow still had its skin on, or if it'd already slipped out of it and was striding around in its proper form. Licking the air and clawing at the metal to get out.

Now and again he'd hear the adults up in the chapel too. On certain nights, when they got on their knees, he'd hear their moans all the way down the hill. He heard them doing that now. The groans, the gasps and the occasional shrill scream. Prosper said that sound should be comforting, but it wasn't.

The only thing to help, Ever decided, was to pray. So he did. He asked Jesus why Milton was guarding his room, and nobody else's. And why he'd said that Ever was going to rebuild the world and 'get his go'. What did that even mean? And the biggest question of all: Why was there a Hollow in their shed?

Prayer, Uncle Dust always told him, was a beautiful way to fall asleep. It was like Jesus putting his hand into ours. And at one point, Ever felt that hand. He felt those cold, carpenter fingers stroking his hair. That touch was the gift it always had been, and he finally drifted off, even as the sounds of wailing and shed-scratching went on. Within moments he was flying to the top of Comfort Hill, only now it was called Comfort Mountain, blazing in daylight. And he was a knight with a glowing sword, skewering the great beast of heaven with ease, while the rest of his family cheered and prayed him on. Even Hope was back, slapping her hands together and whistling with pride. And Micah too, who cheered louder than any of the others, happy and grateful that somehow, Big Man Ever was going to make things right.

CHAPTER TWENTY

Matt waited for a moment, letting the fire crackle fill the air for a moment. Then he leant forward. 'Yes, I saw you with your parents and I don't mean to be nosey but . . . well your dad seemed pretty . . .' Matt sniffed. 'He was going ballistic, Sean.'

Silence. Swig.

Matt tugged his chair a little closer. 'Look, I might waffle a lot, but I'm actually a pretty good listener.'

Sean took another, very deep gulp. His throat sounded like twisted leather. 'We're doing Lord of Steel next, right?'

Matt nodded, and Sean immediately sprang up, and headed to the bar.

They did have a Steel next, and then, when Sean announced a third, Matt had another Steel while Sean went back to the super strong Rinkydink. In fact, he had two of them in the space of Matt's third. And for most of the conversation they talked of anything but Sean's dad. Like teaching and lecturing, and which *Doctor Who* was the most solid series. But it was while Sean chugged through pint number five that Matt asked a seemingly innocent question. It turned the conversation down a new, intense alley.

'So, Sean,' he said, 'I never asked where your head is with all this God stuff.'

'Well, let me tell you . . .' Sean plunged a hand straight into the pocket of his skinny jeans. 'After one more.'

Matt winced. 'Best not, eh? It's a school night—'

'I'm a born-again Christian, just like my parents.' He raised his hand in a high, preaching style. 'Hallelujah.'

'Well . . .' Matt shifted in his seat. 'Good for you.'

'Yep, I've been baptised, I've spoken in tongues, I've done the Alpha Course – twice – I've been to all the festivals, got six Bibles, two on my phone,' he hiccupped. 'Oh, and I thoroughly love the Father, Son and Holy Spirit . . . the whole set.'

Matt waited. 'Listen, I do respect your—'

'But . . .' Sean slapped a hand down on the table and the pints nearly tipped off. Matt had to use both hands to steady them. 'But it turns out that this ever-loving Trinity of yours doesn't stretch it's affection to me.'

Matt spotted some guys playing darts. Both were bald, and both had a heavy curve of gut under the strain of checked shirts. The sound of the table slap made them stop throwing. They looked over and watched for a while.

'Why do you say that?' Matt said quietly.

Sean tapped a finger on his chest and held it there. 'Because God doesn't love anybody like me, apparently. Not unless I . . . erm . . . change one of my interests, if you know what I mean.'

Matt had a quick sense of where this was going, but he didn't want to presume. 'And what's wrong with people like you?'

'That I can't change . . .' Sean closed his eyes in that slow-blink that drink can bring. 'No matter how much my church prays for me

I still love the wrong people.' He laughed. 'Do you know why my dad was shouting at me this morning?'

'No.'

'Because he thought I was trying to pick you up. He said I was doing it right in front of him, just to rub sin in his face.' He sniffed. 'He's an idiot, sometimes. An A-grade pillock. I've never picked anyone up in my whole life. I haven't dared. Kissed a few girls but . . .' He laughed. 'I didn't like it. Or their chapstick.'

'Sean, I'm sorry about your dad.'

'Yeah, me too. But the proper funny bit is when I told him why I really went to see you. I told him I'd been reading your book. I confessed. Matt, do you know that some people read your stuff hiding under a duvet with a tiny torch? Grown adults sneaking your book into their bedroom like a dirty old porn mag. Did you know that?'

He said it quietly. 'I didn't know that.'

'Yeah, well this morning I saw you and I thought screw it. I showed him the book and told him I was widening my perspective on God. Then we got back to the car and he took one look at the contents page and flipped out. Now he's called the pastor to our house for an all-night intercession. That's where I'm supposed to be now, by the way . . .' For the first time, Sean's eyes sparkled with tears. 'Yep. There's a bunch of them sitting in my front room as we speak, all set to "pray the gay away". Which I've tried doing myself since I was twelve but the miracle ain't coming . . .' Sean pulled his wallet out. 'So there you go . . . I can't be a Christian any more . . . game over.'

'Then be both. Be you *and* a Christian. It's completely possible . . .'

'And risk hell?'

And there it was: another throbbing reminder of why Matt Hunter left the church. This morose young man, staring into his pint glass with tears in his eyes, shuddering with self-hate because

God was supposedly a single mathematical unit with no tolerance for difference.

'Let's move on, Matt. It's gin o'clock I reckon . . .' Sean pushed himself up, but his hand slipped off the chair. He dropped to his knee with a crunch and those two bald heads snapped round from the dartboard. They were sniggering now. Sean spoke to the table edge. 'I don't normally drink.'

'No shit.' Matt helped him back up.

'Then I guess this is home time.'

'I reckon so . . . but do you really want to go back to yours tonight? With all those church people waiting for you? You can crash on our couch if you like.'

'You're serious?'

'Course I am.' Matt grabbed Sean's jacket, surprised at how woozy his own head felt once he stood up straight. Then he grabbed his own jacket and bag. He noticed the darts players were staring and whispering to each other now. 'I have an amazing office you can crash in.'

'I'm genuinely touched by the offer but it's fine . . .' Sean's words slurred as they headed for the door. 'I've arranged to stay at my gran's tonight. She's literally a few streets away.'

It was just as Sean put his hand on the door handle that the smallest bald guy said that classic word. Just seven letters, with enough power to set fires. He said 'Faggots', though he was hilarious enough to disguise it with a cough. The other one guffawed into his shoulder.

Matt span his head round. 'What did you just say?'

'You heard me. Couple of faggots, you two.'

'Oh, find a time machine for crying out loud,' Matt said. 'Catch up.'

'Why would we? We're not big into pricks. But you on the other hand . . .'

Matt took his hand off the door and felt the alcohol move his feet and mouth well before his rational brain could catch up. He stepped into the man's space. 'There's only one prick around here, and I'm looking right at him.'

'Whoa.' The barman bounded over just as the darts player slammed his pint on the table. 'Let's just move this along.'

Matt put his hand up. 'Fine, we're leaving.'

The barman between them, Matt turned to see that Sean had already gone outside. He found him out on the pavement, leaning by the wall. Hands buried in his jacket. He was breathing out plumes of cold, frosty air.

'Crikey, I am finished with Rinkydink. It's savage,' Matt said, one nervous eye on the door.

'Thanks for that. For sticking up for me,' Sean said.

'I was sticking up for both of us. Anyway, which way are you walking?'

'I'm five minutes along here.'

'Cool, I'm heading that way too.'

He wasn't really. It was actually in the opposite direction to Matt's house, but he didn't mention that. Might as well make sure Sean got through his front door. After all, new RE teachers found in the street, strewn in vomit, weren't such a hit with head teachers. So he walked with one arm holding his bag, and the other tucked under Sean's arm, helping him with his occasional stagger. He'd done this sort of thing many times before. He knew the ropes with drunk people. When he was first ordained Matt volunteered for a project called the Street Angels. The name was a little corny, true, but the aims of it were actually pretty great. He and a bunch of other church folk would wear high-viz jackets and walk the city streets in the early hours of the weekends. They'd help get drunk people home or offer a listening ear. He'd held a lot of hair during puke sessions back then, but at least Sean didn't look that bad.

It didn't take too long to reach granny's house, which was a skinny terrace with an empty hanging basket above the door. She clearly wasn't deaf because as soon as their footsteps reached the door, the bay window curtain flicked open. A bunched-up, wrinkled eye peeped out.

'I'll be in in a second, Gran,' Sean shouted.

The eye leapt to Matt, gave him the once over, then vanished.

'Do you mind if we keep tonight between me and you?' Sean said. 'For now, at least.'

'Of course. Not a problem. But if you ever want to talk – about any of it – you call me, okay? I'll get my Bible out and show you it's perfectly possible for you to be both.'

He smiled. 'That I'd love to see.'

'Oh, and I almost forgot . . . one free copy.' Matt reached into his bag and fished out a new hardback of *In Our Image*. 'I noticed yours got a bit of water damage this morning.'

Sean stared at it for a long moment, wiped a tear, then took it. 'You know, for an atheist, you're a pretty decent human being.'

'And for a gay fella, you're a pretty decent Christian.'

He laughed out loud. They both did. Then Sean opened the door into a purple hallway where a side table was filled with Victorian baby ornaments. Truly hideous. Sean put out a swaying hand. 'Well thanks. Because after tonight I feel a little more hopeful about my faith. Probably not the reaction you'd hope for—'

'Sean! You're letting a gale in here,' Granny screeched. Her voice was muffled but clear enough from behind the curtains. 'Get yourself up to bed, you've got school in the morning.'

They both looked at each other and laughed again.

'Goodnight, Matt.'

Matt did a relaxed salute. 'Night.'

He walked back the same way he came, down the long straight street that seemed to stretch on for ages. Above him, the moonlit sky was clear so that the stars sparkled through the dark blue. He pictured a lounge somewhere in town, with parents and pastors wringing their hands in despair, praying for a man's personality to vanish and die so he could be someone he wasn't. Someone more generic and singular. The thought turned Matt's walk to a trudge, and he grew angry and glum. Mostly glum, though. Especially when his mind insisted on melding Sean's face with the face of Micah East. Both of them turning to their dads and saying,

Avi, Avi . . . Lama kataltani.

'My father, my father,' he whispered, 'why have you killed me?'

Such an odd way to put it, Matt thought, looking up at the blazing moon. He thought of that train line up near Chervil, which must be glowing from this very same light right now. He crossed the road as he passed the pub, just in case those two tweedle-dummies were out there, looking for him. They weren't.

Finally, he reached the end of the long street and went to turn the corner. He took a quick glance back, all the way up. Two bald heads were shining under the street lamps, but thankfully they were clambering into a taxi, heading the other way. An Asian man was rolling his wheelie bin to the front of his house and in the distance, a woman was walking along the path staring at her phone. It was all quite genteel really. No hordes of drunks crawling along the pavement. Not much call for a Street Angels project in Chesham, he thought. People seemed to like taking care of themselves. He slowed his step. Not far from the woman he could see the front door of granny's house. It was still open. And there he was in the distance, Sean's silhouette hovering in the door frame, light spilling from the gaps and into the street, watching Matt walk home.

CHAPTER TWENTY-ONE

A thoroughly tipsy Matt Hunter crept into their bedroom, convinced it was with the stealth of a ninja, but when he stood on the upturned plug from Wren's hairdryer he let out a pitiful shriek and fell against the wardrobe.

Wren groaned.

'Sorrrrrry' – he pushed a finger to his lips – 'I woke you . . .'

'You woke me half an hour ago.' She turned over. 'When you dropped your cereal bowl in the sink. Got the munchies?'

'Wren, you know as well as I do . . .' he started tugging his socks off, 'breakfast is the most important meal of the day.'

'It's nearly midnight, dimwit.' She watched him clamber out of his jeans in the dark. It was a sad, jerky attempt, which made her laugh. Then she clicked her bedside lamp on and screwed up her face in a squint. 'Nice bromance with Mr Ashton?'

'Yeah, though it was pretty intense at times.'

'Oh?' Her eyes flashed, and she sat up a little more. 'Tell me everything.'

'My lips are sealed . . .' He threw his shirt at the wardrobe, but it was closed. It hit the door and slid down. He pointed at that and laughed, like it was the greatest event in history. Then he slid into the bed, letting out a long sigh flat on his back.

She snuggled in, red hair buried into his neck. 'From the sounds of it, you've had a pretty intense day in general.' She squeezed him. 'Matt . . . I caught the news when you were out. They said you were there when the train hit the boy.'

He pushed a breath towards the ceiling.

'It must have been awful.'

He waited a moment. 'It was. It really was. And the sound of it, too . . .' He shivered and squeezed her.

'Do you want to talk about it?'

He kissed her on the forehead. 'Maybe in the morning, but not right now. This stuff isn't exactly conducive to sleep, if you know what I mean.'

She sat up on her elbow, hand splayed into her hair, waiting.

'What?'

'The police, Matt . . . they expect too much of you. They just throw you into these horrendous situations . . . Hobbs Hill, Menham, and now today . . .'

'They don't force me. I want to help.'

'But what you end up seeing . . . they're trained for that . . . you're not.'

'Hey, I'll have you know I saw lots of dead bodies when I was a reverend.'

'Yeah. Old ladies in hospital beds, not this . . .'

She was right, of course, and the thought of it made the shadows pulse, again. As he lay there, he saw those familiar ghost faces pressing through his ceiling. Folks from Menham and folks from Hobbs Hill. They were part of his brain structure now. Quite the collection he was gathering. They stared down at him silently, like they often did at this time of night. 'The officer I was with today. She gave me a card. Someone I could talk to, if I needed it.'

'Well, that's something at least . . .' She kissed him and the faces vanished. 'I guess I just prefer you standing up in a lecture hall talking about crazy people. Tracking them down in real life, though . . . it scares me, Matt.'

He felt the urge to hug her for a very long time, but she reached over and clicked off her lamp. The room plunged into darkness, and the faces, along with those long animal shadows that always walked with them, were back. He closed his eyes, until they crawled in there too.

'Anyway . . .' She fell against him, cheek on his chest. 'I'm here for you. All right?'

'Cool.'

'And don't forget we said we'd exercise together, before breakfast.'

'Not cool.'

'At least you've had your cereal already.'

'Darn it . . . gonna dream about squat thrusts now. That's way more traumatic.'

She laughed.

They lay there for a long time, enough to feel himself waking up again. Then she whispered one final thing, and he could tell it mattered, even if it was said on the downturn of sleep. She said, 'But I am proud, Matt. Even though it scares me. I'm proud of you.'

He squeezed her hand, then lifted it to his mouth to kiss it.

Fifteen minutes later Wren was snoring. He, however, wasn't. Now that he was in his mid-thirties, beer often did this. It kept him awake. Bored, he grabbed his phone and switched it on under the covers, just so it wouldn't wake her. He couldn't help it. He started reading through the reports from Chervil today. One headline said, AXE AND TRAIN DEATH IN SMALL ENGLISH VILLAGE. Another, SON AXES DAD BEFORE FATAL TRAIN SMASH. Another just said, BLOOD ON THE

TRACKS. Classy perhaps, but not that accurate, since most of the blood was flung quite far to both sides. He'd seen it spread through the air. He read another headline as his breath fogged the screen. TEEN DEAD AFTER ATTEMPTED PATRICIDE.

He gazed at that last word: 'Patricide'.

He pasted it into Google, curious to know how common trying to kill your dad is. His phone threw up a string of articles on patricide, matricide, and the term for both mother and father killing: parricide. Turns out that in the UK and US, the crime was statistically uncommon. Considering the levels of child abuse, one article suggested that the low level of parental murder was, if anything, surprisingly low. Though he noticed that the US idea of 'low' was roughly one parent a day being killed by their kids.

A voice in his head said, *Switch it off and sleep, you idiot.*

He was about to obey when he heard something in the back garden. Like pebbles falling over. He yawned, not sure if he was bothered. Then the pebbles fell some more. Peeling back the quilt he looked at Wren. Her nose was wheezing and her mouth lolled open. Cute, in a baby seal sort of way. He did a zombie walk to the window and pulled back the thick curtains, wide. The church by his house still glowed by those upturned floodlights, and the leaning gravestones set their usual long shadows across the grass. The first thing he'd whispered to Wren when they viewed this house was . . . 'And you're sure you can make love with a graveyard at the window? You're absolutely, positively sure?'

He smiled and gazed down at his back garden and the beloved home office, and the cemetery and church beyond. There were no people walking past, no animals . . . no little black rabbits or tall black rabbits for that matter, which was good because he—

A woman was standing in the shadows.

He blinked.

A silhouette. A shadowy outline with one hand high in the air. The light from the church threw a glistening curve on her shoulder, and her hand seemed to glow. She was under the weeping willow tree, just beyond their back fence.

'The hell?' He rubbed his eyes with his knuckle, just to make sure. When he opened his eyes she was, of course, gone. There was nobody in the graveyard except all those dead folks soaking up the soil. He leant closer till a fog sprang on the glass, and he shook his head.

He checked his watch, 12.43 a.m. *Could you dream standing up? Like horses do?* He swiped a ragged arc through the condensation with his hand and found, once again, nothing but his garden, his cabin, then their fence and the weeping willow and church beyond it. He stared for a moment and all the shadows stared back at him.

Wren's voice, echoing. *It scares me . . .*

There was nothing under the tree. Just his brain coping with trauma. He probably ought to talk to someone, after all. He slunk back to his bed and crashed back into the mattress. He let himself finally drift away. Of course he dreamt of trains all night, but amazingly, the dreams were filled with light and songs and Rinkydink on draught. They raced through never-ending meadows of swaying corn, and most were happy carriages of laughter and love. But only most.

CHAPTER TWENTY-TWO

It was tricky to run. Not so much from all that alcohol, but just from how blurry his eyes were. Tears had a way of doing that.

His dad and mum and . . . wait for it . . . two pastors and two elders from the church had turned up at Granny's door just now. She'd only gone and phoned them just after she made Sean a cheese toastie. *It'll help line your stomach*, she said. No sooner had he eaten it, brushed his teeth and climbed into bed than the front door shut hard and a blundering cacophony of heavy steps tramped up the staircase. He opened his door in his boxer shorts and found them all crammed onto the landing, praying for the spirit of 'unnatural lust' to leave him. One of the pastors saw him in his boxers and covered his face, like a nun at a strip show.

His dad was saying things that sounded kind and wonderfully thoughtful on paper. 'Let God in, son. We can nip this in the bud. It's going to be okay cos we believe in you . . .' Mum was in the corner with her head down and hands locked. As usual her lips weren't moving much. She'd learnt long ago that the prayer stance was a great way to hide.

It was humiliating, pulling on his jeans and scrabbling about for a pair of socks, while they all crammed onto the landing, praying and looking. He tried to close the door, but Rod, the majorly overweight pastor, put his heft against his door, so it stayed open. Sean wondered why they didn't pray the demon of gluttony out of him. But, of course, gluttony was one of the 'okay' sins. Like speeding and gossip, greed and white lies. They were no match for the sick and filthy crime of wanting a life-partner.

So they all watched him dress, which made Sean so angry and uncomfortable that he glared at the two pastors saying, 'Close the door. You're like a couple of peeping Toms!' This accusation threw the entire landing into prayerful wails of horror. It was like what Sean was saying was abnormal, and what they were doing was normal. So, the door stayed open.

Once dressed, Sean had to push his way through them all just so he could get out of there, which was the moment the tears started. It wasn't that they were grabbing him. It was the fact that most of them weren't grabbing him – that's what did it. The pastors and the elders were lurching back, because Sean was carrying the Pink Death. Gay is a contagious disease, after all – everybody knows that. And so their prayers morphed into spiritual tongues. His dad was the only one who put a hand on Sean's shoulder. He'd clearly seen his son's tears because he leant close and said very tenderly, 'This isn't who you are. This isn't the boy I love.' His breath smelt of coffee and toothpaste. 'It's never too late to be yourself, son.'

Sean paused for a second, filtering out the words and grasping at his father's tender tone instead. He'd been such a lovely dad until this. Such a wonderful, thoughtful man before Sean's 'issue' changed his parents into something else. Then an elder started ranting about the spirit of Sodom, which made Sean stumble to the bottom of the stairs.

He saw his granny sitting at the kitchen table, sobbing into her palms.

She looked up and said, 'I'm sorry, Sean. We love you, Sea—'

He slammed the door behind him and that's when he ran. He ran in the direction of the steeple, keeping his eyes on it as it poked over the rooftops, fusing with the moon. Whenever the steeple blurred, he would slow down, lift his glasses and wipe his vision back. At the end of the long street, he looked back, wondering if he might see them all running after him, gathering up the entire town with burning torches to track down a monster. But they weren't even at his granny's door. He pictured them inside, drinking tea. The fat blob of a pastor swallowing a row of biscuits in one and shrugging, *Welllllll folks . . . it were worth a pop.*

Sean's run became a walk for the rest of the way, partly because he was so out of breath and partly because he just wasn't sure what he'd say when he arrived. He was dreading knocking at Matt's door and dissolving into tears. That'd be hideous. No, he thought, he'd spend a few moments pulling himself together. He'd knock and gently say, 'That offer of a couch. Can I take it, after all?'

He turned the lane and saw the Anglican church bright and calming against the cold black sky. And just beyond it was the back of Matt's house, just as he'd described it when they got on to Chesham house prices earlier. The smattering of gravestones and the tall weeping willow looked pretty in the floodlights. Just beyond it was a hedgerow and a tall back fence, and beyond that, a detached house without any lights on. Matt's house.

Okay. He'd nip around the front and give a quick knock. He checked his watch. It was 1 a.m. He stopped walking.

Oh God, he thought. That was way later than he thought. Could he really just turn up? Shouldn't he phone first? He fumbled in his pocket for Matt's card and staggered a few steps. A reminder that Rinkydink possessed a powerful echo. He pulled out the card, looked back up, and froze.

He saw her phone, before he saw her.

Her glowing screen hovered in the thick of the willow's overhang. And being captured in the bright rectangle was a video image of Matt Hunter's house.

He trotted a little closer and whispered, 'Hello?'

The rectangle vanished.

He parted the leaves like a curtain and found her standing under the tree, hidden mostly from view. A backpack was strewn by the trunk.

'Erm . . . what are you doing?' Sean asked.

She spun round, chest heaving, and her eyes started darting left and right, but not at him. She looked older. Fifties, maybe.

'Why are you filming that house?'

She didn't answer.

He glanced at the ground by the tree trunk, where crushed cans and crisp packets lay with two smashed cider bottles scattered in thick shards. 'Are you homeless?' he asked, though he knew she wasn't. She was too clean. Too well dressed.

'Don't rape me,' she said.

His jaw dropped. 'What?'

'Just let me go.'

He was mortified. 'Hey, I was just passing . . .' He was about to back away. 'But wait . . . why are you filming Matt's house?'

For the first time, her eyes locked on his and she bit her lip hard. Her chest started heaving with shallow breath. She was thinking, he could tell. When he stepped forward, she gasped in panic. Then the glow of the phone dropped from her hand and bounced face up on the grass. They almost smacked heads reaching for it, but Sean was fast with these things. Always quick on the buzzer. He grabbed it and quickly backed away, flicking through her phone, a cheap throwaway thing. He saw photos under his thumb, of not just the house, but of Matt standing shirtless at a bedroom window. Then Matt downstairs in his kitchen, eating a bowl of

147

cereal. Then Matt coming out of the Jolly Sportsman pub, chatting to him only hours before.

'What the frig?' Sean looked up. 'Why are you spying on him?'

'Why are *you* spying on him?' she said.

'I'm not. I'm his friend.'

'Who creeps behind his house at 1 a.m?'

'*Who are you?*'

'Give me the phone.'

Sean had an idea. He quickly raised hers high.

She frowned. 'What are you doing?'

'I'm showing this to him. I'm telling him you're taking photographs . . .'

'Don't.'

'He should see this.'

'*No!*' Then a slowing of her voice. A tilt of her head, and after a long moment, a change of response. 'Of course . . .' she spoke very quietly. 'You should take it to him . . . That's the right thing to do.' She started crying.

'Hey . . .' He walked towards her. 'What's going on?'

'I need his help,' she whispered. 'I really need his help . . . I'm so sorry . . .'

She leant against the tree, her shoulders quaking, eyes still bouncing. She kept whispering.

'I'm sorry, I can't hear you.' He stepped closer still, his feet still unsteady from the drink.

'Help me, please,' she put out a trembling hand.

'What's wrong?'

'Everyone's so hollow . . .'

Her cold white hand slipped into his and she tugged him closer. He was utterly confused, and yet her weeping resonated with him. Her comment did, too. So when she guided his drunk footsteps to the tree, he let her.

'How about we go and see Matt together?'

'That'd be nice.'

'And what's your name?'

'I'm Miriam. But my friends . . . they call me Hope.'

'That's a beautiful name.'

She started pulling his sleeve up.

'Wait . . . what are you—'

'You can call me Hope if you like.' She slammed his arm hard against the tree, palm open.

He got the first two letters of the name out.

He shouted 'Mat—' but the 'thew' part was sucked into a strange, jerking gasp. He looked down and saw something utterly bizarre. A dark seam was magically opening in his wrist. It looked so unreal, so fake, that all he could do was stare at the pulsing slit in shock. Then, he felt her finger plunge inside and the sensation of thin threads being pulled taut and far from his hand. The threads snapped, and now his hand was fully warm. He went to scream, but she caught his roar in a pressed palm. God, she was strong. Amazingly so. He heard a dull thud on the grass as the broken bottle fell from her hand. Which was the moment she finally spoke, 'This'll be a better way for you. You'll see. Much better than falling up.'

He screamed against her hand again, his mind a firework of confused agony. He raised his knee to slam her in the guts, but he'd lost all working relationships with his legs. There was no way of standing on them, never mind lifting them. This, he realised, was why the bark of the trunk was scraping up his spine.

Course the tree isn't growing, ya fool. You're sinking.

Hope sank with him, all the way down, with one hand always over his mouth and the other squeezing his forearm over and over. He realised, with a nauseating wave of horror, that she was pumping out all she could. She was milking a cow. In fact, she looked at him like he actually was a cow. Like he was an animal who might have diseases. He tried to shout out 'Matthew' again, but it came out as puffs of blocked air against her palm. He hadn't registered it at first, but his glasses had slid down his nose. Now as his bottom hit the dirt, he felt them fall from his face and bounce off his knee. He thought he could at least grab a bottle to smack off her head, but then she spoke, and it took even that desire away.

'You deserve this, this was always the end for you,' she whispered into his ear. 'Jesus won't be mocked.'

He gave up then and his body went into a shuddering state of shock, which brought a final revelation. The fat pastor's prayers had worked after all because now Sean had met God's fearsome angel. A female messenger with sharp claws, and she'd opened up a hole in him. Something to drain the sin away. Maybe it was the alcohol, or the delirium of pure and violent shock, but his last words seemed like the right ones. And the words were not to her, but to God. He said, 'I repent. Please, take me home.'

The pressure in her hand grew less, then she pulled her palm away completely. He could tell Hope was watching him die. She grabbed her backpack and sat on her haunches, tilting her head. At one point, he felt her pick up his glasses again. She slid them back into place on his head, then she scooped up mud and smeared them on the lens, so he couldn't see her any more. Which was probably for the best.

He started to spasm as the world began to fade, and he wondered whether he was about to open his eyes in heaven or hell. He had no idea which it might be. But at least he'd repented. At least there was a chance. He started to cry.

It was very cold, near the end.

MONDAY

THE SECOND DAY

CHAPTER TWENTY-THREE

'I'm dying,' Matt gasped, as he tried to squeeze the thirtieth press-up out of his flaming arms. 'I'm literally dying.'

Wren was next to him, arms shaking as she did the same.

'How long of this nightmare is left?'

She shook her head quickly, lips pressed tightly together. 'Can't speak.' Her cheeks were as red as her hair.

'All right! Great work, guys,' the bouncy DVD woman hollered into the lounge. She was called Melody Ross, and apparently four sets of these a week was the key to a healthy, new-year heart. After the blowout of Christmas, he and Wren had picked this disc up from a supermarket shelf. It was something to add to their running and swimming. Something they could do as a couple. Which was nice, he supposed, because at least they'd have their heart attacks together. That was something. 'All right, people,' Melody cut him off. 'Up on your feet for a ten-second breather, then it's . . . sixty seconds of high knees.'

They groaned and staggered onto their elbows. They looked like they'd both just stumbled out of a plane crash.

'And I mean *high,* folks. Knee to chin.'

Wren narrowed her eyes. 'I'd like to put my knee on her chin. Over and over.'

They kicked their gym mats to the side.

'Starting in . . . three . . . two . . . one,' she whooped. 'Run for your life!'

The room filled with the sound of cut-price trainers slamming against a hard-oak floor, and through it all was an added humiliation. Amelia sat on the sofa, slurping her cereal and watching them. She was in her school uniform, cross-legged, an iPad on her lap, but she'd turned that off a while back once the burpees started.

'Amused?' Wren said, wheezing.

Amelia spoke through Coco Pops. 'I'm waiting for the best bit.'

'When we collapse and die?'

'When you do the star jumps. They're coming right . . . about . . .'

'All right, guys,' Melody shrieked, 'aaaaaaaaaand, shooting stars for sixty. Go!'

Matt and Wren flapped their arms wide and Amelia hacked out an old man's laugh. It was only when they hit sixty seconds that he turned from the screen. Amelia had set her empty bowl to the side. She was holding the iPad up, filming it all.

They both dived on her, dragging it out of her hands and frantically looking for delete while Melody barked about the power of smoothies. Amelia just ran off with it. 'I'm off to school. See you on YouTube.'

The ordeal now over, they both padded their faces with a hand towel and chugged Council Pop like they were Robinson Crusoe. They slid the patio door back for their usual cool down, out in the cold garden air with open, sweaty arms. They leant and stretched, creaking out muscles and tendons. It was frosty again. The type of morning that might even call for gloves later. But right now, it was exactly what they needed, shorts and all. They filled the air with puffs of hot mist.

'I feel better that we did it,' he said. 'You?'

'Yes. But I do wonder if anyone in the church tower ever looks down at us doing this,' she said. 'Bet they're killing themselves laughing.'

'Then they can feast their eyes.' He turned square on to the church and squatted frantically up and down, then he broke into the running man dance as she laughed out a cloud into the air. They dropped into their garden chairs, red-faced.

'So,' she said finally, 'how did you sleep last night?'

Oh, I dreamt of happy trains for most of the night. Until about four this morning when a tall black rabbit ploughed an InterCity directly into our children and turned them into jam. 'Pretty good, thanks,' he said. 'But I reckon I would like to talk over breakfast. It's just been a bit heavy lately . . . What time's your meeting . . .' he paused. 'Um . . . hello?'

She was ignoring him. She was up on her tiptoes, staring over the fence at the end of their garden. A gang of muttering heads had gathered at the church. That was no big deal. Lots of people cut through here on their way to the train station. But there were other voices unseen, coming muffled from under the willow, right behind their garden fence.

'Ey up,' Matt said. 'What's this?'

'How about you check it and I'll make us some breakfast?'

'Do we have Pop-Tarts?'

'And undo everything you've just done? The pain. The agony . . . for naught?'

'But what a way to go.' Matt grabbed the key for the back gate and jogged across the grass, one hand across his body in a final, tight stretch. He unlocked the padlock and pulled back the bolt. The noise made the voices on the other side suddenly cease. It was only when the gate pulled back that he remembered how he was dressed. Ruddy-faced in shorts and a *Planet of the Apes* T-shirt on a cold January morning.

Phil, the church gardener, stood with another passer-by. Both faces were totally sapped of colour.

'Oh, Mr Hunter . . . we've just called the police.' Phil said it very quietly. Very solemn. 'They're on their way.'

'Police? Why, what's hap—'

'It's a tragedy, is what it is.' Phil stepped aside.

Matt's knees buckled.

Sean Ashton sat rigid and stiff against the tree, his mud-covered glasses frosted to his face. And his arm lay open and strewn to the side, with a large pool of almost-frozen blood, with one single shark's fin swimming through it. A shard of glass.

Phil let out a groan. 'Poor lad's gone and topped himself.'

Matt fell against the fence while behind him he heard Wren's trainers, crunching fast across the grass to see.

CHAPTER TWENTY-FOUR

Ever yawned as he headed up the sloping path of Comfort Hill. They walked in single file, like always, only today they'd done something really unusual. Everyone let him walk up front. This was really quite bizarre. Normally it was Prosper who led the way, or every now and again Uncle Dust. But when they gathered on the path this morning, hands softly touched his back and shoulders. Then his mum leant in and left a kiss and a whisper on his cheek. 'You'll lead us today.' When she said it, Ever caught a glance of Merit's face far behind, crunching into miffed confusion. That threw an enormous smile across his.

So now his were the footsteps that crunched the day's first line into the gravel. Amazing. He turned and looked down the slope. The rest were trudging behind him, about twenty steps back. They slowed for a moment just to look at him and he saw Prosper whisper something to his mum. They were all smiling. It was odd, but it was a 'nice' odd. Though he found his uncle's smile hard to read. It was certainly on his mouth, but not so much in his eyes.

Ever couldn't quite figure that out, but it did annoy him a bit. He'd ask about it after the meeting.

He turned and resumed the march, and finally hit the summit of Comfort. The name was, of course, Prosper's idea, because here was a place where Jesus could tell them it was okay, that the end was coming. That the Hollows would soon die so that his family could go back out and live in the world. He looked forward to that. To enjoy all the good things that he'd heard about. Like playgrounds and forests and beaches.

A cold breeze swept around him and Jesus sent a message on it. *Soon. Ever. Sooooon.*

The rusting metal chapel waited for them in the mist, sparkling with frost and morning magic and not a little danger too. Ever figured if the farmhouse was the safest place in the valley, the chapel was its opposite. It was higher up, so it was easier for outside eyes to see it from a distance. It was supposed to be like a reminder flag to the world, showing them that the last believers of earth were still here, thank you very much. Hiding, but still eager for Jesus to return. More than eager: they were bringing it about.

But this place of comfort had another danger too. One that was harder to grapple with, because it wasn't to do with the Hollows. Simply put, this chapel did something to the grown-ups. When they got inside, the happy, gentle family faces would sometimes twist and contort. Not every time, but often enough to frighten him. And the sounds they made – the wails, the moans, the grunts. He shuddered just thinking about it. Especially Hope, who sometimes dropped to all fours and scrambled around up here. At least he didn't have to see that today. He bit his lip hard, a form of self-discipline, and he told himself it was stupid to be scared of comfort. Of loud, bone-chilling comfort.

The others had reached him now. They gathered round his shoulders, staring at the chapel, just like he was. Some singing birds even swooped up to join them. A nice touch from Jesus, Ever thought. They flew across the roof, slashing curves through the mist. He felt a hand on his shoulder. It was Mum. She dropped to her haunches and he saw the scarf on her throat was a little looser than usual. He could almost see the scars underneath. She took his hand, opened the palm. 'How about you open up today?' She pulled her hand away to see he now held the chapel key.

'Me?'

She nodded, proudly. 'You.'

'Mum . . . what's going on? Why is there a Hollow in the shed?'

'What's going on?' She put her hands around his red cheeks, the wool of her gloves as soft as clouds. 'End's comin' . . . that's what.' She smiled but looked away quickly at the chapel. He heard her sniff and raise a hand to her face.

'Hey, Big Man,' Milton's voice boomed, and the birds scattered like it was one of his gunshots. 'How about you take us all to Jesus.'

Ever waited. Scared of comfort, and of Prosper's bauble eyes always on him.

It didn't help when Prosper's voice rolled like low thunder. 'You heard him. Lead the way.' And Ever finally started walking towards the door, which rattled in the wind. So much so that it looked like something inside was eager to get out. At one point, Ever worried that the large black cross they'd hung on the door might fall off. But no, Prosper had screwed that thing in tight. So, there it stayed – shaking a little but strong, reliable and in its right and proper position. Upside down.

CHAPTER TWENTY-FIVE

PC Briggs, an eager man with ballroom dancer's hair, scratched his pointy elbow then resumed the position he'd held for the last thirty minutes: fingertips hovering over his tablet. 'And is there anything else you want to add . . .' he coughed, 'Mr Hunter?'

Matt pulled his gaze from the corner of the desk. 'Sorry, I didn't . . .'

'I said is there anything else you want to add?'

He shook his head. 'That's all I know. We met at the pub. We drank. He drank a lot. I dropped him off at his granny's house and that was it. Oh, and that run-in with the two guys in the pub. You should definitely track those dickheads down.'

'Yes, I've got all that.' Briggs tapped a finger on his chin. 'And from what you're saying, Mr Ashton was in a suicidal state.'

That seemed to snap Matt out of his staring. He looked up quickly, 'What? I never used the word suicidal. I said he was . . . upset . . . I said he was concerned.'

'About his sexuality' – he scrolled through his screen – 'and his parents' reaction?'

'Yes . . . deeply concerned . . .' Matt felt his stomach turn a little, from the guilt of sharing what was supposed to be a private conversation. Though to explain the whole night, and why the church pastors were at his house, seemed impossible without it. All that mattered now was the police figuring out what the hell had happened under that weeping willow last night. Still though . . . this distant, quiet voice kept nagging at Matt's psyche, saying it really wasn't that complicated at all. That in all probability, this time 'concerned' really did mean suicidal, after all.

'And his father and the church brigade,' Briggs said, 'they planned to carry out some sort of exorcism, you say?'

'I don't know if they'd call it that specifically . . .' Matt leant forward. 'But Sean said they'd planned to cast the spirit of homosexuality out of him. Which really does still happen today.'

'I see.' He tapped some words on the screen.

'I'm just glad he managed to avoid it.'

Briggs frowned. 'Avoid it?'

'Well I told you, he didn't go home. He went to his grandmother's instead, so he didn't have to face them.'

Briggs' mouth rounded into an 'o'.

'Wait . . . what's wrong?'

Briggs sighed.

'Well?'

'Actually, he didn't avoid it. The church came round to his grandmother's house because she called them. So they prayed, after all. The parents, the pastors. Apparently, Sean was extremely upset and ran out of the house crying.'

'Jesus . . .' Matt slid a splayed hand across his forehead, anger blending into sorrow and back again.

'Ah, yes . . .' Briggs tapped his chin the clicked his fingers, 'that's right. The granny was the one who used the word suicidal. My apologies. I'll make a note of that. Mr Hunter . . . are you okay?'

'No, I am not. I'm furious. Did you know how many gay Christians kill themselves? The stats are horrendous. It's an absolute scandal.'

'And just think what it might do to his pupils. Can't be easy having your teacher kill himself. Anyways . . . do you know why he'd do it at your house?'

'He wasn't at my house. He did it in church grounds.'

'Which is right next to your house. Meaning he may have been coming to find you.'

Matt ran his hand across his knee. 'Maybe he wanted to talk. I told him he could, but . . . I was asleep.'

'Unless he was just seeking some sort of spiritual peace in his final moments. Repentance, even. He just found the nearest holy site he could think of. The church.'

'Are you religious, Mr Briggs?'

'Can't see how that's relevant . . .' he said, 'but if you're asking . . . no I'm not. Not by a long shot. But I do know religious people do strange things sometimes. They like their symbolism. Maybe he felt closer to God by dying there.'

Matt thought about it all for a moment. 'If it was suicide then the church should be charged with some sort of—'

'*If* it was suicide? You think it could be something else?'

'Of course. It could be anything.'

'Well . . . not quite *anything* . . . wasn't a bear attack, was it?'

'It could be those idiot bald guys for all we know.'

Briggs pursed his lips together and nodded in the silence. It was long enough for Matt to gradually start hearing the tick of a clock, hidden somewhere in the room. Finally Briggs spoke. 'I hear you witnessed the Chervil boy yesterday. Saw him get hit by the coal train?'

'Yep. I'm a regular dead body magnet at the moment.'

Briggs waited. Watched him, then closed the cover of his

tablet. 'Yeah, I think I'll let you get back to your wife.'

'Good.' Matt pulled his coat from the back of the chair and walked out.

He found Wren standing white-faced by the coffee machine. She was sipping warm pond water from a tiny, plastic cup. When she saw him, she set the cup down and just stood there while her chin trembled. He put his arms around her, slowly. They stood there for a full minute, oblivious to anyone walking past.

She pulled back. 'I don't know how you cope with it. I only saw his hand, but the image. Every time I close my eyes . . .'

He saw her face as it was an hour ago. When she tumbled through the back gate. He'd spun to warn her not to look but she was just too fast. He saw her mouth drop open at the exact same time he stood on a twig, so it sounded like her jaw had clicked horribly loud. He saw the bulge of her eyes and the hand across her face, when she took in the sparkling red ice rink that had sprung from Sean's wrist. After it happened, they both had the world's most morose shower and change, and they sat in the kitchen in gaunt silence, waiting for the police to arrive.

'The images. They'll fade,' he said to her.

'Will they?'

He swallowed. 'Actually, no . . . they won't. Shall we find a coffee shop? Somewhere to talk? I'm not hungry but we should probably have breakfast.'

She nodded. 'Let's get muffins or something. Pancakes. Something fattening.'

'And consumable coffee.'

She nodded again, quietly.

They clasped hands together and looked at each other for a few seconds. It's amazing really, what those looks between people can do. What they can say. How they can heal, even just a little. Then they pushed through the main arched doorway and into the cold mid-morning air. It was just as he put his foot onto the top step that he froze.

'Aw, crap,' he said.

'What is it?'

'That's their car.'

A row of three cars chugged on the pavement. A Ford Focus and a BMW estate had their engines running, but it was the one at the front that had made Matt grip Wren's hand painfully tight. A dirty-looking Land Rover, with a hefty splash of mud up the side.

'Matt?' she said.

'Sean's parents. That's their—'

Just as he said it, all three car engines stopped, one after the other and white exhaust mist wisped into the air. The Land Rover door swung open hard and the wild sideburns of Mr Ashton appeared in the gap. Instantly, the other doors clicked open. A fat guy and a few others hefted themselves from the rocking cars. Ashton wore a saggy, woollen jumper and hefty boots, but the others had suits on. Matt could tell right away they were the pastors, and they were carrying their weapon of choice: the Bible.

'We have to go, *now*,' Wren tugged him towards the wheelchair ramp. He didn't budge.

The fat man had a voice so deep and loud that passers-by stopped to look. 'Do you know what you've done?'

'Ignore him,' Wren said.

'I said do you know what you've done . . . Professor?'

His eyebrows shot up. 'What *I've* done?'

'Matt . . . come on.'

Mr Ashton stayed leaning against his Land Rover, but the fat pastor started his slow walk towards the steps, two disciples in tow. Though he didn't really walk as much as he flopped his body forward. When he spoke it was clear this wasn't conversation. This was a loud, public proclamation in a huge power-voice, trained from millions of hours of standing on street corners, preaching to the lost and depraved. 'So, you think your books and teachings have no consequence, do you?' he called out. 'Do you really think Christ's gonna sit by and let you corrupt the young?'

Another tug from Wren. The hardest yet. He ignored it and leant towards the fat guy, whispering, 'What did you all do to him last night?'

God . . . this guy's expression was so smug. So sure. That was the scary part. He was so *sure*. 'We showed love. Tough, real, heartbroken love.'

'Why couldn't you have just listened to him?' Matt said.

'Listen to what? The spirit of the age? Why on earth would we do that?'

'So, what was it?' Matt stood a little straighter. 'An exorcism? Did you throw holy water?'

'There was no need for gimmicks. We leave that to the Catholics. No . . . it was just prayer . . . that's all. That's all you need to clean the poison out. Just turns out that Satan had his hooks in deeper than we thought.' For the first time he lowered his voice. 'Not only was that boy turned into a pervert, he was also filled with the spirit of suicide. He's got your books to thank for that. Because what else can people like you offer the world except Godless despair?'

'How dare you blame me.' Matt's blood was rushing to his fist. Filling it with weight, ready to strike. Just as it had on the day he found his mum's killer, sitting there in her lounge. He could hear the echo of that old sound. Of the horrible quietness in the room, punctuated only by the quiet slap of skin on skin as Matt pummelled his fists into ribs and stomach, and mostly face. And then the wetness that started to come, under his knuckles, which was the first moment he considered stopping. Matt felt his eyes drift from the pastor to Sean's dad, and he felt the blood in his fists shrink back. He just looked the pastor in the eyes and shook his head. 'How dare you blame me.'

'Because all your lies and bleakness let those spirits in. Stopped him resisting his . . . his interests.'

Matt threw his hands up, aware that his voice was wobbling. 'For crying out loud, Sean was normal and decent, and he loved God a hell of a lot more authentically than you do.'

'Says the false teacher. Says the midnight lover . . .'

Matt screwed up his face. 'The what?'

'Oh yes . . . his poor grandmother heard it all . . .' The fat pastor turned his watery eyes to Wren. 'She says your husband was whispering to Sean on the steps of her house last night. Feeding him instructions. She said it sounded like they'd had a very intimate night together . . . did you know about this, Mrs Hunter? Do you *know* who's in your bed?'

'Wow,' Matt shook his head. 'Just, wow.'

Wren stopped tugging, and now she spoke. 'You might be a pastor, but you sound like the absolute polar opposite of Jesus. Do you know that?'

Thankfully, Mr Ashton still wasn't joining in. He was leaning against the driver's door, as if it was the only thing holding him up. His eyes were puffed and circled with redness. A small crowd had started to gather on the pavement, on the other side of the road, watching it all.

'So, we've come to pray for you, Professor, and lay our hands on you,' he said.

Matt yanked his shoulder from the pudgy fingertips. 'Touch me and I swear I'll knock you out.'

The pastor shrugged and turned his colossal head to shout back to the Land Rover where Mr Ashton now had his huge hand across his face, sobbing against the car. 'Come on, Barry. Come and pray for your child's killer . . . let him know you forgive him.'

Matt saw Ashton's tears, and dropped his voice to a reasonable, tone. 'Pastor. Just let them grieve, please.' Then he turned away. He and Wren both hurried down the wheelchair ramp, heads down.

'Maybe I should offer my condolences,' Matt whispered, as they headed down.

'Absolutely not. They're crazy. You need to just give them space.'

It was just before they turned towards town when they heard the screams. They sprang from those gawkers across the street, outside the pizza place. They'd seen something from their angle that couldn't be seen on this side. It all became shockingly clear, soon enough.

Matt saw her head first, moving along the other side of the cars. It was Sean's mother, Mrs Ashton, clomping her feet directly down the road. Two cars and a van screeched to a halt, but she kept on stomping. And in her hand was something long and black.

'Oh, shit, oh, shit.' Matt pushed Wren back towards the police station. 'Move.'

'What's—'

'*Move.*'

He shoved Wren towards the ramp, but she still turned back and gasped. Which was when he saw the reflection in the police station's window, telling him it was too late to run. He turned slowly and saw Mrs Ashton emerge from between the two cars. She was carrying an old, rusty rifle and was weeping bitterly, her fringe dancing in a sudden wind.

She lifted the barrel.

CHAPTER TWENTY-SIX

There were only two rows of stools in the chapel, and Ever always sat in the back. But when he went to sit down this morning, Prosper got all flustered and shook his head. He dragged Ever's chair and plonked it right on the platform. Now he was facing out and could look at what Prosper saw from his little pulpit: a perfect, freaky-eyed view of everybody's faces and expressions.

At one point, the groans were so loud that he wanted to put his fingers in his ears but Prosper had caught him doing that once before. He'd yanked both of Ever's hands from his head. 'Lament, boy!' he'd yelled. 'There's power in lament.'

That's what everybody was doing right now. They always started their services with lament, which he knew was important. But hearing (and now seeing) them let out their pain was a strange and sometimes upsetting thing to watch. Especially when his mum's tears turned to screams, as they did now. She was on her knees, tearing at her scarf till it slid off like a ribbon. It was one of the only times she ever took it off. He saw her crying and shouting up at the ceiling, chin cocked so he could see the full stretch of those horrendous, twisted lines, all bumpy and shining around her throat. Every now and then she'd claw at them, and if she drew beads of blood it meant her prayer was deep.

Pax was on her knees too, only she kept scratching at her scalp, and the faulty brain beneath it. She had a little wire brush that she kept up here, just for this purpose. She used to use a fork, but she got a little too carried away with that once and tried to dig in way too deep. She hurt herself, so the fork was banned. The wire brush was too small and flat to really dig in, but sharp enough to hurt.

They all lamented, in their own way. Uncle Dust had a funny way of doing his. He sometimes filled his mouth with sand. That's what a Hollow did to him once, he said. When he was a teenager. It just dragged him into a school playground and filled his mouth with dirt, while all the others laughed and chanted. Ever always paid special attention when Dust did that, just in case he choked and Ever had to slap him on the back. But Dust was wise, and he always had a glass of water just in case. He wasn't doing the sand thing today. He was just rocking back and forth on his knees, pressing his knuckles into the floor. And Milton, good old Milton, he would scrape his cheek across the corrugated metal walls. He found places that were rougher than others, with little tears in the metal. Not so sharp that it'd tear out an eye, obviously. But ragged enough to make the lament feel real.

All this was vital to their purity, Prosper said, and he'd often point out that this was precisely what the Hollow churches *didn't* do. Not only did they have a twisted view of Jesus, they also didn't lament because they were empty creatures, terrified of honesty. They'd shuffle in and out of church on Sunday mornings, and the vicar – that was what their leaders were called – the vicar would give out handshakes and say things like, 'How are you today, Fred?'

And Fred would say, 'I'm really fine, Vicar. Thanks for asking. And you?' And the vicar would smile and say, 'I'm really fine, thank you for asking. And your wife?' And so on and so on.

This was all completely insane. A bizarre sort of dance they did. Because Fred was desperate to cry about his dead wife and the vicar still had cancer in his belly. They just thought God would prefer them to be happy about it. It was madness but Prosper said the Hollow churches lived on these lies all the time. 'Dishonesty is the air they breathe,' he said once, 'because they hate to look weak.' Even though Jesus specifically said that his power was made perfect in weakness, and that honesty was vital.

The Hollow churches were never truthful places because they didn't allow their people to scream, and in time, those lies turned them into something less than human. Ever wasn't sure when Jesus let the world revert to demon form, but Uncle Dust reckoned it was about five years ago, which was when they moved here. Up till then, the world had a chance to change. That chance was gone. Now, they weren't people any more – not deep down.

His family, though . . . they were the only real people left, because they never hid their agony. So what if their screaming was scary. At least it was real. Which crucially meant they understood the real horror of the cross too. There were one hundred and fourteen crosses on the walls in here, hanging upside down from pegs and nails. Quite a few were black, smeared with the soot from the birds and rabbits they'd killed and eaten.

Prosper said that if they ever found a cross that was accidentally hanging the way the Hollows liked them to hang, they must immediately turn it upside down. It was a clear way of rejecting what that disgusting symbol stood for. The thought of the Hollow churches turning crosses the other way up, so it became a happy sign . . . now that was dishonest and scary. And deeply offensive too . . . to celebrate a torture device. How hideous.

Prosper finished dragging his arm across his special beam of splintered wood, then he took his place behind the rusty music stand, just next to Ever. The shrieks died down and people wiped tears from their cheeks as they settled into chairs.

As always, Prosper was straight to the point. 'All our lives we've been hurt, abused, betrayed, forgotten . . .' He pointed at the grimy little window and the others followed his finger. 'We've all got the scars from living out there.'

They stared at the rectangle of glass, riddled with awful memories. Ever knew what some of those memories were. Pity made him close his eyes and pray for them.

'But let's never forget,' Prosper raised the volume a notch, 'we don't serve a God that sat on some cloud just observing the mess down here. No . . . *our* God rolled up his sleeves and got his hands dirty.'

'And bloody,' Milton said from the floor. 'He got his hands very bloody.'

Someone groaned in empathy.

'Very true, Milton . . . he saw the world in honesty. He saw it how it actually is.' Prosper raised a preaching finger. 'He didn't stay safe in the comfort of heaven. The Son came down and walked our paths on earth. A master come as scum. Born in a stable. The lowest.'

'The servant king,' Mum said, to ripples of agreement.

'That's right. Which means Jesus has been where you've been. In the gutter. In the piss of cows and donkeys.' Prosper crouched and scooped up dust and fluff from the floor. He rubbed it between his hands and showed his dirty palms to the crowd. 'He refused to stay in heaven, all cosy and clean. He crawled right into the mud to set us free. And how many of us have walked in his shadow?' Prosper started pacing. 'Haven't *we* been beaten and snapped and lied to? Haven't we been used, just like he was?'

More groans and shaking heads.

His mum was rocking back and forth, lips quivering with prayer. She kept stroking her thick and terrible marks.

He knew her story best of all. She got that scar from a Hollow man in an alleyway. He wrapped a chain around her throat and tried to choke the life from her. 'I should have died that night,' she often said, 'but here I am . . . and here you are.' She called that moment one of her miracles.

'But Jesus was there first, wasn't he?' Prosper's pacing creaked the platform. 'The man of sorrows suffered like you, but much, much more.' He opened his arms, 'Crucified!'

That was their cue. With a scratch of chairs on the wooden floor, the others stood to copy the gesture. Ever saw them fling their arms wide, then at the same time they hung their heads to the side like a bunch of broken dolls. They started swaying, as the mumbling one-word prayer grew in intensity.

Kataltani. Kataltani. Kataltani. Kataltani.

Which he knew meant 'murdered', in Jesus's language.

Prosper's eyes rolled across the room and landed on his. Telling him to rise and do the same – especially now that he was at the front. Ever gulped and pushed his chair back, so he could be murdered on a cross too. He opened his arms and lifted them to the side. This part always hurt shoulders.

'And Jesus was betrayed, in the worst way,' Prosper shouted. 'Slaughtered on a filthy, wooden cross. While his Father looked down from his cosy kingdom, laughing.'

Uncle Dust broke his own crucifixion for a second, just so he could screw up a fist and slam it into his hand.

'The King of Kings . . . the Son.' Prosper shouted so loud, it sounded like something in his throat ripped. 'Slaughtered like a fucking peasant!'

Milton let out a roar of anger and glared at the chapel ceiling.

They often did that, whenever talk turned to the Father. They'd fire up glares because heaven was up there . . . the lair of the beast. All those arms dropped from their crosses. Now they were clawing upwards and Ever watched the usual little fountains start to appear. The beads of spit springing up from mouths and dropping in an arch to the floor. One day, he hoped the spit wouldn't come back down . . . that it would smash through the roof, and ride on their lament and would keep on going till it broke down the Father's door and drowned him in saliva, right there on his throne. Though knowing him, he'd probably hide behind the couch and pretend he wasn't in.

'Your time's coming, Pop,' Milton shouted and Prosper cheered, which meant laughter was now allowed in the chapel. 'Jesus won't be dead for long, so fuck your cross . . . we're doing our own version . . . okay? And it's going to split the world in two.'

Prosper was chuckling, eyes straight up. 'That's right. Thought you could knock us off course, did you? With Micah? When the real answer was with us all along . . . ha!'

The lament was well and truly over now. Now came the better part, the dancing part. The moment people hooked arms and skipped around with chuckles and whistles. Then as Ever went to join them, he got a shock, but a good one. The grown-ups rushed over and scooped him up. His trainers left the dust, and suddenly he was on their shoulders, bouncing towards the ceiling. This had never happened before.

'Here he is,' they said. 'Here he is!'

And at some point, Milton called up, 'You're a gift, lad. A gift from Christ. You're going to be a hero, Big Man.'

Part of him wanted to laugh, but he was terrified too because it was all so confusing. So, he just let them bounce him up and down, and their cheers were so booming that it felt like the sound itself was carrying him. He tried to laugh, like they were laughing, but he didn't like the way they kept bouncing him nearer to the ceiling. Springing him up and down like he was another globule of spit. For a terrifying moment he felt himself leave their grip and hover in mid-air. He thought the roof might crack open, and he'd see the Father's huge, manic eye pushing through the gap. Maybe this would be the one time he bothered to leave heaven, just to scoop Ever up with his monstrous claw and stick him on a cross for real.

They whooped and sang, and he found himself pretending to smile.

Pretending? Hmmm?

You're pretending to be happy?

The thought made him gulp in panic.

Everyone's rejoicing and you're smiling and laughing with them, when actually you're just terrified, and all you want to do is cry?

This was precisely what Jesus hated most, wasn't it? The dishonesty.

He shuddered and let his fear for that so-called 'god' up there turn to hatred instead. At least that was real, because Ever really did loathe the Father for many reasons. One, for flooding the world with monsters. And two, for putting his family through lives of hell. Okay, they might have been strange people, but they were good people. And none of them deserved what the Hollows had done.

But the main reason he hated the Father was simply because he had been so unfatherly. Because what was more twisted, more unloving, than murdering your only begotten son on a cruel and shameful cross?

So, he brewed up some spit of his own, and shot it up, and when his went up it was high enough to hit the ceiling of the chapel, which nobody else had managed. And so the place exploded into loud and happy cheers.

CHAPTER TWENTY-SEVEN

Sean Ashton's mother had a very slight voice, but the wind carried it carefully like a loyal butler, eager to serve it. 'Keep still, Professor,' she said, with her raw, tear-reddened eyes fixed on Matt. 'Keep still or I'll keep you still.'

Matt saw a movement in the corner of this eye.

It was PC Briggs, rushing through the police station door. He put a hand out. 'Okaaay, Barbara. Let's just take a few little breaths here.' If this was supposed to be his hostage negotiation voice, it totally, and terrifyingly, sucked.

Matt spoke, as calmly as he could manage. 'Mrs Ashton. Could you please let my wife go back inside?'

She blinked, drew in a breath.

Say her name. Personalise it. 'Wren had nothing to do with this.'

She slowly nodded. 'But you stay.'

Matt quickly turned back to her. 'Get inside. Now.'

There were a few seconds of utter bafflement on her face, and he knew she was considering refusing to budge. So, he did something he never did. He shouted at her. Matt Hunter, the sort of chill-fella who talked stuff out with his wife all calm and Papa-Smurf-style. He shouted 'Go!' The bite of it, the desperation of it, made her face twitch and they caught each other's gaze for a heartbreaking millisecond. Then Briggs grabbed her elbow and yanked her up the ramp. Matt saw Wren's red hair fall across her face and her profile vanished. He considered that perhaps this would be the last image he'd ever have of her, in an almost theoretical, interesting-fact kind of way. Then he thought, no . . . perhaps this really will be the last ever image he'd have of her, which was when his heart dropped through his chest, and his fingers started trembling.

He turned slowly back and noticed the fat pastor was on his knees now, praying in the same way he probably ate cakes, frantically and with wet lips. He did it with such energy and swaying jubilance that Matt had no idea if he was praying to God to stop this, or to let it gloriously happen. The only one in the three-car clan who wasn't praying was Mr Ashton. He'd walked out onto the road and was calling to his wife from behind, not wanting to rush her in case she squeezed the trigger by accident. 'Barb, please,' he kept saying. Or at least he was trying to say it, through tears. 'Put it down, love. Let it be. Let it be.'

Mrs Ashton swayed at her husband's voice, a snake and its charmer, but Matt's eye stayed fixed on the barrel because it kept swinging in tiny arcs. He heard other policemen from the station, ushering people to step back.

She mumbled something that Matt couldn't really hear. It meant he had to awkwardly ask her to repeat it. 'I'm sorry, but I can't hear you.' His mouth had lost all moisture.

'I said, did you bed him?' She sounded like a ruined woman, confronting her kid's heroin dealer. 'Did you turn him?'

Oh, for fuck's sake. 'No . . . I promise you, no. I wrote a book, that's all. He was just trying to find his way, Mrs Ashton.'

She drew in another breath, but this one was horribly long. The length of it felt ominous to him. Like she was brewing up to do something significant. Pull a trigger, maybe.

For a few seconds there was no talking, just the sound of a plane streaking across the sky, and the impatient car horns beeping further down the street. These came from drivers who couldn't see what this was. They probably thought it was some chump up front, taking yonks to park. He watched the barrel sway up then down as if she was weighing up the pros and cons of going for the chest or shooting him directly in the face. Jesus . . . what a choice. His brain scrambled through his memory files, trying to figure out which was best to absorb a bullet. He'd read of hunters who somehow survived rifle shots to the heart, and even the head. And plenty more who'd died. Most, in fact.

There was a low wall to his left. He'd have happily, and most giddily leapt over it. Except some dimwit with an eye for Victorian fencing had fitted a row of pointed, wrought iron railings on it. He'd skewer himself and get shot in the spine as a bonus.

'Barbara,' Briggs again, firmly. 'Put. It. Down.'

Yeah, that's right, Briggs. Try a pissed-off tone. That might work.

She raised the barrel. Stood up straight.

Wren was inside, only because they'd dragged her inside, but he could hear her struggling. She'd be tearing herself from a policeman's grip, like one of those lairy women in a nightclub fight. Typically, she'd be trying to get back to help, but he dreaded her actually doing it. She didn't need to see this. He was learning how trauma can linger. But *this* . . . this would be too much. She didn't need to see her husband shot. He thought of his kids. God, he loved them. He loved his family so, so mu—

A new voice burst into the silence. A woman. 'Mrs Ashton?'

Matt must have closed his eyes. He hadn't realised he'd even done that until he felt them flick open.

'Sorry to interrupt, but I'm a Christian too.'

Matt, and everybody else, dropped their mouths at a woman in a backpack. She casually walked along the pavement, hands by her side. It took him roughly one second to recognise her. It was the woman from the Crooked Church. The one he'd met at the side of David East's hospital bed.

Miriam.

Huh? It was a bobble-hatted Miriam not just walking, but strolling towards Mrs Ashton, like this was a coffee morning and she was handing out biscuits. 'I'm a committed member of a Christian church up the road and—'

'Step aside,' Briggs snapped. Then again more forcefully when she ignored it, 'Step *aside*.'

'—and my name is Miriam Aimes. And all I can say is that Mr Hunter here is not a bad person at all.'

'Miriam,' Matt said. 'Don't.'

She ignored him. 'And I truly think Jesus is working in him. He'll find his way, but he needs time to do that.'

Mrs Ashton raised the barrel and jutted her elbow out. Everybody gasped.

Then, Miriam did something astonishing. She strode between Matt and the gun, putting out her arms to the side, like a human shield. Despite her jolly tone, he was close enough to see her hands were trembling too. She spoke again, but the happy tone was fading. Worry sang now. 'Believe me . . . Jesus wouldn't want you to do this. And to be honest with you, Barbara, I don't fancy it much, either.'

Mrs Ashton tilted her head. 'And what do you know about Jesus?' She cocked the gun.

'I know that he heals the broken-hearted.'

Click.

These sorts of things happen fast.

Matt saw Mr Ashton move first. Then Briggs shouted across the pavement – 'Barbara, no!' And in between them, he saw this silly, mad, amazing woman, Miriam.

Matt lunged forward. He grabbed Miriam's waist to pull her down, and it was just as he yanked the polyester of her coat that the world filled with a cracking sound. It didn't sound like an explosion. It was nothing like the boomy eruptions from video games and action movies. There was no epic echo either, no cool ricochet. Just a short, sharp crack and then the worst part – the jerking spasm of Miriam's body as she slammed hard against him. Then the shot turned into wails from everybody watching. Then the wails turned into screams and the screams turned into shoes running on the pavement.

Matt and Miriam crashed against a telegraph pole and he quickly looked down to see the slash in the material of her jacket. He saw a hole that wasn't there before. He pressed his hand against it and felt the pulse of something warm and wet. 'Shit . . . shit . . .' They both slid to the floor. He heard the gun clatter off the pavement.

Other bodies swarmed around them. A policewoman was on her knees, talking to Miriam, while Briggs already had Mr Ashton in his grip. He kept barking the words 'ambulance' into his radio. Then finally Matt saw Wren flying down the ramp, and he breathed again. She dropped hard and grabbed not only Matt's hand, but Miriam's too.

'You pulled me down,' Miriam groaned. 'Thank you, Matt. You saved my life.'

'What?' he spluttered out a laugh. 'You saved mine.'

Miriam's laughter quickly became a cough, and over his shoulder he saw Mrs Ashton being led into the building. She was looking up into the sky, squinting and silent. Mr Ashton had his arm around her shoulders. He paused to look at Matt and Miriam who still lay heaped on the floor. 'I'm . . . I'm . . . I'm . . .' He let out a quivery breath but couldn't finish his sentence. It was the clearest, most heartbreaking apology Matt had ever witnessed. Briggs hurried the Ashtons inside.

Miriam, of all things, was smiling. 'You weren't hurt, were you, Matthew?'

'I'm fine,' he said, then it hit him again. Harder this time. 'My God, *thank you.*'

Wren said the same, her eyes glistening. 'Thank you. Thank you so much.'

Her smile faded as she winced in pain. Then it came back brighter than before. 'Look at that sun . . .' Her eyelids started to flutter. 'So pretty.'

Somewhere, a siren was wailing.

CHAPTER TWENTY-EIGHT

Ever and Uncle Dust often sat here to talk. At the top of Comfort Hill, on a little bench that leant against the chapel. It groaned and creaked against the metal whenever they moved.

'Probably should have oiled this seat more,' Dust said, flicking his ponytail over his shoulder.

Ever shot up. 'Shall I get some now?'

He laughed. 'Don't bother. Let's just sit and talk, instead.'

Unlike this morning, the mist had cleared now, so the farmhouse looked bright and crisp on the valley floor. He even saw the tip of his tree by his favourite part of the stream, and the shed, of course, sat right near the bottom of the hill's stone trail. The huge, scary rope that was wrapped around it looked tighter than ever, but at least the door wasn't moving any more. Dust must have seen him staring at it, because Ever felt a big warm arm slide around his shoulders and pull him in.

'Don't ever be ashamed of fear, son.'

'I hate it. Fear makes me feel like a little kid.'

'And was Jesus acting like a little kid, when he was scared? When his dad had him dragged to that big old cross? When he started sweating blood in the garden?' Dust swept his hair back. 'He was man enough to admit his fear and weakness. It made him strong, Ever.'

'I know.'

'And you'll never get as stressed as Jesus was. None of us will.'

'We might . . .'

'No way. He was betrayed by his own flesh and blood. But your family's right here,' he hooked a thumb at himself, 'and we love you. *I* love you . . . with every word and step and breath . . . and burp and laugh and tear and song that's in me. Got it?'

Ever chuckled, 'Got it.'

Dust slipped off his glasses and cleaned them on his jumper, while they watched white smoke curl from the farmhouse chimney. Mum had already headed down to make a big lunch. He'd watched her walk down earlier and noticed how she'd walked in a large, curving arc, away from the shed.

He could tell that the time had come. The moment to ask his big questions about what was going on. But neither he nor his uncle seemed ready to go there just yet. The others were. Ever could hear them inside the chapel behind them. They were right up against the metal, whispering prayers through the cracks.

He thought of a new subject. 'How can the Hollows worship the Father, after what he did to his son?'

'Who knows? It's baffling. They sing songs to him, build cathedrals for him. They wear crosses around their necks like it's no big deal. It's barbaric and . . . weird. That's the truth of it, Ever. The Hollows aren't just dangerous. They're weird.' He spun a finger at his temple. 'One time, I saw a hundred of them in the park and – get this – one of them was dressed as Jesus, carrying a cross. And this Hollow had fake blood all over its face, and twigs were pushed into its head because they love that he died. They're obsessed with it. It's their favourite part.'

Ever screwed up his face. 'I'll never understand them.'

'I'm not even sure they understand themselves. They've lied to each other for so long and hidden their weakness, they've started to believe the biggest trick of all. They think Jesus did it on purpose. That he died willingly. Can you believe that?'

'It's stoopid.'

'And sick too.' He patted Ever's knee with a hand covered in decades-old scars. Slashes from knives, mostly.

'The Hollows . . . they'll be coming for us soon, won't they . . .?' Ever said, just as the breeze moaned.

'The closer to the end we get . . . yes. Prosper's sure of it . . .' He looked him in the eye. 'But don't be scared. We're all here for you. Just like the family was there for me, when I needed them. Took me off the street and dusted me off. Gave me a home and love. And you . . . I got to be an uncle. That was best of all.'

He heard a surge in the prayers. It told him that it was time.

'Okay . . . so why's there a Hollow in the shed?'

The prayers sank into quiet. Ears, not mouths, touched metal now.

'Well, you know how Jesus is coming back to take the Father's place and give this world a proper God for a change?'

'Yeah. Second Coming.'

'And that he'll make everywhere like this valley? Take all the Hollows away?'

'Yep, nice and safe.'

'Well, the thing is, sometimes . . . sometimes you need a symbol to unlock that sort of power. And the Father seems obsessed with them. The Bible's filled with people doing seemingly pointless things – they build an altar of stones, they lift a snake in the air, they slaughter a ram on a hill – and somehow those acts change things. I mean, think of Jesus. He didn't just heal people, he often did some sort of ritual to make it happen. Like the healing of the blind man . . . what did he do first?'

Ever looked up. 'He spat on dirt and rubbed it into his eyes . . . and then he was healed.'

'Exactly. He was only healed *after* the symbol.' Uncle Dust leant a little closer. 'Now the Hollows' big symbol is the cross, and they reckon it saved the world, but we know better. We know that symbol ruined everything. But we don't throw those crosses away, we turn them upside down, and make something new. That power. So, we're going to show the world a new symbol that'll make things right . . . but listen to me . . . it's our faith that really matters. The symbol . . . that's the key. But it's our faith what makes the key turn . . . do you understand?'

'You need to just tell me. What do we have to do?'

'Okay . . .' Dust pointed down the hill at the shed. Ever's heartbeat flicked up a notch. 'Prosper, me and Uncle Milton caught a Hollow in the city.'

'On purpose?'

'Yes. We brought it back and put it in the shed.'

'Why on earth would you—'

'Jesus wants us to kill it.'

The praying started again, and the corrugated metal behind Ever's shoulder creaked as they all leant up against it inside.

'Is that what Micah was supposed to do? Kill a demon?'

'That's right. But it didn't work out.'

Every bone in his body started to contract. He could feel himself shrinking, literally shrinking into the bench. 'But, I thought . . . I thought we had some other path to try. Milton keeps talking about another path.'

'Forget the other path. We're on the same path, just with a different person. Micah tried and now . . . well, now it's going to be you, Ever.'

'Wait . . . you want . . . you want *me* to kill it?' He started shaking his head.

'But listen to me, my beautiful boy.' Dust's arms clamped around him. 'We're going to make it super easy for you. You'll do it way better than Micah. All you have to do is stop its heart. Once it's gone, me or Milton can do the rest.'

Ever couldn't speak. His chest pumped in and out. 'But why me?'

'Cos you have to get used to killing.'

'I don't want to get used to it.'

Squeals of lament now. Hammering on the floor and walls inside.

'You'll have to, okay?' he said. 'Or Jesus won't come back. We'll be overrun with Hollows and lose this place for ever.'

Ever had his face in his hands but something else was stirring. He spoke into his palm, 'Jesus was scared too.'

'Terrified.'

'But he was brave . . .'

'Exactly. And you'll be brave as well, because he's *in* you. He's in all of us.'

'And you're absolutely sure this'll bring Jesus back?'

Dust opened his mouth, then just looked away for a moment.

'Hey . . . what's wrong?'

Dust shrugged. 'Nothing. Nothing's wrong.'

The prayers of the chapel grew to screams.

'Okay then . . . so what if I can't do it?' Ever said.

'You can.'

'Then what if it gets me first?'

'It absolutely won't. There won't be a chance of that.'

'But why me? Why can't you do it?'

Uncle Dust looked back and wiped a sleeve across his eyes. 'Because *you're* the gift. Not us . . . you are. You'll know what it all means, when the time comes.'

Ever slid his hand away. 'Then why do you look so scared?'

Dust breathed, waited, breathed some more, but said nothing.

So Ever looked down at the shed, which was pulsing again. Only now he could see his mum on the front porch of the path, praying on her knees and looking up at them.

CHAPTER TWENTY-NINE

Matt set the wide, bobbing plant on the table as he and Wren sat into the plastic chairs.

Miriam smiled. 'It's beautiful. You shouldn't have.'

'Oh,' Wren said. 'I think we should've.'

Miriam wasn't in a bed. She was sitting in a tub chair in a small hospital room, with a cup of hot coffee misting the air. She was fully dressed in jeans and a jumper, with her boots and bobble hat set neatly in the corner of the room. Matt noticed her thick socks had tiny white moons on them. 'They've said I can go home in a couple of hours. How great is that?'

'That's fantastic news.' Matt bit his lip awkwardly. 'But doesn't it hurt?'

'Not nearly as much as you'd think.' She hitched her jumper and turned a little. A square patch of bandage covered her side, just above her hip. 'I reckon what'll hurt the most is when they peel this darn tape off.' She laughed.

'So, it just grazed you?' Wren said.

'Yep. They said if Matthew hadn't pulled me down it would have hit me right in the tummy.' She let the jumper drop and slid back into the chair. 'So, thank you, Matthew. Like I said, you saved my life.'

'Listen to her.' Wren shook her head. 'Miriam, you saved *his* and I am . . . insanely grateful.'

Matt nodded. 'We both are.'

'Well' – she swished a dismissive hand – 'all's well that ends well, right?' She sipped her coffee and Matt was conscious they were both just staring at her. Especially Wren, who looked at Miriam like she was an angel who might flutter away at any moment.

'Miriam?' Matt broke the silence. 'Why were you in Chesham, anyway?'

She giggled. 'A miracle, I guess.'

He faked a giggle back, 'Yeah, but . . . why were you?'

She slowly set her cup down and waited.

'Are you okay?' Wren asked. 'Are we tiring you out?'

Finally, she spoke. 'You gave me your card, Matthew. You told me I could get in touch.'

'So, you were looking for me?'

'Yes. I knew you lived in Chesham. So I came to find you in Chesham.'

'But how did you know I was at the police station?'

Matt felt Wren's eyes on him. She had that look on her face. The stop-interrogating-people look. He got this glare at parties sometimes, when he battered guests with silence-filling questions like 'Where do you work?' 'Who painted that?' and 'Do you like airports?'

'Just interested, that's all . . .' he said.

She spoke slowly. 'I was driving, trying to find your house, and I hit this traffic jam. I got out to see what was going on and who do I see but Matthew Hunter, standing right there. I could tell you were in trouble, right away.' She whispered the next few words, 'Some would probably call that a fluke, but it's a miracle, like I said.'

'So, what did you want to see me about?'

'I wanted to know if you'd figured it out.'

'Figured what out?'

'Why Micah attacked his dad, of course. The church is baffled and distraught, and we need answers.'

'We're working on it.' A breeze rattled the blinds, and as they sat in silence, something came back to mind. Something that had been bugging him. 'Miriam, you said something interesting last night. You said that perhaps Micah did what he did because he simply didn't like his dad.'

She shrugged. 'Lots of people don't like their father because not all fathers are good, are they?'

'Yes, but most people don't grab an axe and—'

'Do you like your father, Matthew?' She leant towards him. 'Do you love him? Does he love you in return? Is he affectionate and caring, and kind?'

Matt blinked, and a snap of Barnabas Hunter flopped from his brain. He saw his dad in the front seat of the car, turning back to look at him with those tiny eyes, though actually they could have been quite big eyes for all Matt knew. It's just that they were always narrowed when they looked at him, so it was impossible to tell. And he had that fifties-style slick of hair and grey, skinny lips that could boom out tones that could shake an entire car.

Matthew. You do NOT talk when I drive. I have TOLD you.

'My dad left when I was young.'

Miriam smiled. 'So, you didn't like him?'

'Not really, no . . .' He waited. 'But I didn't try to decapitate him, as I recall.' He felt Wren's hand on his arm, pressing him to ease off. 'But, Miriam, do you know of any concrete reason why Micah's dad would be . . . unlikeable?'

'No. David was a lovely man and I have no clue why Micah did this. I think it's possible we might never know. Till heaven, that is.'

'We're planning on finding out way before then. Finding Micah's mum might help.'

Miriam closed her eyes.

'You really have no idea where she is?'

'She's travelling, Matthew. You know that, already. Could be in Timbuktu for all I know. I hear she liked foreign things.' She yawned.

'You're tired,' Wren said. 'We should go.'

'The drugs, I guess.' She sniffed. 'Sorry.'

'PC Bowland gave you her card too, didn't she?' Matt said. 'If you were curious about the investigation why didn't you ask her?'

'Oh, give the woman a break, Matt.' Wren blushed and hooked a thumb at him. 'This brain of his. It's always fizzing with questions. I apologise.'

'No, I'll answer,' Miriam looked at him. 'PC Bowland is a policewoman and you're just a university lecturer. I figured you'd be a lot less busy.'

Wren burst into laughter and Miriam started to smile.

'Can I ask one more question?' Matt said, and Wren groaned. 'Why did you risk your life to save me? We only just met.'

Wren stopped groaning. 'Actually, I'd like to know that, too.'

'That one I'll gladly answer . . .' she said. 'Too many Christians sit in their little church bubbles and ignore the pain of the world. But that's a dishonest way to live. I read the Bible differently, Matt. I believe Christians should get into the situation and help out, at any cost. Jesus was extremely hands-on and I think we should be hands-on too.'

'You could have died.'

'Oh, I knew I wouldn't, because Jesus said so. I prayed in my car, see.' She smiled, and her eyes started to sparkle. 'So, I didn't even have to think about it. I just heard the Lord say, *Help him*, so

I did. He said, *Save that man*, and look . . . I'm fine, you're fine and heck . . . even the lady with the gun is fine.'

Wren reached for Miriam's hand. 'Well, I think it's amazing.'

Miriam blinked slowly. 'I heard you used to be a vicar, Matthew. Is that right?'

'How did you know that?'

'I saw you on TV. They said you were a reverend.'

'Ah, but that was a long, long time ago, in a galaxy far, far away.'

'Well clearly not that far . . . because judging by today your God is clearly still looking out for you. You'll always be marked out as a father of the flock.'

'I'm not sure I agree with you on that.'

'Oh, I know it. It's a lifetime identity.'

Wren spoke for him. 'Well I don't know about him, Miriam, but I'm starting to believe in miracles.' She squeezed Miriam's hand for the hundredth time. 'Now listen. If you're getting out of hospital today, you've got to let us treat you.'

She tilted her head. 'I like the sound of that.'

'At the very least we're taking you out to dinner.'

'Oooo,' she smiled, 'I'm free tonight.'

'Perfect. Name the place.'

'How about your house? I do love home cooking' – she winced – 'unless that's too much troub—'

'Shush,' Wren said. 'That's decided. You're coming to ours for dinner tonight. Let's say 7.30 p.m? Do you have any food allergies?'

'None.'

She smiled at Matt. 'I love this woman.'

Matt checked his watch. Visiting time was almost done. 'How are you getting home? We could drop you back.'

'Oh, I'm sorted for that, and thanks again for the plant. It really is beautiful. I'll treasure it.'

'And thank you,' Wren stood, 'for all that you did today.'

'No biggie, really . . . and Matt?'

'Yeah?'

'Try not to get shot again, okay?'

'Will do.' He nodded to her and they both headed out into the hospital corridor, weaving through the nurses and visitors.

'You know something? I think she's astonishing,' Wren said.

'Mm-hmm.'

'All that stuff about Christians getting stuck in and actually helping. I mean, after what she did today, that's pretty damn inspiring. Don't you think?'

'Mm-hmm.'

'Like, if the churches put themselves out for people like that, it'd make a lot more people consider religion.'

'Mm-hmm.'

They reached the lift and as they waited for it to arrive, he listened as Wren talked about how sacrifice was, in many ways, the absolute key to a healthy society. He just nodded and hummed his responses. Deep in thought. The doors slid open. They went inside. It was empty.

It was when the doors finally closed that she changed the subject. 'Er, Matt?' she said to his reflection. 'I have something to say . . .'

'Uh-oh. What?'

'I think you could be grateful for what she did.'

'I am grateful.'

'I mean, more grateful. Like, a lot more. She saved your life.'

'We don't know that for certain. I could have just got a flesh wound, just like she did.'

Wren snapped at him, 'Matthew.'

You do NOT talk when I drive. I have TOLD you.

'Sorry.' He turned to her. 'But don't you think she's a little . . . peculiar? A little, I don't know . . . off-piste?'

'Matt, you think all Christians are off-piste.' She waited for a moment and took his hand. 'What's bugging you? Is it Sean? Are you thinking about that? God knows I am. Or what happened in Chervil?'

His eyes followed the white circle of light, blinking its way down the numbers. 'I just find her a little odd, that's all.'

'Well, she's awkward, I'll give you that. Not so great at eye contact, either.'

'Oh, she's terrible. She'd be crap in a job interview . . .' He turned from the lights and threw his arms around her. 'But listen . . . I *am* grateful. I really am.'

'God, that gun . . . I was so scared. What a day . . .'

She squeezed him, and he squeezed her back, his nose and mouth lost in a mass of red hair. They both heard the lift door open, but it was a little too soon to break it off.

She kissed his cheek as the bodies pushed by them for space. 'Here's to miracles,' she said.

CHAPTER THIRTY

Ever lifted his plate from the table and, as usual, went to wash it in the sink, but Mum rushed over and tugged it from his hand.

'Nope. Not today,' she said. 'I'll wash yours.'

He frowned at her, but a smile quickly replaced it.

As scary as this new development was, it was kinda fantastic to be treated like one of the men for a change. He turned to make sure Merit was seeing all this, but her chair was empty.

Darn.

He'd find her and tell her, but for now he just watched everybody else smearing the last lines of soup from their bowls with torn chunks of bread. Prosper, by contrast, had his elbows on the table, both hands in a steeple under his chin. He wasn't saying much. Just thinking and blinking. He'd spilt a little soup down his jumper, which he dabbed with his thumb and sucked.

'We'll do it tonight,' Prosper suddenly announced.

Everybody looked at each other. They knew what he was talking about. And now Ever did too.

'When the sun goes down, we'll get the Hollow and . . . practise. It'll be easier than you think, Ever. Heck, you might even like it. Might even love it.'

'Well, my mummy says . . .' Pax spoke into her palm and rocked in her chair, 'killing's a nope. Not a nice.'

'Hope said that?' Milton burst into laughter. 'I think you've got the wrong end of the stick there, ya retard.'

Pax stopped rocking.

'Milton, take that back.' Uncle Dust reached out and touched her hand. 'Hope hates you calling her that.'

He coughed. 'Sorry, Pax.'

Ever nodded to the empty chair, changing the subject. 'Where's Merit?'

'Daisy rope,' Pax whispered.

'Huh?'

'Daisy rope.'

His mum leant in to translate. 'She went to make daisy chains in the front garden.'

'Can I join her?'

She looked at Prosper for permission. He glanced out of the window. 'Okay. We can watch you from here. But don't go far.'

He pulled on his jacket, stepped into his trainers, and clomped out onto the porch, but Merit wasn't in the garden after all. There were, however, a trail of scattered daisies near the shed. He glanced at the shed door and saw no movement. But he knew that beast was in there. The same breed that wrapped a chain around his mother's throat and stuffed Dust's mouth full of sand. He saw himself grabbing an axe, kicking the shed door in and chopping the Hollow into chunks. Maybe he'd peel the skin right off its face and snap off one of its fangs or claws. He could throw it on the kitchen table and take a bow. How brave would he look then?

But no . . . because he wasn't that brave. Not yet, anyway.

He followed more flowers, scattered along the grass. They led to their old rusty white van, which apart from last night hardly ever came out. He breathed fresh air in and smelt lavender on the breeze, then he rested his chin on the kissing gate. This gate, he knew from repeated lessons, was the most important boundary for the children. 'Never ever walk beyond it. Not *ever*, Ever!' It was a sentence chiselled into his brain. But he was allowed to look across it, at the dirt road.

'Where is she?' he whispered to himself and could hear the blossoming worry in it. Determined to get a higher view, he clambered onto the gate. It creaked as he climbed but it was an ideal ladder to survey the area and track Merit dow—

'Jesus.'

He saw it.

He saw it and his heart stopped.

Right at the end of the dirt track, just around the curve. He saw a long cream car.

The shock made him step back without thinking. His foot trod air. He dropped into the dirt, arms flailing. He'd lost his height now, so the parked car was now hidden behind the tall grass. But he saw something move behind a bush at the side of the road up there.

He gulped.

Merit was stumbling through the thick hedge, thorns snagging her long hair as she staggered onto the track. Her face – he gasped at this – was white with terror, and across her mouth he saw something bizarre. A thin and dirty cloth was tied tight, so that it pressed her cheeks back and showed her teeth. Then the worst part of all came up over the hill, from where the car was waiting. A lanky figure was striding out, straight out of hell itself. It looked young, probably about Pax's age, and its long spindly arm reached out, trying to grasp her hair.

No!

Ever's fingernails snapped into the beams of the gate, as he watched Merit rip the gag clear of her mouth. She let out a heart-stopping, hill-splitting scream, but it was too late.

The thing grabbed her hair in its fist and yanked her hard, backwards.

'Get off her!' Ever yelled, then he jumped in shock.

The thing jerked its head towards him. Eyes wide and wild, ready to hypnotise.

He threw his hands across his face, covered his eyes.

Then he spun around and darted back to the farmhouse, racing with every ounce of strength he could pump into his legs. The field and hill filled with the sound of two things only. The pitiful squealing of Merit, and the panicked cries of Ever calling out the same word over and over again.

'Hollow! Hollow!'

CHAPTER THIRTY-ONE

Matt sat at his desk in the warmth of his cabin, and clicked on a video-call. He heard Skype beeping out it's jaunty tone. The screen flickered into life, and Jill Bowland sprang onto screen, sitting in front of a row of filing cabinets.

'Hi,' Matt sat back into his chair. 'Is this still an okay time to talk?'

'Yes, but my word, Matt . . .' she said. 'I heard about what happened this morning in Chesham.'

'I'm fine,' he said. 'Nobody got badly hurt, thankfully.'

'Having quite the forty-eight hours, aren't you?'

'You could say that . . . hey, is that your daughter? The one who lives overseas?'

She turned her head towards a photograph, sitting on the cabinet, of a young woman holding a laughing baby. 'That's Sara, yes, and my granddaughter, Bethany. She made me this,' she lifted her wrist and her thin little wristband jiggled. 'Wear it every day.'

'I noticed it. How cute . . . and how old's Bethany these days?'

'Oh, she's much older now, but I haven't . . . I haven't spoken to her in . . .' She trailed off and tugged her sleeve over her wrist.

He saw her face change, and he tilted his head. 'I'm sorry. Didn't mean to pry.'

'It's complicated, but then most things are . . . but anyway, back to it. What did you want to talk to me about?'

'Firstly, how's David East doing?'

She swung a little on her chair, looking more Uhura than ever. 'He's actually making remarkable progress. They're hoping he'll be out of the coma soon.'

'So maybe we could talk to him, together? Get to the bottom of this Micah thing.'

'Potentially, yes.'

'And what's the latest on Micah? Any new theories?'

'So far we're still classing it as a domestic. Or at least not some big satanic conspiracy. We found more stuff in his locker at school, but it was very pro-Church. Old paintings torn from books of Jesus healing the sick, walking on water. The usual stuff.'

'And were the eyes torn out?'

'Jesus, no. The disciples, yes. The Pharisees too. Everyone but him, basically.'

Matt blinked. 'So, he'll piss on altars and upturn crosses, but he leaves Jesus as he is.'

'It's rather inconsistent, isn't it?'

'And he uses an ancient biblical language when he tries to kill his dad.'

'Which he learnt online. We found it on a thumb drive in his school locker. Mostly Jesus stuff. His files were like a shrine to the guy.'

'Any other pictures on there?'

'A few. Some celebrities. Quite a few politicians.'

'Don't tell me, he'd scribbled the eyes out.'

'Not quite. He'd just pasted a black rectangle across their faces.'

Matt started tapping a rhythm on the side of his desk. 'Okay, so he smashes his laptop, takes out the fuses to his TV and XBox . . .'

'Ahem . . . you're assuming *he* cut the cables. What if his dad did it? Did you consider that?'

Matt blinked. 'Actually, no. I didn't.'

She waited. 'Look, maybe this is more than a domestic issue and maybe it isn't. We'll find out when Reverend East wakes up. Until then, it's not like anyone else is in danger.'

Matt ignored her. 'I've been thinking about what Micah said to me. When he grabbed me near the train. He said he was scared of me . . . of all of us . . .'

'Course he was. He was on the run.'

'No, he called me . . . a demon. Said I was empty inside or something. He wouldn't look me in the eye. And he . . .' Matt stopped. His eyes widened. 'He said . . . he wanted to stop the father.'

'Well, he didn't manage it, did he, cos his dad's going to be fine.'

Memories slipped into focus. The pounding of rain on the shoulders of Matt's jacket, the rumble of the death train cutting an eager line through rain. The fear in Micah's eyes as he stared at Matt's chest and called him . . . hollow. That was it. Hollow. 'He didn't say he wanted to stop his father . . . He said the Father.'

'You think there's another dad involved?'

'*The* Father, Jill.'

She looked confused, then suddenly twitched. 'Oh . . . hang on. You mean—'

'God the Father.' Matt grabbed a notepad and scrawled a few words down. 'Offhand, I can't think of any belief systems who venerate Jesus but hate the Father. Do you?'

She shrugged. Looked at her watch.

He jotted some more words down:

My father, my father . . . why have you murdered me?

'As fascinating as this is' – she coughed – 'I've got another call coming in. But thanks for your um . . . input. I'll be in touch.'

'Okay, but—'

'Glad you're okay, Matt. Bye.'

The screen vanished into blue.

Matt looked at his notepad and chewed his lip for a moment. He took the pen, scrawled a hard circle around his words and tore the sheet off.

Pro-Jesus, Anti-Father.

He grabbed the edge of the table and pushed his chair back. The wheels rumbled across the hardwood floor, something he often did with Amelia when she sprang up onto his lap. He'd perfected the distance now, and so the chair came to a sliding stop in perfect reach of his many bookshelves. He stood up and slid his finger across the spines, fingertip rattling as he went. He stopped on his section on cults and new religious movements. There were at least fifty books in that section.

He pulled the first copy out.

'Here we go.'

He was fourteen books and three swigs into his third coffee when his mobile started ringing. He frowned and tapped the screen. It was Bowland again.

'Miss me?'

'Matt, hi. What are you doing for the next hour?'

'Why?'

'It's David East. He's awake.'

CHAPTER THIRTY-TWO

Ever scrambled closer to the farmhouse, gasping for air. The front door flung open with a hammering crash while Uncle Dust and Milton bundled out onto the porch steps, both with shotguns.

'What's all the squawking?' Milton shouted while his mum and Pax stood behind him, white-faced.

Dust rushed down the steps. 'Ever, are you hurt?'

'There's . . .' he could barely breathe, '. . . there's a . . . there's a . . . Hollow at the gate. It's got Merit. It's dragging her away.'

'Jesus.' Milton cocked his shotgun, and span towards Pax. 'It's got your little girl.'

Pax was slow, but not so slow that she didn't understand this point perfectly. Her hands flew to her face, and a horrible moan burst through them. Then Prosper was in the doorway, booming and stomping, 'Then get her back!'

Boots pounded dirt and Ever ran with them. He looked back and saw Pax wriggle and yank herself out of Mum's grasp. She came running despite Mum's yelling for her to stop.

Ever saw the skies change above them. Each new step made the clouds turn dark and heavy. Swirling and throbbing with the evil that lived above them. He pictured the Hollow dragging Merit into a car and clawing her eyelids open as she kicked and screamed. Soon she'd have no choice. The thing would make her stare too long and she'd change for ever. No matter how annoying Merit was, this was not what she deserved. Not in the slightest. The fear in him, which consistently ticked and throbbed, started winding into something else, something even deeper. He felt . . . fury.

How dare they, he thought. *How dare those filthy, twisted losers take her away? What right do they have?*

They reached the gate in thirty seconds and slammed their hands against it, panting, but the dirt track looked empty simply because it was empty.

'It was right there.' Ever jabbed a finger at the ridge. 'It grabbed her by the hair and it had a car too. A big white car—'

That made the adults look at one another.

'White car?' Pax said. 'White car . . . *white car*?' She let out a howl of despair then dropped to her knees by the gate, sobbing uncontrollably.

Prosper kicked the gate hard and it swung wide open, then he hissed them all into silence. Though for Pax to stop, it took a hard slap from the back of Prosper's hand.

'Shhh. Everybody shut up and listen.' He pressed a sharp finger on his puckered lips. 'An engine. Just over the ridge. Shhh.'

Milton lifted his shotgun ready to rush forward, but Uncle Dust shoved the barrel up and away with his. 'It's no use, Milton. What if he's halfway down the track already?' He quickly tugged the van keys out of his pocket. 'Come on. It's the only way to keep up. Pax, take Ever back to the house . . . and pray!'

She was still sobbing on the grass but even Pax knew the power of prayer. She clambered to her feet and went to take Ever's hand, to guide him back.

'No,' Prosper pushed her arm away. It made her yelp. 'He's coming with us.'

'I don't think that's a very—'

'Don't fight me, Dust, not today. He comes with us . . .' Prosper said. 'And Milton drives.' Dust waited, then tossed the keys to Milton. Ever saw them whizz in a high tinkling arc until Milton plucked them out of the air. They clambered inside, Uncle Dust and Ever in the passenger seat and Prosper in the back. He hammered his palm against Milton's seat. '*Move.*'

The engine burst into life and Dust immediately reached over to check Ever's seat belt was tight. The tyres sprayed dry mud all the way to the top of the ridge, and they saw it soon enough. Just like he'd told them. The white car was a little way down the road, facing towards them. Only now its wheels were spinning because it'd heard them coming. The wheels locked in a hard turn, and dirt filled the air.

Milton shouted over the growling van. 'Bloody hell, it's him. It's Bill.'

'Don't you call it that,' Prosper barked. 'Now move.'

The white car was off, rattling down the dirt track while old rubbish from the dashboard showered onto their knees.

Ever pointed at the car. 'Look! It's got a cage in the back.'

'He used to keep his dogs in that.'

Ever looked at Milton, confused, while Prosper pressed a sharp whisper into the old man's ear. Milton stopped talking.

'But . . . but . . .' Ever was frantic. 'Is she in the cage? Will we need a key?'

'Breathe, Ever,' Dust said, as the engine wailed around them. 'She isn't in the cage. She's in the front seat. I can see her hair bobbing.'

'Faster!' Prosper tapped a skittish rhythm on the seat. 'Get alongside it.'

Dust frantically turned the window handle and the wind rushed in.

Ever's fringe started dancing. 'What are you doing?'

Dust hung his head from the window, hair blowing wild, then he cocked the shotgun over his forearm and slid the barrel forward.

Ever called out, 'You'll hit Merit.'

'Quiet, Ever. I'll try for the back tyre. Just get me closer.'

'Just shoot,' Prosper hollered. 'Shoot the whole bloody car into hell.'

Praise Jesus, they were catching up, because now he could see into the back of the car. He saw the shocking silhouette of the Hollow's face through the back window. The curve of its huge nose, the bulge of its buzzing lips. How weird it was, that it could make itself so normal. He thought the Hollow was shouting at Merit or mocking her, but then it reached over to pat her shoulder. He could hear her screaming, even over the engine. Trees and bushes scraped the van.

'I know this road better than he does,' Milton laughed. 'We'll get the little Judas just you . . . *shiiiiit*!'

The white car screeched and missed a thick, roadside tree trunk by what looked like ten centimetres. Milton turned the wheel and skidded. They missed the same trunk by a matter of one.

Defeated, Dust pulled the shotgun back. 'It was way too bumpy for a clean shot.'

Ever realised something, just then. That this was the furthest he'd been from home since he was little. Even in the terror of it all, he caught snapshots of the landscape and held them in his mind. The terrifying beauty of new scenery. It made him long for a Hollow-free world more than ever. How selfish, he thought, that these monsters keep the world's treasure to themselves.

'It's losing it, look.' Milton chuckled. 'It's all over the place.'

He was right. The white car bounced violently, as the gap closed even more. Ever caught a glimpse of the demon inside. It kept turning back to glare at the van. He threw a hand across his face, but not before he saw the Hollow's grim face. It swiped a hand across its eyes because it must be gearing up to poison him to . . . Ever blinked and looked harder . . . because . . . because . . .

No, it wasn't. That wasn't poison.

It was crying.

That's why it couldn't see straight. That's why the car was all over the place.

This Hollow was crying.

'I'll get it at the turn,' Milton nodded at a long stone wall up ahead. 'Last chance before he hits the main road.'

Dust put one hand against the dash, to steady himself. He threw the other across Ever. 'Just don't flip his car. Merit might not have a belt on.'

'She does,' Milton said. 'It must have put her belt on for her, I saw her hanging onto it when we almost bumped.'

Ever looked through his fingers. 'Why would it do that?'

Dust ignored the question. 'Well still, just be careful in case—'

'Shhh, this is it.' Milton cranked the gears, and the van roared like a lion finishing off a gazelle. The van's bumper nudged the back end of the car. It was only a slight contact, but it worked.

Its wheels span out of control, its entire back end swung to the right, missing the sharp turn, and with a horrific-sounding crack the car pounded directly into the end wall. Then stopped.

Milton hit the brakes. Seat belts sliced into shoulders in the skid. 'We're gonna hit!'

In the blackness of his lids, he heard Uncle Dust shout, 'Jesus, save us.'

Jesus did. The van gouged deep grooves into the track until the front bumper reached the other car. The van tapped its rear lights and stopped.

Milton burst out laughing, 'Halle-fookin-lujah. That was close.'

The van doors sprang open. The men leapt out. Ever heard birds singing in a nearby tree.

'Stay put,' Dust said.

Ever just sat there, gripping his seat belt, watching it all through the grimy windscreen.

The Hollow frantically tried to open its driver's door, but the door wouldn't budge because the frame was too twisted. The passenger side looked okay, though – another prayer answered. That's where Uncle Dust went to first. He flung the door open and in a flash of her dress Merit sprang into his arms, whimpering and holding her shoulder. The Hollow's arms reached for her, flailing across the gearbox, but her little feet vanished from the car.

Prosper was already at the Hollow's side, yanking so hard at the driver's door that the car rocked from side to side. Ever watched Merit run to the van, and as she went to clamber up to get inside she squealed in pain from her shoulder. A deep purple line ran up along her throat, from the seat belt. Her lip was split too, and her chin was quickly growing thick with blood. He helped her clamber up the step and she fell against him, streaming tears and shock, so he hugged her and stroked her hair, and promised himself he would never ever treat her badly again. 'You're safe, little one. You're safe.'

When he looked back up, he got a shock. Prosper was staring back at the van, staring at him. He curled a finger to call Ever outside. 'You need to see this,' he shouted.

It took a while to untangle himself from Merit, mainly because he didn't want to leave the van. But Prosper kept shouting for him, over and over. So, he dropped from the cab and his trainers thudded into dirt.

'Come here, Ever,' Prosper said.

Dust was frowning. 'What are you doing?'

'We can use this moment.'

As Ever walked slowly to the rear of the car, he could hear this hideous voice coming from the passenger seat. His blood ran cold. *They even sound like monsters.*

'You can't do this.' Its voice bubbled, as if the Hollow spoke with a mouth half-underwater. It made his flesh crawl. 'You're all lunatics,' it spluttered. 'You're all mad.'

'Ever! Get round here.' Prosper lifted the gun barrel to the car. 'The only mad one here is you, leper. You could have killed us. Could have killed a little girl too.'

'She belongs with me.'

'No, she belongs with her mother. With Pax.'

'Pax? *Pax?* What sort of fucked-up name is that?' the demon sobbed, blood spurting from its broken teeth. 'You're sad, you know that? You're all sad. Couldn't cope with a bit of suffering in life so you made up a religion to make you feel better. You don't even know who God is!'

'*Religion?*' Prosper jerked his head towards Ever in a reptile snap. 'This isn't religion. This is reality! Now get around here, boy, *now.*'

Chest heaving, Ever came forward a few steps, and now he could see it all. The Hollow sat crushed into metal, with a steering wheel somehow buried in its chest. Blood was pumping from his throat in a strange, jittery rhythm. He could hear the splash of it. And Ever noticed how the Hollow hardly had any teeth, either. Just a mouth full of gums, sticky with thick blood. Wow, he thought, it's changing right in front of us. It's transforming. The wobbling, underwater voice said, 'Just let me take her home. She's mine. I'm begging you.'

'Why should we?' Ever shouted suddenly.

The men stared at him and Prosper smiled.

'Why should we?' Ever took a step forward. 'So you can turn her into a demon? Like you are? And fill her with lies? No way.'

Prosper broke into a hard, wheezy laugh, then he motioned for Ever to come closer. 'Quickly, there's not much time left.' He lowered the barrel. 'Take it, Ever. Take the gun.'

Ever froze.

'Take it,' Prosper licked his lips. 'End it.'

'Wait,' Dust called across the roof. 'Not like this.'

'Forget the shed . . .' Prosper was smiling. 'He can practise on this one. It's a gift.'

Ever stared at the shotgun, as Prosper turned the handle towards him. The blood pulsed through his temples while the Hollow slowly turned its head, rasping out air. It raised its face and opened its mouth to a sickening, bloody hole. '*Connor?*' it said. Then a mad, desperate laugh that caused dark strands to slop from its mouth. 'Is that you, Connor?'

'I'll do it,' Dust lifted his shotgun high and Ever clamped his eyes shut while Prosper ranted that 'Ever should be the one'. Then the battling voices trailed off, and all Ever heard was a long, watery breath that seemed to go on for ever. And on that breath was a strange, wet whisper . . .

'*Wait till they're asleep, Connor,*' the Hollow said, '*then run away. You and Merit run and don't stop till you're safe . . .*'

When he opened his eyes again, the sky was much, much darker and the wind was up. The Hollow stopped moving and Ever felt his own legs fill up with stone. What frightened him most of all was that this demon's last act was a wide, mad stare directly at him.

'Too late,' Milton said. 'He's gone.'

'My old name . . . how did it know my old name?' Ever asked as the dead eyes stared on.

Silence.

'How did it know my—'

Dust bundled Ever back towards the van, but Prosper was calling out, shouting to the hills, to the world. 'Ever. Do you know what it was going to do to Merit? Shall I tell you what awful, forbidden things it was going to do to her?'

'Prosper, please . . .' Dust said. 'Get in the van, son.'

This was the first moment Ever realised that he was crying. And he could tell that he'd probably been doing it ever since he saw the car in the first place. He felt horribly small and hopelessly young, but Uncle Dust was always so good at reading his mind. He dropped to the ground and did exactly what he needed. He covered the back of his head with his palm and rested Ever into his neck. He held him there for a long, shuddering moment. He heard Dust sniff, like he was crying too.

'Can't you see, Ever?' Prosper kept calling to him, even as Dust pulled back from Ever and helped him into the van. 'Can't you see how it's starting? There'll be more of them coming soon. Hundreds of them . . . thousands . . . might be a million of those things running through the fields as we speak.'

Ever reached for Merit's shivering hand and held it.

'Unless we do what's right and show the world . . .' Prosper glared at the dead, dripping Hollow. Then he picked up rocks from the floor and started flinging them at the body. 'Spread the word . . . tell the others. End's comin'! End's comin'!'

Ever shivered at the cruelty. The manic, laughing hysteria of it, and though he closed his eyes, he could still hear the sickening wet thuds of rock on bone, which was when Ever realised what was happening. Even when they were dead, these Hollows could corrupt good people with little more than a constant stare. Prosper was strict, but he wasn't evil. But now as he danced and hammered rocks at the car, he was changing into something that Jesus wouldn't like or approve of.

If this was the world, if this was what these enemies of Christ could do to good people, Ever had to join the fight. He clicked the van door open, slid back on to the grass and walked to Prosper. He slipped a hand into his. Prosper tore his gaze from the staring demon and looked at Ever's hand.

'We better get back,' Ever said. 'We better pray.'

Prosper waited for a long, scary moment but then he dropped the rock from his other hand and nodded. 'Okay.' There was a smile on his face, but it was a thin, desperate, heartbreaking thing. He nodded to the car. 'Milton, Dust? Get the tow rope. We'll drag the car back and hide it.'

It took a while to get the car tied and connected, but they did manage to drag it all the way. Nobody spoke on the way back. Mum and Pax came running to meet them. When they saw the mangled car, they threw up tears into the darkening sky. Especially Pax, who immediately ran up to the chapel, pulling and scraping at her hair, looking for her wire brush. Prosper shouted for Mum to join Pax in the chapel to pray. He said she certainly wasn't to see the Hollow in the ruined car, not under any circumstances.

They hauled the car around the back of the shed, and they all pulled a massive tarpaulin over it. Ever helped with that. Now they had one dead Hollow, just a few feet from a fully living one, still in the shed. It was when the living one started battering on the shed walls that Prosper dropped to his haunches and looked Ever in the eye.

'Don't be scared, son,' he said. 'Remember Jesus chose you. You're going to open the doorway.'

'But I am scared.'

'You're not.' He put a hand on Ever's chest. 'You see, this shiver in here, I know it feels like fear . . . but it's not. This is courage, Ever . . . it's courage that Jesus is pulling out of you. It's feels like a bad thing, but it's a good thing. This shiver is glorious.'

Ever put a hand to his own chest and tilted his head.

'Can you feel it?' Prosper said. 'The tremble? The coldness?'

He nodded.

'Well, that's courage . . . and calling. That's what you're feeling. And all you need to do is do the things we say over the next few days . . .'

He trailed off, because the shed door started rocking and the voice of the Hollow moaned from inside, asking to be let out. It could obviously tell someone was out there listening, but Ever didn't run. They both just listened to it speaking. Saying its name was 'Sam' and that it had 'done nothing wrong'. And just as it sounded kind and almost human, it asked them to take the tape off its eyes, which showed Ever what it really wanted.

Ever kicked the shed hard and shouted, 'Shut up in there.'

The Hollow obeyed. It gave up talking and the horrible scrape of fingernails on metal came to a slow and laboured end. Prosper just ruffled Ever's hair and said it was time to go in, so they did. Ever stopped on the porch and looked out across the field, and the dirt track where so much had only just happened.

In the air, he heard a distant rumble. It sounded like the strangest thunder he'd ever heard.

CHAPTER THIRTY-THREE

Matt and Bowland stood waiting at the door of Rev. David East's private ward. Through the glass square they could see the nurse leaning over him, changing a dressing. He lay on the bed looking frankly as comatose as before, and he still had tight bandages around the back of his head, but there were less of them now, and less machines and tubes, too. All the main lights in his room were off, except for one single Pixar-style lamp on the bedside table. If it was possible for an intensive care unit to look cosy, this one did.

'Look at them,' Bowland nodded down the corridor to the waiting room where the church pensioners milled around a coffee machine. They were laughing and hugging, amazed and excited that a resurrection had come. They were desperate too, to get in this room and see the faith-building sight of their very own Reverend Lazarus, but the nurses were keeping them at bay. Bowland had special permission to ask a few 'brief' and 'non-taxing' questions. Quite how they'd keep topics like axe attacks and dead sons in the 'non-taxing' category was something Matt was eager to see.

Matt turned back to watch the nurse, fixing some sort of wired clip to East's earlobe. 'Does he know about Micah?'

'Yes. I told him earlier.'

'How'd he take it?'

She whispered it. 'He screamed.'

Matt jumped when the nurse opened the door. 'Keep it under ten minutes, please.'

They both nodded and stepped inside the dim, blinking room. Matt assumed Bowland would start with a gentle whisper. Something soft to ease the fella in. But she dived right in with a clean, loud, clipped approach, with gaps between each word. A sort of William Shatner voice people use with deaf folks, or when they order lunch in a very foreign restaurant. 'Reverend East . . . I'm DS Jill Bowland . . . and standing next to me . . . is Matthew . . . Hunter . . . he's assisting us with—'

'Volume.' East's voice came out as a croaking rasp. 'Please. It hurts . . . my head. And I can hear you fine.'

'Apologies.' She dropped her voice. 'It's good to see you're speaking again. Your congregation say it's a miracle.'

'So, do the doctors . . . I'll keep my eyes closed, if you don't mind. The light's a bit much.'

'Shall I turn it off?' Matt said.

'Best not. Don't want you tripping over and yanking my mains plug out.'

For a short and welcome moment, Matt laughed.

'We'd like to ask you some brief questions.' Bowland and Matt went to sit.

'About why he did it?'

'That was my main question, yes,' she said.

The grinding strain of his voice grew a little harsher, but he pushed on. 'Well the first thing you need to know . . . is that Micah wasn't a bad boy, and he wasn't confrontational. Conflict isn't in his nature. Or mine, either.'

'So why did he—'

'Attack me? Isn't it obvious?'

'Actually, no,' Matt added. 'It isn't.'

'Ah, but it is, Mr Hunter.' He swallowed, and winced as he did it. 'Are you aware that the most underappreciated form of abuse is neglect? It's when a caregiver . . . through forgetfulness, or disinterest' – he winced again – 'when they take the attention they ought to give to a loved one and they squander it on other matters. And the worst type of neglect, the easiest type, happens through presumption.'

Bowland flicked a look at the clock, for time.

'We presume those closest to us will always be there, so we spend our time with those on the fringes instead, because we think the fringe is fleeting. Then you wake up one morning in a hospital bed with the police staring down at you, and you find that the ones you thought were for ever were actually on short-term loan. And you realise it's your neglect that caused them to go. Both of them. I've preached on this topic many times. About the importance of family. But I only preached it to others. Never to myself, it turns out.'

His eyes were still closed, and he had an astonishing calmness as he spoke, and though his voice was raspy and quiet (they both strained forward to hear it), it was steady and clear. Amazing, for his condition. Miraculous, even. But then Matt also knew that vicars were trained to hold things together under extreme stress. He remembered sitting in a class full of ordinands at Bible college, where the tutor specifically said: *When you lead a funeral, even a heartfelt one of a little kid, you can never be the one who needs consoling. Others may weep, but you must stay strong. You must lead the ship.*

'Is neglect the only reason for the attack?' Bowland said.

'Isn't that enough? The power of rejection is profound, Sergeant. Even more when it's a father to a son . . . I ought to know because my own father did the same to me. He was a doctor, you know, and his patients were always more vital than us. I admired that for a while. Then it made me sad, and lonely . . . which became anger. And it stayed like that until he died. Today the irony is . . . I'm now him.' With some effort, he finally started to open his eyes. Matt saw the sticky lids peel, tug, then finally pop apart. The narrowed gaze fell on Matt, and he was taken aback for a moment. The whites of his eyes weren't white any more. They were a mixture of milky red and glazed yellow. He looked like a horror movie zombie – a talkative and erudite one yes, but a zombie none the less.

Now the eyes were open, Matt said, 'Hi.'

'Hi,' East tried a smile.

'You said you caused them both to go . . .'

'Yes. Micah and Zara.'

'We're having trouble tracking her down,' Bowland said. 'Do you know where she's travelling?'

For the first time, East's chin started to shudder.

'Reverend East?' Bowland said. 'Are you okay?'

'That's just what I told the congregation.'

Matt and Bowland looked at each other. 'You mean she isn't travelling?' Matt asked.

He shook his head. 'That was a . . . well, it was a lie.'

Bowland frowned. 'Then, where is she?'

'In the hills . . .' His chest started to heave, the emotions of it all whirling inside like a personal hurricane. But like a good, steady vicar, he battened the hatches down. 'There you are. This is the first time I've told anybody about this, or at least anyone who wasn't God. She left me. She found somebody new. Somebody who paid her attention, which makes him infinitely wiser than me. I don't know his name . . . but he lives in the hills. You'll find her there. Happier, no doubt. I followed her there, you see.'

'When did you follow her?' Bowland said.

'A couple of months ago, after we argued. It was a rather loud one. She said I loved the old ladies more than her and more than Micah. I called her selfish, said she was losing her faith, and then she told me she didn't care any more. Which is when the penny dropped. Micah heard it all, I'm sad to say.'

Matt tugged his chair forward. 'Where are these hills?'

'The Chilterns. The beautiful Chilterns. See, she drove off after our row and so I got in my car and followed her. It was like a sordid little soap opera. I drove after her, and the higher we got, the more I knew. I just knew she'd found someone. I watched her pull off the main road and stop at a gate. Then a man opened up to let her in. She drove up a long dirt track and I was furious enough to trespass on his property. I followed her up thinking she was some sort of Judas or Jezebel. Imagine that, being furious that she was ignoring me. The irony . . .'

'Did you confront her?' Matt said.

'I parked my car on the dirt track and looked through the bushes down this big hill, and there she was, sitting on the porch of a pretty little farmhouse. There was a field and a stream nearby and birds in the air too. It was heaven – no more, no less. And the man with her was holding her hand.' A tear glistened in his zombie eye. 'And do you know what? All my anger vanished at that precise moment, because I spent a good ten minutes watching him listen to her. I could see it, even at a distance. When they embraced for a long time I heard God's voice. He said, *David, this man is more worthy than you. He should have her.* So, I came back down the hill and I drove home and I led a funeral that afternoon for an eighty-year-old man I'd never met before. The family asked me for dinner and of course like always I said yes. Always the last one to leave, that's me. Zara came back that night. I found her in the church praying at the altar. I tried to talk and beg for forgiveness but she . . . she wouldn't even look at me. I was heartbroken. Next day her things were gone. She'd left a note saying she wouldn't be back. The only thing that really shocked me was that she'd leave Micah behind. They were very close. So, I'm not surprised Micah blamed me for her leaving, because he was right. And do you know what she called our marriage? In her note, I mean. Do you know what word she used?'

Matt nodded for him to continue.

'She said our marriage was hollow . . .'

Matt tilted his head. 'Hollow?' The same word Micah used, just before the train.

'Yes, she said our relationship was hollow . . . and that I was hollow too. And do you know something? She was right . . .' His lip started to tremble. 'I thought that was the perfect way to say it.'

Bowland shifted in her chair. 'Did Micah know about this other man?'

'Yes . . . but I made him lie. I told him to tell the congregation she was travelling, and he wanted to lie. To protect her reputation, you see? I told him that his mum might change her mind someday, but I knew she wouldn't . . . to be honest, I knew she *shouldn't*.'

Bowland said, 'Well, she needs to know what happened to Micah . . . and to you.'

He didn't answer. He wept instead.

They sat there for a moment, staring at this minister quaking. He wasn't even able to reach up and cover his face with his own hands. So Matt reached out and placed his fingers on East's kneecap. Then he said something he hadn't heard on his lips in a very long time. A quote from Psalm 20. Back in his vicar phase, he'd found this particular Bible chunk to be pretty effective medicine for those in despair.

'May the Lord answer you when you are in distress,' Matt said it softly, 'and send you help from his sanctuary.'

The fact that there was no God to comfort Reverend East was kind of by the by. Mere facts didn't strip these verses of their psychological power. Placebo or not, East gradually stopped crying and he looked up through his fluttering lashes at Matt. They held each other's gaze for a moment, and East mouthed the words 'Thank you.' To which Matt did something he didn't expect. He asked one more question. 'Did you ever see the upturned crosses in your son's bedroom?' But the man winced and shook his head. He was through. Spent.

The clock ticked over into ten minutes, and at that precise moment the door clicked open.

'That's all, folks,' the nurse said.

'Wait, where was this farm?' Bowland said.

He peeled his lips apart. 'Old Moat Farm. In the hills . . . near Speen.'

'Sergeant,' the nurse snapped. 'That's enough.'

'And tell her . . .' East was sobbing now, all his vicar power dissolved. 'Tell her that the church isn't crooked . . . and that I'm sorry. For forgetting what we had, for turning hollow . . . and tell her I wish her well with this man . . . that she deserves it . . .'

'We'll tell her,' Matt said.

'Personally . . .' David stared at Matt. 'You must tell her personally, Mr Hunter. She needs another Christian voice—'

'Shhhh.' The nurse threw a killer stare at Matt. 'That's enough for one day, don't you think?' Then one of the beeping machines upped its rhythm and the nurse snapped one more word. 'Out!'

They both hurried into the corridor, where Bowland was checking her phone.

'That poor man,' Matt said. 'What an absolute nightmare.'

She nodded, and they started walking.

'Well, I'll be fascinated to hear what Zara has to say,' Matt said. 'I'm around in the morning if you wan—'

'Around for what?'

'To head up to Old Moat Farm.'

Bowland slowed her pace.

'What?'

'And you want to be the one who tells Mrs East that her son's dead?'

Matt slowed too.

'I'll send an officer up to inform her in the morning, then I'll chat to her at some point.'

'You're not sounding very urgent.'

'That's because I'm not.' She fixed her eyes on Matt. 'For now, I'm satisfied.'

Matt stopped walking, 'Really?'

'Look. It's coming together. Micah had a lot of pent-up emotion about his dad. Now we know his dad might have even driven the mother from the home. Eventually all that anger exploded, and he lashed out.'

'The magazines . . . the pissing on the church altar . . .'

'You said yourself that teenagers lash out symbolically . . . at the things their parents value. Urinating on the altar was just mocking his dad's job.' She smiled at him. The kind of look a teacher gives to a dumb kid. 'Do you realise what most murder statistics boil down to?'

'Killing?' He didn't hide his frustration.

'No . . . it's emotional, relational breakdown. They're almost always domestic issues. What I'm saying is that life isn't always epic. Sometimes death isn't a conspiracy. Sometimes' – she looked away at the women in the waiting room, then put a hand across the band of beads on her wrist – 'sometimes the world isn't about big miracles or evil curses. It's just broken people lashing out at the ones they love. And that's about it.'

He looked back at her, biting his lip. 'He just told me to talk to Zara personally. He wants me to reassure her about church.'

'And how are you going to do that? Give her a copy of your book?'

He frowned at her. 'Steady on.'

'I'm sorry. But look, I'll get an officer up to the farm to inform her, and I'll keep an eye on this. I'll be back to see Mr East too, but let's be honest . . . it's not like we're tracking down a mystery murderer here. I have a church full of witnesses who saw Micah attack his dad, and yes, we'll follow up this Old Moat Farm thing. But this is turning into what I've suspected all along. A tragic domestic case which is, granted, a little more dramatic than the hundreds of others that cross my desk each year . . . but essentially, it's the same. Okay?' She waited. 'Okay?'

Eventually, he nodded.

'Besides,' her face softened, 'maybe we should listen to what he did say in there.'

'What do you mean?'

'I mean go back to your family, Matthew. Hang out with them, laugh with them, spend time . . . that's sure as shit what I'm going to do. I'm going to call my daughter.'

He smiled at her. 'Good for you.'

'It's been an intense couple of days, for both of us.' She started to button up her coat. 'I reckon it's time to turn the dial down a bit.'

They passed the waiting room, where East's nurse was informing the church women that the good Reverend wasn't available for visitors, after all. She did this elegant spin and tapped her fringe into place to walk back, leaving an explosion of groans and hands against brows behind her. 'Quick,' Bowland said. 'Let's leave before they revolt.'

He and Bowland stepped into the lift, silent until it started to hum downwards.

'That's odd,' Matt said suddenly, as the doors closed over. 'Miriam wasn't with them. She was all over this place when he first came in.'

'Um . . . she was shot today.'

'Oh, she's been discharged.'

'Then she's probably recuperating at home.' She pulled a small umbrella from her bag, and the gesture of it, the slap of it against her hand, was her way of closing the conversation. 'You should carry one of these at all times. Especially with this psycho weather.'

'My kids bought me one, but I keep leaving it in the car.'

'Not much point in that. You know they say there might be tornadoes this month.'

'Yeah, I read that.'

'Little ones . . . but still. Tornadoes in the Home Counties. Imagine that.'

CHAPTER THIRTY-FOUR

It was dark outside. Not that it was fully night. It was actually late afternoon, so the moon was yet to arrive. The day was dark, simply because the end of the world was coming.

This was the darkness that comes when the clouds get organised. When they thicken themselves and join hands in the air, because they have instructions from Jesus to block God's sun out, ready for a son to dawn. But paradise wasn't here just yet, which meant the trees, the stream, the house and the hill were now a very dark, very stony grey.

They'd asked Ever to decide where they should do it. That was amazing, really. To be in charge of a decision like that. Both Mum and Milton said it should happen on Comfort Hill, right in front of the chapel. But Ever said they should kill the Hollow in his favourite spot by his own stretch of stream. If they did it up on the hill, he told them, the light and smoke would draw the attention of the Hollow towns. The fact that he'd considered that factor seemed to impress everybody no end. Wisdom was growing, it turned out.

Along with the courage that was making his chest shiver more than ever. Enough to make his little hands shake so much he had to hide them in his pockets.

Now the decision was made and the prayers were over, they all stood as a solemn little crowd, listening to four sounds blend into one. The first was the trickle of the stream, a sound he'd always loved; the second, the high-pitched whistle of a very cold wind; the third was the deep groan of thunder, and finally there was the fourth sound. The weeping and whimpering from the lump on the floor. Milton had found some thick black tape. As soon as he'd dragged it from the shed, he'd wrapped this tape around the Hollow's eyes. Thankfully then, nobody was going to fall into its hypnotic traps.

It was very reassuring that the eyes were covered because when the Hollow died in the car, it had been staring at them all. This made the grown-ups way too twitchy and intense for Ever's liking. Shouting at each other, falling back into worldly ways. Now this one had its eyes covered, his family were themselves again – all calm, if a little sad, that the world had come to this. Prosper explained how the killing would work and it seemed, well . . . straightforward. They'd kept it easy for his first step into maturity.

Prosper slowly walked towards the Hollow on the floor and started speaking to it. He used his gentle voice. The tone for compliments and kind, treasured blessings. 'Hey, lost one. It's time to see light.'

A murmur came, a movement.

'That's it. Sit up straight. You're gonna help us heal the world.' Prosper nodded to Dust, and they both tugged under the Hollow's armpits, so its spine was flat against the thin tree trunk. Then Milton flung a rope over, which uncoiled like a snake in mid-air. Dust looped it around the tree, but he did it way too slowly, so Prosper pushed him aside and took over. He set the Hollow in place really tight and well.

Everybody gasped when the Hollow spoke. It had that bubbling, rasping voice they all seemed to use. 'Who are you?'

'We're the honest ones. The ones that never changed.'

'I've got nothing to give you, all right?' Its mouth flapped like a hole, underneath all that thick eye-tape. 'I've got nothing worth taking.'

'That doesn't matter. We want to give you something.'

The mouth curled. 'Give me what?'

'Freedom . . . from your condition. You know I'm a big believer that when a Hollow's set free it gets the chance to be born again one day. Back how it was. A fresh start. Isn't that right, Milton? Don't I always say that?'

'Yep,' he said. 'He always says that.'

'But for that, we need Jesus back . . .' Prosper stroked the Hollow's shoulder. 'And who knows . . . maybe you'll help us build a wonderful new world, someday. The Father gone for ever, the Son in charge. That'd really be something, wouldn't it?'

'Let me go,' the Hollow said, 'for the love of Christ.'

'Yes!' For the first time, the reverent atmosphere shifted and Prosper chuckled to the others. 'See, Ever? It knows what it needs, and that's good enough for me. I think it's time to let it go.' He nodded a signal to Milton and turned back to the heap on the floor. 'Did you hear that, Hollow? We're going to do exactly what you've asked. We're going to let you go.'

'You are?'

Milton hauled a canister over, then he lifted it.

'Yes. Because you said his name. You said the name of Christ.'

A sobbing thank-you came from the Hollow but the mouth that was giving out gratitude was quickly filled with the gushing liquid from the petrol can. Panicked, it tried to close its mouth, but Prosper shoved his fingers right inside, teeth scraping his hand, then pressed hard until the jaw clicked down with an aubible snap. 'Fill it,' Prosper said. So Milton kept glugging more petrol.

Dust wasn't watching any of this. He was over by the stream on his haunches, fingers trailing in the water, but Ever found it impossible to look away. The smell of petrol stole the air, and so, in time, did the wet, gulping screams. Because Hollows aren't stupid. They knew what petrol could do. It quickly started vomiting, and the screams of 'why' turned into painful retching. In fact, it became so hysterical that Prosper nudged Milton to pull out his roll of black gaffer tape. He tore a strip off and slapped it right across the Hollow's mouth, trapping the petrol inside. Black tape across the mouth, black tape across the eyes. Now the only part of his face on show was a pointy nose sticking out, and a crop of petrol-wet hair sprouting up top.

'Did you bring them?' Prosper looked up. 'Hey. Dust. You listening? I said have you got them?'

Dust pulled the matches from his pocket and stared at the box. Then he said something that was very confusing, in a tone that Ever wasn't used to. There was a desperation there. He turned his head, so that his ponytail fell against his cheek, and he whispered to Prosper, 'What if there's another way?'

Prosper froze, then he leant close to Uncle Dust and said, 'You know full well there is. Are you saying you want to do that instead, because we could do that right now, you know . . .' He turned his eyes to Ever. 'We could take the other path right—'

'No, I don't mean . . . I . . . mean . . . perhaps if we pray . . .'

Prosper snatched the box from Uncle Dust. 'Go back to the farmhouse, right now. Wash your face . . . and your eyes especially. You must have looked at the Hollow in the car for too long.'

Dust stood up finally, looked at Ever and seemed to reach for him.

'Hey,' Prosper shouted. 'I said back to the farmhouse.'

Ever tried to smile. 'And wash your face, okay? And Uncle Dust? Really scrub it, and you'll be better.'

Uncle Dust stared at Ever, then he closed his eyes, as if he couldn't look at the world any more. Ever watched him trudge away.

'Okay,' Prosper turned back to him. 'Remember . . . the light came into the world and overcame the darkness . . . but the darkness could not understand it. Jesus is the light, son. So, share the light. Set this Hollow free.'

He told everybody but Ever to step well back, then Prosper pulled out the match. He struck it and it fizzed into life. He lit the rag on the end of Ever's stick, but the actual dropping of the stick . . . that was for Ever to do. For a moment Ever looked at the dancing ball of light and thought that maybe Uncle Dust was right after all. Maybe there was some other way. But when he turned to him for advice, Dust wasn't there. He'd already crossed the ridges of the field and was back at the farmhouse. He got there so quickly, he must have run.

'Rain's coming, Ever. Throw it now,' Mum said, and when she saw him staring back at Uncle Dust she added, 'You're braver than him, Ever.'

Milton had poured a little stream of petrol in a long line from the Hollow, just so they wouldn't be too close when it finally lit up.

'Now,' Prosper said. '*Avi, Avi, lama kataltani.*'

What would happen if he refused? Ever wondered. If he told them he didn't—

Prosper shoved his shoulder and Ever dropped the stick. The ball of light just fell from his hands, like the earth was tugging it downwards.

Faces lit up with a flash and the little stream of fire raced and crackled towards the Hollow. Then the fire line hit home with a huge *wooosh* of sound. It sounded like the flapping of one single, giant wing, whooshing across them all and leaving a panicked scream in its wake. It seemed to rise in pitch after each desperate breath. They gasped as the heat hit their faces, then the sky joined

227

in, because streaks of lightning were now dancing across the horizon. Too many to count. A moment later, a loud smack of thunder rattled heaven. Prosper pointed to the clouds and said, 'Hear that? That's the door to paradise cracking open, just a little. We'll kick the bugger wide open soon.'

The Hollow screamed again, only this time the tape had burnt away, so that flames shot out of its mouth. That was terrifying enough, but the absolute scariest part was the way its legs seemed to kick in and out in weird spasms, like it was climbing an invisible ladder. To heaven perhaps, and hopefully rebirth. That's what Ever told himself as everybody's lips pressed together, as hands clasped hands to make a chain. They hummed the melody to a sweet hymn. *Jesus, Jesus, your name is like honey on my lips.* The music turned the screams into tiny sparks of light that twisted up into the dark air. Then the Hollow was silent, and Ever felt a fat raindrop slap hard against his nose. This was signal enough. The Father was trying to put the fire out. One last-ditch attempt.

Prosper found this hilarious. He chortled to the sky and said, 'Bit late for that now, isn't it?' Then he looked at them all and whispered eagerly, 'Notice how the Father's getting weaker and slacker, now that our faith's up? I'm telling you, this is going to work.'

'It's dead,' Milton said, 'praise Jesus . . .'

'See, Ever? You can do these things. You're gifted at it . . .' Prosper smiled then turned to Milton. 'You might as well take the head, now.'

Milton leant over and grabbed the axe. It was sitting in the grass, but then the sky flashed again, and rain started to hammer off their shoulders. This would usually have been a cue for them to go running and giggling back to the farmhouse. But today they waited and watched Milton start whacking. After a series of smacks, and a few moans from the others, Ever heard an odd little series of thuds on the wet grass as the still-burning head rolled off. He didn't look at it. He didn't want to.

'Today we've seen that the end is almost here,' Prosper called out above the thunder, as Milton tried to yank the axe from the tree. 'They've started coming for us, they've tried to take our children. And if we wait much longer, they'll be on our land, and in our house. And all they want is to make us forget who we are. To forget the truth.'

The rain hit hard, but it wasn't putting the Hollow out. Not completely, anyway.

Milton had to shout over the rain and thunder now, looking at each of them in turn. 'And if they drag us into their world, we'll be back with every monster who ever beat us, or raped us, or chained us up, or slaughtered the ones we love.' He looked across at Milton when he said that. 'And they'll make you forget her. You'll move on, and you'll let it be. Do you really want to betray her like that, old man? Do you want to let them win?'

Milton squeezed his eyes shut and shook his head, 'Never.' He said it in a whisper.

'Well, you don't have to, cos Jesus came to bring light to the world and he's made us the light-bringers. Just look at how even this little symbol is changing the atmosphere. Just think when we do this for real because look . . . Ever here is ready to fight for our lives.' Thunder boomed, right on cue, then he clamped both wet hands onto Ever's shoulder. 'Round of applause, for Ever. You did it, son!'

Wet hands slapped against each other, as the final flames died under the rain. Then Prosper hoisted Ever up, against his hip. He never did that, because that's what Uncle Dust always did. His hip felt much sharper, like the bone was broken in there, and Ever could smell the stale hum of his sweat, and he could see the strange bulge of his eyeballs. 'But we have to do it soon.'

'How soon?' Mum whispered.

'How soon do you think?' Prosper laughed. 'We leave tonight.'

'Praise be,' Milton said. 'Praise be.'

Prosper carried Ever all the way home, his chin resting on his shoulder. It meant that all the way back Ever was facing the dead, headless Hollow and the smoke-filled tree. He suspected that Prosper carried him like that on purpose, just so he could look at what he'd done. It was too dark to make out any of the Hollow's features, but there were pockets of light and sparkles coming from its chest. Latent fire perhaps, or the regeneration of a soul that he'd helped to save. It was the latter, Ever decided. Or hoped.

'I'm proud of you, Ever, and Hope . . . Hope's going to be over the moon.' Prosper creaked him up on to the porch steps. 'Just one more of those and we're done. But we have to travel for it.'

'Are we really leaving the valley?'

'Yep, but you'll be safe, don't you worry. Let's just get some food before we set off.'

They hurried inside, stinking of smoke, and Ever rushed upstairs to wash his hands. He found Uncle Dust on the landing, rubbing his face with a towel.

'Did you scrub your eyes? Did you get it all out?'

Dust just stared at Ever, then out of the window at the tree. A swirl of smoke still curled into the air.

'Uncle Dust? Are you okay?'

'Mm-hmm.'

'So, how come you didn't even watch?' Ever said. Hurt now. 'You didn't stay to see me do it.'

'I had to come back to the house. Prosper said.'

'Did you watch from the window?'

He shook his head, slowly.

Ever's voice started to quiver. 'You aren't even proud of me, are you . . . of how brave I'm being?'

Dust looked at his feet and pulled in a long breath.

'Why are you angry with me, I've done nothing wrong—'

Dust immediately pushed himself from the window, then dropped to the floor. 'I'm not angry with you. Not at all.'

'So why are you crying?'

Dust sighed and put his arms around him. 'I guess I'm just scared.'

'Well don't be. Cos the fear you've got inside yourself isn't really fear. That's courage bubbling up. That's Jesus.'

Dust grew stiff in his arms.

'So we should go downstairs and get some hot food. It's a big journey ahead.'

Dust pulled back and looked at him. For the first time, he smiled. It wasn't the beaming glow of his usual grin, far from it, but it looked like the gentle upturn of a man reaching for hope. 'You know something . . . *you're* why I believe. You're my evidence.'

Ever smiled, not really understanding what that meant.

'I guess it was just that Hollow in the car. Guess I caught its eyes for a little too long, but look' – he popped his eyes open and shut a few times, a theatrical blink – 'I'm all scrubbed up now.' He sniffed his final tear away and pushed himself to his feet. 'So yeah, let's get some food.'

Ever took one last look through the window. The smoke ladder was reaching high up into heaven, slowly starting to vanish. *Wow*, Ever thought. *I saved a Hollow today. I saved a soul.* Then he turned to head down the stairs where he saw one more thing. Something that startled him. It was Milton, standing at the bottom of the steps. It looked like he'd been watching them both, the whole time.

CHAPTER THIRTY-FIVE

It was dark when Matt slammed his foot hard into the brake. He lolled against the seat belt and only just missed the car that sat in his usual spot. There on his drive was an old green Rover 200, with a registration plate from the late Jurassic Age – 1998. He sighed at the thought of company and had to back out onto the street to find another space. He parked under the church lamp post instead.

Back on his drive, he peeked inside the Rover as he passed it. The passenger seat was strewn with screwed-up tissues, and on the dashboard a packet of liquorice perched in an open position. A disgusting and nigh-on demonic flavour in Matt's considered opinion, but this driver clearly loved to dip into these en route.

He felt the call of wine on his tongue and pushed through his front door. He heard a shriek of Wren's laughter echo down the corridor followed by a huge guffaw of another woman. A laugh he recognised and knew. He groaned and clicked the front door shut. The laughter died away.

'Matt? Is that you?' Wren called out.

'Yep, just a sec.' He kicked off his shoes and threw his jacket on the peg. When he opened the kitchen door, he saw two heads swing to greet him. Both held large and very full glasses of red wine.

Miriam raised her glass. 'Welcome home.'

Wren raised an eyebrow. 'Didn't you get my text?'

The phone was in his hand, which made it even worse that he hadn't bothered to look. He quickly glanced at it and saw the long string of eBay notifications he'd been ignoring earlier. And amongst it, a text from Wren saying *Remember Miriam's coming tonight. We're eating at 7.30 p.m.*

Matt glanced at the clock on the wall. A plastic Elvis – whose pelvis swung on each passing second – said 8 p.m. 'Darn . . . sorry, ladies.'

Wren snapped up the oven gloves and opened the oven, but rather than shove him in it, she thankfully pulled out dinner instead.

'I got caught up with something.' He loosened his collar. 'I really do apologise.'

'No need,' Miriam shook her head. 'To be honest, I was late myself . . . I only just arrived.' She raised a glass towards the oven and winced. 'Sorry, Wren!'

'No need for you to apologise,' Wren said, while Miriam pulled a chair out for Matt. Without asking, she sloshed a hefty measure of Shiraz into the third empty glass, just as Wren set some skillet veal on the table, grating some parmesan across it. Tea lights twinkled in the centre of the table, and he noticed their best plates were out. She'd done that thing she did when she really made an effort too. The chef-style arc of olive oil, across the side of the plate. Just that thin splash. Seeing the trouble she'd gone too stoked his guilt at being late. So he decided to do something nice. He prepped himself to say grace along with her, figuring of all people, Miriam would be the type to appreciate that. But when he looked up at her, she'd already opened her mouth and was shoving a forkful of food in. 'Dear me . . .' she moaned, 'this stuff is heaven.'

'Thanks,' Wren said, and they all got started.

Relieved of his prayer duties, Matt cut a chunk from his meat. 'So, Miriam, how's the injury?'

She swallowed. 'It's amazing. I don't even need the pain relief they gave me. Course, if I press it, it hurts. But if I don't, it doesn't. So . . . *ta-dah* . . . I don't press it.'

Wren eyed him over the candles. He cleared his throat and said, 'Well, look . . . I just wanted to say once again how very grateful I am.'

'Hey, it's no big deal.'

'Yes, it is,' Wren said. 'You're a superhero.'

She shook her head and pointed upwards. 'If anyone's the hero, it's him.'

'Elvis?' Matt nodded to the clock above her and she laughed.

'Point higher.'

Matt raised a glass to the ceiling and nodded a cheers, then just as it touched his lips he added, 'Oh, and guess what.'

'What?'

'He's awake.'

'Elvis?'

'Reverend East . . . David . . . he's woken up.'

She scooped some more food up. 'Well, that's lovely news.'

'Isn't it?'

She ate a little more and closed her eyes. 'Wow, Wren, I need this recipe.'

'To be honest, I thought you'd be there at the hospital,' Matt said. 'Your whole congregation's camped out up there. They're calling it a miracle.'

'It is . . .' She raised a glass. 'Maybe I'll pop in tomorrow.'

Maybe? She was surprisingly underwhelmed.

He hadn't hidden his puzzlement very well, because Miriam ran a palm across the table. 'Well, I wouldn't want to crowd him, would I?'

Wren nodded. 'Quite right. And I bet you've had enough of hospitals for one day.'

Conversation lulled into the banal, including chats about Miriam's work. She helped at a dry-cleaners in Chervil but seemed way too bored with her job to talk about it much. She preferred to keep talking about a prayer meeting at St Bart's tomorrow night. Just an hour of thanks and praise that David hadn't died, and that Matt was okay, too. Both he and Wren were, of course, invited, and Wren, of course, happily committed them to attend it.

Throughout the evening he noticed how Miriam tended to look at him and not Wren. Just a few sly glances at first, then lingering stares that he caught in the reflection of the dining-room doors. He'd look back and these stares were politely broken off, because as ever, she was really crap at straight-on eye contact. But he still caught her looking at him, or at least at his forehead, a fair bit. For a wine-fuelled moment, he wondered if Miriam might simply fancy him. Like the occasional student each year, who'd sit right up front and fawn whenever he opened his mouth. Who knows, maybe that explained everything. Miriam saved his life for love! What a slayer of hearts he was. This theory amused him, precisely because he could tell full well that it wasn't true.

He noticed that Miriam lifted her wine to her lips a lot, but the level barely seemed to go down. He and Wren, on the other hand, were sinking the bottle at a steady clip. Drink was a necessity after the horrendous two days they'd had. Something to numb the memories of Sean, Micah and Mrs Ashton's rifle. But neither he nor Wren could talk openly about any of these horrors. They were too busy discussing mundane subjects that Miriam started bringing up, like how hard it was to get grass stains out of jeans. Neither Wren nor he complained, since she was, after all, their hero. But Matt did often phase out of conversations and found himself thinking of Micah East instead. Sitting in his little cupboard of upturned crosses, working out ways he could stop *the* Father rather than *his* father . . . whatever the holy heck that meant . . . and all those eyeless magazines. And how . . .

And how . . .

Matt stared for a moment . . .

And how Micah seemed terrible with eye contact too.

He blinked. Miriam was talking to him.

'Matt?' Wren said. 'She asked you a question?'

'Oh, sorry, go ahead.'

Miriam leant on the table, eyes on his hairline. 'I was just wondering how you could have been a Christian . . . an ordained pastor, no less . . . but these days' – she scrunched her face up – 'you're not a big fan of the *G-O-D*.'

Wren laughed into her wine. 'He's not a big fan of the *C-L-O-C-K*. either.'

Miriam smiled gently, but she still went on. 'What turned you away from your faith?'

For a moment, all he could hear was the generic dinner party playlist oozing from the speakers, and he saw Wren look over at him, sympathetically. They'd replayed this scenario a thousand times at dinner parties. The big reveal of why Matt Hunter left the church. But right now, he had no intention of talking about his mum's murder and about him being suspended from the pastorate for almost beating her attacker to death. These may well have been the catalysts for his faith-drop, and they weren't secrets either, he'd even mentioned them in his book – but he had no intention of talking about his mum with this woman. He wasn't sure why, he just didn't. So, he gave her a different reason instead. Just as a new track of slinky jazz began. Something he'd been pondering ever since hearing that tape recording of the attack.

My Father my Father, why have you murdered me?

'Actually, what put me off Christianity was the Trinity.'

She looked up, 'Oh?'

'Yup. I don't mean Jesus. He was progressive and wise. It was the other one I struggled with.'

'The Holy Spirit?'

'No . . . The Father. Or, at least, I struggled with how the modern church presents him.'

Miriam had plastered a smile across her face since the moment he'd walked in. It was only now that he saw it shrink at the edges. 'And what problem did you have, exactly?'

The plates were now empty, but Wren had laid out some after-dinner mints. Matt grabbed one and bit into one as he spoke. 'Well, I was brought up evangelical, right? And they're always singing about the wrath of the Father. It's like he had all this pent-up anger about sin and he had to let his fury out on someone . . . so he picks his own son and pummels him on a cross. If I met a dad like that in the street, I wouldn't call him noble. I'd put him in anger management.'

Wren cleared her throat. 'Isn't this a little heavy for a Monday night?'

'No, I'm fascinated. Go on, Matt.'

'I'm just saying, in the New Testament Jesus forgives people and he repeatedly calls on his followers to forgive without expecting retribution. But according to the evangelicals, the Father only forgives after retribution . . . on his own son. That reading of the atonement always felt . . . contradictory to me.'

Miriam said it softly, '. . . like the Father and the son have different personalities.'

Matt clicked his fingers. 'Exactly . . . In fact, you could say they have *conflicting* personalities. Like a good cop, bad cop situation. I mean, look . . .' Matt pushed his seat back and went to the kitchen window, knowing he was oversimplifying the cross, but he kept going – because it seemed to do something to Miriam's expression.

He leant over the sink and opened up the blinds to show the view they had. Every time he did the washing-up he had to stare at the symbol of the religion he'd abandoned. A stubby, stone crucifix was perched at the top of the church. He turned around, just to see her reaction to it. It's not like she lurched back like a vampire. But she did narrow her eyes, and, for a very brief moment, she glared at it. He wasn't sure what he was trying to achieve with all this, but his mind was racing with Micah's upturned crosses, and those Aramaic threats to the Father.

'Millions of people have this symbol hanging round their necks, right?' He leant against the sink, cross hovering over his shoulder. 'Tattooed on their forearm, printed on tea towels for crying out loud . . . and they forget what it is . . . an instrument of execution. I mean, Wren . . . can you imagine if I bought you a necklace for Valentine's Day and it was a little dangling noose . . . or a pair of electric-chair earrings? This isn't a sign of love, it's a symbol of aggression. Heck, you could even call it a sign of murder, from the Father to the Son.'

She was biting her lip, and nodding.

He went on, 'But what's interesting is that Christians weren't always obsessed with the cross. The key symbol for the early church was the Ichthus, you know, the little fish you see on the back of cars? That fish was just a shorthand way of saying Jesus was God and Saviour, and that symbol defined Christianity. So, for the first millennium, sanctuaries were filled with images of Jesus in life. Teaching, preaching, healing. But then sometime in the medieval age the church started fixating on the idea of redemptive violence. Out went the fish and in came the cross.'

'Are you saying the cross isn't important?'

'Not in the slightest. It's still vital, but what if it wasn't to satiate the bloodlust of an angry Father? To me, that sounds more inspired by the pre-Christian gods of the pagan world. No, the cross was still key, but we've made it too much about anger and punishment. What if it's more like an amazing demonstration of God's character? That the true way of life is love, forgiveness and sacrifice.' He looked back over his shoulder at the window. 'But when we spin it as being all about punishment, we start thinking God's primary role is to judge and punish us. And shock horror, that's what some Christians end up acting like. Follow a God who majors on judgement, and you major on judgement yourself. Follow a God who majors on love and sacrifice, and you see that instead. I think the Bible shows God as a Trinity . . . as a community of love, and the cross is the ultimate expression of that.' He cleared his throat, conscious he'd been talking for a while. 'So, um yeah . . . in answer to your question . . . that's one of the reasons I left the church.' He caught her eye. 'I suppose as a Christian you'd find all that a little blasphemous. In which case, I apologise. It's just, you asked.'

'It's not blasphemous at all.' She set the glass onto the table and finally said, 'In fact, I take your point. The Father is distasteful. And the cross too . . .'

He cleared his throat. 'Miriam, do you think that Micah shared your distaste for the cross?'

Her eyes flicked to the table, as if a cog was falling into place in her mind.

Matt pressed again. 'Did he?'

'I wouldn't know . . .' Miriam said. 'And just hold your horses, Professor. Just because you make a few interesting points about the Trinity doesn't mean I'm anti-Christianity. I'm as traditional as the next person.'

'But you say you're not a fan of the cross. That's a rather unusual—'

'Course I'm not. No Christian is . . .' She threw up her hands. 'It's what killed Jesus, for Pete's sake.'

'But I'm told that your church in Chervil is quite traditional. They revere the cross. You don't share their theology?'

'Matt,' Wren put her hand up. 'Rein it in.'

He looked at Miriam. 'Listen, I'm not trying to be disrespectful but—'

'Are you sure about that?' She stared off into space like she was suddenly tempted to cry, but Matt could see it, he could *see* it in the way she was holding her jaw, and how she looked back and forth all dramatic and busy-eyed. She even held her side as if her wound was hurting, even though she hadn't needed to do that for the entire evening. She was pretending to look sad, just to wrap the conversation up, but he knew he'd touched a nerve.

Wren had clearly fallen for it. 'Bloody hell, Matt. Stop hounding the woman.' She put a hand on Miriam's forearm. 'I'm sorry. He's drunk too much.'

'That's okay,' Miriam looked at her watch. 'It's getting late any—'

'Why were you in Chesham this morning?' Matt said.

Wren glared at him.

'I told you,' Miriam stood up, 'I wanted updates.'

'Yes, but—'

'That's enough,' Wren snapped loudly. 'I apologise, Miriam, but religion and wine clearly bring out the idiot in my husband.'

'That's okay,' she said. 'But I really better go.'

The two women vanished into the hallway and Matt heard them chatting. When he came out, he saw Miriam throw a huge hug around Wren.

'Miriam, I didn't mean to be hurtful,' Matt said.

She smiled at him, and this one looked genuine. 'You know you may have left Jesus, but he won't leave you. I think you should just accept that he clearly didn't want you to die today. You should thank him for that.' She leant over and kissed Wren on the cheek. 'So remember, prayer time tomorrow night. 8 p.m. at St Bart's. It'd mean a lot to me if you both came.'

'He'll be there,' Wren said then closed the door. Alone

now, she turned and aimed her eyes directly at him. 'You know something . . . you can be a real dickhead sometimes.'

'Wow.'

'Just because you have issues with religion, doesn't mean you have to treat all Christians like they're pieces of dirt.'

'I don't . . . and it's not even like that.'

'Then what the hell is going on with you?' She paused, softened for a second. 'Is it the stress? These last few days?'

'No, it's just . . .' He looked over her shoulder at the door. 'I don't trust her, Wren.'

'But why?'

'Because . . .' He shrugged. 'She can't even look us in the eye.'

'Who cares? She saved your life.'

'And don't you think that's weird? She barely knows me.'

An exasperated breath crossed her lips, then she looked him up and down and shook her head. 'I'm not doing this. I'm going to bed.'

'Fine.'

'And don't come up to talk about it, either.'

'*Fine.*'

He watched her stomp up the stairs then did his own, slightly staggered stomp to the kitchen, so he could swig a glass of water at the sink. The church cross beamed its fire at him. 'Oh, don't you start.' He reached for the blind cord.

And paused.

Around this time last night . . . he thought to himself . . . Sean Ashton was digging a glass into his own wrist . . . right under that black-looking tree, right in the shadow of that damn crucifix that had once felt so beautiful to Matt, so hopeful. The cross his mother loved and ended up dying for. *How can you expect people to believe*, he thought to himself, *when you just stand back and let people die, even your own son?* He snapped the blinds shut.

241

He checked the front door was locked and slow-walked up the stairs. He and Wren passed in the hall. She took a leaf out of Miriam's book and kept her gaze fixed forward.

'Night,' he said. He got back what he expected. Silence.

He brushed his teeth, clicked off the bathroom light and paused when he saw street light seeping through the curtain on the landing. He went to close the gap when something made him open them instead.

Just a touch.

He leant forward and looked down.

Miriam's car. The Rover 200.

It was still in their drive. The bag of liquorice still sat on the dashboard.

He frowned and checked his watch.

Ten minutes had passed since she left, maybe fifteen. Why was her car still here? Then he figured it out. Those few sips of wine had been too much, and she'd called for a taxi home instead. Or worse, walked to the bus stop. They should have called a cab for her and paid for it too. Now her car was taking up their drive.

Then the engine of her car started.

He jumped and pushed back, but then he quickly leant forward, so he could get a better look. His nose hit the glass and he looked down.

She was looking up at him through the windscreen.

His entire body stiffened, and though he wanted to pull himself back again, he didn't. He just noticed how the light made her face look as white as paper. He held her gaze and he wondered why her mouth was moving. Like she was whispering something to him. But then of course, she looked away, and the headlights finally clicked on.

He watched her back out onto the street, and slowly, very slowly, she drove away.

Eventually he crawled into bed, exhausted. Wren was pretending to sleep. He touched her shoulder. An apology. She shrank from it and turned away. He stared at the ceiling, his mind a whirlwind of questions. Sleep was desperate to come, but his busy brain refused it entry. So, he grabbed his phone and the glow filled the room. Wren tutted, so he pulled the covers over his head, and started tapping the screen.

He typed the words: *Old Moat Farm, Nr. Speen*, and there it was. A pixelated dot, floating on its own in a mass of green. He gradually zoomed out, and eventually spotted a long thin black line. An actual road. And then another which led off it, and a B road that led off that. It was quite isolated in one sense, but actually not that far from the surrounding villages. He tapped the phrase *Old Moat Farm* into Google Images, and kept misspelling it repeatedly as his thumb slid and his head bobbed.

He felt the screen touch his forehead and slept.

CHAPTER THIRTY-SIX

There were four of them in the van, with Uncle Dust driving. Prosper sat in the passenger seat, and Ever in between. Milton sat in the back. As they headed up the ridge Ever stared at the wing mirror, where his field, stream, farmhouse, home and everything he knew shrank in the reflection. Then they tipped over the ridge and the black hills split open and devoured it all.

Somewhere in the belly of those hills would be Mum, Pax and Merit. They'd be praying by the fire tonight, with heads and hair resting on each other's shoulders. An all-nighter, Mum had said, with duvets strewn and pillows stacked. There was a version of himself that ached to be there. He called that version of himself 'little boy Ever' and he was the one who hadn't killed a demon last night. It was this version of Ever who kept begging Jesus to make them turn the van around and send him back. That version of Ever said 'Take this cup from me'. But the older Ever, the wiser one, the one who dropped the fire and saved a life . . . that version was quietly sitting here, trying to regulate his breathing. This

Ever knew that sometimes the right thing could be the hardest thing of all.

It took him a long time to pull his eyes from that mirror, and when he did, he saw what he expected to see. A jet-black world swooping around the van. They looked eager, these shadows, and were probably whispering to other shadows, further away, saying *Spread the word! Pass it on . . . Ever is out.*

It was just a waiting game, he knew that. At some point he was bound to see the flash of demonic eyes in the darkness but so far, there was nothing. Once they got through the main front gate, the van rolled up onto the smoothest stretch of road Ever had ever known. Even the tyres fell silent. The headlights fell across two buildings over the smooth road. Not just buildings, either . . . they were houses. The skin of his arms grew into bumps and he stared at the two little cottages passing by. He saw full gardens and chimney smoke and – freakiest of all – glowing windows.

'Hollows live there?' Ever was awestruck. 'Right at the end of our track?'

'Just one or two,' Dust clicked the indicator. 'Most are in the villages and the towns.'

The smooth, silent, unearthly road curved round and he soon saw the distant lights of the next village. Only they weren't so distant any more. Then lights zoomed towards them, loudly whizzing by. It was way too dark to see the creatures behind the wheel, but he wasn't an idiot. Cars didn't drive themselves. There were Hollows hurtling past him, right at this very second, and it was more than just frightening. It was confusing.

'Why don't they drive into us? They could run us into the trees . . .'

'They can't,' Prosper said. 'Jesus is keeping us protected.'

Just as he said that, a Hollow appeared at the side of the road. A thin, lolling creature, leaning over and holding its thumb out.

It held a strange plate of numbers and its cold eyes flashed as the headlight struck its face. Milton suddenly leant through and pushed the steering wheel towards it. 'Watch this, Ever.'

'Hey,' Dust shouted, gripping the wheel. 'Don't.'

Prosper said, 'Milton, he's right. Don't.'

Milton shrugged and let go. Instead of smashing into the Hollow, the van just sprayed dirt all over it instead. Ever watched it in the mirror, glowing red in the tail lights, hopping up and down and raising a claw.

'Speed up,' Ever said. 'It's angry.'

'Angry? That's nothing,' Milton said. 'You know one of the angriest I ever saw was Hope's husband.'

'Wait . . .' Ever's mouth dropped. 'Pax's dad was a Hollow?'

'Course he was. And he got way more angry than that one did. Did some proper bad things to her and Hope. Beat Pax senseless, for a start. Used an old cricket bat, too. When Prosper found them both, Pax's head looked like a squashed tomato. Isn't that right?'

Prosper nodded, silently.

'You know, if Pax hadn't been smacked so much, that girl could have been a doctor or something.'

'She will be, one day.' Prosper turned to the window again. 'Felt good to watch her turn that bat on him.'

Dust cleared his throat. 'Remember, I'm going to have to stop here for diesel. All right?'

Prosper nodded. 'That's fine. We'll be okay.'

Up ahead a very strange large box of lights appeared, with a bright red strip glowing on the roof.

Ever's eyes bulged. 'What is that?'

'It's where we get fuel.'

The indicator clicked, and the van pulled in under a glowing red and yellow roof. Hollows were everywhere. Climbing out of cars, walking the pavements and drinking what could well have been hot blood from steaming cups. He felt his heart shrink like never before as terrifying figures passed the windows. At one point, he even heard the zips of their jackets and coats scrape against the van.

'I suppose we could just kill them all,' Milton said. 'Before they rape us and stuff. We could run them down with the van. Blow this whole place up.'

'Shut up, Milton,' Dust said, just as a laughing demon passed the window. 'Just pray for me, because I have to get out.'

Hands slapped together as Uncle Dust stepped out of the van. Ever watched him chug the fuel in, looking over each shoulder constantly. Thankfully, no Hollows were coming near. Then once he was done, Dust took a deep breath and walked away from the van towards a little glass window. Ever saw something astonishing. His uncle was standing in front of a woman Hollow who sat behind the glass. It smiled at him, and even started to talk.

At the same time, Ever saw a little Hollow girl standing near to Dust. She had long straggled hair, and wore what looked like pyjamas. She chewed her thumb hard and stared at the van, at Ever particularly. He caught her eyes and saw her mouth edge up at the corner. Then she turned and walked through some doors and amazingly, she used her powers to open them without even touching them.

He felt dizzy for a few seconds and realised that he'd looked at that little girl for far too long. He could already feel the corruption of it, the bloom of their clever mind control. His mind was filling with ridiculous, corrupting ideas.

They look just like us, he thought. *It's like they're just people.*

A chill went through him. Then he looked back at Dust who was handing money to the Hollow behind the glass. She said something, and Dust seemed to step back from her. Then he turned and quickly jogged towards the van.

He slammed the door shut and fired up the engine.

'What did it say?' Ever asked. 'You should tell us.'

Dust pulled out onto the main road again. 'It asked if I'd like some chocolate.'

'Huh?'

'I said no.'

They drove the rest of the way in silence, until the van slowed so it could head up a dark, lonely road. For a silly, immature moment, he thought they were back at the farmhouse, heading up their track. But then he saw a very long wall made of stacked stones and large pebbles, and beyond it, a sight more terrifying than anything he'd seen so far.

'Is that . . .' He put a hand across his chest.

Dust nodded. 'It's one of their churches.'

The church cut a black hole in the sky and it had the strangest slope to the roof. Like it was falling down. And right on top was a cross, upright and prominent. It was so blatant. So obvious. Like the murder of Jesus was something to venerate and be thankful for. Like a parent had stabbed their baby to death then mounted the knife on their mantelpiece and wrote songs about how wonderful it was. He felt nauseous, and for a while, terribly sad.

'The church . . . it's so big.'

'Alright, we're here. Everybody out.' Dust parked behind a dark, old house, then they popped the doors open and dropped into the mud outside. But not Ever. For a moment he simply couldn't move. The van door lay wide open, but he was frozen to the passenger seat.

'Okay so we'll just . . .' Dust turned back. 'Ever? It's time to get out.'

Ever stared at the dashboard and felt Dust's reassuring arm patting his knee.

Prosper turned too. 'Right now, Ever. We need to get to the church and pray.'

'We're going in there?'

Dust nodded. 'But we're protected, remember?'

'How do we get in?'

'Hope left us a key,' he said. 'She says it'll be empty all night and all day too. So how about you relax, and we get things ready for Jesus?'

Prosper took a step forward, his voice calm. 'Get out of the van, Ever.'

Ever didn't move. 'Is Hope coming tonight?'

'No,' Dust said. 'In the morning. She's busy tonight.'

'Doing what?'

'Ever . . .' Prosper's voice. Another step.

'Watching over someone . . .' Dust caught the dread in Ever's face and soothed his tone with a smile. 'But hey, just think, this time tomorrow it'll all be over—'

Prosper suddenly exploded. He slammed one hand against the van and with the other he reached up into the van, frantically grasping at his jeans. 'Dammit Ever, I'll drag you out, I'll *drag* you out.'

Dust's jaw dropped, and Ever spasmed against the clawing fingers, 'I'm coming. I'm coming out now. Prosper, I'm sorry.'

Prosper grabbed Ever's jeans and yanked him out, his voice a pure whiplash snap. 'You'll do as you are told and you will pray.'

Ever tumbled from the van and dropped into a clattering heap on the track. His palms slammed into the dirt. Dirt, he realised instantly, which wasn't from his valley. He was deep into the Hollow world now. Touching, smelling and hearing alien things. Around him, what felt like a hundred gigantic trees of pure dark swayed towards him and giggled against the black night.

Prosper got his breath back and ignored Dust's glare. Instead he started walking to the church, one hand swiping back across his bald head, as if he still might have hair there. He did that when he was stressed.

Ever sat there, trying not to cry, though when Uncle Dust hurried to hug him and help him to his feet Ever thought he might just burst into tears. But he quickly reminded himself of an important fact. The frozen boy in the van just now was Little Boy Ever. The real Ever, the true Ever, calmed his heart down and said, *Focus. Breathe. This time tomorrow, this'll all be paradise.* He took his uncle's hand.

They walked in silence as the looming, black monster of a church grew and leant across them. They had to wait for a moment in the porch while Prosper scrabbled under rocks, looking for the key. As he searched, Dust, Milton and Ever stood there in the moonlight, saying nothing. They just watched the breeze pushing and tugging at all these grey and withered flowers that sat scattered in various pots, standing near these weird stone markers that were around the building. Some were shaped like crosses, some had angels on them. All had names. He didn't ask what they were for. He didn't want to know.

Then just as Prosper found the key he heard the breeze again, only this time a voice was on it. A familiar, melodic moaning. It was the voice from the farm. The one that told him to walk down the staircase and offer himself to help. The cold, distant and lonely voice of Jesus, he assumed.

Ever . . . it said . . . *come inside and let me look at you . . .*

Then louder.

Come inside and look at me.

Then the key finally clicked, and the door slowly opened with an animal creak. The others took a breath and hurried inside.

Everrrr . . . loooook . . .

He turned towards the voice coming from the doorway, knowing he was about to see the spirit of Jesus, waiting there. And Jesus was a very tall black shadow, standing in the doorway, curling a finger to welcome him inside.

TUESDAY

THE THIRD DAY

CHAPTER THIRTY-SEVEN

Matt sat in the car, engine running. He'd been here for about three minutes. Maybe even five. Just tapping his fingers on the wheel and listening to the voices in his head. At first it was Wren's voice, or more specifically, her text message. She'd left for work early this morning, so he hadn't seen her all day. But her text was loud enough.

Don't forget. Miriam's invited us to that prayer thing at Chervil at 8 p.m. Don't be late. YOU OWE HER!

Then, he heard the cautious tones of Bowland in his head. She kept telling him to step back from all this and relax. That the last few days had been nothing more than another dip into life's great crapola. To be honest, he'd taken her advice so far. All morning and all afternoon, he'd been living the normal Matt Hunter life. He'd dredged through a pile of work emails and answered annoying student questions like 'please can I submit my coursework as a vlog?' He'd finished a magazine article about the many-breasted statue of Artemis in the Vatican Museum in Rome. His main point:

they weren't really boobs after all. She was laden with bull testicles. Yeah, it'd been a fairly normal morning.

But the main point was that he'd given plenty of time for the police to do their thing. They'd have been to Old Moat Farm by now and if Zara East really was there, she'd know all about her dead son, and nearly dead husband. He just wanted to know why Zara was up there, that was all. And what she might know about Micah and Miriam – two folks who seemed into Jesus but had some issues with eyes and the cross. It wasn't rocket science. It wasn't unreasonable. He just wanted an answer to the very first question of this whole experience. Why did Micah East take an axe to his dad? Besides, David East had specifically asked Matt to pass a personal message to Zara. That the church wasn't crooked. Ironic that he should deliver such words but deliver it he would. It was such a nifty excuse to get up there.

So he shrugged, decision finally made, and pulled out of his drive. Old Moat Farm wouldn't take too—

He slammed the brakes.

Right over at the other end of the road, he saw it again. Miriam's car.

It was sitting at the far side of the church. That damn Rover.

'Right,' he said and surged the car forward, ready to pull up alongside her and stomp right out. But as he drove closer he realised it wasn't hers at all. It just looked like hers. Sitting in the front seat was actually a chunky-looking old man, looking at his fingernails. There was no Miriam sitting in the back. No bag of liquorice on the dash.

He sighed and let the most important voice of all take the lead: the Hal-9000 voice of the satnav. It led him from Chesham, through Great Missenden and then up towards the Chiltern Hills. God it was beautiful up here, with long swooping hills peppered with golf courses. He saw a few little villages which reminded him of Hobbs

Hill – and millionaire houses nestled at the end of long drives. The mad weather was finally playing nice today, so he had the window down. A fat sun baked his arm and a breeze ruffled his hair.

Twenty-five minutes later, the car announced they were on the final main road, but he noticed the signal on his phone grow intermittent. Then it cut out completely. He turned a curve and saw two white cottages at the side of the road. Across from them, a wide wooden gate blocked a dirty track leading up.

He crunched his tyres, stopping right in front of the gate, and stepped out to see a hand-painted sign. KEEP OUT – STRICTLY NO VISITORS. There was no mention of the words 'Moat', or even 'Farm', so he just stared at it, hearing those cautious voices telling him to head back home. But then he heard a series of hard, echoing slaps from across the road.

He turned to see that one of the cottages had its front door open. A white-haired woman was in her garden, smacking a pair of walking boots off the doorstep. Even from here, he saw chunks of dry mud flying everywhere.

Matt hurried over the road, calling out a cheery greeting, 'Nice to see a blue sky again, isn't it?'

The smacking stopped, and the air filled with a Cornish accent. 'Well make the most of it. The radio says it's the only slot of sun we'll get all week. They reckon it's gonna chuck it down, tonight.'

'Shame . . .' He nodded to her boots. 'Been walking in the hills?'

'Yep. Though at my age, it feels more like they walk on me.'

He laughed. 'And have you been walking on that hill?' He jerked a thumb over his shoulder.

'Ooof, no. It's private property is that, and they don't like company neither. Anyway, where are you trying to get to?' She gestured to his car by the gate. 'You're lost, I take it? People never stop here for the view.'

'Actually, I'm looking for a friend. My name's Matt Hunter.'

She doffed an invisible cap. 'Bessie Major. Who's your friend, Mr Matt Hunter?'

'Zara East.' He looked for some recognition in her face and saw none. 'She's a woman, in her fifties, short black hair. I'm told she's staying up on Old Moat Farm. Have you spotted anyone like that at all?'

'Sorry, no.' She shook her head. 'And I reckon if she's gone up there, she'll never come back anyways.'

'That sounds rather ominous.'

She laughed. 'Sorry, I don't quite mean it like that. I mean the folks up there never come out.'

'You mean the man? The one who owns the farm?'

'They all own the farm. There's a bunch of them up there but you never see them. Not since they turned up a good few years back. Took that old place on when it was falling apart. They knew the old owner. I see their van now and again, but not very often. And I hardly ever see them. I thought they was being rude, but my husband said to leave them be. Told me that people like their peace and quiet. He certainly did.'

Matt nodded to the cottage. 'Is your husband inside?'

'I hope not. He's dead.'

He sniffed. 'Sorry to hear that.'

'Don't apologise. He's getting all the peace and quiet he ever wanted up there.' She laughed at herself, then threw a wink up to the clouds. 'Anyway, they've got no telly or anything, is what I heard. Got a couple of nippers too. Keep themselves to themselves. Shame, really.'

'But don't you see them when they go to work? When they take the kids to school?'

'You don't get it. They don't go anywhere. They're religious folk. Got one of those "communities" up there,' she said it with finger quotes. 'Like them Amish types, off the telly.'

Matt leant on her gate. 'Is that so?'

'I suppose you'd call it a commune.' She gave her boot another whack.

'Allow me.' He took the boot and hammered the last chunks of dried mud out.

She folded her arms as he got to work. 'They do this home-schooling thing. Every now and then I spot someone from the government turn up. They check the kids are fed and watered . . . the usuals.'

'How do you know this?'

'Cos one of the inspectors backed her car into ours, years back. I got her chatting, while we sorted the insurance. But other than these little inspections, they're as private as they come up there. Some sort of Christian thing. Bit daft when there's a perfectly good church in the village. There's churches dotted all over these hills.'

'And have you ever popped over to say hi? No cups of sugar?'

'Ha ha!' She threw her head back. 'Don't be daft. I used to see the van leave every couple of weeks, but I stopped waving a hello years ago. There's only so many times you can stand on your front step beaming and waving at folks who won't even look you in the face . . .' She broke off when her cat came strolling past. She leant over and gave its chin a stroke. 'It's Matt, you said?'

'That's right.'

'And is your friend in some sort of trouble, Matt? I only ask because I saw a police car headed up that track, first thing this morning. Tell you the truth, that place has been busier than ever these last few days. Seen the van come back and forth a couple of times. So is this Zara lady . . . is she on the run? Them lot shielding an international art thief, up there?'

He laughed. 'Nothing like that. We have some bad news to share with her. A family tragedy.'

'Oh . . .' Bessie's mischievous grin faded. 'Well, why don't you just head on up? And if you don't come back, I'll assume you got converted.'

Matt looked over at the gate. 'Did the police car come back?'

'Now who's sounding ominous?' She patted the cat on the head and stood up straight. It started slinking against her legs. 'Coppers were there for twenty minutes and that was it. Look. I've got some overpriced gloop to shovel into this underpriced cat. So, if you don't mind.'

He handed her the boot. 'Good to meet you, Bessie.'

'And you. Oh, and tell your friend' – she looked across the road – 'if she ever wants an ear, and a hot cup of tea, there's a daft old lady here with a bucketful of biscuits and lots of time to listen.'

He shook her hand. 'I certainly will.'

He turned to cross the empty road and stood beside his car. The 'No Entry' sign shook a little in the breeze.

Some sort of Christian group . . . he thought. *A religious community* . . .

His heart upped its pace as he started to undo the rope on the gate.

CHAPTER THIRTY-EIGHT

Ever felt a kiss on his forehead and his eyes fluttered open.

He yawned and peeled a puffy cheek from the cold, church carpet. Uncle Dust had called this the choir vestry, saying this was where the Hollows prayed their most hollow prayers. Light streamed through the dirty window, and in the corner he saw something super weird. A rail of white robes, hanging like a rack of ghosts. This was for when they'd wear dresses to mock the power of Jesus. It was so shocking.

Even though he hated this room, it was way less disturbing than being out in the huge church that lay on the other side of that old wooden door. That was the biggest room he'd seen in his entire life, with ceilings that could break clouds. They'd crept around in there last night, praying and weeping and letting out their final laments – only they did them as quietly as possible. And mostly in the dark too, so as not to draw attention. Thankfully he hadn't seen that shadow again, which made him think it was just how the light fell. At least, that was the theory he was clinging to with most enthusiasm.

After praying for a few hours last night, they'd all slept in here, with one person on watch every few hours. Apart from him, of course. He was told to sleep and keep his energy, and he must never, ever leave the side of the grown-ups.

He blinked and rubbed his eyes, then froze.

Something was making a noise behind him. A breath, slowly drawing in, and slowly pushing out. He turned and jerked in fright.

Hope sat on her knees, a foot away from him. 'Did my kiss wake you?'

He stared at her.

'Ever? Aren't you going to say hello?'

He pushed back a little.

'Come now . . .' Her smile twitched. 'Why aren't you looking in my eyes?'

He waited. Said nothing.

She put a hand on the carpet and started to crawl slowly towards him.

'It's just—'

She stopped. 'Yes?'

'You've been living with them so long.'

She tilted her head. 'And you think I might have changed, is that it? Become like them?'

'You've been gone for ever.'

'A few months is not for ever, Ever.' She smirked and crawled forward for one more knee drag.

'But . . . but are you okay?'

'Don't I look okay?'

A table leg pressed into his back. 'I . . . I . . .'

'I missed you, Ever. I missed all of you. But what I really want to know is, how's my little Pax? I missed her most of all.'

'You avoided their eyes for months?'

She started laughing. 'Oh, I'm way stronger than you think and so are you. I mean look at you . . . coming down here with the big men. Ready to fight.' She wrapped her hand around his toes. 'And to think we were messing with Micah East, when Jesus had you in mind all along. It's all so perfect.'

'Uncle Dust says I have to kill another Hollow.'

Her eyes flashed. 'I'm very much looking forward to it.'

'And after that it'll all be—'

'Look me in the fucking eye, Ever!' She yanked his foot.

He twisted, fell back, and his shoulders smashed against the floor. He heard her hands and fingers gallop along the carpet and stop near his shoulders. She pushed her face into his. 'Look at me. *Look*.' He felt one of her thumbs, clumsily try to prise his eyelids back open. Then she let out a breath. 'Where's your faith?'

Her thumbs were gone. She pulled herself off him.

'I'm sorry,' he said.

'Faith makes a family, remember? So you need to trust me.'

'I know.' He waited, then he sucked his lips in. 'Pax talks about you every day.'

She closed her eyes. 'She does?'

The door creaked open.

'Hey, Ever, you need—' Prosper broke off instantly and ran across the room, throwing his arms around her. They tumbled onto the floor together. 'Hope!' he laughed. 'I never saw you come in.'

For a moment they were lost in brief, open-eyed kisses. Ever looked away and saw Uncle Dust standing in the doorway, feigning sickness and jabbing a finger down his throat. They both laughed, silently.

'I came in the back, just now,' she said, then eventually clambered to her feet. 'God, it's good to hear my name again. If I hear Miriam one more time, I'll scream.'

'Did Milton find you all right this morning?'

'Yes. He's watching over Matthew right now.'

Dust bit his lip. 'And you're absolutely sure the police won't come back here?'

'Relax. The police have all they need. And besides, I'm the only one here on a Tuesday.' She held up a little swinging set of keys. 'Cos today's my volunteer cleaning day. They think I'm dusting off the altar, but I thought I might slide my bare arse off it, instead.'

The men burst into laughter. Ever did the same.

'So, have a little faith, Dust,' she giggled. 'We're safe. And tonight, it all comes together.'

'So, you've kept this Hollow safe?'

'Haven't I just?' She hitched her jumper up to show the white bandage, taped across the curve of her hip.

Prosper's jaw dropped. 'What the hell is that?'

'I got shot.'

'What?' Ever gawped.

'A fat, floppy Hollow tried to kill Matthew, so I had to stop it, didn't I? Had to save him for us. So, I um . . . I stood in the way of the bullet.'

They stared at her.

Prosper whispered, 'Your faith is . . . well . . . it's just magnificent.'

'I can't lie. I was scared; in fact, I was petrified. But I had no choice. And listen, Jesus was there the whole time. He said it'd be okay, and it was. When he swatted that bullet away it showed me something . . .' She moved her gaze to each of them. 'That he's obviously in this, I can feel it. We're doing the right thing. As crazy as it sounds, we're doing the right thing.'

'Wait.' Dust's eyebrows drew together. 'Why did a Hollow want to kill Hunter?'

She ran both palms down her jeans. 'Because I had to kill its son, and Matt kind of got the blame. It saw me—'

'You killed someone?' Dust's mouth dropped.

'Some*thing*,' she corrected him. 'It saw me watching over Matt's house and said it was going to tell. What choice did I have?' Her face grew cold when Dust didn't respond. 'I said what fucking choice did I have? They would have found the farmhouse through me. And you'd all be back in your dark places. Especially you, Dust. You'd be getting buggered by a Hollow in the common room, just like the old days—'

'Shhhh,' he said quickly. 'Fine. You did the right thing.'

'Yes, I did. Which means tonight, those Hollows are going to fall up into the sky. For now though, me and Prosper need to get a few things ready, but Dust, you stay with Ever. And if he doesn't know everything, then tell him now.' The two of them vanished into the wide gaping cavern of the church, kissing as they went. Then the door creaked shut. For a moment Dust didn't say a word.

Ever broke the silence. 'Will the Hollows really fall tonight?'

'Well, that's what we believe, isn't it?'

'Do you believe it?'

He didn't answer. He looked away.

'Well, do you?'

'Yes, it's just . . . don't mind me . . .'

'Why . . . what's the problem?'

Dust walked quietly to the door and made sure it was shut. 'No big problem. It's just last night, when we got petrol, something happened . . .'

Ever's skin prickled.

'When I paid the woman at the counter. She looked at me.'

He groaned. 'For how long?'

'A while. She looked really . . . normal. Like any of us.'

'But she's not normal.'

'But she really seemed normal.'

'Not deep down.'

He waited. 'You're right. Deep down she . . . *it* is a monster . . .' He shook his head. 'It's amazing, though, isn't it? How a little glance can make you wonder. It's a very clever trick they do. But I looked away and I'm getting back on track now.'

He thought of the little girl, smiling at him. 'Why didn't you watch me kill the Hollow on the farm? You didn't celebrate—'

'Ever . . .'

'You even looked sorry for that thing.'

He grabbed his hand. 'I said, I'm fine, okay? I'm fine.'

'And is Hope fine?'

He frowned.

'What if she's changed? We've been away from the farm for ages. What if you've changed, or me, even . . .' He took a breath, frightened of his own doubts. 'And who is this Hollow, anyway? This . . . Matt Hunter?'

That question plunged the room into an even deeper silence, and Uncle Dust just walked to the window and stared out. Rain trickled down the pane.

'Well?'

Uncle Dust took a long breath in, and finally turned. 'He's your dad, Ever.'

Ever laughed at that. He actually tilted his head back in a chuckle, but Dust wasn't smiling, so the laughter died away. In fact, Uncle Dust looked like he had a great pain in his head because he kept pressing it with his fingers.

'Well . . . that's silly.'

'Why?'

'Because he can't be . . .'

'Why not?'

'Because he's Hollow.'

Dust sighed. 'Hope's dad was Hollow. Prosper's too. Pax's father certainly was . . .'

'And yours? Was he Hollow?'

266

'Extremely so,' Dust said. 'But that doesn't change who I am. Or who you are.'

'He's my dad?' Ever put a hand across his mouth. 'Does Mum know?'

For the first time, Dust laughed. 'Course she does, that's how it works. But listen . . . he's nothing but a rotten-hearted, Jesus-hating beast and he even used to run one of these churches. Probably turned a thousand people away from Jesus.'

'So, he's powerful . . .'

'Yes, he is, but listen to me . . . none of that matters because we're your family now. Do you understand? And Jesus is with us.'

Just as he said that, the window started to rattle. Something was hitting it hard and loud. And as they both watched it, the tension in Dust seemed to slip away. 'Wow.'

'What is it?' Ever said.

'It's . . . it's hail . . .' His smile slowly – and brilliantly – started to form again. 'You know, I think I might be just a silly old fool who needs to read the signs. Because the earth declares the glory of Christ, and the skies proclaim the work of his hands. Look . . .'

They had to open the door in the end, just to see it. A billion balls of ice hammered the church. Each chunk bounced in springing arcs from the grass and gravestones. He'd never seen anything like it. None of them had. At one point, the hailstones were so rapid and heavy that the rattle grew into a thunderous roar and Ever covered his ears. But the louder it got, the bigger he smiled. And Dust too. Even Prosper and Hope rushed to see it and they did something next that made Ever cry, because it showed him who his true family was, and whatever this Hollow may be was totally irrelevant. Hope rushed out into the hail and started to dance in whirling circles around the graves. Then Prosper joined her, and so did Dust and Ever. The hail hurt, but they carried on dancing.

'See,' Prosper shouted. 'The heavens know.'

Ever sniffed, and Dust wiped his cheeks, as they both stared at what sat in Prosper's hands. A marvellous, beautiful sign of a universe in panic. An ice ball was already melting in the cup of his palm, fresh from a dying heaven.

CHAPTER THIRTY-NINE

It took a while for Matt to make it all the way to Old Moat Farm. Longer than he expected. The dirt track ran between a couple of hills, and it was so uneven the entire chassis of the car rocked horribly. It didn't help that there were tiny shards of glass scattered at the base of a low wall, either. He had to slip up on the ridge to fully avoid them.

He pondered as he drove, realising that he had no idea if Zara East would still be up here. The police had already visited, so she might be back in Chervil by now, hopefully at David East's hospital bed. It'd be good if they patched things up. If at least something positive came from all this despair.

He headed up the slight incline, wondering if it'd be best to park and walk the rest of the way, but then he pictured an Amish family on a farmhouse porch, all black hats and white bonnets, hiding pitchforks under floor-length beards. They might see his car and wail 'Satan has cometh!' Or more likely, it'd be an everyday farmer rising from a bush and shooting him with a rifle. Nah. He'd had enough of bullets this week. He wouldn't walk, he'd stay in the car till the very last minute.

He saw the bonnet rise up as he hit the top of a ridge, and then the car tipped down to a wide, swaying field. It looked like it was tilled and prepped for spring planting. Though to be honest, he knew sod all about farming. He wondered if the recent bizarre weather might help or hinder growth. At least that epic hailstorm had stopped. That was so balls-out intense he'd thought he might lose a headlight. He even parked for a minute just to film it on his iPhone.

As well as a field, he saw a trickle of a stream to the far right and a patch of trees hanging over the water. But at the very end of the dirt road sat a little farmhouse, with white walls and thick, heavy beams. Wow, he thought. Developers must be frothing at the mouth to snap this patch of land up. They could build another Lego-set housing estate up here. Or failing that, rent this place out as a holiday home. True, the house looked tired and in desperate need of a *Grand Designs* visit. Probably a double episode. But the location was amazing and deceptive too. It was the quietness and rise of the hills that did it. Old Moat Farm felt like it was in the middle of nowhere, a hundred miles from civilisation. Certainly not a mere mile from a bustling little town with a gastro pub and a Tesco Express. Which it was. Yes, Matt thought. If the Amish-style commune project went tits up, they'd at least make a killing turning all this into a trendy glamping site.

He pulled his car in next to an old metal shed, tyres sliding into a puddle of ex-hail. Then he took a breath and checked his fringe in the mirror (important to get that right, in new situations – God, he really was nervous). He stepped out and immediately almost tripped on a rope. It lay in a thick bundled heap by the shed door. He stepped over it, breathed the air in and listened to the birds. He briefly considered commune life as a potential but serious life choice. Then he walked towards the farmhouse, ready to stick his hands in the air if a gun came pointing out. He shook his head. He'd be fine. He just knew it. He headed up the little path, lovingly lined with pebbles on each side. Each in contrasting colours, dark and light in turn. It must have taken ages to do that. It was all so intricate. He also saw a bunch of bamboo poles sticking out of the ground. For growing some sort of climbing plant, maybe? Or for hanging their tall black hats and buckled shoes?

Okay. The plan.

He'd ask for Zara East, straight out. If they said the police had already been, he'd say, 'Yes, I know. But I have a personal message from her husband . . . the church isn't crooked.' If they got shirty with him, he'd put up his hands, and say 'Hey, don't shoot the messenger, and by that of course I really mean don't shoot the messenger.' Then he'd chat a little more and ask about their beliefs. He'd act all fascinated. He'd want to hear more. He'd do the starry-eyed look of your classic, spiritual-seeker, and if they told him off for trespassing he'd apologise and say the gate was wide open and he saw no sign. Blame it on those pesky police who popped in earlier.

He put his foot on the porch step and the wood instantly creaked beneath him. He thought he heard a commotion from inside, though it could have been the breeze against a window shutter. He looked up. The house had no shutters. Heart ticking fast, he tapped a knuckle on the door. He waited. Tried again.

'Hello,' he called out, in as friendly a voice as he could muster. 'I just have a message to pass on, then I'll be on my way.'

He heard nothing inside. He knocked again.

'I have an important, personal message for Mrs Zara East, which I'm sure she'd be keen to know. I understand she's staying here?' He knocked. A little harder, this time. 'Hello?'

A noise came through the wood, proving there really were people in there. The whine of a child – a very young one, from the sound of it. The cry started sharp and loud but was quickly lost in a rumbled muffle. The way the sound changed made him picture a hand sliding across a toddler's mouth.

'I'll just wait out here till you're ready to come out. No worries at all. It's a lovely day.' He stood at the door, hovering for an entire minute before he prepped his knuckle for one more smack. He paused in mid-air when the locks in the door suddenly rattled and slid on the other side. It slowly creaked open, but only for a hand's width. A face didn't appear in the gap, but an ear did. Not an eye, but an ear.

'Hiya,' Matt said. 'Beautiful day, isn't it?'

'What do you want?' A woman's voice.

'I'm sorry but I can't quite hear you,' he lied. 'If you could just look out of the door?'

He got the distinct sense of whispering voices, then the face turned a little until half a mouth and half a nose were visible. A single eye looked out now, but it was firmly fixed on his shoes, not his face. She had a scarf tied around her throat. It looked painfully tight. 'You've already been this morning.'

She thinks I'm with the police, Matt thought. He was in no rush to change that. 'Yes, but I'd like to speak to Zara.'

'I told you people already. She doesn't live here any more.'

'Is that so? Since when?'

'Since over a month back.'

'I see. I was told she may be living—'

'Goodbye.'

Matt pushed a hand against the closing door. 'Then where is she now?'

'She left us. She didn't believe any more.'

'Ah, well that's a real shame, isn't it? Too many people are losing faith these days.' Matt pushed the door a little more. 'You know, I'm fascinated by your beliefs. Would you be willing to tell me—?'

'Please, go.'

'But—'

'You're scaring me.'

'I'm just looking for answers. For guidance.'

Finally, she looked up and caught his face at last. Which was the strangest moment of all, because when that single eyeball finally rolled up, she gasped with fright and actually stumbled back. 'Why are you here?' she said.

'Wait.' He caught her face, or at least one side of it. 'You know me?'

She crunched her eyes shut.

'Hang on a sec . . .' He frowned. 'Haven't I met you before?'

The door shoved hard against Matt's hand, but this time it was way harder than this woman could do alone. Someone else was behind the door, too. His arm snapped back, and the door slammed hard in its frame. He stepped back, looking up at the house, searching for a face in the window. He saw nothing. His mind flipped through the files, trying to place the woman's face, but he came up with nothing. Maybe she just had one of those generic looks that you see all the time.

He let out a breath and headed back down the steps to his car, then his shoe left the gravel path and hit wet dirt. It was like pressing a button on the world. A fierce and howling breeze suddenly rolled across the hill. He could see and hear it approach, flattening the sprouts of grass so it could slide a wave up into his body, face and fringe. He considered marching back to the door and demanding they open – then he remembered that stalkers and psychopaths do that sort of thing. Best to leave it for now. But at least he had something here. Something new. These guys were some quirky religious group who didn't like eye contact, and what's more they recognised him.

But how?

Confused, but relishing the puzzle of it all, he climbed into the car. Then he checked his rear-view mirror for a three-point turn, so he could head back the way he came. He reversed backwards, turned and noticed himself parallel with the metal shed. Which is when he saw it. Something was tucked behind it, out of view from the main track.

Just behind the shed was a large sheet of dark-green tarpaulin, stretched across something big. It was obvious what it was, too. There was a car under there. He knew it because this sudden, wailing wind was lifting the edge. He could even see what type of car it was. It was a smashed one. There were heavy scrapes down the side, and the front grille and bumper were warped and folded.

Yet it wasn't the ruined state of the metal that made Matt get out of his car again. It was what the helpful wind showed him, as it lifted the tarp higher still, just for a split second. Enough to show a strip of a colour that seemed at odds with the white paint of the doors. That's what made him move. The browny-red streak and splatter that seemed to spill down the driver's door in long crusty rivers. It made no real sense until he'd grabbed the tarpaulin and lifted it higher.

What he saw made him drop the tarp instantly.

'Oh . . .'

He wasn't consciously aware he was staggering backwards until his spine smacked into the door of his car. The tarp was back in place, but it didn't matter much. What he'd witnessed was now etched in his mind. Another Grand Guignol act to add to the growing cast of his nightmares. He fumbled for the door handle behind him, then sense shocked him into life. He shot his eyes towards the front of the house, and then the back, where a long, empty washing line danced in the whistling breeze. What if they all came running around from both sides, clambering over each other to pull him inside?

Crap.

He realised he was pulling at the passenger door. He gulped and rushed around to the driver's side. He jumped behind the wheel, locking the door behind him. Locked all the doors, in fact. He was so disorientated that it was impossible to avoid wheel-spinning. Chunks of mud churned and sprayed behind him, and for a horrifying second he was both incredibly noisy and horribly stationary. He heard the front door of the house slam open.

The tyres slipped and slid.

Shit.

He heard voices yelling and porch boards rattling.

Shit.

The back of the car seemed to swing to the right a little, and he had to look back over his shoulder to see if there were fifty of them, grabbing the car to stop it moving. But the turning tyres had only slipped up and out of the puddle. He got traction suddenly and the whole car lurched forward. He cleared the shed and threw a glance up to the left of the farmhouse where a panicked face stared out through an upstairs window. A terrified child was smacking her palms off the glass.

Jesus.

The car skidded up the track as women's voices hollered and wailed behind him. He only got distracted once: by a small metal hut at the top of a hill. A winding path of stones led up to it. Then he checked his mirror again and saw two figures running behind the car, mud was spattering their long skirts with every step. Then, knowing it was useless, he saw both women drop to their knees and scream at the sky.

The car bounced hard across the dips and holes, but he saw no other car coming after him. He just knew he had to call the police as soon as possible. They had a petrified little kid in there who looked like she was screaming for her life. He'd left the gate wide open before, just to make it easier when he headed back out. That little move saved him precious seconds, as he ploughed the car through. He felt, and heard, the front bumper scrape against the empty main road, then he was up onto the wonderful Nirvana of tarmac.

He grabbed his phone. *Dammit. Still no signal.* He held the phone up, waving it around for some sort of reception. Nothing. Panicked, he looked up and saw the old lady Bessie emerging from her doorway. She was shouting something, between cupped hands.

He buzzed the window down.

She shouted, 'What's going on?'

He called out across the road. 'Bessie, do you have a phone?'

'Course, I have a—'

He spun his wheels into instant reverse and rolled back off the tarmac. He backed against the gate, clipped the side of it, and heaved the car back until it clamped the gate hard into its frame, probably smashed it too. Either way, it was a nifty move. They'd not get a car out of there in a hurry. He leapt from his seat and sprinted towards her house.

'Young man, this is not Formula One.'

He looked back and saw nothing, but he heard their distant groans rising on the wind, and the sound made him shiver. They were coming. From the corner of his eye, he was sure he saw something else too, and he gasped. Was that Miriam's Rover, parked way down the track?

'Get inside. I need your phone,' he said. 'And lock the door.'

CHAPTER FORTY

Wren stood at the lounge window, watching the sky turn dark. Both hands were wrapped around a coffee, and she sipped at it slowly, listening to the rain crackle against the glass. Her eyes kept moving back and forth between the clock on the wall and the blackness of the clouds. Clock, clouds, clock, clouds. Both were always there. The one other constant was the element that wasn't there when it should be.

Matt.

Lucy was sprawled on the sofa, scrolling through her phone, but she set it aside and propped herself up on her elbow. 'Mum. Why don't you just call it off?'

'I can't. I won't.'

'But the weather's getting awful.'

'That's not stopping you going out . . .'

'That's different. That's the cinema. I'm not going to a crumbly old church. With no heating, I bet.'

'Yeah . . . well, it's just rain.' She turned from the window. 'Besides . . . I've already booked a babysitter for Amelia.'

'All so my parents can go to a prayer meeting?' She tapped a finger against her temple. 'Can you hear that? It's the sound of my mind, boggling. You're really going to go?'

'After what she did? Absolutely.'

'But will you actually pray?'

'Dunno,' she shrugged. 'Might give it a whirl.'

'Well Dad won't. He'll probably burst into flames.'

Wren smiled at her. How refreshing that she was back calling Matt Dad again. At least for now. 'Well, I reckon Dad'll just treat it like a research trip and he'll cough when he's supposed to say "Amen" so it doesn't count.'

That's assuming he ever turns up, of course. She grabbed her phone and tried Matt's number yet again. It went straight to voicemail.

Hey, this is Professor Matt Hunter, but alas I can't come to the—

Pfft. She waited for the answer tone. 'Matt . . . hi. Listen, I keep leaving messages because the babysitter's arriving in a bit and Lucy's going out soon after. I know you said you're following up this police thing, but you better be on your way, because we have to make an appearance at Chervil. And Matt . . . bear in mind that if you don't call me back . . . I will shoot you myself.' She clicked it off.

'Marriage is brutal,' Lucy said.

Wren turned back to the window, and the room was silent for a while. Just rain.

'Mum?' Lucy's hand touched her shoulder. 'I bet it's just the weather holding him up.'

'Maybe,' she said. *Or maybe*, she thought, *my husband is just way more selfish and prejudiced than I ever thought.* She stared as the rain raged on and saw her own glum face staring back at her. She saw a silent flash of light in the distance, but though she waited for the sound, it never came.

CHAPTER FORTY-ONE

Matt slammed Bessie's front door shut, turned, and squinted through the red circle of glass in it. He saw no sign of them. No figures running down the track.

'You need to lock this . . .' he said. 'Bessie? I said you need to lock this.'

He turned to see her standing in the hallway, panting. One of her hands was splayed against some daffodil wallpaper, the other on her chest.

'Hey. Are you okay?'

'Young man, I've barely met you. So if you think I'm locking myself in with—'

He took another quick look through the window. 'Then where's your phone?'

She jabbed a fat finger at the lounge. 'But be careful of my ornaments.'

'Keep an eye on the gate and tell me if anybody comes down their track. You're sure you're okay?'

'I'm fine. But what's going on over there?'

'Murder, from the looks of it.'

Her jaw dropped a little and he actually saw her grey-looking dentures settle into place.

He left her and scanned the lounge for her phone. It took a split second to picture her sitting in here. The high-backed chair by the crackling fire, the bargain TV and the digital radio. The circular table with a doily and teacup and two Sports biscuits lying on a plate – both were high jump. He never even knew you could still get those. And a large print cowboy novel called *Chimaroo*, open at the spine.

One second later, he saw the little grey phone resting in its cradle. It had huge, easy-to-see numbers, and it stunk of perfume. He quickly jabbed Bowland's number. He waited, hearing the low tick of her mantelpiece clock. 'Bessie?' he called out. 'See anything?'

'Just your car blocking their gate in. Bet you've buggered their fence up. Oh, and the bumper on your—'

Bowland's voice buzzed into his ear. 'Matthew?'

'Listen to me. You've got to get up to Old Moat Farm.'

'Huh?'

'Send police to Old Moat—'

'Calm down, we've been there already. Zara left a month ago—'

'Get back here now, there's a body . . .'

A moment of silence. 'I beg your pardon?'

'There's a shed near the house—'

'You're *there*?'

'Just now. I found a smashed-up car covered in tarpaulin.'

'Why the hell are you there?'

'Listen!' he shouted. 'I found a car by the shed, and inside it, I saw a corpse. Do you hear me? There's a fucking cadaver, Jill. So, no, I won't calm down.'

Her breath crackled into the phone, clearly on the move. 'Who is it?'

'I've got no idea. A man. Early twenties, maybe.'

'And how do you know he's actually dead?'

'Cos somebody's scooped both of his eyeballs out. Is that enough?' He caught his breath. 'And get this . . . there's at least two women in the house, and I saw a little girl up at the window, looking terrified. All this while a body rots outside. So get here now, all right? Swoop in. Cos those two women are coming for me.'

'Where are you calling from?'

'Mr Hunter?' Bessie's voice sounded higher. Panicked.

'Give me your location, Matt.'

'One sec.' He rushed into the hall to see why she'd called for him, the phone still clamped to his ear. She didn't need to explain because he saw it over her shoulder, through the red-tinted glass. Two figures were sprinting across the road, towards them. Their dresses were flailing, either from the wind or sheer speed.

'Shit, *shit*.' Matt pressed his mouth to the phone. 'Listen, we're in a little cottage, across—'

It's all he could say, because a hand reached out of nowhere and swatted the phone against the wall. The plastic shattered and he noticed a breeze that wasn't there before, icing up his shoulder. The back door of the kitchen was half-open. Matt felt two hands shove him forward, and he toppled to his knees.

Bessie screamed, 'Get out of my house!'

He tried to turn, to see who had pushed him, but the two women's faces suddenly filled the little red window in the door, eyes wild, heads flailing. The door handle started yanking up and down rapidly. Bessie tried to hold it, but she wasn't strong enough. The door heaved inwards.

He sprang forward to help her, but Bessie shouted, 'Leave my stick alone. That's *my* stick! It's *mine*.' He knew what that meant soon enough, when something long and sharp smacked off Matt's shoulders. His arms gave way. His chest hit the pink fluffy carpet and he belched out air. He saw Bessie stagger forwards, hands flailing, skin white. Her teary panic fixated on the stick. 'That's mine! It's *mine*.'

The women started slowly pushing through, and Matt saw the fire of daylight throw a very thin, long line on the carpet. The opening door hit Betty right in her hip. She stumbled away from it and fell against the wall and quickly slid down it. Then the strip of light grew fat and wide, and Matt saw the women's hands, curling around the door frame like mad spiders, filling the gap, eating all that sunlight away.

His shoulders were stinging, absolutely throbbing, so he flipped himself over to stop that damn stick from hitting him again. He saw a man standing over him in the hallway. He wasn't what Matt expected. He assumed it'd be Jason Statham, all skinhead and uber-tight muscle-top, but he saw a man in his sixties looking like a veteran sailor, or an old boxer, with a wild mop of grey hair and a heavy knitted jumper hanging. And while Matt expected the guy's face to be all anger and violence, he saw something else instead. Sheer, blind panic. The old boxer's wrinkled, puffed-up eyes darted to a million places, and he swayed on his feet, gasping, while Matt heard an odd, unexpected sound from outside. The wailing scream of a child, scurrying through the back door.

'I just called the police.' Matt nodded at the shattered phone. 'They know my location. They'll be here any second.'

The man shot out a hand to steady himself against the wall. 'Jesus . . .'

'So, it's pointless, isn't it?' Matt pointed to Bessie's walking stick, still clamped in the man's hand. 'So, it'd be better for you if you just put that down.'

One of the women spoke from behind him. And her voice sounded strange and childlike. 'Don't listen to it, Milton. Got claws. Got worms in its eyes. Look. A liar, liar.'

Then the other woman, the one with the neck scarf, spoke much clearer, but her voice was riddled with panic. 'Milton, we've got to go right now.'

Slowly, Matt turned to see Bessie wheezing on the floor, and realised that for her sake, it'd be best to just let these nutters go. The police would catch them in the end. Forget the grab-the-stick plan. Forget the big rescue.

But none of them were leaving yet. The old man just kept staring at Matt's legs.

'Milton . . .' The second woman again, who really did look familiar. She shouted it, incredibly loud. '*Now.*'

The old man groaned. 'Let's get it in the car.'

Wait. What?

'I'll get its legs. Grab his arms. We'll bundle it in.'

Matt bolted forward on all fours and lunged into Milton's legs. He took two handfuls of the old coot's mud-spattered jeans and started dragging his body down. The guy screamed, and Matt landed a punch in his groin. Impact. The guy let out a wet gasp of breath and scraped his nails down the wall. Sharp enough to tear a gaping triangle of wallpaper. Matt reached for the walking stick but then two pairs of female hands were on him, pushing him down. And another moment, a sensation that chilled him the most, the feel of that little girl who he'd seen at the window. She was helping them. Her hands were grabbing his hair, helping to pull him down.

Milton whacked him with the walking stick again right on the back of his neck. Pain burst across his shoulders. Then another smack, just where the sun don't shine. He shouted into the carpet, 'Where's Zara East? Where is she?'

'Make it quiet,' one of them said. 'Hit it hard.'

Furious and desperate, Matt roared, 'Where is she?' Deliriously thinking that his anger might fill him with power, he tried to grab them again, but the stick smacked against his fingers and head and the white hot pain mushroomed across his body. Bessie hadn't said anything for a while. Strength faded. His split, throbbing knuckles started trickling.

They slipped something round his wrists.

'She ran away, if you must know . . .' Milton shouted, as they tied Matt up. 'Said she'd bring the whole world on us cos of what we were planning. And look, she has! That vicious little slut . . . she *has*.'

'Milton, there's no time.' The woman again. Desperate. 'We've got to get him to Chervil. Get the car.'

'Okay. Right. I'll bring it round now.'

Matt tried to pull his hands apart, but he couldn't. Tried his feet too and couldn't.

He felt a deep, profound panic bloom, just then. That he hadn't managed to finish his conversation with Bowland on the phone, to tell her to call Wren straight away, and to insist that under no circumstance must she go to Chervil church tonight. But even the panic of that thought seemed to drown, just as the light faded.

The last thing he heard, as his brain powered down, was when one of the women said, 'For crying out loud, cover its eyes.'

And then the old man said, 'No . . . it's okay. It's closing them anyway. Praise Jesus. Look. It's closing them anyway.'

CHAPTER FORTY-TWO

They'd dried the melting hail from their bodies with the white robes from the vestry. It felt fitting and wonderfully symbolic to take the mocking dresses of the Hollows and turn them into towels. They scrubbed the holy garments into their hair and blew their nose into them too. Prosper shoved one down his trousers and marched in a circle. Everybody laughed. Then they scrunched them up and tossed them into a corner where they sat crumpled and damp, as pathetic as they always were.

The amazing hailstorm, bigger than any of them had seen before, was a wonderful touch from Jesus. A rapid and timely reminder that they weren't alone. After that, they'd spent a good hour prepping the church. He helped line up all the candles then watched Uncle Dust light each of them in turn. Every new flame unleashed a horde of monstrous shadows.

At one point, Prosper asked Ever to give him a hand with some rope. There was a thick and heavy pile of it in the van. When they went outside to get it the sky had turned crazy dark – a mixture of the coming night and the thickest storm clouds he'd ever seen. It looked terrifying up there and he tried not to look at it. They dragged all that rope into the church and he tried not to think about how much of it there was. This special Hollow must be seriously powerful. When he asked about it, Prosper just smiled and said, 'Don't worry about it.'

At one point Prosper almost slipped, carrying a metal bucket from the van to the altar. He dumped it on the stone floor and a twirling puff of black powder burst up from it.

'What's in there?' Ever asked.

'What's left of that Hollow you burnt,' he grinned. 'Milton scooped it up with a shovel. Wanna see?'

Ever closed his eyes. 'No, thank you.'

He looked around the church instead, staring at the long, dark and painful benches that the Hollows liked to sit on. It all looked very glum and cold, except for one little section near the back. That part had bright, curvy chairs with happy yellow-face cushions. Instead of icy stone, the floor was covered with a sweet little carpet of roads and fields. The walls were different in this part too. Crayon pictures draped the wall, scrawled by the Hollow children. They showed Jesus healing the sick, feeding the five thousand. walking on water . . . all the really great stuff. Which made it all the more infuriating to see what the death-obsessed adults preferred in their art. The rest of the church had paintings of Jesus being beaten with a whip and carrying his cross while crowds cheered. They'd even made the large back window show a giant Jesus dripping on a cross, while the Father rejoiced in heaven.

It was baffling to see how the Hollows could get the Lord so wrong, while their kids appeared to have gotten him so right. The first thing he'd do, once this was all over, would be to tear down all those paintings glorifying death, and he'd stick up the kids' pictures instead. Plaster the whole church with them and throw smiling cushions on the altar too.

But not now. Because now they were stuffing all that rope under the altar, hiding it with the white sheet. Once that was in place, Prosper put a hand on his shoulder and dropped to the floor next to him. 'I have something to show you. It's in the kiddies' section. The bit you keep looking at. Come on.'

They walked back up the aisle and Prosper sat cross-legged on the roadmap carpet. 'I notice you're enjoying their pictures. So, I want you to see one that I drew myself, last night.' Prosper reached for a large sheet of paper tucked into the bookshelf. He placed the sheet on the carpet and pressed his palm into the centre.

Ever stared at it. 'It's blank.'

'That's cos it's upside down, ya dingbat.' He smiled. One of his gentle ones. 'I drew this for you, Ever. Just for you.'

'Is it Jesus?' he smiled. 'What's he up to this time?'

'Crikey, it's not Jesus.' Prosper shook his head slowly. 'Hope just thinks it's time you saw one.'

The hair on his arms bristled.

'You know all those Hollows we've seen so far,' Prosper said, 'they look like us on the outside. But not if you peel the skin away.'

'I know that.'

'But you've never actually seen one, have you?'

He stared at the paper and shook his head.

'Do you want to see?'

He heard the sound of his own breath. He shook his head again.

'It's not a choice.' It was Hope, sitting in one of the creaking pews. He hadn't seen her before.

He saw her rise to her feet then stride between them, as tall as a tree, with her eyes rolled down. Then the tree sank to be with him, and a coldness from the sky came with it. 'You have to know what you're dealing with.'

He turned back to Prosper, 'How many have you seen? I mean, without their disguise.'

'I've seen a couple, without their skin on. Hope's seen more.'

'Plenty more,' she said.

'But I drew this one the best I can, cos this is what you'll be killing tonight. And when you do, we'll walk in the world, and we won't have to hide—'

'And Pax . . .' Hope trailed off. 'My Pax'll be clever again. So you'll do it, won't you? You won't let her down?'

He wanted to reach over and touch her hand. He felt like that might be the right thing to do, for a woman who so often wept over Pax. But he didn't want to touch her that much, so he just said, 'I won't let her down. Or any of you.'

'Good. And if you ever think the one tonight is normal . . .' Prosper went to turn the sheet. His thin bald head and naturally bulging eyes made the moment even more intense. 'Just remember this is how they really look. And deep down, where it really counts. They're Satan's sons and Satan's daughters. And they'll crucify us, Ever. They'll crucify us all.'

The picture, scrawled in crayon, was now in sight.

And it was vile.

He gasped.

On the paper, in jagged and unkempt black, was what looked like a tall thin rabbit standing on its hind legs. Its head was lean and pointed, with ragged but stiff ears protruding into a strange downward curve. Its spindly arms were reaching forward, claws outstretched, desperate to grab. And hundreds of little razor teeth lined the thin black lips. The only other colour was red. With it, he'd drawn drips of blood hanging from its mouth, and the same colour was repeated for the eyes. Scribbled, thick vertical lines. Those eyes looked up, and Ever wanted to turn and run as far from the church as he could.

'I saw one in the park one night,' Prosper said, sliding a finger across its eyes to block the stare. 'It was sleeping in a subway and it came at me, creeping up the tunnel. And it was reaching for me, like this . . .' Prosper reached out to him, grasping and wriggling his fingers and Ever flinched. 'It was desperate to touch me. Made the weirdest sound you ever heard. Like bones cracking, over and over.'

'That's how they talk,' Hope said. 'Sounds like a spine being twisted underwater. Like insects scuttling. But they must do a clever little trick, so we hear it like a normal voice. It's not normal, though. It's how the Father talks. Yeah, I've often thought the Father might be some sort of insect.'

His mouth was open. His heart thudding. The thing at the door . . .

'I . . . I think I saw one.'

They looked at each other, 'When?'

'Last night, over there,' he turned and slowly pointed to the church doorway. Squinting when he did it, in case it was still there. 'It's gone now.'

'Good. We must have scared it off,' Hope said. 'And this Hollow tonight hates Jesus, but Jesus hates it. So you won't hesitate, will you Ever? Because Micah hesitated and it all went wrong.'

'Micah . . .' Ever thought of their newest member, and how the grown-ups always sat with him on the porch. Always talking, always planning. And Micah's mum, sitting there and listening, but never really speaking. 'He's dead, isn't he?'

'Yes,' Hope said. 'But that's okay. He was weak and that's why he failed. But you won't fail, will you? Prosper said you killed that one at the farm like a hero.'

Don't cry, don't cry. He pressed his lips together.

'So, you won't hesitate here, will you?'

Finally, words came out. 'I won't hesitate.'

'Good. And remember it'll be way easier than you think. You just have to stop its heart and we'll do the rest . . . You don't even have to touch the axe . . .' She slapped the paper hard into his hand. 'So you put this in your pocket, Ever, and you remember who they are inside. These are the demons that put a chain around your mummy's neck and threw Prosper onto the street and hounded your Uncle Dust and filled his mouth with sand, and these are the ones . . .' she paused for a breath, 'who smashed my little girl's brain to mush . . . and turned her into a . . . a baby.'

He put his hand on her knee.

'God,' she said. 'She was always so bright—'

'*Car!*'

Ever jumped and Prosper too. They snapped their heads to Dust whose panicked voice was echoing from the other side of the church. 'There's a car coming. It must be Hunter.'

Hope shot bolt upright and checked her watch. 'It can't be.' Her voice was calm, her face wasn't.

Headlights flashed through the tall church windows and a swooping white block of light swept across the walls. Ever threw a hand across his silent scream.

'They're way too early.' Hope hurried towards Dust, who was starting to open the door so he might see.

'Does it matter?' Prosper quickly dragged a black bag to the altar. 'The sooner the better, if you ask—'

'It's not them,' Dust stood at the open door. 'It's . . .'

Hope gasped. 'Milton?'

'And there's no other car. No Hunter.'

'What the hell? He's supposed to be watching Matt.' Hope slammed the door fully open and ran out into the blackness. Prosper followed. For now, Ever and Dust stayed at the door, as Milton backed up Hope's car.

'Uncle Dust?' Ever said. 'What's happening?'

'Shhhh.'

'Where's the Hollow?'

'*Shhhh, dammit!*'

Trembling, Ever watched Milton stagger out of the car like he was gasping for breath.

'Jesus . . .' Dust said, 'he's got Verity . . . and . . . and . . . holy shit, he's got Pax and Merit.'

'Mum!' Ever rushed outside, and the wind slammed into him instantly, pushing him into a side stumble. Dust was close behind, grabbing Ever's hand and pushing down the blustery gravel path. Hope got there first, desperately trying to get everybody to quiet down.

Milton was propped against the car, while Prosper barked questions at him, but Dust walked right up to him and set two hands on his shaking shoulders. 'Just breathe, Milton, okay? Just catch a breath and tell us what happened . . .'

'It came to the farm. The Matthew one.'

Prosper moaned, raked a hand through his scalp and spun.

'It found Bill's body, too,' Milton said.

'What?' Hope stomped to Milton and pushed Dust away. She shoved her hands hard against the old man's chest. 'What the hell were you doing? You were supposed to be watch—'

'I did . . . I . . . I was at its house, like you said.'

'And?'

'You said to stay with it, so I followed its car. I had no idea where it was going. But it went . . . it went to the farm.'

'But how?' Dust said. 'How could he even know about that?'

'It just knew, and I couldn't let it see me so . . .' Milton was wheezing now. 'So, I couldn't stop it going in, and I couldn't very well kill it, could I?' He glared at them all. '*Could I?* Tell them, Verity . . .'

She was hugging Ever by now, but she pulled back and nodded. 'Matt came to the door, and I turned him away.'

'He saw you?' Hope shouted. 'He saw your face?'

'Not fully. He didn't recognise me. Then he found Bill's body in the car,' Mum said. 'Hope, he's called the police.'

She flung her head back, and the sky filled with the most terrible sounds of lament.

Prosper said, 'Jesus Christ, it's over, it's over . . . we'll have to use the other way . . .'

'No, it's not over . . .' Milton shouted. 'We weren't followed. Nobody knows we're here.'

'But what's the point if Matt's not here?' Hope kicked a chunk of gravel at him. It clattered on the car. 'Is he with the police?'

When Milton responded, it was with a roar. 'Listen to yourselves!' he shouted. 'Listen to what you're saying. You've been away from home for way too long already. He is not a frickin' "he". "He" is an it . . . and *it* is not with the police, okay? Where's your damn faith?'

'Then where is . . . it?' Dust said.

Mum pulled fully back from Ever and rushed to the back of the car. She stood there, framed by a sea of glowing, fast-moving clouds. Her hair glistened with starlight, and the loose threads of her scarf danced in the night wind.

'Wait. You're saying it's in the boot?' Hope said.

'See? *See?*' Milton nodded. 'There's always hope.'

'But he still called the police.' Dust looked at the road. 'And the other one. The wife. You said they were coming together.'

Hope was laughing now. 'She was the only way to get him over here. He wouldn't have come himself . . . but look . . . now he's here anyway.' She slapped a hand on Milton's shoulder. 'The Lord's in this. He's got better plans, even than me.'

'But what if she comes?' Dust said. 'What if she comes after him?'

'Easy. We get his phone and fob her off. And if she does turn up, I'll deal with her. We're friends, don't you know?' Hope smiled. 'Now get that boot open.'

CHAPTER FORTY-THREE

Matt had been blindfolded with a foul-smelling rag for what seemed like an hour now. At least it felt that long since he last saw the light of Bessie's hallway. Just before he'd lost his sight, they'd smacked him on the shoulders with that damn walking stick. Just one last thwack. *One for the road!* Then he passed out. They must have dragged and yanked him out of her house.

He'd only become vaguely aware of movement when they dropped him into something. Even in blindness, he could tell it was the boot of a car. It was the way it sank as he crashed into it, on his side. Then all those hands fought to keep his limbs inside. He started to struggle and kick out but was rewarded with a heavy thud above him. The wind and their voices grew muffled. The engine rumbled.

As he rocked from side to side, sliding on the turns, he tried to kick his way out. Tried a lot of things, actually. But when you have plastic cable ties on your hands and feet, your options are severely limited. Eventually he just lay there, shoulders and legs throbbing, feeling baffled, hurt and something else too. Something major and true, that threw an icy shadow across his entire psyche. He was scared. He was very, very scared.

The engine noise sometimes blended with muffled voices from inside the car. They frequently seemed to be shouting at each other.

He'd made a foolish attempt to mind-map the journey. Frantically doing a mental satnav to confirm the way they came. Surely he could figure that out? He was clever, supposedly. He lost track after thirty seconds. There was all the sliding around and junk falling across his face to contend with. And the thought of impending death. There was that too.

So he felt both relief and dreadful shock when the car finally stopped. When the boot opened, he heard a new voice, a man say, 'Get him in the church.' Matt thought he might laugh just then and say, *Wow guys, in my day we just invited people to a carol service and offered them hot chocolate. None of this rope and car-boot malarkey.* But he didn't laugh. He didn't say anything, at all. Because every time he had opened his mouth before, that crazy-eyed old man whacked him with the stick. He thought of Bessie. How she never answered when he cried out to her. Just before he drifted from consciousness.

Still blindfolded, he heard more voices now. Then many more hands heaved him out and dumped him onto a surface that had no in-built suspension: the ground. They lifted him by the armpits and dragged him. He felt the cold sting of rain slap his face, and the tips of his shoes scraped lines through gravel. Then that sound soon changed, like they'd stepped into an echo chamber. The ground became smooth and the air musky. He instantly knew he was in St Bart's. He could just tell by that smell and the familiar echo, designed by centuries-old architects to strike reverence into the faithful. He was now, rather ironically, a prisoner inside the very institution he'd once described as a prison. He'd used that specific word in a recent article about oppressive biblical texts. And, of course, he'd headed that piece with a picture of this place – just at the very start of its meme wave. WELCOME TO THE CROOKED CHURCH, the headline read. How witty he'd been. How droll.

He could smell David East's three-day-old blood, stubbornly clinging to the air.

He couldn't tell how many people were around him, but it sounded like a lot of them. And they kept speaking over each other. Words tumbling over words. At one point he felt a set of fingers grab his hair and lift his head up. Then a voice boomed near his ear and said, 'Look everybody. Daddy's home!' Which made the church fill with wails and screeches that were either excited or panicked, he couldn't tell which. He knew which one he was, though. Holy shit, he was panicked. He was trying to be calm, for survival's sake, but holy shit, it was scary not being able to see.

Then the voices grew louder but more compact as he was dragged into what sounded like a little room. He braced himself, expecting to be dropped to the floor, but then he heard a woman's voice say something odd. 'Put him in that chair, Dust.' Heavy hands placed him carefully onto a rickety, creaking seat.

Voices filled the space. A mixture of strange Jesus prayers and barked instructions like 'Watch him', 'We'll get things prepped', 'You, you and you . . . watch all the doors'. And finally, a strange sentence that made no sense whatsoever. 'Where's Ever? Get Ever ready.' Someone asked about Matt's phone too. Where was it, did they bring it with them, who had it, was there enough charge in the battery? He heard a lot of mumbling about how to operate it. It was the one time he had the energy to call out. He said, 'Dammit, leave my phone alone,' shouting into the void of his blindness. He sounded so pathetic that he wasn't surprised when a couple of them laughed. Then something hard touched his thumb, and a finger pressed into his thumbnail. He heard a familiar, light-sabre swoosh. The sound of his phone opening. He snapped his hand back. They laughed again, and somebody said, 'Halleujah.'

'Phone's ready,' a man shouted.

After a while, it grew quiet, then suddenly muffled. He couldn't be sure, but it sounded like they'd all moved back into the church, leaving him behind. For a few moments he listened to them singing wild, frightening hymns of a valiant Jesus, slaying the father who first slayed him.

Matt waited. Caught his breath. He risked a voice. 'Hello?'

No answer.

If he really was alone in here, he'd smear his face down a wall or something and get this damn blindfold off. Look for a way to fight. Then a voice spoke up. A man's voice.

'Quiet down . . .' it said.

'Dust?' Matt said. He recognised the tone. 'Is that your name? I heard them call someone Dust . . .'

'Don't look at me.'

'I can't see you . . . not through this . . .'

'Good. Now, how did you know about the farmhouse? Did Zara tell you? Prosper's right, isn't he? She betrayed us.'

'She didn't tell me anything because I never found her.'

'Then why were you there?'

'Her husband, David, he's awake. He said Zara was up at your farm, but she wasn't there . . .' Matt shifted his hands again. The plastic cable-tie on his wrists felt tighter than ever. He wanted to strangle the guy, but he opted for calm. 'Why am I here?'

Silence.

'What have I ever done to—'

A woman's voice, extremely close to his head, said, 'You mean you don't know?'

Matt jumped.

'Verity,' Dust said. 'Shhh . . .'

'It's fine. I can talk.' The woman's voice came closer. He felt her breath on his cheek. 'You don't remember me, do you?'

'I've never met anybody called Verity.'

She laughed. 'Fair point. But surely you recognise my voice?'

'I'm better with faces. Can I see your face?'

'It's shocking . . .' Dust said. 'Evil's so mundane to them, they can't even remember the crimes they do . . .'

Matt started tugging at his wrists again. 'What crimes?'

'. . . it's like destroying folks is just another thing to do on a summer's day . . . like it's no big deal.'

'What's no big deal? What do you think I've forgotten?'

'Just a sin you did. A sin that's obviously got lost in the Hollow pile. But we're not like you, we remember. And we don't cover the past with lies, we tell it how it is, with all the pain and all the sorrow. So how about I dig this sin out and see if it rings any bells . . .' Dust came close. 'You know . . . you remember . . . that time you raped Verity here.'

Confused fireworks blasted at all levels of Matt's mind, rendering comprehension and articulate responses a luxury. All he could manage was a sound that was supposed to act as a question. He said, 'Huh?'

'Bet you've done it a million times. Made a million little Evers all over the world.'

'Huh?'

'To a million wives. To a million husbands, too, I'll bet.'

'What the hell are you talking about? I've never even met a Verity.'

'Oh, really?' Her voice again, closer than ever. Her breath on his chin, now.

'Wait . . . Verity,' Dust said. 'Don't . . .'

Her fingers were spider-walking up his cheeks, scurrying around the sides of his head.

Dust said it again. '*Don't.*'

'I want him to see my face . . . I want him to remember.'

The blindfold dropped around his shoulders and he squinted at the bulbs of the small room. They seemed fiercely bright. But he slowly opened them, and eventually he saw her face appear, pushing through the forest of his lashes.

'Reverend.' She nodded as she came into focus. 'Hello again.'

Matt's voice said, 'Jess?'

But his brain said, *Oh, my God. Oh, my God. Oh, my God.*

CHAPTER FORTY-FOUR

Wren marched around the kitchen, swinging each cupboard open in a gruff, sped-up version of her usual babysitter routine. 'Tea and coffee. Hot chocolate. Help yourself to any food you want. Wi-Fi code is here.'

'Ta.' Tracey, their new babysitter, was scrubbing a towel across her head.

'Your hair won't survive out there. Amazing colour, by the way. Where do you get it—'

'Gotta run, sorry.' Wren spun and grabbed her coat as the lightning lit up the hallway, then she sat on the bottom stair and pulled on her boots, yanking the laces way tighter than she needed. There was something satisfying about the feel of it. Like she was garrotting someone. Someone called Matt Hunter. All laced up, she leant through the lounge door where Lucy and Amelia were squealing playing Mario Kart. 'Amelia, show Tracy how to work the TV. And you do NOT make her watch *Troll 2*.'

'Oh, but I bet she'd love to see—'

'I said, no!' she snapped and zipped up her parka. 'Look, I'm not in the mood.'

Amelia was staring at her, her face gentle and serious. 'Maybe the roads are closed. Maybe he's stuck somewhere.'

'Yeah, well if he turns up you just tell him I've already left.'

'Mum . . .' Lucy put her controller down. 'Maybe you shouldn't go out in it either.'

'I'll be fine.' Wren caught the clock on the wall. 'Crap. Gotta go. Enjoy the cinema, Lucy. And Amelia, be hospitable.'

Amelia saluted her. 'Well, you know what they say about hospitality. You can't pi—'

'Bye,' Wren said.

She scooped up her keys from the bowl and flipped the parka hood over her red fringe. She looked like a cartoon character staring back in the mirror, all padding and just face, then she stepped out into Waterworld. The wind instantly caught her. It seemed to pick her up in four hurried steps down the path. She ran the gauntlet to the car, zapping her keys and throwing herself inside. It was shocking how soaked she became. Drenched in ten seconds. This weather at the moment, she'd never seen anything like it.

She shivered, pushed the ignition button and the car purred into life. Then she pulled the belt across her and yanked out her phone. She stared at the screen as the car rocked in the wind. She couldn't help it. She tapped onto the astonishing message she had just received and read it for perhaps the eighth or ninth time.

Wren. I'm not going to that prayer meeting at Chervil any more. I hate that stuff. And you can't go either. I'm serious. Be back late. Explain tomorrow. I heard it was cancelled cos of rain anyway. Love you.

'Well, I'm bloody well going.' She threw the phone on the passenger seat and surged off.

She tried to stop thinking about him as the wipers danced and the sky kept flashing, but he kept coming to mind. Which was strange, because Wren's therapist had taught her such nifty techniques to block him out. But still, she thought of her first husband Eddie. She didn't often do that. She was getting better at burying his shouting echoes and not feeling the flash of his stubby fingers, pressed into her throat. But there he was again, Eddie Pullen, sitting in their horrible little flat, telling her that baby Lucy *had* to be her priority now and that her architecture dreams would obviously have to wait. That she shouldn't *have* to work. Which became *you mustn't* and ended up as . . . you will *not* work. She felt that hot press of Eddie's mouth against her ear, because that was the way Eddie always shouted best – in a whisper.

She started firing up her methods to block Eddie out, and tried her favourite tool. She said, 'Wren Hunter and Matt Hunter' over and over, because the therapist said she had to remind her brain that she had a new life now. That the controlling beast of Eddie was locked away in a prison cell. But saying Matt's name along with hers didn't soothe her as much as it usually did, because she couldn't stop thinking of Matt's text.

And you can't go either. I'm serious, he'd said.

The rain was remarkably loud, and it was a strange, long and lonely drive.

CHAPTER FORTY-FIVE

Matt shook his head, frantically. 'No, no, *no.*'

'Yes, yes, *yes.*' Verity sat cross-legged in front of Matt, tilting her head as she curled a thick strand of her very straight hair. It was much, much longer than it used to be, but now she had it down, and wasn't hiding behind a farmhouse door, he saw those old echoes in her face. Around her neck, a thin scarf was wound tight. He knew why.

'Careful of its eyes,' Dust said. 'Not too close.'

'Oh, shush, he's tied up.' She turned back. 'So, you're denying it then, Rev?'

Rev. She always used to call me that.

'Rev? Can't you speak?'

'Jess, come on. I didn't—'

She blew a puff of air into his face, while Dust twisted his hands and paced the floor. Trembling, Matt looked into those bright, familiar eyes.

'Then why did I catch you?' she said. 'You were holding my hand after. And you were the only one in the alley. Hmm? Fiddling with my clothes?'

Matt couldn't stop blinking. The harshness of the light, no doubt. But every time he closed his lids, a very old world sprang up. He saw a cold night, light years into his past. He was in his twenties, helping out with the Street Angels scheme. He and a posse of local Christians were hanging around the city nightclubs, every weekend, from 11 p.m. to 5 a.m. They helped drunk people get home and got homeless people into shelters. This church-in-action stuff really appealed to him, back in the early days. He could see himself then, all denim shirt, jeans and cheap trainers, back when he was as naive about fashion as he was about life. When he thought TV panel shows weren't scripted and that God cared about him.

During one Street Angel shift he was standing awkwardly by a nightclub, pounding out muffled beats at four in the morning. He and the other volunteers handed out free shoes to anyone who might have lost one that night. It was a surprisingly common and incredibly dangerous injury, they'd been told. People staggering home shoeless could easily slash a major artery on broken glass. Unless the trusty Street Angels swung in with a two-pound plimsoll to save the day. The Angels held people's hair as they vomited into drains. They got between brawls on the steps of pubs. And they looked for the forgotten, the lonely, the hurt.

Like her.

'Jess, I was helping.'

'Helping yourself.' She nodded. 'All those sweet little women.'

'It wasn't like that . . .'

'All those teats hanging out, and too drunk to stop it. Oh yeah, I get it. You and your clan . . . prowling the city and hungry with it.'

Another flash of him and the team and their usual patrol of the backstreets. They'd hunt for people face down in puke or bloodied and shivering from a pub brawl. They all wore high-viz jackets and goofy-looking caps, so that everybody knew who they were. Despite the few accusations – 'You're parasites, you're trying to convert us' – most of the drinkers knew it. They seemed aware. That when a little old lady in a Street Angels baseball cap held the hands of a weeping woman on rickety heels, there was something profound going on. He'd seen complete strangers break down and tell the Angels secrets, crimes, regrets.

Then there was that one snowy night, where the Angels had to slip through sleet to help people home. He happened to turn a corner and saw her hair first. A short tuft of dirty blonde, pressed into a melting pavement. He hurried closer, clicked on the torch and groaned in shock. He saw a very young girl in a baggy pink tracksuit, passed out. Clearly not a clubber, clearly not a night out. This one was homeless. For her, every night was a night out. He remembered thinking she was about twelve, though he later found out she was seventeen. She had a strip of blood, smeared from the corner of her mouth. It ran across her cheek and up into her ear. He remembered the pattern of it quite vividly, and what he thought was a really tight, ridiculously thick necklace that turned out to be a bike chain wrapped multiple times around her throat.

He dropped to his knees and quickly pulled it loose and let that grim circle of torchlight move down to see her skinny legs strewn, tracksuit bottom and pants gathered at her ankles, like a binding rope. Trembling knees were locked together. No socks. No jacket. Just snowflakes melting on her bare kneecaps.

'Oh, God,' he'd said, which had been one of his purest ever prayers.

She'd groaned in response. He'd already torn off his gloves, so he could grab her frozen hand. Then he dragged his big, Street Angels puffa jacket off so he could cover her bottom half up. He'd considered pulling her tracksuit back up, then realised that might not be the right procedure. There'd be evidence to gather. So, he just sat there heartbroken at how pitiful it was, and how shameful she must have felt, shivering under his coat.

Throughout all this, Matt had called for the others to come. His booming shout filled the alley and made her open her eyes. So, he squeezed her hand and said, 'It's okay.' She flinched so sharply that he apologised and set her hand down. He called for the others again. When they didn't arrive, he did the only thing he could think to do. He prayed frantically, saying, 'Father God, be with this girl.' That's what he said. 'Father God. Be with her. Be with her, father God.' Which is when she screamed and tried to scramble away. Then the others came, and they seemed to scare her even more than he did, so she reached out and held his hand. She looked up into the falling snow, utterly confused. He told her there was help and hope.

He blinked again and the cold of the snow vanished. The cold of the vestry replaced it.

'You're wrong, Jess.'

'Verity!' She smacked a fist on the floor. 'My name is *Verity* now because that means truth. And I am telling the truth.'

Matt stumbled on his words, '. . . Verity, I didn't do anything to you.'

'You were leering over me.'

'I was checking you were alive.'

'You were getting dressed.'

'I was dressing you. I called the others over.'

'After you were done.'

'You know this. I turned a corner and found you, then I called them over. Remember, we all carried you to the ambulance? Remember a few of us slipped in the snow and you laughed about it?'

Dust looked over, frowning. 'You said he was alone, Verity.'

'He was alone. At the start.'

Dust bit his lip and turned silent.

'Jess . . . you were out of it. You'd been on something. The whole team took you to hospital. Me and a lady called Dee came with you. You couldn't remember who attacked you, but you never said it was me, Jess. In fact, you asked me to stay in your room with you the whole night.'

'But you wouldn't, would you?' she said. 'You said a woman had to do it.'

'That was the policy.'

'Then the next morning, when I asked for your address, you said you couldn't give it out and gave me a helpline instead.'

He nodded. 'There were procedures in place. I had to follow them.'

'And that day? A month after. Was that procedure?' A tear dropped from her eye. It exploded on the floor. He saw that gaunt look of shame in her face, and the thick bandage wrapped around her throat, as she stood on his doorstep weeks after the attack and all he could think was not, *Is she doing okay?*, but rather, *How did she find my house?* 'And when I came to the vicarage,' she said, 'I was standing in the rain with nowhere to sleep. And I asked if I could stay on your couch for the night and you said you'd call a shelter instead, like you couldn't bear to be near me.'

He'd told her she couldn't come inside, because the church had strict child-safety rules. Grown-ups were not allowed to be alone with kids. It protected everybody from abuse, or accusation. She'd gawped at him, and said she wasn't a child, and he'd said that technically speaking she really was. Then she cried and said he cared more about church gossip than child safety. Which was actually quite true. That and the thought she could be a thief and that he might wake up tomorrow with an empty wallet and a hole where his laptop used to be. Then the moment when she said, 'What's wrong? Don't you trust yourself with a girl?' He remembered that part, especially.

That was when he'd flung out a leaflet for another shelter. He tossed it like meat to a whimpering dog. Then as she tried to step inside, he closed the door in her face. She kicked it hard, but only once. He sat on his welcome mat, feeling like crap until her whisper came through the letter box, sharing her little revelation.

'Ahhhhhh, I see . . .' she'd said. 'So you're not angels at all. You're devils. You're devils in a world full of devils.' She'd laughed as she'd said it, crouching at his door, then eventually she went. He watched her through a gap in the curtains, vanishing into the rain. The echoed voice of his Bible college tutors tried to reassure him – *Got to be wise as serpents, and as innocent as doves – Mustn't be alone with a vulnerable teenager – Don't give the homeless cash, they'll spend it on drugs.* He remembered how rotten it felt to be so professional.

Matt opened his eyes and saw the vestry carpet flashing from the lightning outside. He looked up and saw her wiping tears across her cheeks.

'I'm sorry I didn't give you more help,' he said. 'I was trying to . . . to be wise. I'm sorry.'

'Wise?' She cleared her throat. 'Yeah, well I moved away after that and I found a brand-new family and a brand-new faith. A real faith. They didn't turn me away, and they even helped me raise my baby in the end.'

'But I swear to you, I didn't—'

She was oblivious. 'And the moment I saw him born I knew. Like, I'd been blinded up until then . . . but then I knew full well why you didn't want me at your church . . . because you couldn't bear to see what you'd put inside me—'

'*Ah, but he'll see tonight . . .*'

A new voice split the space. It came from across the room.

Of course he knew who it was, even before he saw the face. He just heard the slow creak of the vestry door swing open, and there she was, walking in like it wasn't a big deal. Strolling up with her hands clasped across her tummy, not even looking awkward about it. She sat herself into an old rickety chair opposite and just smiled. The type of smile you do when a kitten runs past, or you see a gameshow win, or your host refills your glass with some more red wine.

He said her name, but it came out more like a long, distant breath. 'Miriam.'

She laughed. 'Aw, come on Matt. We're friends now. We're buds . . .' She looked relaxed, heartfelt and horribly psychotic. 'You can call me Hope.'

CHAPTER FORTY-SIX

'Do you know what the amazing thing is, Matt? Or should I call you Reverend?' she said. 'The amazing thing is you were always meant for Ever.'

He stopped struggling and squirming for a moment. 'What does that even mean? What the hell are you talking about?'

She smiled at him.

They all did.

She put both hands on her knees and leant forward in the chair. 'I've been listening at the door just now, cos I just love to hear Verity's story. About what you did to her. She told us about it the other night, Matt. The full detail. And it wasn't easy for her – to tell us all where Ever really came from. There was a lot of shame in it, but she was very brave, and of course it changed everything.'

'You can't keep me here, you can't—'

'And it's a pretty story, Reverend. Shall I tell you why? Because it shows how Jesus takes the very worst of the world and turns it very good.' She ran her gaze around the vestry, shaking her head in disgust. 'We thought if Micah killed David it would work. A son killing a holy father. That'd be our symbol to change the world, but he couldn't bear to do it properly. It all felt so . . . it felt so wasted. But it wasn't wasted, because with Jesus, nothing is wasted.'

'What are you even saying?'

'I'm saying that we make our little plans, but Jesus has a far bigger vision. I'm saying that Micah was only ever meant to bring you in. It's amazing. It's all connected. You know, when Verity saw you on TV that night she cried out hallelujah, and she wept at the grace of it, Matt. We all did. We wept . . .' Her eyes were glistening, and there was something in those brimming tears that was scarier than anything else. They were real tears, and this was real belief. 'Back in that alley, you thought you were hurting her . . . but he was working out a far bigger purpose. And all you did was create the very one that'd hurt you eventually. You made Ever in hate, and now he'll kill you in love, Reverend.'

'Stop calling me Reverend, dammit,' Matt shouted, truly shaking now.

'And that love's going to bring Jesus back, see? Because symbols and rituals . . . they're powerful. I mean listen to what it's doing to the weather. Listen to the rain! Have you ever heard anything like it?'

'Symbols are symbols!' he shouted. 'They do nothing.'

She started laughing. A huge belly-laugh of hilarious disbelief. 'Ah, but symbols and ritual do everything because they're doorways. They change things. Think of that cross . . . a father killing his son ended up ruining this world, but . . .' she raised her finger, 'what if the sight that'll set things right is when a son kills his father? A reverend, no less . . . a Hollow. Dead at the hands of . . . his only son . . .' She laughed against her hand. 'It's . . . it's . . . it's fucking poetry.'

Matt writhed against the ropes. They tore into his skin. 'The police are coming.'

'No, they aren't.' It was Verity, finally looking up from her hands. 'They'll be here.'

She shook her head, 'No, think about it, Rev. You said you were at the farmhouse, remember? Not here.'

His breath came out, sounding thin and jittery.

Miriam smiled and was up on her feet, because the thunder was crashing harder than ever and it must have been like the sweetest music to her. She started to dance around the room, twirling and laughing in the white-hot flashes. Then Verity was laughing too, even though she was weeping at the same time. And in the corner, Dust was on his knees, hard in prayer. The women turned and embraced, and laughed and cried and sang of old things made new.

The sheer, flashing shock of it all threw Matt deep into his own mind, and he tumbled through blackness to find himself in a plush banqueting chair, watching himself speaking at a conference in Berlin. A memory of two years back, when he spoke on 'The Psychology of Religion and Cults'. He heard himself saying how cults isolate themselves and create 'well-controlled feedback loops'. A phrase he liked. And how even the most rational, professional people can fall into a kind of group psychosis, as long as outside influence was kept away.

'Let me tell you the truly scary thing about cults, particularly the very small ones,' he'd said, to that distinguished hall of the learned and loved – and he'd said it with a mocking grin on his face, because they were all amused at his extreme examples too. Like it was all a sad joke. He said, 'Some cults preach the most whacky things you've ever heard – that God wants his people to move to Venus' – pause for chortle – 'that mushrooms are satanic' – pause for snorts – 'or that sex with pigs will bring heaven to earth' – pause for guffaw – 'or that God demands commuters are poisoned on a Tokyo subway' – pause for awkwardness. 'And you'd think most folks would see these gonzo ideas for what they are – kooky and totally irrational. Until you realise these are all true cases.' Which is when he stopped smiling and threw up shots of the happy folks at Guyana.

And oh, how they all laughed afterwards, he and the civilised delegates. Oh, how they'd laughed as they'd mingled in the exquisite ballroom with the painted ceiling. When they asked if the Chardonnay was laced with poisoned Kool-Aid. Oh, how they'd laughed at that joke, because it was better to snigger into their glasses than to think that all those little children, folded onto each other on the Jonestown floor, were real children from a non-fiction world.

And here he was, two years later, watching the true believers dance. And they were the ones laughing now.

Beyond the turning women he saw a bizarre, skin-tightening sight. The rest of the group had now bundled themselves against the door frame. A mass of faces not looking evil or even manic, but reverent and awestruck at his presence. He was, after all, a gift delivered. They were the shepherds and wise men at the stable.

Then Miriam stopped dancing and simply said, 'Now,' which was like a match to petrol. They spilled into the room, tumbling over one another. And though he forced himself back and willed himself to vanish, they reached out their arms and their hands slid across his body.

Matt heard himself whimpering and wondered, if he survived this, whether he'd remember this as the moment his mind collapsed. When they danced and wailed and covered him in hands. He said, 'Please, *please*, don't . . .' as they dragged him up.

Miriam led the way. Her happy voice echoed into the church as she skipped, even ran, to the altar. 'Remember, everybody,' she shouted, 'don't let it look at you, but we'll keep its blindfold off so it sees Ever. It's important that it knows what it made.'

Then something happened, just as they were dragging him through the vestry door.

A bizarre sound that stopped everybody dead. One that none of them were expecting. It took him a few seconds to realise exactly what it was.

A call you have! A CALL you have, A CALL you HAVE!

Holy shit, he thought. *My phone.*

Heads snapped towards the vestry desk, where Matt's iPhone rattled and vibrated. The screen came on for a few seconds. By now Miriam was still out in the church. She'd run right up to the chancel. She called back, 'What's going on?' Then that old boxer guy from Bessie's house stomped in. Milton. He rushed across the room and stared at the phone. Scared to touch it. 'It says Bowland . . .' He looked up. 'Who's Bowland?'

The screen winked out, like a candle.

Miriam shouted from the church, 'Just leave it. Come on.'

'Says she's left a message . . .'

It was Dust who moved first. He plucked the phone up and dropped next to Matt and spoke his words, fast and frantic. 'Make it work.'

'What?'

'The phone. Make it work again, so we can hear.'

'Again?' Matt blinked for a moment and remembered being half-conscious as they pushed his thumbprint into the phone earlier.

Sick of waiting, Dust just grabbed his hand and did it. 'I want to hear. Just in case the police are coming.'

'Don't. We'll be done soon.' Miriam was rushing back through the church. 'Then we won't have to worry about any Hollows.'

'We need to listen,' Dust said. 'Just in case . . .'

314

Milton glared at Dust. 'In case what?'

'In case all this doesn't work.'

The old man's mouth dropped open. 'You're doubting it?'

'Put that fucking thing down.' Miriam was at the door, trying to push through them all, 'and get Ever and this thing to the altar, now.'

But Dust took the phone into the corner just as Bowland's disembodied voice entered the room. For a moment, everybody froze, transfixed by it.

Matt, it's me, Bowland said. *You were right . . . we found the car, and the body inside. One of the local coppers recognised him. He's an ex-member who used to live with them. His five-year-old daughter still does. The mum's, um . . . handicapped . . .*

'We haven't got time for this,' Miriam said.

Dust pressed himself into the corner and held the phone higher. A magical box, buzzing out secrets.

. . . No sign of anyone. Found a chapel up on the hill, though. It's filled with upturned crosses, so I guess Micah really was in with these guys . . . but Matt there's another thing. A big thing . . .

'Turn it off,' Miriam said.

On the other side of the hill, not far from the outer gate . . . we found a bunch of birds pecking at the ground . . .

'Turn it off!' She rushed in, but Matt managed a hard lean into her. He could do that much, even tied up. She was moving so fast that she toppled to the side for a second. She fell against a bookshelf.

We've found her, Matt, in a shallow grave.

Miriam scrambled to her feet.

Dust closed his eyes.

It's Zara East, no doubt about it.

'Stop it,' Miriam shouted.

Dust's hand slid across his own gaping mouth.

Someone's strangled her—

'*Stop!*' Miriam swatted the phone from Dust's hand and they all watched it shatter against the wall. Bowland's voice vanished in a crackle.

All those arms that were dragging and holding Matt suddenly weakened because the bodies attached to them seemed to stagger. Confused voices filled the room and, for a strange moment, even the rain and thunder seemed to stop dead. Milton shook his head, stared at the floor and walked into the church.

Dust was the only one to speak. He pulled the palm from his face and said it calmly. 'What did you do, Hope? What did you do?'

CHAPTER FORTY-SEVEN

The church filled with an explosion of voices.

Ever looked up from the altar, where he'd been told to wait. He'd been on his knees, praying with Prosper, with an intensity he never thought possible. But then he heard the commotion from all the adults. Prosper sprang to his feet and gulped because Milton was stumbling away from the vestry door.

'What's happening?' Prosper ran down the aisle and Ever ran after him. 'What's all the shouting about?'

'She lied . . .' Milton shook his head. 'She killed her.'

Prosper's face changed instantly. Ever saw it as clear as day. The skin flicked to white.

Ever ran up. 'Who lied?'

'Hope,' Milton strained his voice out. 'Zara didn't run away at all. She didn't leave us. She's been dead and buried the whole time.'

'No way.' Ever shook his head. 'That can't be right.' Though deep in the dark of his gut he thought, actually yes, that probably is right. Because that just feels right. Like it was something Hope might do. Desperate to find Dust he rushed to the vestry door, where the grown-ups were lamenting at full tilt. He had to climb up on a chair just to see over everybody's shoulders. Hope was standing in the middle of the room, pleading with them, and now Prosper was shoving through them all to join them.

'We had to, okay?' Prosper said, and everybody stared at him. He stood with Hope and took her hand. 'Zara was going to tell the world about us.'

'You knew about this?' Dust barked at him.

'Of course I knew.'

'But she believed. She wasn't Hollow, she was one of us.'

'Hope thinks she was a plant. Some sort of Hollow spy come to turn us.'

Verity was on the floor, nodding her head. 'She always was . . . quiet.'

'Bottom line is, she was going to tell,' Hope said. 'She didn't want Micah to do the ritual. She acted all supportive in front of you lot, but she was struggling with it. Then I made her tell me the truth. She was going to tell Micah's dad what we were planning.'

'But you said she ran away,' Dust said.

'It was better that way. We thought if you knew she turned Hollow while she was on the farm, it'd . . .'

'It'd what . . .'

'Rock your faith.'

'Yeah, right. You lied because the truth would have sent Micah running.' Dust laughed, but it quickly fizzed into anger. 'We don't lie.'

The room was in chaos, and the more they shouted, the more that Ever understood why this was happening. It was this special, powerful Hollow, sitting in the middle of the room. The one they'd dragged from the car. It was on its knees, tied up, but it was adding its voice to the rest. It shouted its words especially at Uncle Dust, and the scariest part was that Dust was listening.

'See?' the Hollow said 'You can't trust her. And if Hope lied about this, how can you trust this ritual of hers?'

'We'll use the other way,' Milton said. 'The world can still end.'

The Hollow turned its head to Hope and Prosper. 'But why do you think they're so desperate for it to end now? Your farmhouse life was over the minute they killed her. They knew full well the police were gonna track Zara down. That's why they want the world to end . . . because you're running out of time. But listen . . . the world won't stop. You'll just end up in prison because none of it—'

Milton said, 'We won't end up in prison.'

'Ah, but you will, because none of this ritual, this belief—'

Verity slapped the demon hard across the face. It kept talking,

'—none of it is true. So, get me out of these bloody cables before the police get here.'

After the slap, the Hollow turned its face to the side and spat out a large globule of blood. Which was the worst image of all. The moment that explained everything. He hadn't realised it until now, but here was the solid proof that it was tricking them all.

They'd taken its blindfold away.

This Hollow, the special one, the one for which all this was for, sat tied in the middle of the room. Only those plastic cables around its wrists were irrelevant because it was staring at each person, and they were all staring back. And nobody seemed to realise that Uncle Dust was turning against the others and soon, the rest would too. Dust called out, 'It's over. We're ending this.' And Ever heard a smack of thunder so loud that he thought the entire building would collapse. As they argued, the Hollow held them in its gaze, orchestrating the chaos, with a blood-filled mouth and an animal gaze. Any second now, his entire, beloved family were going to turn Hollow, and their eyes would all roll in their sockets to find him.

319

His heart gave him the answer. His heart said: *Run*.

As they all raged he turned and sprinted into the church. He found Pax sitting there oblivious. She was drawing crayon shapes of Hollows on sheets of white paper. He grabbed her hand. 'Something's gone wrong,' he whispered. 'We've got to get Merit and go.'

She narrowed her eyes at him. Licked her lips.

'Come on!'

'Gonna tell on you . . .' she sang her words, '. . . gonna tell.'

He hated the way she gazed at him and how the lightning flashed against her bared teeth. He wondered if blood might suddenly come trickling between the gaps and tumble over her chin, and in the light, he thought he saw her eyeballs start to shrink into slits. He stumbled back as she reached out a clawed hand. Then he hurried to the door as the others screamed and wailed in their chaos. He looked back at the vestry, desperate to find Merit and to call for Mum, but he ached to call Dust most of all. But the fear of his uncle scrambling out on all fours was sure to throw Ever into total madness. It'd be impossible to bear such a sight. So, he pushed the door open. It took both hands and before he knew it, he was out.

He avoided the gravel path, because he knew more Hollows would come that way. A whole army of them were probably crawling here right now, just for this final, brutal and cruel moment. So he turned left instead, where a dark wood ran alongside a field. He bolted towards the swaying, shaking trees and was battered with rain, assaulted by thunder and blinded with flashes of light. The Father was throwing the entire universe at him, trying to stop the escape. Behind him, he could hear that their screams were changing. They sounded different now, which meant the Hollow must have won. He tried to fight the image of their spines splitting through their skins and those long black ears (maybe they were horns) cracking up through their skulls, as they stood as they really were. Then he froze inside, when he heard the smack of wood against stone.

The church door was flinging back, and his family howled his name. *Ever . . . Ever . . . Eveeeerrrrrrr.*

He screamed as he ran. In fact, he screamed a great deal. But mostly . . . mostly he wept.

CHAPTER FORTY-EIGHT

Wren tapped the lever for her windscreen wipers, hoping she might increase the speed they turned. But they were stuck at their top clip, which on any normal day was more than enough. Yet on the night that an entire ocean fell from the sky, they could barely keep up.

She'd had the radio on at first. She'd hoped it might help scrub away those echoes of Eddie, but all this storm-of-the-decade talk was starting to freak her out. At least she knew it was pointless to turn back and go home. She'd come too far for that. So she turned off the doom-voice of the radio because the rain was getting too loud to hear it properly anyway and splashed the car through bottomless puddles. For most of the journey, the weather hadn't been quite so epic. Yes, it was stormy and dramatic, but nothing that threatened to stop her car. It was just when she turned into Chervil that the sky seemed to click into full chaos. She looked up at it now and saw the amazingly frequent flashes of white. Each burst of light lit up the fast and frightening clouds that were swirling around the world. Like something from a sci-fi epic, projected on the biggest screen she'd ever seen.

A large, substantial part of her deeply regretted coming here and there were moments when she cursed her stubborn insistence on proving a point to Matt. Her principles might well put her in a wet ditch. But the intermittent satnav told her she was now only a mile down the road from the church, and she figured she'd be better off getting there to wait out the storm with Miriam.

The glow of her lights picked out a long low wall to the right, stacked with rocks and large stones. Then she saw a huge beast of a puddle taking up almost the entire dirt track. There was no way she was driving through that, so she slowed down and aimed for the little ridge. She swung to the right and the ridge pushed her front end up. Her beams spilt across the field and picked something out at the end of it. She saw a row of dense woodland, but what made her stop dead and stare across the wide field was something else entirely.

Someone was running through the trees at the other side.

It was a small figure, leaping over logs and racing between tree trunks. Whoever it was kept looking back over their shoulder, like they were being chased. The wipers weren't fast enough to clear the view, so she flicked up her parka hood and opened up the door. The roaring hiss of rain blasted her eardrums, but she stepped out anyway and stood as high as she could, one hand cupped over her eyebrows like a visor. Which is when she gasped.

God.

It was a boy. A terrified little boy was running through the trees and he wasn't even wearing a coat. Just a flimsy, sodden sweatshirt from the looks of it. She looked to her right and left and saw nothing but the gaping black void of a road hanging in space. Until the heavens flashed, and the Crooked Church announced itself with a heart-stopping, Gothic crash. It was less than half a mile up, standing proud and twisted on the hill. This was what the boy was running from.

She couldn't drive to him; the wall stood in the way. She'd have to hop over it instead. She kept her headlights shining, and though the glow only barely reached the woodland on the other side it was enough to make him out. She swung her jeans over the piled stone and slapped her boots into the mud of the field.

A horrifying fork of lightning fired across the church again and she wondered if those bright fingers were trying to find her. The laser guns of heaven, taking closer and closer shots at their target. She closed her eyes every time the blind, giant, clumsy forks of light jabbed their way across the field, fumbling to find her as she ran towards the now-screaming boy.

CHAPTER FORTY-NINE

Ever gasped for air as he staggered through an entire army of shuddering, shaking trees. Tall trunks towered above him and he could hear them whispering to each other to get him, to slow him down. The wind joined in, whirling leaves and twigs so they slapped into his face and made him squint. Now that he was out in the Hollow world, he was starting to see that the rules were different. These trees would probably bend over and crouch with a creak. They'd slip their sharp fingers through his hair and hold him in place for Hope and the other new Hollows.

He winced. This was too much to bear.

He kept looking back over his shoulder, but it was way too dark to see any sort of movement. Then something happened that made him shriek. He saw a pair of car headlights swing around a bend. All he could think to do was to keep running. Then the headlights slowed and turned. Like vast eyes, they scanned across the field, and stopped . . . on him.

'Jesus, Jesus.' He upped his pace. 'Help me.'

He heard a car door opening.

The headlights were too bright to make out what was behind it, until he saw a sight that almost floored him it was so shocking. The Hollow in the car had seen him. Of course it had, and now it was slithering over the wall so it could run at him, across the field.

That's when he slowed down and burst into tears. That's when he decided it was time to give up. But then the sob was scooped up with a thick arm. It slid around his stomach and pulled him close. He went to kick, but the figure behind him spoke.

'Ever, it's me,' Milton said. 'Calm down.'

He turned to see the old man. He looked normal. His eyes as kind as ever.

'I thought we'd lost you, Big Man.'

'Are . . . are you okay? Are you still . . .'

'Still me?' Somehow in the madness he laughed. 'I'll die before I turn Hollow.'

Ever lifted his finger and pointed across the field. 'There's one of them now.'

Milton groaned in shock when he saw the female demon staggering across the field.

Another voice crackled from the darkness. It was Hope, panting but looking . . . normal. 'We have to get back to the church,' she gasped. 'Right now.'

'But . . . but . . . Uncle Dust . . . he says you lied. About Zara.'

'Listen . . . your Uncle Dust looked at the Hollow's eyes for too long. That's all.'

'You all looked at it.'

'We're fine, but we have to get back cos . . . look . . . that one's getting closer!' Hope pointed across the field. The Hollow was halfway across, wading through thick mud.

It called out suddenly, 'Get off him, let him go,' in a horribly human-sounding trick-voice.

'See?' Hope whispered. 'They want you. They know you're the only one to stop this. And they're going to take you away and hurt you every day for eternity. Look at how it calls for you . . .'

The Hollow was getting closer, but it was slowing and out of breath.

'And Ever, I know about this one. It's a nasty, cruel demon. Got twenty kids in her cellar, and she goes down every night just to rip off their toenails.'

Ever could barely breathe.

'And when she's finished with the toenails she takes the fingers as well. And when she's finished with the fingers, she takes the tongues . . .'

Ever turned to her and burst into tears. 'I'm sorry. Take me back, take me back.'

She nodded to Milton. 'Take him to Prosper and don't wait for me. Get this finished now. I'll stop her.'

'Just leave her.'

'I can't you idiot. Look at her hand.'

'It's glowing,' Ever said, shocked at their powers.

'It's a phone. She's calling the police. Now move!'

The sky cracked again as Milton ran with Ever, back the way they came. As they headed to the church, he kept sobbing and saying, 'I'm sorry, I'm sorry.' But he stopped to hear Hope calling out to him over the rain, just before she ran to the Hollow. And her words made him better. Just a little.

'Jesus loves you, Ever,' she said. 'Never forget that. Do his will and he'll make this right.'

CHAPTER FIFTY

Wren watched the man rush back through the trees, the crying kid locked in his arms. She cupped her hands and shouted through the rain. 'Get off him, let him go.'

The boy looked back, but the man only ran faster.

She quickly grabbed her phone and tried to tap out 999 again, but the screen became instantly wet, and it must have affected the sensitivity. None of the numbers worked. Desperate, she wiped it against her jeans and went to call out again, which was when it fully sank in. The woman wasn't going with the man and the boy. She'd actually started a mad sprint across the mud, running so fast that she didn't seem to get slowed by it, not like Wren had. This woman was skimming across the very tip of the squelch and was somehow never bogged down. That was shock enough, to see a woman come pounding towards you in a rain-soaked field. But what made Wren's heart stop, for a long beat or two, was when the lightning flashed again and lit up the field like a photo shoot from hell.

It was Miriam.

Eyes wide, mouth screaming, wet hair slimed against her cheeks.

At first, Wren was so horrified and confused by all this that all she could do was slowly walk backwards, slipping in the mud. Then the lightning flashed again, because the world seemed keen that she see Miriam open her mouth and scream out her name.

Wrennnnnnnnnn.

She was getting closer, moving at a freakish pace. The thunder boomed loud enough to knock Wren over. But she managed not to fall down. She just pulled her trainer free from the ground with a loud sucking sound, her mind an impossible jumble of shock.

And ran.

CHAPTER FIFTY-ONE

Hands, many of them, pressed Matt to his knees, then the cold wood of the Communion altar hammered off his cheekbone.

Funny how life can throw up certain mockeries, he thought. The last time he knelt behind a Communion table he was all collared up, praying over the sacred offering of bread and wine. Jesus's body, Jesus's blood. Since he jumped the church-ship he'd never expected to take part in such a ritual ever again. And now here he was, at the most literal Communion service he'd ever attended, not just as a participant but as the integral elements themselves. There'd be no wine and no bread at this Lord's supper.

Only real blood and real flesh.

His.

The sheer, mind-fuck bizarreness of this entire experience was something he hoped he could mentally process later – he told himself there would be a 'later', over and over – but for now, he just kept his cheek where they told him, and tried like mad to figure out a plan. His first attempts at a solution had been feeble so far. He'd kicked and struggled against the cable ties, but it didn't work. At one point in the aisle he even tried to nut one of these maniacs, but he got punched in the stomach and dragged back in place. So, he tried conversation instead. He'd always been a good schmoozer. Great at parties, was Matt Hunter. Always worth putting him on your list. But every time he opened his mouth he got whacked in the face until they decided to be done with it and slapped a chunk of black gaffer tape across his lips. Now it was impossible for him to clearly say stuff like 'Had a nice Christmas?' Or 'Do you come here often?' Or 'I have a family, please, please, please . . . let me go . . .'

He had no idea where Miriam was. That guy Milton and Dust were gone too. But he did see Verity. She stood there looking at him, only because of the angle of his head he saw her at a strict ninety degrees. Sometimes she was smiling, sometimes not, and now and again she shivered as if frozen with snow. She seemed to flit between Verity in the cult and Jess in the alleyway, like a flickering old bulb. It chilled him to see it.

That habit they had, of changing their names, wasn't uncommon in groups like this. The whole name changeroo happened in the Bible all the time. God got a kick out of taking a Simon and making him a Peter, a Saul and making him a Paul. There was something powerful in the forging of new identities. It helped with the brainwashing side of cults, too. A key tactic was to give their members an identity that was impossible to define apart from the group. Course they always picked religious-sounding names. You never got a James becoming a Fred, for example. It was always Malachi this or Joshua that, or in this group's case Puritan names, based on virtues like Blessing or Peace.

The bald-looking one, who looked like a gargoyle – Prosper, he'd learnt – was standing over Matt right now, with his arms folded. He'd just come back from the choir vestry, where the arguments about Zara East's body seemed to have died down – at least for now.

His head shone, and he pressed his hand across it, like he was holding his brain in. He whispered strange prayers over Matt. But he kept his big eyes wide open since he was making sure Matt didn't move. He saw Verity shake her head at him, like Matt wasn't up to snuff, then he watched her move to the pews. She sat next to a young woman he'd learnt was called Pax. Pax held the hand of a little girl who looked no more than five. It was the kid from the window at the farmhouse.

Pax would giggle every now and then, and wipe spit from her lip. It was pretty obvious that this was the mother Bowland mentioned on the phone. And that the kid on her lap was the child the man had tried to rescue from the farmhouse, before he got a steering wheel wedged in his throat and they took his eyes. The others, as far as he could tell, were fetching the other one called Ever, because without him this whole ritual was a no-go.

Seeing them all gathering around him, lighting candles, and checking all was in place, was strangely reminiscent of any other church prep he'd seen. These were just people, waiting for a service to start. He even saw an accordion lying on a pew, ready to play. As if Matt's impending – and he assumed bloody – death would somehow be a happy, celebratory affair. Which sounded so depraved and sick, until he thought of the ancient Aztecs lopping off heads to appease the Sun God, and a million trendy Christians with lattes in one hand and the other raised in wonder at the cross. What was about to happen to him wasn't so strange after all – since so much of religion flowed on the streams of blood sacrifice. It was helpful to theorise about all of this. To judge it all as an interesting object lesson in anthropology. It'd make for a killer PowerPoint one day, when he got back to his uni job. *When* he got back. And all this pondering was an attempt to drown the other voice out. The voice that said . . .

No, Matt. It is neither a matter of when nor if, because you are not going back to anything other than this. Consider this instead . . . when an axe takes a head, how long does it remain conscious? Will you see your twitching body, from a once-impossible angle . . . and will brain and vision last four seconds or maybe even five? You can see a lot in four seconds, wouldn't you agree? Enough to turn you mad, perhaps? Count it. Count four seconds. One Mississippi, two Mississippi, three . . . That's a lot of time to notice things—

His chest shuddered so hard that his ribcage hurt.

He had to focus. He had to theorise on a solution. He had to watch.

He swallowed and let his brain take the wheel again.

Bowland was bound to come. She'd visit the farmhouse, find his abandoned car and somehow, they'd track him here. Somehow, it'd be okay. The voice that said these things was growing more and more quiet, he noticed.

So, Matt waited, and stared at the drunken sway of the candles. They'd put candles all across the altar, and on the floor too, so the shadows of the ceiling bulged above him. He'd spotted a bundle of rope under the altar, too. He'd bet money on what it was for.

Got to keep you steady when they sever that old noggin off—

—but for now, they seemed content with these agonising little cable ties. He even saw them drag out a metal bucket filled with ash and strips of material and there were chunks of what looked like white sticks or branches in it. This bucket of black and grey powder stank of smoke. Whatever they'd burnt, they started to scoop handfuls of it into heaps, just so they could smear a metal cross that lay on the altar as well as scrawling shapes across the church walls. All around him he could see, and smell, the violent swipe of endless upturned crosses. Then Prosper smeared inverted crosses on Matt's cheeks, forehead and clothes. He only stopped smearing when the church door suddenly swung open.

Matt shifted his head as best he could. It was the big guy, Milton. He was walking in with another kid in tow, older than the little girl. Ten, maybe. Verity saw the boy and ran towards him.

'They found you, praise Jesus . . .' She snaked her hands around the boy and held him close, looking over at Matt. That look of hers sent the whole church into a strange quake and spin. She caught Matt's stare and pushed her lips forward. It said everything he needed to know. That here was the result of whatever happened in the alleyway that night. And my God, he could see it in her eyes – *She really does think it was me.*

'Look, Ever,' she said. 'This is your father.'

Matt started shaking his head, pressing his temple into the altar. He tried to shout *No. No, I'm not,* but it came out as pure noise.

The boy had already been chewing his fingers. Now he started gnawing at them.

Prosper planted two hands on the boy's shoulders and hurried him down the aisle towards Matt. The kid kept staring at the floor, petrified, while Matt struggled hard against the cable ties and kept groaning desperate, yet pointless, words against the tape. Prosper just smacked him again with something heavy and sharp – a metal crucifix, smeared in soot.

'Where's Uncle Dust?' Ever said.

Prosper turned. 'He's in danger but we can still save him if we finish this, first.'

Ever shook his head. 'No . . . tell me what happened.'

'A bunch of Hollows came from the woods, all right? They've dragged Dust off.'

'What?' Ever gasped. 'But I didn't see any outside.'

'Dammit boy, they weren't in their skin. They came crawling out as they are . . . as shadows, and they've taken him to the woods, but there's still time to stop them. So come on, boy, let's throw all those Hollows to the sky.' Prosper nodded to Milton to hold Matt down, then hurried to the side door of the chancel and threw the door open. Matt knew this was the door Micah had escaped from the other morning. Outside he saw a world in wild, flashing chaos. Some of the candles instantly went out, swallowed by the screaming wind.

'Look at it out there!' Prosper said. 'End's comin' . . . Jesus is coming . . . resurrection day. As soon as Hope gets here we can—'

'Don't wait.' Milton's breeze-block hands pressed Matt's head down. 'She said just do it.'

Prosper's smile quickly faded. 'What? Where is she?'

'Keeping us safe, like always. So, mate, there's no time. She said to just do it.'

Prosper looked frantically into the rain.

'Prosper . . . now.'

He sucked in a breath of courage and quickly grabbed something from a stone shelf: a black pouch. He turned the Velcro flap open and pulled something from the inside by the handle. A stubby little Stanley knife. Verity and Pax immediately started singing in the pews, and so did the little girl on Pax's lap. They stood to their feet and began a solemn walk to the altar.

Matt flung himself back from the table, but Milton's hand smacked it back into place. Pain sliced deep into his cheekbone. The hand stayed locked, then other hands pushed him down, too. Verity, Pax, Prosper, Milton, and then the little girl, holding him in place. He saw Milton drag something long from a bag.

'That's too heavy,' Ever said. 'I can't lift it.'

'Don't worry about that: you use the knife, and when it's dead we take the head.'

'Why can't we do fire?'

'There's no time. Just cut him. Just cut his throat.'

Matt screamed just then, staring at the axe, shining and brand new. A replacement for the one Micah lost. He screamed, right against the tape, and let out great hisses of desperate breath.

'I need Dust, I need him . . .' Ever sobbed and turned to Verity. 'Mum, I can't do this. Not alone.'

'You're braver than you think.' Verity was crying too. 'So kill it. Kill the Father. Kill the Father for Jesus.'

'But what if we're wrong, Mum . . .' He gulped his words out. 'What if we're—'

'Kill it!' Her shout ripped his voice away, and her eyes bulged with pain and madness. 'Kill it for me, Ever! For what it did to me. Kill it. Kill it.' She tore her scarf from her neck and rubbed and clawed at her throat. Her terrible scars looked like they were moving and wriggling.

Matt heaved against the altar and Prosper slipped the knife into Ever's hand. 'Careful, it's sharp. But the blade's pretty small, so you'll have to push it in him then drag. Like this, see?' He stuck his hand forward, then hacked a line in the air. 'Milton? Flip him over.'

The singing grew louder.

All those hands turned him around and Prosper cupped a wet palm across Matt's forehead. He was face up now, throat bared. Arms and wild faces hovered over him and the little boy with a knife in his hands stepped slowly closer, staring at the twitching veins in Matt's exposed throat. The kid was framed by the huge arched window behind him. Matt watched it flashing with holy figures in furious stained glass.

The inevitability of the moment sank in just then, from a body and brain that finally admitted the truth. That he was pitifully unable to throw all these hands off. The realisation hit Matt like a hammer. Actually no. It felt more like a fast train on a wet day. Because up until this moment there really had been at least some hope. But now the black tar had swallowed it all up, and Matt's brain exploded with ridiculous, distracting questions – anything that would stop those thoughts of the axe. The types of questions he'd ponder in the dentist chair, just to take his mind off the coming pain of the drill. With his mind an utter tornado of shock he thought, *I wonder which one of them plays the accordion, I wonder what happened* to that Dust guy, I wonder if this church roof leaks, I wonder if my beautiful daughters get married, I wonder how many candles there are in this room . . .

Yes . . . yes!

I'll count the candles. I'll count while I die . . . maybe it'll help . . .

One . . . two . . .

Life flashing. Lurching panic.

'Now, Ever.'

Three . . . four . . .

Counting like that silly Dracula puppet from Sesame Street.

Five . . .

Yes . . . I'm a kid again, watching the Count and I'm sitting on my dad's lap. Hi, Barnabus Hunter. Fancy seeing you in my final moments.

Six . . . Seven . . .

In the days when his dad acted like a dad. In the days when I loved him . . .

Eight . . .

Before he stopped being a dad and became a father, and somehow turned into a beast.

Nine . . .

And the desperate panic that the final image of his life wouldn't be his family or even his mum on Sizewell beach. It'd be him sitting on his damn father's lap counting for ever . . .

Ten . . .

At last, their names blossomed on his lips . . . Lucy . . . Amelia . . . and . . . Wren . . . then nothing came but the rain and thunder and the strangely beautiful singing that filled the church. Then the rain went quiet as Milton gripped the handle of the axe and locked himself into strike position.

Pax's voice. 'Now, Ever, Now! Make me clever again.'

Prosper's groan . . . 'I can hear Dust screaming . . . he needs you, boy. He needs you. Say the words . . .'

'I love you, Ever.' Verity whispering through her hands. 'Be brave, Ever. Kill it for me.'

'Say it . . .'

Then everything moving into one bone-deep breath as Ever spluttered out his pre-rehearsed line . . . '*Avi, Avi, lama kataltani.*'

My father, my father, why have you killed me . . .

'Well done.'

'Good boy.'

Pats on his shoulder.

Applause.

Then the last thing. The only thing.

The diorama snapshot of Milton, gripping the axe handle, eager to finish it, while the boy raised the knife with two hands above his shoulder then slammed the blade down with a wail of terror and rage, so loud that it was hard to tell if it was coming from the boy, or from the flashing glass Jesus who also happened to be dying in agony behind him.

CHAPTER FIFTY-TWO

Wren sprinted across the field, slipping and stumbling her way back to the car. Her thoughts were a whirling mess of information. She had no brain space to consider why this was happening. Only that it was.

Kind, lovely, self-sacrificing Miriam was now running at her at full pelt, shouting in a voice so brutal and guttural that Wren felt dizzy with the terror of it. '*Holloowwwww.*'

No time to scream.

No breath to scream it.

Finally, the stone wall came into view. It blocked her from the car, so she figured the best way to clear it was to grab it with both hands and fling herself over. She just needed to slow down a little to make—

Wet footsteps, close behind her.

Thud. Thud. Thud.

Miriam wailed, 'Come and die, you fucking ghoul.'

Getting closer.

Wren's hands were not builders hands, but architects hands. They were creamed with Nivea every night and were exceptionally good at sinking an eight ball. Now those hands slammed into the top of the rough stone wall. She moaned at how sharp it felt. Then she sprang up and over with a picture of herself vivid in her mind – clearing the wall in slow motion, like this was a parents' race at the school sports day, while all the other school mums cheered her escape.

Then her right knee slammed into the wall. She fell against it on the wrong side. Miriam's side. Not nearly high enough. She dropped and heard Miriam panting.

Shit, shit, shit.

Frantically she clambered up onto the wall and shrieked, when a strong, slapping clamp of a wet hand grabbed her ankle. She twisted, flipped over to her back and looked down her body. A mass of wet hair was snapping its teeth at her feet. She dragged again at Wren's leg, tugging her down.

'Why are you doing this?' Wren said, close to a sob she noticed. Then a mad thought. Maybe she just didn't like the meal the other night. Everyone's a critic.

Miriam slowed for a moment and her wet mouth opened in a smile. The type that would scare children in pantomimes. 'Because I believe it. Because it's real. And the storm believes it too.'

A gust of drenching wind pushed at them both, and Miriam almost toppled over. Wren kicked out. She shoved a clear foot into Miriam and made contact with her chest. Her mad ranting got lost in a puff of air as she fell back. All this gave Wren a perfect, golden moment of time. Enough seconds to spring up and slide across the toppling rocks and drop to the other side. Mud slapped against her belly as she dropped on all fours, then she flung herself up and stumbled towards the car in a wild, skittish escape. Thank heavens their car had that fancy feature where you didn't have to take your key out of your pocket. The sensor picked up the fob and you just grabbed the door handle and flung it open. In the dealership, Matt had said that this feature was a great idea that'd really be handy. She called it a pointless, pricey gimmick. How insane to know that a sales clerk's skills of persuasion would be the very thing that might save her life.

She flung the car door open and dived inside, slamming the door shut against the booming thunder.

She jabbed the ignition on, flicked on the lights.

She gasped.

The harsh glow of the headlights lit up Miriam who was spider-walking over the wall and reaching for the bonnet. She threw the car into reverse. The tyres churned back. The rear end of her car dropped a little as she hit that deep, colossal puddle she was trying to avoid earlier. A quick glance to the right showed there wasn't enough of an arc to turn the way she came. She'd wedge the car into the wall while Miriam scrabbled at the door.

So she locked the wheel into a hard left, and scraped the front right bumper along the wall, barely clearing it. Now all she had to—

Glass shattered.

She leapt in her seat when the rock came through the passenger window. It landed in a mass of glass in the footwell and leering through the broken hole was an actual Disney witch. The car was moving, and Wren had locked the door, but that had little effect on her terror. Miriam was now running alongside the car, grasping at the jagged glass teeth of the window which slashed her fingers. She was trying to climb in, reaching an arm into the car, always calling her name.

Wren picked up the pace on the turn and the tyres soon hit thinner ground. She ploughed ahead at last and Miriam quickly slid from the window, raking her arms on the glass, and landing in a tumbling heap of glass. Soon, she became a horrible, red-lit figure in the rear-view mirror.

But she was still coming. Still running and bleeding through the rain.

Her car threw water high on each side while she grabbed her phone and smeared the rain from the screen. She jabbed 999 and finally it was dry enough to register. She shouted out her location . . . but the voice on the other end was quiet and small, and soon fizzled away to nothing.

Wren thought, *I should've run Miriam over.*

Then she thought, *But that's good, isn't it? That my natural instinct was to get away, and not to just kill a person.*

Then all thinking stopped, because a mass of white filled up the windscreen. She slammed the brakes hard. Too late. A parked, dirty, white van was jack-knifed across the road. When she hit it, the airbags of her dashboard burst and flung her back into her seat. She tried to reverse, but the wheels just span. She pressed the airbag down and looked to the left at the shattered passenger window. Panic bloomed. She checked her mirrors. It was clear for now, but there were screams on the air that weren't the storm.

There was no other choice. She opened her door and fell out into the rain.

A house was on the left, looking black, deserted and incredibly lonely. She considered getting in there to grab a kitchen knife, a fire poker, anything. But then she heard this strange wailing coming from the church, and what seemed like an open door spilled light and screams into the graveyard.

The little boy.

Jesus Christ.

She could hear that little boy, crying out.

She ran towards the church, but she'd avoid the front doors. She moved around the building, looking for a safer entrance. She quickly found another door at the back. It was closed, but she saw light shining from underneath. Petrified that Miriam might suddenly rise from the mud, she pushed through.

When she got inside, she saw someone else instead.

A man with long hair was lying on the carpet of what looked like a vestry room. His face bulged and bled from a very fresh beating, his glasses lay smashed by his head. Another victim, she thought, just like the boy. He moaned through the gag in his mouth, asking her to set him free.

No time to think.

No strength to think it.

So she dropped to her knees, and quickly undid the rope.

CHAPTER FIFTY-THREE

When the knife came plummeting down the tip of it wedged hard into the wood of the Communion table. Any closer and it would have buried into his shoulder. He'd managed to heave himself to the left at the very last second with a Hulk-level burst of latent energy (fuelled by desperation and the sheer terror of death), but something else had helped too. It was the boy, Ever. He'd slipped on the way down because he'd been distracted by something.

A man's voice calling his name from across the church.

Locked in position by all those hands, Matt couldn't see who was shouting, but he did see all their faces spasm in shock when they looked up.

'Don't do it, son,' the voice said. 'Don't kill him.'

It was the man, the one they called Dust, though his voice sounded very different to before. Now it was strange and spluttery. Prosper eased his hand off Matt's forehead in pure surprise, which meant that for a while, Matt could look too. Dust was slouching in the far end of the middle aisle, keeping himself upright by gripping the back pew. His smashed face dripped blood and loose teeth seemed to slide down his slimy hair, but it was who stood just behind him that made Matt explode into life, so he might wrench himself free.

Wren.

She was standing by the vestry door, drenched with rain and smeared with mud. Her eyes were wide and both hands covered her mouth, because that's the sort of reaction wives have when they see their husband tied on his knees behind a church altar, with tape across his mouth. In the sudden, gaunt quiet, Matt yanked his chest from the altar and somehow pulled free from Prosper's hand, but Milton helped shove Matt down, harder than ever. The two men swooped to each side, using all their strength to stop him throwing them off again. He writhed like a mad asylum inmate.

'Get off him!' Wren called out and started to come forward, but Matt shook his head, desperately trying to warn her off. She saw the sheer fright in his eyes and slowed down.

'This isn't the way, Ever.' Dust staggered to the next pew. 'You have to put the knife down.'

Prosper immediately leant close. 'Look at him. They've turned him Hollow. See how awful he looks. Hear his voice? Just like the one in the car.'

Dust took a shambling, zombie-step forward.

'The monster's coming through, it's splitting the skin.' Prosper yanked the knife out from the wood. 'So Ever, try again. No distractions this time.'

'They did this to me,' Dust shouted, in a voice so loud it shook the entire church. 'And Ever, they killed Zara and lied about—'

'Dammit, Dust, that's enough. Zara tried to stop Micah from doing this,' Prosper shouted in desperation. '. . . Just like you're trying to stop it now.'

'You said lies were for Hollows . . .' Dust took another shambling step forward and almost fell. 'How can we trust you with anything?'

Matt couldn't hold it any longer. He called out to Wren, with a groaning plea against the tape, 'Run!' he shouted, though it sounded little more than a muffled roar. '*Please. Go.*'

He saw her wipe tears from her face, which were instantly replaced with new ones. Then she shook her head at him, refusing to leave. Instead, she darted her gaze around the church, looking, he assumed, for a weapon. And through it all, his wrists were burning because those damn—

He blinked.

He tilted his head. Blinked again.

Something clicked into place. A moment that his old self might have called miraculous while his new self simply called it physics. He felt the heat from the candles.

The candles.

Holy shit, Matt thought. *The candles!*

He immediately leant back a touch. Just so his wrists grew closer to the flame. He heard the hair on his arms quietly crackle, but they were all too distracted to notice. He ground his teeth as the scorching pain began. Which was when the mother of all lightning bolts crashed outside. They all swung their heads at the side door, as if they might see the entire world on fire. What the lightning bolt had actually left behind was a figure, stumbling up the church path.

Miriam.

Wren screamed.

The drenched, bleeding figure scrambled in from the rain; her hair was a writhing nest of wet, wild snakes. She looked across them all with disgust. 'End it, come on!' Then she threw a pointed finger at Wren. 'Pax, Verity, keep her back.'

The two women let go of Matt and ran to stop Wren, who was now running down to the altar. His arms felt lighter, but the two men still locked him in place. He leant back a little and jammed his teeth together at the pain in his wrists.

Miriam hobbled over and tore the tape from Matt's mouth, which felt so sharp and searing. Then she spat on him. 'When we see you, we see the Father . . . but you can't hurt us any more. All the hate and abuse you threw at us . . . it ends here . . .'

He could see Wren struggling. Now his mouth was free he screamed at them. '*Let her go.*'

Miriam leant closer. She was trembling. 'You are the Father, and we reject you completely. We serve the Son who you tortured and killed on the cross . . .'

'Jesus chose to go . . .' Matt groaned. '. . . It wasn't murder . . . it was love . . . it was the Trinity . . .'

'Fuck the Trinity,' she laughed. 'That's the biggest lie of all. There can only ever be one God. So, Father . . . it's time you stepped down.'

Matt stared at her. 'You're mad.'

She pushed a hot, wet whisper directly into his ear. '*Eloi, eloi . . . Lama kataltani,*' then she grabbed Ever's hands and squeezed his palms around the knife handle.

Aaaaand . . .

She plunged Ever's hands forward.

The boy's sobbing body jerked like a rag doll, without any sense of aim. She just went for anywhere on Matt's body. He heard Wren scream for what felt an incredibly long time. Then the pain arrived, and he lost any sense of where the candle was at his wrist. He felt the bizarre presence of something cold inside his shoulder. A foreign invader. Then the sickening sensation of it slipping back out as a wet soak of blood spurted down his arm.

Wren broke free, heaving Verity and Pax to the side.

'Stop it!' She scrambled down the slope ready to leap onto Miriam's back, so now Milton had to let go of Matt too. He rushed towards Wren to stop her. At the exact same moment, a loud and wild crashing sound came from the side wall, near the door. A few panels from the stained-glass window had blown in.

'It's working, see? It's working,' Miriam shouted, 'but you have to get his neck, Ever, his *neck*!'

Prosper splayed Matt's head back and yanked open the collar of his shirt, so his throat was clearer. He had a horrible look in his freakish face. He looked lost and confused, and when he looked at Miriam, deeply afraid.

'End's coming.' Miriam was laughing as she slammed Ever's hands, and the knife, down. 'End's come!'

Snap.

Matt heard it. He actually heard the tiny pop of the cable tie. Over all this commotion, the candle flame had burnt all the way through the multiple threads of plastic and half into his skin.

Just a little *snap*, and everything changed.

People were too shocked to even comprehend it. Their faces just twitched in surprise, almost in awe, when Matt suddenly rose. It was one of those flickering moments from a dream, where his hands sprang apart and the cable ties split in two. He moved fast enough and with enough deliberate aim to aim his opening hand for the black metal cross that sat upturned on the table. Just as he'd been planning for what seemed like months now, he grabbed that cross on the upswing. He saw it out the corner of his eye as if another arm and another hand was doing it. The muscles in his shoulders and forearms screamed in pain, but he welcomed the agony because with it he saw the black cross rise in his fist, soaked in ash. He even saw a line of soot shed itself through space, as he sliced it hard through the air.

Crack.

When it smashed against Miriam's temple, at the very sharpest edge, the impact shook every bone in his arm. He saw her eyes widen, that was all, then she whispered something inaudible as she keeled over to the side. It was like the slow-motion felling of a tree, which everybody stopped to watch. The thinnest jet of blood

348

fountained from her temple and traced a perfect arc through the air as she fell.

In panic, Prosper, Pax and Milton threw out arms to catch her, as she toppled onto the steps. All three fell with her, crashing in a heap on the stone floor. Milton still had the axe in his hand. The only sound was the clank of metal as Ever dropped the Stanley knife and after that, the sound of his little feet pounding on the stone as he ran to Dust, who had now completely collapsed and lay wheezing on the floor.

Matt grabbed the knife and liberated his feet with one sharp cut.

The lightning flashed again, only it was now a completely different colour than before. It was blue, which was when Milton dropped the axe too. For a silent moment, every single person just stared at the light. They watched the stone arches flicker and Pax started laughing as she stroked Miriam's hair. She talked about angels, swooping to 'rescue her mummy'. Ever was the only one to speak. His jaw dropped at the bright-blue miracle and with tears in his eyes, he said, 'Dust, look . . . it's working. Jesus is coming . . .'

The sirens grew loud enough to sting the ear, and Matt noticed Verity was crying at the lights. It meant Wren was able to wriggle from her grip with relative ease. She rushed over and scooped her hand under Matt's armpit and they both turned to the open church door. The world outside was a flashing disco of colour and each long shadow turned, like a time-lapse sundial. Yet the police cars were still too far away, struggling to get up the hill, which by now was a gauntlet of sliding mud. And in those moments when he and Wren slouched to the door, Matt kept looking back at the people's faces. He didn't see the chaos of criminals caught in the act. Or the fury of fighters, ready to stand. He saw the horribly silent phenomenon of many hearts breaking, all at the same time. The dawn of a bleak reality: that the world, or at least their world, truly was at its end after all. *End's coming . . . end's come.*

It was strangely hypnotic, to watch them like this, until he saw something that broke the moment completely. Miriam was crawling along the floor towards them, glaring at Wren with her gore-soaked eye.

He grabbed her hand. 'Move.'

He was losing blood of his own, but he could still walk straight, just about. Thank God the kid was a crap aim, though he wondered if Ever had deliberately swayed to the side, on those early blows. As they staggered to the side door they both noticed a gut-wrenching sight. The little girl he saw earlier was cowering behind the curtain, by the door. When Matt looked at her, she covered their eyes and looked away. 'Please! Please, don't eat me.'

He grabbed the girl's hand and after a nod to Wren she grabbed the other hand. They pulled her through the side door, out into the dark, wet world, and the sky filled with the screams of an abducted child. It was only when they'd cleared the door and stumbled onto the gravel that Matt hugged a shell-shocked Wren and gave her Merit's other hand. He went to turn back to the church. She stared at him, jaw dropping. 'Wait . . . what . . . what are you doing?'

'The boy,' Matt said. 'Ever.'

'Matt, the police . . . they'll get him . . .'

It came out as a desperate gasp. 'There's no time.' He nodded to the police lights. They were still making their laboured rescue up the hill. Even from here, he heard wheels spinning in the mud, and for a moment he was back in his lecture in Berlin yet here at the same time. And those images of Guyana and Waco were being projected against the rain, reminding him of how these stories tend to end. He just knew it, as sure as the sky was flashing and the blood was seeping. That Wren was wrong. There was no time.

She had to keep this little kid out here to stop her running back into the church to her family. If she did that, she'd be lost too. And it had to be Wren that stayed out here, because he'd struggle to hold on to the girl, what with this damn pain blazing in his shoulder. It was him or nothing, because the old man had said something earlier, that there was 'another path'. He saw Wren stare at him, mouthing desperate words.

'He'll die . . .' Matt said, because he knew it was true.

She winced and shook her head. Tears fell.

He touched her arm and thought of Sean Ashton, bleeding by the tree, and Micah exploding in a boom of thunder, and Ever on some future lecture screen, and he told Wren with his eyes . . . *If I don't go back he'll be one of my slides one day. And I can't bear the thought of it, Wren. I can't.*

She was about to speak, but she looked back over his shoulder first, staring at the broken window into the chancel. She wailed in horror. 'Oh, Jesus.' Whatever she'd seen was a revelation because she looked at him, nodded and handed him something. The Stanley knife. She must have grabbed it from the floor. The little girl struggled against her, yanking her little arms so hard they almost dislodged from the sockets. But Wren didn't try to stop him any more. When she spoke again, it came out as a gulping sob of despair, but she said it anyway.

'Go,' she said. '*Go.*'

CHAPTER FIFTY-FOUR

Ever rushed to Uncle Dust on the floor, while Prosper dragged the heavy ropes out from under the altar. Milton flung them over the beam, each in turn.

'Close the door, please,' Prosper said. 'And block it. Use anything you can find.'

Ever turned to the doorway and saw the woman Hollow staring back from outside. She was covered in flashing blue light and horizontal rain. Then she vanished as the wood rattled shut.

Hope was back on her feet now. She took a staggering step towards the altar. Steady rivulets of blood were pulsing from her head. It made her stumble. 'Ever?' she said. 'Where are you?' She ran her eyes across the church, until they locked on him. 'Ahhh . . . there. Can you hear him? Can you hear Jesus singing?' She tilted her head to listen and blood poured from the hole. It made her eyes flicker. 'Verity . . . can you collect him, please?'

Mum nodded and came to him. She put a hand on Ever's shoulder, and they both watched Milton throw the final rope over.

Prosper counted them up. 'Thanks Milton. Looks like we're ready.'

Milton nodded quietly, and the two men shook hands, cupping a hand over each other's shoulder.

'Wait,' Ever stabbed a finger at the other rope, coiled under the table, 'Isn't that for Merit? Shouldn't we get her back?'

'No time,' Prosper saw Ever's panic and he smiled, 'but Jesus . . . he'll reach her. We'll just have to meet her on the other side, that's all.'

Now that the ropes were out, people were being polite. Ever liked that, and he knew the reason was simple. The Hollows were gone. It meant they could finally be themselves again, but he still found himself chewing through his lip, staring at Uncle Dust on the floor.

Mum dropped to his level. 'It's time, Ever.'

'But . . .' He lowered his voice to a whisper. 'He said Hope lied. He said her and Prosper hurt him.'

Mum placed a single fingertip against his lips. 'That's impossible. The Hollows must have tricked him.'

'But—'

'But nothing, Ever. The Hollows lie. That's their language.' She saw him staring at the blue flashing ceiling. 'And those lights aren't angels. It's them. It's another trick. So, it's time, okay? Time for the other path.' She leant towards him, eyes brimming, hands trembling. 'And we have to hurry, cos I can't be in heaven without you. And if we stay, they'll take you away from me. They'll put Mummy in a cage.'

His face started to crumple. Hers too. 'I messed it all up, I got scared.'

'You were brave, you tried . . .' She straightened his hair. 'But it's okay, cos if Jesus isn't coming to us, then we can go to him . . . right? Just like we always said.'

She went to stand, so he stood with her, but he held onto Dust's hand. He looked down at him. 'What if they get inside and kill him?'

'Baby, he's already gone.' She tugged their hands apart and his uncle's arm dropped like a stone. 'So how about we find Dust and Merit again? Let's meet them on the other side of the stream. He'll—'

They both jumped.

Someone was hammering on the church door, trying to get in.

'Come on,' Prosper said. 'Hurry.'

The six dangling ropes had stopped swinging and, in the stillness, Ever heard the most beautiful sound he'd ever heard. It was Pax, starting to sing. She sounded so . . . so normal.

'Jesus's hands were kind hands . . . doing good to all . . .' She was the first one to climb up on the altar. 'Healing pain and sickness, blessing children small.'

Prosper lifted his voice too, as Pax helped him up. Then Milton joined in. 'Washing tired feet and saving those who fall.'

There was a surprising, and yet very unsurprising, peace about it all. Even with the church doors hammering. Even with the flashing blue lights and the thundering of his heart, Ever felt peace. Milton put his big fat thumb up and winked at him. 'Chin up, all right? We're gonna be grand. You've proved your faith tonight. Hell, we all have, and he's seen every bit of it. We still get a happy ending, okay, Big Man?'

'Take my hands, Lord Jesus, let them work for you. Make them strong and gentle, kind in all I do.'

'Will it hurt?' Ever asked, as Milton lifted him up.

Hope said. 'Sing. Just sing.'

So he did, as the doors boomed, and the storm raged on.

'Let me watch you, Jesus, till I'm gentle too, Till my hands are kind hands, quick to work for you.'

When they'd all climbed up they thanked each other for the helping hand. They stood together in the Crooked Church and kissed one another, then they all hugged for one last time, before leaning their heads forward to help each other with the ropes. There was no lament. No weeping or wailing. The time for that was over. Just a sense of rightness that the weakest one of them all, Pax, was now singing like an angel, leading them home.

CHAPTER FIFTY-FIVE

Matt smacked his fists off the side door. Hard enough to send shooting pains through his wrist and forearm, but especially his shoulder. Then he slammed a boot against the wood. The door creaked and strained, but it was stuck solid. All he got for the effort was a searing pain through the gash in his shoulder. He was about to try the door again when he heard Wren shouting. 'Use the side door. The choir vestry.'

He nodded and hurried around the church, scraping his foot from gravel to grass. The police had abandoned their cars now, and were finally running closer on foot, but even a minute away still felt like the world.

When he turned the curve outside of the chancel, an ice wind slammed into him with a force he hadn't experienced in years. In his entire life, actually. It was astonishing really. The power of the gale, the way it screamed through the gaps in the church stone, and all that relentless rain from a flashing, End-Times sky. He could see the headlines tomorrow: STORM OF THE CENTURY HITS

BRITAIN! No wonder they thought it was the end of the world, in there. It sure as hell felt like it was out here. The wind pushed him into an unexpected, jogging stumble. He planted his hand on something to steady himself. A gravestone. Lightning flashed. He almost laughed. If God was up there, he was getting zero points for subtlety.

He found the door easily because a thin strip of light glowed from under it. The wind made it rattle wildly against the door frame. He thought it might be locked, but he just turned the handle down, and the wind wrenched it inwards with a loud snap. The rain hushed to a low white noise, once he was inside. The choir vestry was a mess, with a wooden chair on its side and a mass of broken glass on the floor. The chair was bent and smashed, and . . . odd. One of the legs had been wrenched off. It lay in a wet circle on the carpet, the splintered, spiked end soaked with blood. A stake for a vampire – a sword for a Hollow.

God, he thought, as he scooped it up, *they must have beaten Dust with this*. Stabbed him with it too, from the looks of it. Gripping the dry end, he loped towards the door that led into the church, then paused before going in, just to catch some breath.

He pushed through.

The first thing he noticed, when he creaked the internal door open, was how quiet the place was. No more shouting, like before. As he slouched past the pillar and planted his hand on a pew, he saw them all, and realised that his instincts were right. These groups might embrace the most preposterous and illogical world views, yet at least they knew when it was time to quit. Especially when the end wasn't really the end to them. Just the end of the beginning.

He looked down the aisle at the sunken chancel and shuddered.

They were holding hands, standing on top of the Communion table. With songs and strange smiles, they reached out their arms to help the others up. Six of them. Prosper and the big guy Milton stood next to the young woman Pax. She was singing, while Verity and Ever stood beside her. And finally, Miriam stood at the right edge of the altar with her blood-drenched eye blinking, and her arm in the air worshipping the storm.

He knew instantly what was happening. When he saw the ropes under the altar earlier, he'd assumed they were for him, but of course, they never were. He was the first path . . . but this . . . *this* was the other.

He saw Ever, the little boy, lean forward, politely waiting for his noose.

'No!' Matt's shout sounded pathetic, flat and pointless.

Ignoring the pulsing throb in his side he slouched down the aisle, surprised at how they didn't seem to notice him. They were oblivious to anything except this moment. Matt had to step over a massive heap in the middle of the aisle. It was Dust. Blood pumped from a few ragged puncture wounds. He'd bet money they'd match the splintered tip of this chair leg he was carrying. He patted his pocket for the Stanley knife. Still there, and ready to use.

He gripped the weapon but didn't raise it. Not yet. He moved forward instead, feeling that familiar pressure of going down a slope. *Welcome to the Crooked Church*, he thought. *Har-dee-haar.* The altar sat on the other side of the knee-high Communion rail, where the penitent knelt for their weekly bout of spiritual cannibalism. A gulp of flesh, a swig of body. Nothing barbaric about that, until you spend three seconds thinking about it. This was a fitting place, then, for these poor, brainwashed seekers to make their sacrifice.

The wooden beam was just a little bit in front of the table. A perfect stride's width. Like it was all meant to be and written in their stars. The Communion rail had a gate on it, which they'd closed now. He called to them, as gently as he could manage and said, 'Please . . . *please* don't do this.'

Only three of them looked at him. Prosper, Milton and Pax. They already had their nooses in place and Pax smiled when she saw him. It was a pretty, happy face she had. He noticed the curve of their shoes were already peeking over the edge of the thick heavy table, like divers set to leap. He saw a pair of muddy black boots, brown shoes, purple pumps, grey pumps and blue trainers.

'This won't work.' Matt spoke so quietly that it came out as a whisper.

'I see paradise . . . I see the end of lament . . .' Prosper said, smiling. 'I see home . . . I see a vast—' He dropped.

Matt's eyelids slammed shut. But the sound got through.

A deep, heavy thud, and somewhere hiding in that thump was a soft crack, which could have been the wooden beam or could have been Prosper's neckbone. A conundrum that could drive you mad, if you considered it for too long. Matt opened his eyes again and saw Prosper swinging forwards and back, forwards and back. His feet and arms twitched like a mad, dancing puppet. His swollen eyeballs, rolling up. The others kept looking forward.

Matt rushed forward, desperately hoping to reason with them but knowing they could all just step off at the exact same time. If they did that, he could grab at least one of them, maybe two. He'd keep them up while the others dangled. It was like a gameshow from hell.

Choose one to save, and four to swing!

Actually, I've had a great day. I think I'll just go home.

He knew full well what his choice was: Ever and Pax, but what about the others? Weren't they all children once? Perhaps they still were. He had a vision of himself bunching all their legs together and holding them up before the police arrived, like a bizarre, fumbling Atlas. He knew that wouldn't work. Matt started to climb over the rail.

Verity already had her noose in place, pressing down against the ugly scars from the bike chain, but she was having trouble with Ever's. It seemed like it was too big for him, so she was yanking it tighter. Sensing his moment Matt shot forward, but just as he did it, Milton tearfully said, 'I've loved you all.' He dropped too.

Matt's eyes were open this time and as Milton's bulk stepped forward the knees buckled, and his hefty weight knocked the table back an inch. The whole altar wobbled and then Verity slipped off. Matt saw her turn her head to her son. He saw her open her mouth to say something meaningful, just as the rope snapped taut with the loudest crack of them all. That crack was louder than humanly possible, until he realised it was the beam itself starting to buckle. Prosper, Verity and the heavy Milton danced and dangled. Arms, chins and toes pointed down in spasm. Ever's raw eyes were locked forward, but now they were fighting, *fighting* the urge to slide right and look at his mum.

When Miriam saw Verity fall she moaned, then she looked at Matt. 'Does this please you, Hollow? Does this feed you?'

'Mummy, don't look at it,' Pax said. 'Wanna be clever. Wanna fall now.'

'Ever first.' Miriam went to finish what Verity had started. She tightened the noose around the boy's neck.

Matt lunged forward and grabbed Ever's legs.

'It's got him,' Pax shouted. 'It's got him!'

'Then jump, Ever!' Miriam screamed, and when he hesitated, she started shoving him off instead. But Matt was smacking her arms with the chair leg. She winced and pulled her hand back. Matt reached up to drag the rope off the boy's throat, then he yanked it over his chin where it snagged hard and stuck against his teeth. Ever's eyes were shut tight now, and his shoulders rocked with sobs.

Suddenly, a crashing sound came from above them. Even Ever

looked up to see it. Another small panel of stained glass blew in with the wind, leaving a wild, flashing hole. And something else came too, from up above the beam. A shower of powder that poured like sand. They all looked at it, transfixed. Then Matt blinked and knew.

It took all his strength, both physical and emotional, to force that rope over Ever's mouth. To rip the skin of the boy's top lip away, and try to pull it over his nose, while whacking Miriam across the fingers as she shoved and pushed at them both. But she soon gave up when he pulled out the Stanley knife, and she turned back to Pax who was unable to sing any more, because she was crying. From the corner of his eye he saw them hug one another, and Miriam whispered the kind of loving, reassuring words Matt said to his own daughters, before a hard exam or a tricky appointment. Then finally the noose was over Ever's now-bleeding nose, and once that happened it was off the boy completely. Matt yanked him off the altar. He expected a scream but Ever had nothing left. The stones above him cried out instead. They started to moan and creak.

Despite the agony, Matt held the boy and started to run, though it was more of a gasping stumble back down the aisle.

'Close your eyes, Ever,' Matt said. 'Don't look.'

They were halfway up the aisle when Matt heard the two thuds. They hit at almost the exact same time. And soon after, he heard what the powder had promised would come. A horrendously deep, pirate-ship creak that shot through the wooden beam and burst into a splintered explosion. He couldn't see it, but he heard the beam collapse and smash to the floor. He could picture them all and their attempt at a graceful death, sliding off like curtain rings into a grotesque heap.

The kid was trying to push his head up.

'Don't. Don't look.'

The back of the church suddenly swarmed with mud-soaked police, wet and panting, and when he reached the end of the aisle he saw their faces drop in horror at what they saw in the chancel. Matt couldn't resist it any more. Ever still buried, he joined the police in one last look. The beam had cracked in the centre then dropped. It made a stark and clumsy V at the end of the church. The silly hope that Matt had, that Verity and Pax might be getting up and just rubbing their necks after sliding off, vanished when he saw the heap of arms, and Miriam on top. He saw her fixed stare, the vile angle of her neck.

That was when the stones started to fall, and a voice shouted, 'Everybody out. Now!'

But Matt didn't move, even as he saw the statues smashing onto the chancel floor. He didn't move because Ever was pointing at a shadow in the far corner of the church. 'Look,' he said. 'The Hollows.'

The police strained to see but saw nothing but darkness. They tugged at Matt to leave, dragged at him in fact, but he waited for a single second because it was simply impossible to look away.

Ever said, 'You can see them too?'

And Matt thought, *Yes*. Though he refused to say it. But he did think it. He thought, *Yes. I see them too.*

He saw tall shadow things, animal things, insect things that walked like people and stepped from the corners of the church like ballet dancers, like puppeteers after a show. He saw them stride towards the bodies on the floor to crouch and touch and sniff the broken necks, while the other shadows stood tall with arms open wide in pride and achievement. Then the one squatting on the altar, the one that Matt recognised, turned to face him. It lifted its twisted rabbit arm and opened its mouth to tell. Because there were two people here who could see.

A hand slammed onto Matt's shoulder and dragged him back. It was Bowland. 'Move!'

Matt looked away, too shaken and confused to cope with it. So, he buried it. He locked it away in a box marked 'hallucination from blood loss' and he set it from his mind. He let unseen hands drag him and Ever into the rain.

They all gathered a good distance away, standing by the stone wall in the muddy road and together they waited for the Crooked Church to fall, just like it had always wanted to. At one point someone gasped because the building let out this God-awful groan, and he assumed it might topple completely. But it didn't, so people put their phones away and stopped recording. And soon Matt was shouting at the medics to get back inside, as if there might be hope. Wren clambered out of an ambulance, just then. He saw her a little way down the road, and beyond her shoulder he saw three paramedics trying to restrain the screaming little girl.

'Merit . . .' Ever reached out a hand. Then the ambulance door slammed shut.

Wren ran close and put a hand on both him and the boy. Matt saw the fear and shock in her eyes. She saw the fear and shock in his. Two medics rushed behind him, with a small torch firing into Ever's face. 'Can you open your eyes, son? We need to see your eyes.'

Matt felt the vigorous shake of his head.

'Wait. Your shoulder.' The medic looked at Matt. 'You're bleeding.'

'Yes, I suppose I am.'

'Then set him down, please.'

'He won't let go.'

The medic slapped a piece of material on Matt's shoulder, just as Ever spoke. He heard a little whisper settle in his ear. 'Are you my dad? Or is that a lie, too?'

'I'm not. Your mummy made a mistake.'

Ever waited. Said nothing. 'Then what are you?'

'Set him down, now,' the medic said.

Matt said, 'I'm your friend. And I promise I won't hurt you. None of us will.'

The boy shivered against him, but Matt felt the arms hug tighter.

'Matt.' Wren grabbed his arm. 'Look!'

He squinted through the rain, and for the first time in hours a bright smile filled his face, engaging muscles he thought were long gone. Matt span the boy around to see. More paramedics were coming from the church, carrying a stretcher through the rain, and one of them was talking to the man lying flat on it. The man was talking back.

'Uncle Dust?' Ever's manic grip vanished, and Matt set him gently into the mud. Before running off, Ever paused and caught Matt's gaze. The boy held this look for what felt like a very long moment. Then eventually, with a nod, Ever spun on his feet and rushed to the stretcher, where Dust was reaching out for him.

Matt jerked in shock at the feel of so many fingers on him, but it was just the paramedics, hurrying him to the ambulance. Somebody pressed a fresh piece of material hard into his shoulder while Wren held his other hand. They climbed into the back and he winced at the sharp, interior light. The two men got to work, cutting his shirt. They lay Matt down on his side. The cuts weren't deep they said, and that was good. As they fixed him, he noticed Wren's arms and elbows were wrapped in tight bandages too.

He looked at her from the bed and said, 'Best date night, ever.'

She smiled at him, and it was heaven to see it, but then her chest shuddered, and she kissed the back of his hand. He pulled her hand close and did the same to her. They never lost sight of each other, even as the medics leant and tugged and lifted.

At one point he saw her lips press together. She was trying to keep it all in.

She lifted her hand to her mouth. Embarrassed. 'What? What is it?'

'It's okay, Wren,' he squeezed her hand.

'What's okay?'

'It's over . . . so it's okay to cry now . . . if you need to.'

Her eyes filled, and she laced her fingers into his. 'And you too.'

So they did.

CHAPTER FIFTY-SIX

Matt and Wren sat at their dining-room table, watching Bowland set out three teacups and a bright orange teapot made of cast iron. This teapot was crazy expensive, but it always seemed to impress guests. He'd won it at a posh raffle. Some black-tie uni dinner. He watched the honey-coloured tea falling from the spout. Listened to the gentle glug and trickle as it fell. It made him think of rain.

Bowland was pouring the tea because this super-pricey teapot was also super-heavy. It wasn't easy to lift, when you had wounds. So, when Bowland arrived and saw all their bandages and steri-strips on sides, shoulders, elbows, chins and knuckles she insisted that she serve. So here she was, all power-dressed and perfect skin, with her sharp sculpted grey hair pointed, getting milk from their fridge. They sat and watched her in silence.

The kitchen window was wide open. Amazingly it'd been wonderfully warm for a while. After the 'storm of the decade' pummelled southern Britain two nights back, newspapers warned there'd be more rain on the way. But the heavens seemed too traumatised by it all. They'd given all the drama they could muster in that one, apocalyptic night. Now it was an exquisitely sunny day for January. He wondered if Bessie might be out in her front garden today. He'd heard she was okay after the attack at her house. Shaken but unhurt. He'd go up and check on her soon. Take her a massive bunch of flowers and a pile of cowboy paperbacks too.

Bowland's spoon clinked against the cups as her earrings swayed, then she finally broke the silence. 'So, Wren. How are you doing? I hear you were pretty bruised after that tussle with Miriam.'

Wren openly shivered.

'Sorry, I didn't mean to—'

She raised a hand. 'Just bruises and scrapes. Nothing broken. Though I'm thinking of burning this entire dinner table with a flame-thrower.'

'Oh?' Bowland started pulling out a yellow paper file and set it in front of her.

'That psychopath ate an entire meal off it.'

'Kinda puts you off a stir-fry,' Matt added.

Bowland put a palm on the file. 'You know, if you'd both rather I fill you in later I can give—'

They both said 'No' at the same time. It made them look at each other. They gave one of those quiet laughs couples do when they speak at the same time.

'No,' Matt said. 'Go ahead.'

'We want to know all of it . . .' Wren stared at the file.

Bowland set her cup down and waited for a moment, eyeing them both with a slow, surveyor's blink. Then she slipped her glasses on and opened the file. 'Well, first things first. Sean Ashton wasn't suicide. We found DNA on the shard of glass and we've traced it back to Miriam.'

Wren shivered again, but Matt said nothing. He'd thought as much. He stared at the file. 'Go on.'

'Seems like he stumbled on her watching your house. She must have thought he might tell someone, so she killed him under the tree, with a broken bottle. I think she just panicked.'

Wren shook her head, 'Or maybe that's just what monsters do.'

'Maybe.'

'And she was watching the house to keep an eye on me?' Matt said. 'So the cult knew where I was?'

'More than that. She was making sure you were safe. They couldn't have you hit by a bus. It'd screw up their ritual. So, she watched and kept you protected. Which of course is why she stepped in when Mrs Ashton tried to shoot you. She couldn't let you die. That was for the boy to do.'

The nerves in his stab wound started to crackle, but he resisted another scratch. 'You know, the fact that she stood in front of that muzzle makes this case very simple.'

Bowland looked up. 'It does?'

'It shows she really did believe it. That she genuinely thought this . . . this symbol was going to change the world. They all did, I guess.' He looked away at the open window, at the stone cross on the church. And he saw them all in his back garden. Prosper, Milton, Verity and the rest, hugging and weeping and climbing up on his picnic bench. He often saw them out there, since it happened, like last night when he heard Pax singing at two in the morning. He came downstairs and stood at the window watching for them. He snapped the image away by grabbing his cup. 'And how's Ever? And Merit?'

'Well it's going to be a very long, very complicated process of therapy, but they're in the care of counsellors and they're together. We have specialists who've helped lots of other kids with re-entry.'

'Re-entry?' Wren said. 'So this happens a lot, does it? Kids and cults?'

'It's more common than people realise . . .'

'And Ever's uncle?' Matt said.

'He was uncle only in name.'

'Um, yeah . . . Dust.'

'Physically he's improving. Might even regain sight in his left eye, but it's early days. He's getting the same sort of counselling too. He's asked to be called by his real name now. He refuses to answer to Dust.'

Matt set the cup down. 'What is his real name?'

Bowland ran a finger down her file. 'Marc Coombs. An orphan. Had a long history in children's homes all across the country. And not the good ones, either. Had a tough time at secondary school, from the looks of it.' She started flipping through her file. 'Milton was um . . . Billy Fenton. Used to be a farmer till he had to sell up ten years back. Lost his wife around the same time. Drunk driver. Almost drove him to suicide till he found this group.'

'And Prosper?'

'He was a petty criminal called Jason Meek. In and out of prison for most of his life. He tried to murder his dad once when he was a teenager. Understandable, to be honest. I've seen the file.'

'What about Miriam?' Wren said, quietly.

'Her name was Miriam Croft, who became Hope. She had a pretty normal life, as far as we can tell. Ran a dry-cleaning shop, went to church. But her husband beat her daughter one night. Quite out of the blue. She was ten at the time.' Bowland turned a picture round. A happy, bright little girl in a school uniform beamed back. 'She suffered major brain trauma. Miriam gave up work to care for her full time. Her husband ran off and was never found.'

369

'So this is Pax . . .' Matt whispered, gazing at the picture.

Bowland nodded. 'Real name, Jenny Croft.'

Wren reached over and held the picture. She just kept staring at it.

'And Verity. She was Jess . . .' Matt bit his lip, searching.

Bowland flipped a page. 'Dean. Jessica Dean.'

'That's right. Dean. Jessica Dean.'

'She ran away from home in her early teens. Classic scenario. Drunk dad, easy with his fists, absent mother. She lived on the streets for a while. A long while, actually. Two years, from the looks of it. She was raped in a back alley, as you know. Which seems to have gotten her pregnant. Eventually she found the group, though we're not sure how. Found a home for her little boy, anyway. She called him Connor, but he became—'

'Ever . . .' Matt said. 'And Merit?'

'Was probably always called that. She was five, so she never knew anything different than the group. The man you found in the car was Merit's dad, Bill. Seems like Pax and him had a short relationship, but clearly he couldn't accept living on that farm, and left. Dust said his leaving was an early sign.'

'Sign of what?' Matt asked.

'That the end of was coming.'

Wren hadn't spoken for a while. She just stared at the picture of Pax. Eventually she set it on the table then slowly slid her head into her hands. Her fingers became lost in the red of her hair. 'My God,' she said. 'No wonder they thought the world was filled with monsters . . .'

'Yeah, for them, it really was.' Bowland gazed down at the files in front of her. 'We reckon the man who raped Jess was caught, by the way.'

'Really?' Matt looked up. 'How?'

'Kevin Parsons. Police caught him about six years ago, doing the same to another woman in the city. Seems like he'd stolen one of those Street Angel jackets so he could get alongside people. Pretty insidious fella by all accounts. Explains why Jess got confused when she saw you in the same gear . . .' Bowland caught the look in his eye. 'I'm sorry, Matt. This is a lot to take in.'

Matt and Wren were holding hands. He wasn't sure when that had happened, but he noticed it seemed to be automatic at the moment. This holding on to each other. 'So, what about Zara East? How did she find the others?'

'Marc Coombs . . . Dust . . . he told me that Miriam was trying to connect with a bunch of vicars' sons to recruit them for their ritual, but it didn't take them long to find Micah. Miriam really clicked with him, only he brought his mum along too.'

'Who was drifting from the church anyway . . .' Matt said.

'Yep. Dust says Micah was fascinated with their teaching and was besotted with Miriam. They worked on him for at least three months. Thoroughly washed that kid's brain. The mum got drawn in too, until she heard their plans for Micah. She must have threatened to tell. Looks like Prosper and Miriam strangled her and told the rest of the group she'd run off and turned demon. Told Micah that too. He thought the only way to save her was the ritual but then David East didn't die. The miracle of St Bart's.'

Matt sniffed, 'They might call it a miracle but I'm thinking Micah just got cold feet. Maybe he deliberately failed, in the panic of it all.'

'Or he was a crap aim . . . but it didn't matter in the end, because that's when they found you.'

Matt punched the air. 'Yay.'

Bowland didn't smile, but she did look at both of them in turn. 'So, I want to say thank you. Because if it wasn't for the two of you I'd have two dead children on my hands. You didn't have to go back in to that church, Matt. And Wren . . . you didn't have to let him, either. But you did. In fact, Matt, you didn't have to get involved in any of this, but you did.'

He looked down at the table. 'You could look at it another way. If I hadn't got involved, they'd have never seen me and this could have all been just a failed murder attempt at a church.'

Wren squeezed his hand. She knew this line of thinking.

'Erm, excuse me, young man.' Bowland pointed her pen at him. 'If you have any sense of guilt about this, then you better nip it in the bud right now. Because you know, as well as I know, that after Zara, Miriam was going to end their world one way or another. We'd have tracked Zara down to the farm and found a pile of hanging bodies. Merit and Ever included. You know this is true, don't you?'

Matt looked at the table. 'I know it in my head.'

For the first time, Bowland slid her hands across the table and grabbed his and Wren's. 'Give it time. It'll sink into your heart too. You got involved, you saved three lives, including Dust.'

'But Sean Ashton . . . he'd be alive today if—'

'Stop it. I'm serious. Stop it and listen to me right now.'

He looked at her as Wren wiped her cheek.

'I've seen what you've done in Hobbs Hill and in Menham. Now for me in Chervil. I appreciate you're an academic and all, but what I'm saying is, you're saving lives here, Matt. That's kind of a big deal.'

He felt Wren's arm slide around his back; her sniffling head fell against his shoulder.

'So thank you, both of you,' Bowland said, and shut the folder softly, 'but I reckon that's quite enough for now. You two need rest. So Matt, how about you go and play some of your trendy, silly video games you told me about?'

'Hey,' he raised a palm, 'enough with the trendy.'

'And don't forget to eat.' She hooked a thumb towards the fridge and cupboards. She'd already packed them with goodies she'd brought. Cakes, biscuits and a few bottles of very decent wine. She stood to her feet and patted her jacket down, then after shaking Wren's hand she said, 'Walk me to my car, Matt?'

He nodded and led her out.

When the front door opened sunshine splashed up their bodies, and when Bowland tapped out her sunglasses, he grabbed his from the side table and did the same. How amazing to actually have a need for these, after the black skies of recent days.

'Good weather for the structural engineers.' She stared up into the sky. 'They're assessing St Bart's today. I hear once the chancel's properly reinforced, it'll be fine. I guess the Crooked Church refuses to die.'

He laughed. 'Ain't that the truth.'

They walked into the street where her car sat perched on a kerb. She swung her door open but didn't get in. She turned back and spoke over the roof. 'And don't forget to call that number I gave you. You both need to talk through what happened.'

'Will do,' Matt said, then he saw her gaze drop. 'Jill, what is it?'

She sighed, 'Nah, it's fine. Another time.'

He put his elbow on her car. 'No come on, there's something else.'

She tilted her head. Her earring jiggled.

'Well?'

'The boy, Ever. He keeps asking about you.'

'Asking what?'

'He says he'd like to meet you again, sometime.'

Matt shrugged. 'Sure. If it'll help . . .' He broke off. 'Wait. He does know I'm not his dad, right?'

She smiled. 'Yes, he does. That's all confirmed.'

'Fine, then how about I come this week? Tomorrow maybe?'

She shook her head, 'Not for a while, yet. He needs time. And so do you. Besides, his doctor says it might not be helpful for him to meet with you this soon.'

'Cos I'll bring the memories back . . .'

'No . . . they're just worried you might confirm what he saw at the end.' She searched his face. 'He says you both saw demons, just as the stones fell. Walking through the church, crouching by the bodies.'

He didn't speak.

'Matt?'

'There was a lot going on. The place was dark. It'd be easy to be mistaken . . .'

'Did you see something?'

He shrugged. 'Just a few shadows walking around.'

'Walking shadows?'

'Just a trick of the light, I guess . . . wait, what's wrong?'

She was taking her sunglasses off.

'Tell me, Jill.'

'What if I told you something? Something that's been getting under my skin for this entire case?'

'Go on.'

'What if I said I saw those walking shadows too?'

The sun pulsed. A child in a neighbour's house started to cry. 'I'd say there were a lot of candles in that place and we were all a little stressed.'

She turned something over in her mouth. 'Actually, I mean in Micah's bedroom. When I went in there by myself, that first morning. What if I said I saw one of those things crawl out of his cupboard and stand up straight? What would you say then?'

He looked at her, but he kept his sunglasses on. 'I guess . . . I guess I'd say that we both need rest.'

She slid her glasses back on and put out her hand. They shook across the car roof. 'Well, thanks again, Matt. And call that number. Talk it out.' She sank into the seat and closed her door.

The engine started, and she buzzed her windows down. 'Feels good to need aircon again.' She snapped her CD player on. The low slink of a guitar riff pumped from the speakers. Dolly Parton, 'Jolene'. 'God, it's a beautiful day, isn't it?'

'Glorious.' He tapped his palm on her roof and she pulled away. He stood on the pavement, watching her car dwindle down the street, while above him a fat sun blazed and five birds flew in wild, diving arcs. He closed his eyes for a moment, just to concentrate on the novelty of outdoor heat. It didn't last long. When he opened them again, Bowland was gone, and the birds too.

Strange. He took his sunglasses off, because his street had turned oddly grey. He looked up and saw a huge bank of cloud creeping past the sun to block it. He wondered if it might rain one final time, or if he'd hear Pax and the others in his garden again, like they were last night, singing and dancing in twirling circles, while the whispering shadow things hopped and sprung and wandered between them, approving of it all.

Then he heard a voice.

'*Hollow*!'

He jumped.

A child's voice from the pavement.

He twitched and turned towards it. It was Amelia, tugging at his sleeve.

'What did you just say?'

She cupped her hand around her mouth. 'I said, helloooo, Daddy. Is anybody there?'

He dropped into a crouch and winced at the ache in his shoulder. 'Hello, you.'

'We're having the cake your friend brought. Mummy says she's cutting giant slices. Want one?'

'Absolutely, positively, yes,' he said.

'Good,' she said. Then she hugged him. He noticed how she held it for a lot longer than normal. She knew he needed it.

They walked back up the path together, hand in hand, and he closed the front door just before the sun went to hide and the drops began to fall.

ACKNOWLEDGEMENTS

So there you have it, my novel about rejection. What, you say? You didn't realise the book was about that topic? To be honest, neither did I. But I just finished writing it an hour ago, and I'm sitting here in a pub (waiting for a burger to arrive) and I'm pondering the intense journey I've just been on. And I'm thinking . . . wow . . . this book is about rejection. The pain of it, the sad isolation of it, the depressing regularity of it. Flick back through and you'll see a steady trail of people pushed aside, of fractured relationships, even in the heavenly realms.

The fact that rejection should be a core theme of *Severed* shouldn't be a shock, now that I think about it, because it was inspired by the first novel I ever wrote. That was called *Congregation* which got me a literary agent (yay!) but it was rejected by every publisher who read it (non-yay!) To be fair, it wasn't that good, and it was very different from the story you just read. But it still explored the same bizarre theological question: what if Jesus and his dad weren't loving any more? What if they wanted to strangle each other instead? That concept could have made for a funny sitcom I suppose, but my mind turned it into a pulpy, tragic, hopefully okay horror-thriller.

So, my first thanks go to every editor or agent who rejected *Congregation* and the three more novels that came after, also rejected. You guys were doing your job. You were following your tastes and instincts and lists. I think that's fair enough, because I never thought I was destined to get a book deal, only that I was destined to try and get a book deal – there's a big difference. So yeah, thanks for saying no. It made me sad and all. I remember I cried about it one night, sitting at my kitchen table. But still, I think it made me a better writer, and maybe a more rounded person too. Because what sort of adventure has everything going right? The best adventures – the scary ones that actually mean something – they are a wild mixture of springboards, and shocking brick walls.

So big high fives to my springboards, too. To Joanna Swainson, my splendid agent, and to Therese Cohen, who has helped my books appear in other countries, I say thank you. Hardman and Swainson always feels like a cool literary agency to me. So, I'm chuffed my face gets to gurn out from their sleek website. I also want to thank the crack team at Allison & Busby, who gave Matt Hunter some room at the inn. What's more, you've let him stick around, so thank you Susie Dunlop, Lesley Crooks, Kelly Smith, Daniel Scott, and Simon and Fliss Bage. And Christina Griffiths too, who gives the books such a lovely look. Hat tips go to Debra Reid and Harry Derbyshire too. Thanks for helping me put strange Aramaic words into Micah East's mouth. Thanks also go to Icon Books, who just published my first ever non-fiction book (in all good bookshops now *wink*). Seriously though, *The Frighteners: Why We Love Monsters, Ghosts, Death and Gore* was fuelled by rejection too. When it looked like my fiction would never be published, I came up with a non-fiction idea as a backup. I'm astonished – nay, elated – that I'm now getting to do both. A hearty handshake also goes to so many of you who've come to see me at book signings at events and festivals, who have come to hear me speak or who follow my strange images and left-field utterances on social media. Travelling around and connecting with readers is one of my favourite things to do, so don't be shy. Come and say hello in the flesh or online. And if you're looking for a speaker for something, please cartwheel with haste to your nearest email machine and drop me a message.

Next I'll thank a special trio of trios, starting with Jean, Julie and Norman (better known as my mam, sister and brother). They're the longest running relationships of my life, and they're brilliant. You should invite all four of us to your Karaoke Night some time. Thanks also go to that other well-known trio: God the Father, God the Son and God the Holy Spirit. As far as I can tell they don't want to decapitate each other. Phew! Instead, these three individuals are so close that they are actually one. Yes, the concept of the Trinity fascinates me, not least because it tells me that love and unity really is a plausible goal, even amongst wildly diverse individuals. Then I offer a massive, hugging thanks to my own, blessed little Trinity – Joy, Emma and Adam. Along with me, we're four individuals that create one unit. That's kinda divine if you ask me.

And finally, I want to thank you, the reader. Especially if you feel rejected right now. Maybe it was a crappy email, or an unexpected phone call. Maybe it was a throwaway comment, or a formal letter in the post. Maybe it was the depressing discovery of a betrayal, or just the unbending rules of an institution. I don't exactly know what's left you feeling like you've been kicked off the ship, and that you're plunging into cold while everybody else is dancing on deck. But I do want to thank you most of all. Not least for noticing, and even reading, my book *Severed*, which was once the much-rejected *Congregation*. Who knew that you'd be there for this story one day. As I sat in my kitchen years ago, staring at a 'no thanks' email in panic, thinking that this story (and every other I had) would only ever be trapped in my own head. Who knew that many years later, someone as cool as you would pick it up, see it's face and say, 'Yeah. I think I'm going to take you home.'

So thank you. Thank you for saying yes.

Peter Laws, eating a Cluck'n'Ale Burger (just arrived) in a
Bedfordshire pub
Thursday 13th September, 2018

PETER LAWS is an ordained Baptist minister with a taste for horror. He writes a monthly column in the *Fortean Times* and also hosts a popular podcast and YouTube show which reviews thriller and horror films from a theological perspective. He is also the author of *The Frighteners* which explores our fascination with the macabre. He lives with his family in Bedfordshire.

peterlaws.co.uk   @revpeterlaws